THE DETECTIVE
and
MR. DICKENS

THE DETECTIVE
and
MR. DICKENS

Being an Account of the Macbeth Murders

and the Strange Events Surrounding Them

A Secret Victorian Journal,
Attributed to Wilkie Collins,
Discovered and Edited by

WILLIAM J. PALMER

St Martin's Press   New York

Production Editor: David Stanford Burr

Design by Judith A. Stagnitto

Library of Congress Cataloging-in-Publication Data

Palmer, William J.
      The detective and Mr. Dickens : a secret Victorian journal
   attributed to Wilkie Collins / discovered and edited by William J.
   Palmer.
            p.   cm.
      ISBN 0-312-05073-9
      1. Dickens, Charles, 1812-1870, in fiction, drama, poetry, etc.
   2. Collins, Wilkie, 1824-1889, in fiction, drama, poetry, etc.
   I. Title.
   PS3566.A547D4   1990
   813'.54—dc20   90-37334
                                                           CIP

First Edition
10 9 8 7 6 5 4 3 2 1

This book is dedicated to
William J.
and
Ellen Jane Palmer

EDITOR'S NOTE:

This memoir, written in the style of a novel as befits its author, was recently discovered amongst the papers of Sir William Warrington, bequeathed to the University of North Anglia by the estate of Mr. George Warrington. Sir William, the renowned Lincoln's Inn solicitor and, as he was to many famous persons during the latter half of the last century, counselor to Queen Victoria in the final decades of her reign, was Wilkie Collins's personal solicitor from 1866 until Collins's death in 1889. These papers have recently been opened to the research scrutiny of scholars. This manuscript is a discovery destined to add more than a mere footnote to literary history. The revelations contained in this document redefine the "myth" which, thanks to reticent and overprotective biographers*, has grown up around the life of England's greatest novelist, Charles Dickens. This manuscript revises the accepted view of Dickens as eminent Victorian and presents a fierce chimera of a restless man pushing against the restraints of his place, his fame, his whole society. I wish to thank the University of North Anglia for permitting me to edit and publish this hitherto unpublished (and almost certainly suppressed) literary document.

—WILLIAM J. PALMER

---

*Principally John Forster, Dickens's closest friend, colleague, first biographer and guardian of the holy flame, and Edgar Johnson, the dean of the twentieth-century Dickens biographers, whose fine and nearly definitive two-volume *Charles Dickens: His Tragedy and Triumph* studiously avoids dealing with the material contained in this memoir. Fred Kaplan, Dickens's most recent biographer, in his eloquent *Dickens: A Biography*, rejects this earlier biographical overprotectiveness.

THE DETECTIVE
and
MR. DICKENS

REMEMBERING

(June 14, 1870)

It seems only yesterday that we were young, and he would set aside his glass of port or burnt sherry, and, springing to his feet with a hungry gleam o'erspreading his countenance, say, "Young Wil, we need a walk. Come, let 'the Inimitable' show you his favorite streets." He always gave himself that appellation in the same half-joking, half-serious tone. I didn't like it. I found it vulgar. I'm sure he really believed it, though he wanted you to think it was a joke. From the earliest confidences of our lifelong friendship, I was always resentful of that arrogant appellation. With him in the field, writing novels has been twice as difficult because he is everywhere and you must, else you cannot call yourself a novelist, struggle to avoid imitating *him*.

I was beardless then and twelve years younger than he. I was already in small, tight spectacles but his eyes were still clear and eagerly searching for new material in the world. Sitting in the *Household Words* offices in Wellington Street, Strand, or in the Garrick Club, the actor's spot, he would say, "Come Wilkie, let's see what's abroad this fine English night." We would put on our hats, and perhaps a scarf if the wind was up, or a greatcoat if it was getting on past Michaelmas Term, and together we would head out into the foggy night streets of London.

He is dead, "the Inimitable," how ironic. We will all imitate him in this. The funeral drones on. They will bury him in the Abbey. The faces of his family and friends, lined up in the pews like wax figures on the shelves of a candle shop, mourn

1

him. The church is filled with friends, the curious, those whose business includes the death of a great man.

About halfway back, alone in a small side pew, is a face I know, a face from our past when we used to walk the streets in search of adventure.

Ah, the streets. For more than twenty years, beginning in 'forty-eight it has been my good fortune to share his night streets. He took me up after reading some articles on murder and shipwreck which I had published in the *Daily News*. I was so young, and trying to be a writer. I was quite fit then, and he told me he felt safer with me along. He was obsessed with the streets. He would gaze out the windows into the black night eager to escape the warm, safe confines of his well-appointed *Household Words* office where he often slept when his wife and children were down in the country (which they were more often than not). Imagine giving up warm rooms, brandy, the capacious chair and good fellowship of friends like Lemon and Forster and Leech at the Garrick Club to walk out among thieves and beggars and the fallen women who crowded the gaslit streetcorners offering their only portable, perishable property for sale to any stranger attracted to their wretchedness. It was as if he needed the streets to satisfy something in his restless personality, perhaps to convince himself that he was real, and not just some figment of his own overactive imagination.

"As for me, I went along willingly—no eagerly. It was an exciting time for me, an honor to be taken up by the writer who commanded the field. I would, however, be remiss not to admit that I could have been observed frequently and nervously glancing back over my shoulder as we strode boldly into some of the darkest, most labyrinthine pockets of damnation in that city of night. That familiar face in the mourning pew, halfway down the aisle, brings it all rushing back into my memory.

"The Inimitable" is dead now, and soon the Vultures will descend upon his life and pick it to pieces. Things will be made known which have remained hidden and secret. Surely some

2

clever young Grub Street hack will find out about Ellen sooner or later. But they'll never learn the whole truth of it. Only I, and that solitary mourner halfway back, know the whole story, the real story.

And he knows more than I. He knows how it was all settled. Perhaps if I approach him, he will tell me what sort of gentleman's agreement he and Dickens arrived at which gave "the Inimitable" the focus of his last twenty years.

He sees me looking at him from my pallbearer's chair sideways to the aisle up next to the ornamented, brass-handled casket. I want to lean around the corner of the catafalque and wave to him. But that would be out of place here and now. We exchange grave nods, but our eyes hold on each other, and I know that he is remembering exactly as I am. Without warning, he tips me a quick sly wink, and I have to suddenly cover my mouth with my black-gloved hand, and pretend to cough, in order to hide from the mourning multitudes an irresistable grin. By heaven, we had some times together, the three of us.

My familiar friend is a burly, balding man. He looks different without his hat. Whenever London's guilty (and are not we all?) saw that hat approaching, they tried to escape its relentless jurisdiction. I remember it as a flat square brown hat that could slice right through a crowd. His shoulders are wide, and his neck thick, yet he isn't hulking. He stands below six feet, and his face, through proportioned to that powerful neck, is not overwide. His eyebrows are dark black and strong, but it is his keen eyes which rule. Nothing escapes those eyes; they move like pickpockets, dipping deep into every soul without anyone ever realizing until they have passed on. His sharp hat and sharp eyes can cut to the heart of the matter as deftly as might Lord Jarvis Hillis-Millar, the Queen's Surgeon-General.

But now, across the funeral congregation, those clear eyes are misty. He is a man I never could have imagined shedding tears. Yet he is on that verge. We are both, perhaps, getting old.

It has probably been a year since I have last seen him, my

familiar friend. "The Inimitable" hadn't much time (or strength) for the streets in recent years. I had ceased accompanying him on his fierce night walks years ago. God only knows when the last time was, that Charles and this familiar friend had been together. Yet our friend was there, sizing up the crowd, catching my eye, tipping his ironic wink which said to me: *Do you remember the heat of the chase? The pleasure of the game?* He raised his forefinger, crooked in that familiar way, as if just lifted out of the trigger housing of a pistol, to scratch softly at the side of his eye, as Deacon Hornback's voice rose to some crescendo of elegiac nonsense.

That forefinger, yes! It was his most powerful weapon. He had a tendency toward tapping people familiarly on the chest with that forefinger as he questioned them. He had the abrupt habit of suddenly punching his forefinger over his left shoulder and spitting, "Now hook it," when terminating a conversation with some vagrant or street boy or powdered whore. But his forefinger was always the most intimidating when pointed directly at his target like the barrel of a gun. With his sharp hat, his sharp eyes, and his exceedingly sharp forefinger, my familiar friend had gained quite a reputation for cutting to the bone of reality, cutting across the whole fabric of society, cutting through all the appearances which clothe the truth.

My familiar friend, alone at the funeral, was one of "the Inimitable's" closest associates, though few—not Forster, nor Wills, nor Dolby, nor any of the members of the family—would recognize him. He was "the Inimitable's" one firm friend of his beloved streets. Ah yes, they were colleagues indeed. My familiar friend was Detective Inspector Field, of the Metropolitan Protectives, Bow Street Station.

Field, his sharp brown hat restored to his head, was standing outside the door of the Abbey when I emerged, waiting to take me into custody. The street in front was flooded with people, horses, cabs, and the inevitable street vendors who were the first profiteers on Charles's death. There would be many more to follow. When I finally made it to his side, he had already been recognized and accosted by another denizen of the madding crowd, an eager young newspaper reporter intent on probing his presence at the funeral of the great man.

"'Ee and I were acquaintances and colleagues. I greatly admired the man." Field scratched the side of his eye with his forefinger.

"Colleagues?" the young man probed.

"No, no, not a'tall," Field assured him. "Just an acquaintance I greatly admired. Now please, do you mind? An old friend."

Field shouldered his way through the crowd to my side.

"Field, how good to see you, how good indeed."

He caught the true enthusiasm in my voice and smiled.

We both suddenly remembered where we were and our faces fell.

"A bad business this," he finally said gruffly, nodding toward the emptied church. "I'd rather 'ave met up with you and 'im any other place on earth."

"I agree. I agree," I agreed, stupidly.

"We did 'ave some strange journeys, put on some intricate little performances, the two writer swells from the West End and their detective friend, didn't we?" He gently broke the awkward silence with three affectionate taps of his forefinger to my cravat.

"We certainly did," I nodded. "He had no better friend than you."

Dickens was there in both of our minds, in black waistcoat and black silk scarf, walking briskly beside me, perhaps smoking a cigar, as we hastened to follow Field's Juggernaut pace down the dark maze of streets, into some pestilent London rookery.

"'Ee 'onored me with 'is friendship," Field was gravely saying.

"He honored us all."

The awkward silence ebbed back in.

The desire not to mourn alone built within me. It didn't seem right to just shake hands, throw off a meaningless "So nice to see you again" fare-thee-well, and then go our separate ways. I think Field felt the same attraction for my company. We lingered in the awkward silence of the street.

"Let's have a wake," a voice, which turned out to be my own, said. It was an inspiration that could have come from only one source. I felt his presence as palpably as if he were standing there in the street. "We'll have a pint in his memory." I was positively grinning, as if Dickens were elbowing me in the ribs at the hilarity of the idea.

Field smiled again—twice in mere minutes. That was more than he normally budgeted for a month. "Least we can do, two old campaigners, lift a glass to a departed chum."

We found a quiet table in the window of The Merry Thistle. Field stood his stick in the corner. It was a straight one, thin and shiny black with a fierce knob on the top. I'd seen him use it as if it was an extension of his body.

Our pints arrived, plus a small portion of Irish whiskey. "It's been a strong day, so we might as well 'ave strong drink," he said.

"To 'the Inimitable,'" I toasted. Violently he threw off his glass, then chased it with a generous draught of bitter. I sipped mine. The whiskey seemed to loosen and relax him.

"Remember the Mannings? That's where I first met 'im . . . and you, when we 'ung 'em. The Mannings were my case."

"Yes, how could I forget a night and morning like that?"

"As long as I live I'll never forget the way 'ee looked at me that first time, as if I was a scarf or a bowler 'at or a pair of gloves in a store window. 'Ee 'ad this look on 'is face and this gleam in 'is eye that seemed to ask, I could almost 'ear it, 'Will 'ee fit? Is this my man? Is 'ee well made? Will 'ee hold up and wear well? Is 'ee in style?'"

"It's the way *you* look at people when *you're* sizing them up. It is your look that says, 'I'll have you in my custody soon, no doubt.'"

"I suppose it is."

"If he hadn't met you, he surely would have invented someone like you."

"'Ee did invent someone like me. Bucket indeed!"

"You never liked that name, did you?"

"A silly name for a detective. I told 'im as much, and 'ee just laughed. 'Ah,' 'ee said then, and 'is eyes told me 'ee was jokin', 'but not a bad name for a receptacle for the garbage of society.' All I could do was shake my 'ead. 'Bucket indeed!' was all I could say. Then 'ee laughed, and clapped me on the back, and said, 'You're a good friend, Field. Bucket's just a jumble of words on a page.'" Field was a great mimic. His imitation caught the playful tenor of Dickens's voice. *'Inimitable' indeed!*

The waiter brought two more small glasses of the Tollamore Dew.

"I'll never forget 'ow, months later, 'ee just walked in one night off the streets. Just walked in and said 'Owdeedo' as if we wuz expectin' 'im, looked 'round as if waitin' for someone to kiss 'is ring or 'is sleeve or 'is arse, for God's sake."

Field's animated telling had me laughing then. Despite the day, the death, it couldn't be helped.

"I busied myself with my pipe while 'ee looked 'round," Field went on, "takin' everythin' in, in that detective's way 'ee 'ad. I think you were right behind 'im, a stout drippin' young fellow, 'oldin' a waterlogged bumber, and wearin' fogged spectacles."

"The blind leading the blind." We were both smiling in the memory.

"Finally 'ee spotted me, and marched right over with 'is hand outstretched sayin', 'Field old man, 'ow are you?' as if we'd been friends for years. Everyone in the station 'ouse recognized 'im immediately. They were significantly impressed. For weeks after, I was really quite a 'ero, 'eld somewhat in awe for my 'eye connections. 'Field old man' indeed. That's 'ow it all began Collins. You remember it, don't you?"

"Field old man," I tried to imitate the voice, but I couldn't

7

do it nearly as well. "I don't remember if I was there that first time, but I can hear him saying it nonetheless."

"Do you ever see 'er?" he inquired.

"Quite often," I answered. "She stayed near him to the end."
He nodded.

I saw my opportunity. "What went on in the chapel at St. Mark's that night?" I said, mustering the courage to ask. "Why did you let her go without even so much as an inquiry?"

"That was about all you weren't in on durin' that case, I'd say. I let 'er go because I'd taken a likin' to 'im, and I saw from the beginnin' 'ow valuable 'ee could be to me. 'Ee 'as been exactly that valuable over the years. You know of much of that."

Indeed I do, I thought. *Indeed I do.*

We two old soldiers spent the greater part of that afternoon in that warm pub. The waiter brought us pints of beer. We remembered it all. It was a fitting wake.

As we were leaving, Field adjusting his sharp hat and picking up his murderous stick, looked at me and said: "'Ee was the most creative detective I ever knew. 'Ee would 'ave worn well in my line."

That conversation with Inspector Field set me thinking of the sort of memorial that I, a writer of novels, might make to my dead friend. I went home that day, and started a new commonplace book, but not one of the usual sort. I began writing a record of events that had happened more than twenty years before, a record of the man only I, Inspector Field, and, of course, his beloved Ellen, knew.

AT THE RAREE-SHOW

(Nov. 12–13, 1849)

Dickens first met Inspector Field at a public hanging. It was an event of great notoriety, the execution of the murderess Sylvia Manning and her sniveling husband.*

It was a foggy November, fog everywhere, fog invading one's very pores. Charles was working on *David Copperfield*, at a pace which left all of us in awe. I was one of Dickens's "new-found friends," as that petulant boor, Forster, would say to Dickens. "Your new-found friend, young Wilkie, is a ubiquitous presence lately, is he not?"—followed by some fragmentary remark about "clinging vines" generally turning out to be "climbers." I never have, through all the years, gotten on well with Forster. He and I were often in each other's company and always civil, but it was no secret that neither was comfortable in the presence of the other. Dickens was attached to each of us for different reasons. Forster was his closest advisor and confidant. I was his court jester and dining companion; he liked me with him when we walked out at night because I was young and stout. What lurking robber was going

---

*Hangings as widely-covered social events were something which the English had a tremendous fondness for and gave up grudgingly. In fact, though hangings were not nearly so public later as they were in Dickens's time, it took the English over 100 more years to outgrow them. In 1955, Ruth Ellis, who had shot her high-society lover in the head, had the honor of being the last woman to be hanged in England.

to accost a tall man with a powerful stride accompanied by a wide-shouldered, thick-wristed bulldog?

As we walked, he noticed everything, pointed out the smallest details, the light on the water, sinister bills posted on dirty walls, shadowy wretches slouching into dark byways, or sleeping in doorways. He was constantly making writing plans. "I can use this place," he would say, as we looked out over the Thames from the railing on London Bridge. Or, "That sound, mark it, it's perfect!" he would exclaim, as a posh coach, its velvet curtains drawn tight, clattered past, and was swallowed by the fog, only to leave its receding sound lingering in the air. None of our night walks were ever planned. The night of the Manning hanging, however, was different.

Leech, his illustrator, suggested it. It was to be a historical moment in the annals of London crime and *Punch* had commissioned Leech to capture this triumph of British justice, morality, and barbarism. Leech invited Dickens to accompany him to the hanging, and Charles, in turn, invited me.

"Leech will be at his sketchbook the whole time," he insisted. "You must come, Wilkie, I'll need support in this."

As usual, he was manifestly right.

Though the expedition had been Leech's idea, once underway, it became Dickens's project. He made all the arrangements, like some playwright blocking out the movements of his actors. He reserved space for our dinner, and rented space on a rooftop overlooking the gallows so that our view would be unobstructed.

"Young Wil," he said excitedly, "it is going to be a night we will all remember." *Night indeed!* In all his planning, he only overlooked one small detail: sleep! When I had the temerity to point out that his schedule demanded we remain awake all night, he snorted once, then chuckled slyly. "I'll wager it is not the first time you've watched the sun rise, Wilkie, in rather unwholesome circumstances."

The hanging was to be carried out at dawn on November thirteenth, but our plan was to spend the night at the site of the command performance. Both Forster and William Wills, a man Dickens had met at the *Daily News,* joined our party that evening. At Dickens's urging, we all muffled up, and walked out to dinner. On the way, Dickens engaged Forster and Wills in animated conversation concerning a plan for a new periodical, a weekly, that he wanted to start up. Leech and I walked silently behind, he carrying a small carpetbag containing his sketchbooks and the utensils of his trade.

"We'll call it *The Shadow,*" Dickens insisted to Forster and this Wills person, who seemed the real target of his arguments. "To bind it all together will be the ubiquity of its conductor, a mysterious personality called the Shadow, who may go into any place by sunlight, moonlight, starlight, firelight, candlelight, gaslight—who may be in the theatre, in the palace, the House of Commons, the prisons, the churches, the railroad, in the sea, in every dirty byway and crumbling tenement and pestilent alley of every rookery and rats' castle of this great verminous sinkhole of London. I want him to loom as a fanciful thing, so that everybody, from the Queen to the most destitute crossing sweep, will be wondering, 'What will the Shadow say about this? Is the Shadow here? Does the Shadow know?' I have not breathed this idea to anyone, but I have a lively hope that it *is* an idea, and that out of it the whole scheme may be hammered."

Wills seemed interested.

Forster scoffed. "Sounds like the scheme for some profane novel!" he barked. "*Adventures of a Fly on the Wall of a Gentleman's Brothel.*"

"Ah, are you conversant with that species of literature, old man?" Dickens teased him. Little did we know that there already was such a shadow as Dickens had described in London, and we would meet him for the first time that very night.

We supped in a private room at the Piazza Coffee House, Covent Garden, just a bit after eleven p.m., on smoked chops with boiled potatoes, a steaming cauliflower with cheese melted atop it, and a delicate plum pudding. We smoked cigars as we walked over Hungerford Bridge to Horsemonger Lane

Gaol, the site of the executions. The closer we approached the actual scene of the evening's entertainment, the more subdued Dickens became. It was almost as if he were having second thoughts about all the elaborate arrangements for the celebration of such an inhumane event. But he was never one to back away from experience or reality, and we pressed on, though not the jolly troupe we had been earlier.

We went first to inspect our perch on the rooftop. The landlord had dragged every available stick of furniture out for the accommodation of his influential (not to mention highpaying—he had charged Dickens two guineas for each of us) guests. Below, at the closed end of the street, built against the front gate of the gaol, stood the gallows. The gibbet posts and the crossbar shown silver grey in the cold moonlight, and cast skeletal shadows against the white stone of the high gaolhouse wall. The crowd had already gathered in the street, and the wardens of the gaol and a detachment of Metropolitan Protectives had thrown up barriers around the sinister scaffolding to keep the crush of people some small distance from the gallows itself.

Dickens's plan had been for us to walk down amongst the spectators to observe their behavior, and, perhaps, even collect their opinions of the event. But none of our party seemed immediately so inclined. That gallows, ghostly in the moonlight, sobered us. We sat in the landlord's chairs and finished our cigars. Only Leech showed any inclination toward activity. His hands were already moving across the first *tabula rasa* of his sketchbook.

The crowd below grew increasingly restless. Sounds of impatience and anger and laughter and obscene flirtation floated up. The street was flooded with humanity, and it was still five hours until dawn. Leech's pencils flew over his pages.

"Let us descend into this inferno," Dickens said, finally breaking in on our private rooftop reveries. "We didn't come here to sit brooding over our cigars like a tribe of tired old voyeurs."

"Ah, by all means," Forster piped up, sarcastically. "Maybe we can wangle an interview with Jack Ketch."*

Dickens ignored him. We descended the tenement staircase, but at the street door to Horsemonger Lane we were stopped momentarily by a crush of bodies moving in a slow stream. It was an unruly crowd. There were constables in blue uniforms everywhere, each carrying a bright bull's-eye.* Even as we were pushing our way out of the door, a young woman, carrying a basket, slipped to her knees or was pushed in the street. Before she could right herself, the crowd came on and trampled over her like some blind Juggernaut. She would have died but for a young bobbie who rushed in swinging his bull's-eye like Samson's jawbone through the unfeeling crowd to where the poor girl lay stunned on the grimy stones. She was dazed and breathless, but, aside from a few rising bruises, seemed to have no serious injuries. Her basket was gone forever, crushed, then carried off like shattered jetsam on the human tide. It was a warning to beware the ugly wave that could engulf us and batter us into shipwrecked splinters. We made our way toward the gallows, which rose above the crowd like some perverted altar. More than once, I was forced to shove an uncouth ruffian out of our way, who would turn with a murderous glare and his hand rising to strike. But each immediately noticed that we were gentlemen, and backed away snarling, but unwilling to risk attacking us. Leech disappeared almost immediately upon our entering the street. He was sketching madly. Foul language floated in the air. Dirty clots of people had staked out their territories for viewing the proceedings. All were drinking openly, and howls were raised from time to time, which could remind one only of that

---

*The generic nickname for a professional hangman.

*A gas-filled hand-torch which was also frequently used as a weapon.

place where such disturbing sounds were commonplace—Bedlam.*

Other groups yelled and caroused to the tune of parodies of the vulgar Negro melodies of the day:

> Oh, Mrs. Manning,
> Don't you cry for me.
> For I'm goin' to hell this morning
> My true love for to see.

As the crowd grew, thieves, low prostitutes, murderous ruffians, and filthy vagabonds of every size and shape and species of wretchedness flocked onto the ground, displaying countless varieties of offensive and foul behavior. Men and women alike fainted in the crush, and were carried out by the constables. Other women, swooning, clearly victims of more than merely superficial liberties, were dragged out of the crowd by the police with their dresses disordered. As these poor victims passed, the crowd greeted them with hoots of obscene speculation.

As we loitered in the shadow of the gallows, Dickens spotted a reporter from the *Daily News*. The man, pen flying in a small notebook, was conducting an interview. Dickens maneuvered closer, to eavesdrop. The man under interview was of burly composition, wide of shoulder and thick of neck, wearing an unobtrusive brown longcoat of a heavy military cut with round collars lying across his shoulders. Jammed tight on his head was a low, square hat. As the interviewer plied him with questions, the man stood as if sculpted in stone, unmoving, attentive, yet his eyes darted over the crowd, missing nothing.

"Ought to be done inside the walls," the burly man in the hat was saying as the reporter's pencil flew. "Look at 'em! Bloodthirsty mob!"

---

*The generic English name for Asylums for the Insane.

14

Dickens turned to us: "Who is Axton interviewing over there?"

"Inspector Field, of the Peelers," Wills answered.

"Good Lord, that's Field?" Dickens exclaimed, openly excited.

"Who's that?" Forster harumphed.

"The famous Inspector Field," Dickens explained in the voice of a ha'penny broadside enthusiast, "the Detective Genius responsible for the apprehension of the Mannings. I must meet him."

Dickens quickly turned back, and hailed the reporter. The sharp-eyed man's attention throttled Dickens immediately. *What have we here?* The sharp-eyed man tried to place him. *Tall, urgent, foppishly bearded man interrupts my interview.*

"Young Axton, halloa," Dickens clumsily intruded.

"Mister Dickens, sir," the reporter said, recognizing him, and replying respectfully, in fact with a certain amount of awe.

At the mention of that name, the burly, sharp-eyed man's attention immediately relaxed. His face softened into a congenial smile of recognition as if he were thinking *Dickens, indeed, I want to meet this duck.*

"Working hard tonight, heh Axton?" Dickens moved in, and clapped the startled young man congenially on the shoulder, all hail-fellow-well-met.

"Yes sir, quite sir," Axton stammered.

The burly man waited, amused.

Dickens froze in awkward silence, as the befuddled Axton groped for his wits. Finally, the young man, realizing that all eyes were upon him, waiting, did what was expected.

"Mister Dickens, sir. Detective Inspector Field of the Metropolitan Protectives." His introduction complete, young Axton, trailing his pencil and pad, dropped immediately out of existence, and, to my knowledge, was never seen nor heard from again.

Dickens and Field stepped toward each other, and shook hands warmly.

"My great pleasure Mister Charles Dickens, sir. I 'ave read

a number of your creations. I 'ave admired your work for many years."

"And I yours, Inspector Field," Dickens laughed, as he nodded up toward the sinister scaffolding towering above us. *

Field didn't join in the levity. His grim, crook'd forefinger snaked out from under his coat and struck at the side of his eye. "Can't say I'm too fond of all this," Field said evenly.

"I couldn't agree more," Dickens, taking the cue, also sobered. "It is a barbaric spectacle."

"That certainly is the case from a philosophic point of view," Field agreed, "but, from a practical point of view, this is a criminal's convention. Every thief, pickpocket, gonoph, woman molester, and strong-armer in London is in attendance today, workin' this crowd."

"The crowd is getting out of hand," Forster complained from Dickens's elbow. "We ought to get back, out of this crush."

Dickens and Field ignored him.

"Thanks to ingenious men like you," Dickens said, bestowing the compliment warmly, "Scotland Yard is gaining a reputation."

"Don't spend much time there," Field replied matter-of-factly. "Bow Street Station is my beat. All of the West End to the river's where I spend my evenin's."

I had been watching the man's incredible darting eyes. Not for a second, though by all evidence the conversation was the object of his full attention, did they cease roaming over the crowd like two swift birds of prey, gliding, waiting for their victim to break cover.

"Excuse me one moment, sir," Field suddenly brought their

---

*One subject of interest which weighs down the pages of first the *Daily News* and then *Household Words* and *All The Year Round*, yet which few biographers have observed or commented upon in any depth, is Dickens's fascination with detectives, with the London underworld, with the intellectual aspects of crime solving.

conversation to a halt. "I've just marked an old friend whose acquaintance I expressly came 'ere to renew tonight."

With that, Field took off his hat, and passed it once through the air above the heads of the crowd. Within seconds, two uniformed constables in stovepipe hats materialized. "Against the buildin' in the grey overcoat and bowler," Field ordered.

Dickens couldn't take his eyes off of the two constables making their way through the crowd. Coming up, one on each side, they took custody of the designated man easily. The crowd was never aware of the tiny drama in its midst.

"Ah," Field turned back to Dickens, "now it 'as been a profitable evenin'. I've got the man I came for."

"Who was that?" Dickens asked eagerly.

"'Arry the 'Oly," Field's eyes were alive with satisfaction, "one of the most proficient swell mobsmen* in all of London. Does 'is best work in well-dressed crowds leavin' church on Sunday mornin's. I was sure this would be too promisin' a ceremony for 'im to decline attendance. I've been after 'im for two months. Knocked down an old lady name of Summerson outside a church in Russell Square during a bungled purse snatch. Old lady died later of the shock of it. 'Ee's been lyin' low ever since. With good reason. But I knew this would bring 'im out."

Field was soft-spoken of voice but strangely commanding in tone. His speech had but a lingering trace of the cockney. He chose his words carefully. Even in one of his novels, Dickens couldn't have invented a more interesting place for the two of them to meet than there in the middle of a ghostly, moonlit night, in the shadow of the gallows.

"Would you join us for some tea, Inspector Field? I would very much like to pursue our conversation," Dickens said, and went on to explain how our party had accommodations on a nearby rooftop.

---

*Criminal slang for thieves who dress as gentlemen and, usually in groups, work crowds at public gatherings.

"With 'Oly 'Arry taken up," he answered blithely, "I 'ave time for that. But I must be back on duty down 'ere before the festivities begin."

With that, we all withdrew to our aerie, and I brewed the tea. We sat in a tight little circle on common kitchen chairs near the edge of the roof, where we had a clear view of the street below all the way to the gallows. Dickens asked Field for the particulars of the Manning case, and that worthy was more than willing to regale us with the story.

He told how Mrs. Manning, originally Sylvia de Roux, of Swiss-French extraction and personal maid of Lady Blantyre, the daughter of the Duchess of Sutherland, simultaneously contracted sexual liaisons with the Irishman Patrick O'Connor, a customhouse officer and stock speculator, and Frederick George Manning, a guard on the Great Western Railway; how she married Manning yet continued to welcome O'Connor in her husband's house and meet with O'Connor alone in his rooms. Dickens listened to every prurient detail.

Field told how she and her husband found out about O'Connor's great wealth in foreign railway stocks, and invited O'Connor to dinner; how Frederick Manning purchased a large shovel, and had a bushel of lime delivered to the house; how O'Connor appeared the fatal night, and smoked a cigar on the back porch while talking intimately with Mrs. Manning; how Mrs. Manning led him to the kitchen on the lower level to wash his hands, raised a pistol to O'Connor's head as he bent over the wash basin, and fired without hesitation; how, when her husband joined her in the kitchen and found O'Connor still alive, he battered him to death with a ripping chisel; how, after they covered the body with lime and buried it in the kitchen beneath two flagstones, they sat and feasted on a goose dinner in the very room where they had murdered and buried the man who was to have been their dinner guest. Dickens never blinked at the utter savagery of it.

Field told how he collected all of the circumstantial evidence which pointed to Mrs. Manning, then went to the house to question the suspects. Dickens hung on every word.

Field was an eloquent, graphic and economical storyteller. No wonder he and Dickens hit it off so well from the very beginning.

"'Ma'am,' says I, 'I work at the customhouse with one Patrick O'Connor, who 'asn't appeared for work in more than a week. Some friends 'ave said 'ee was last seen on 'is way to dine with you last Thursday night.'

"'Friends must be mistaken, 'Aven't seen 'im,' says she.

"'Is landlady says you came to 'is rooms and made 'er let you in last Friday.' says I.

"'Landlady is mistaken," says she, cool as a three-day old corpse.

"'Neighbors say they saw man of O'Connor's description, smokin' cigar on back porch Thursday even' last,' says I.

"'Neighbors mistaken. Don't allow smokin' on the premises. Filthy 'abit," says she.

"We went away but when we returned the next day with the writ the Mannings 'ad both fled. That was when I thanked the Lord for givin' me sharp eyes. The back kitchen was all large flagstones. I noticed a dark damp mark 'ad spread along the edges of two of the stones. We quickly borrowed a shovel, a crowbar, and a boathook in the neighborhood, and took those two stones up. Beneath 'em we found what was left of Patrick O'Connor. That was it. We 'ad 'em. All we 'ad to do was find and take 'em. They'd split up. It took three days, but I tracked 'er to Edinburgh, and took 'er myself. Others took Manning, drunk, in Jersey."

I could see in Dickens's face that he was not only fascinated with the story, but with the teller of the tale.

"Int'restin' study, wot? The Fair Sex. The Innocent Sex." It was that man Wills, speaking with an almost cockney mumble.

"How could a woman lose all that is womanly, and kill so coldheartedly?" It was my own voice posing that question. I had meant simply to listen and observe, but the question seemed to rush to my tongue.

"I've noticed in my experience that the criminal mind don't seem to know if it 'as been bestowed on a male or a female,"

19

Field answered. "Women are a sticky lot to deal with as criminals. They are generally smarter and more cunning than the low-life men who dominate the criminal classes. They are also 'arder to crack, to scare, to break down with empty threats. They are just all around 'arder, because no man, whether a detective or not, wants to believe that a 'andsome woman can be guilty. But the fact of the matter is that they kill just as dead as any man and they lie even better."

Thus, I was with Dickens when they first met.

Soon Field had to leave our jolly tea-party, and Leech returned wrist-weary. "Wasn't that Field of Bow Street Station I passed going down?" Leech inquired.

"It certainly was," Dickens answered.

"Made a sketch of the two of you shaking hands down below before," Leech remarked. "God knows what for! All *Punch* will want is the climactical picture of the lady herself walking on air."

"I must have that sketch, the one of Field and me." Dickens's voice was eager.

Morning approached, and nervous anticipation hushed the straining crowd below in the street. Soon a door opened in the wall of Horsemonger Lane Gaol, and Mrs. Manning, followed by her sniveling wretch of a husband, was led slowly to the gallows. Luckily, the espoused murderess did not have to pass through the screaming, spitting, hissing, bestial crowd. The constables, all armed with heavy truncheons, had cleared a path and thrown up barriers to insure the safe passage of the two guests of honor.

Mrs. Manning, always leading, climbed the gallows steps with determination as if hiking up the side of a Scottish loch. Her husband, faint, terrified, had to be helped up the steps by two constables.

"She seems singularly composed, for a woman only moments away from one of the lower circles of Hell," Dickens said quietly.

The woman on the scaffold turned and glowered at the crowd. She writhed at the hanger which held her hands securely behind her back. Her dark wild eyes flashed. The whole of Horsemonger Lane became still, waiting.

In broken English, at the top of her voice, she unleashed a curse upon the crowd which was both magnificent in its defiance, and comic in its clumsy grasp of the language. "DAMN SEIZE YOU ALL!!!" she screamed. "DAMN SEIZE YOU ALL!!!" she howled again.

Her husband sagged pathetically at her side. As a haughty gesture, clearly performing for the crowd, she turned, and bestowed a mocking kiss on the poor ashen man's cheek. At this bit of bravado, this Judas kiss, the crowd went mad, and surged against the barriers. It was all the constables wielding their truncheons could do to beat back the crowd. The crowd wanted to tear her flesh, rip out her eyes, draw and quarter her. Dickens silently shook his head at the obscenity of the spectacle. We actually learned later that a thirty-year-old woman, one Deborah Thomas of St. Giles, was driven against the barrier by the rush of the frenzied crowd, and crushed to death.

As the hangman placed the thick noose around the murderess's neck, the mob below grew more and more brutish. Nor were the roof dwellers any more compassionate or sympathetic toward the two poor wretches.

"She dares to wear black satin, that harlot!" gasped a well-born woman in an expensive black satin gown and shoulder muffler, who was observing the proceedings through a small set of opera glasses. "Well! I'll never wear black satin again, you can be assured of that!" she announced.

"No respectable woman should be watching such a thing as this," Dickens muttered, "nor any respectable gentleman either. Collins, Field is right. These things should be done inside the walls of the gaol."

"Quite so," I agreed wholeheartedly, "exactly the solution."

"And deprive all these nice people of their fun?" Forster piped up sourly.

"It is not funny," Dickens was subdued, not angry. "That a woman in this age should be driven to this is deplorable."

The traps were sprung. With a sharp downward thrust, the Mannings stabbed through the floor of the scaffold, and imbedded, quivering, in the empty air. The crowd gasped and panted at this moment of completion. Howls of satisfaction and murmurs of ecstacy rolled like waves through the crowd. The husband and wife were hung side by side. Like demented marionettes, they performed their dance of death. The woman's legs kicked out, as if trying to reach the faces in the front row. The husband died more meekly. He spasmed once or twice in mid-air, before going as limp as his backbone had been all his life. The unspeakable crowd spewed hate.

"TO HELL, HUSSY!" they screamed.

"BURN, DEVILS, BURN!"

"DIE, WHORE! DIE AND BE DAMNED!"

Dickens turned to me, "It's a bloody raree-show!" he exploded. "Worse, it's a bloody damned pagan sacrifice to Satan!"

I wasn't surprised at his emotion, his anger; what surprised me were his words. The man never cursed. It was as if he had too much respect for the language which was his constant companion to profane it.

As we walked back over Hungerford Bridge, talk turned to Inspector Field. "That man is London's real 'Shadow,'" said Dickens. "I'll bet he knows every inch of this city as if it were his own parlor. That man's a good man for us to get to know, Wilkie."

AT THE STATION HOUSE

(April 5, 1851)

Dickens started his weekly magazine that next year. He discarded the idea of "The Shadow." Instead, he and Forster and Wills named the new periodical *Household Words*. I became one of its regular contributors.

I continued as the favoured companion of Dickens's night walks. During that period, when he was working so hard to get *Household Words* underway, his nocturnal forays served purposes much more complex than mere post-prandial exercise. They were his physical and psychological outlet. It was as if the long day working in the office brought him slowly to a boil, and his walks through the dark streets were his way of letting the pressurized steam escape. He prowled those streets like an obsessed spy. He had ordered a large brass bedstead brought into the Wellington Street offices, and had fallen into the regimen of spending the first four nights of the work week— Monday through Thursday—there, living like a bachelor. He, of course, rejoined his family in the country for the weekends. Mrs. Dickens, Kate, had been afflicted with a strange undiagnosable dizziness and headache since February of that year, and had been under the private medical care of Doctor Southwood Smith at Great Malvern.

His father, John Dickens, died late in March of that year, rather suddenly, of an old urinary complaint which years before had forced him to retire from the Navy Pay Office. Dickens had known nothing of his father's condition until summoned from Malvern to his father's bedside when a bladder infection cast the old man into a violent delirium.

23

John Dickens died the next morning with his son in attendance. Dickens had been a dutiful son, and had loved his father well, though there was evidence that he didn't take the old man very seriously. Forster, for one, had accused him of creating Mister Micawber of *Copperfield* out of the raw material of John Dickens, but Dickens had always steadfastly denied it. When his father died, Dickens took it hard, sank into a near wordless state of depression for days afterwards.

Two days after the funeral, I supped with Dickens. The offices of *Household Words* were in a homey, three-storey building with a gracefully bowed—out front about halfway up Wellington Street, Strand, on the right hand side. It wore the number sixteen on its right lapel. Its bowed front provided its character. The bow reached up for two storeys, and was all expansive bay window, which provided a perfect flood of light of the sort absolutely necessary for literary work. The master's office was on the drawing room floor, ten steps up from the ground floor entrance, where Wills guarded all comings and goings like some overly polite Cerberus. Dickens's desk and the cushioned wooden chair in which he sat were nestled into the curve of the bay window. His office more closely resembled a handsomely furnished study in some wealthy bachelor's flat than a newspaper office. Two smaller offices, sparsely furnished with desks and chairs, took up the back of that second floor, and provided spartan work space for itinerant contributors who needed to be on hand to consult with the master in the process of readying their articles for the magazine.

Dickens had put in a feverish day. He had, by my imprecise count, bounded up and down that short flight of stairs to consult with Wills on editorial details no less than twenty to thirty times. When not vaulting the stairs, he paced back and forth before his desk, like some caged resident of the Zoological Gardens. It didn't require a high degree of intelligence to realize that his father's death hung heavy on his mind, and to sense the pressure building within him. I was there, working in one of the back offices, the whole afternoon. About five, Dickens popped his head in with a strained smile.

"Wilkie, can you stay and dine with me? I've got another hour or so of work, and then perhaps some bachelor fare, brandy and cigars, eh?"

He wanted company, and I, as always, was honored to provide it. Being a friend of Dickens then gave me a status in the London literary world which I had not yet earned with my pen. People didn't identify me as Collins, the young writer with the rough edges, but rather as "Dickens's *protégé*, who would soon, no doubt, produce great things."

It wasn't a very witty dinner. We dined on chops catered in. He picked morosely at his food. We sat silently smoking our cigars afterward.

"Wilkie, this will simply not do," he said, finally breaking our morbid silence. "Let us walk out and get some air, see what amusement might be abroad tonight."

I was more than happy, in fact eager, to oblige him. In short minutes we were hatted, gloved, scarved, walking-sticked and on our way.

It was a cool (verging on raw), damp April night. A slight mist hung in the halos of the gas lamps in the Strand. He walked briskly with his typical long stride. As usual, he headed into the darkness of the city in the direction of the river. For some reason, some kind of magnetic attraction perhaps, he was always drawn toward that pestilent ribbon of water that bisected the great city.

As we walked through darkened neighborhoods, his pace quickened. Normally, his head swiveled from side to side, eyes darting into every doorway and dustbin, alleyway and dusky mews, but not this night. He wasn't looking for the chance encounter with some rookery character, whom he could observe and file in his capacious memory for use in some future novel. This night he walked as if he knew his destination.

Somewhere in the West End—we had moved so briskly that, in my struggle to keep up, I had lost all sense of direction—he braked to a sudden stop beneath a lone gaslight at the dark junction of three streets.

"I wonder . . .," he mused aloud, as I came up puffing from the exertion of our mad gallop across London.

"You wonder what?" I gasped.

"If that could be the very station house out of which our friend Inspector Field works?"

It took me a long moment to figure out what he was talking about. It had been more than fifteen months since Dickens had met Field for the first and (to my knowledge) only time, yet the Detective Inspector was suddenly our mutual friend. A street marker bolted to the brick wall of a building immediately behind our position on the street corner beneath the gaslamp read: "BOW STREET, West London."

"Perhaps it is," I finally answered. "It has been more than a year, but I believe he did say Bow Street Station that morning at the gaol."

"Splendid!" Dickens exclaimed, and set straight off across the street.

"Let us go in, and see if our friend is on duty," he said, as we read the words etched on the glass of the door:

METROPOLITAN POLICE
Bow Street Station

"Let us go in," he urged, and, of course, we did.

The reception area of the stationhouse was a drab open room with a blue-uniformed constable sitting at a desk near its back wall. Low wooden benches sat along both side walls. A door, closed, in the back wall directly behind the constable's desk, was the only break in the whitewashed monotony of the room's interior decoration.

"My name is Dickens," he said, addressing the constable on duty, "a friend of Inspector Field. Might I inquire if he is in tonight?"

"Oh, aye, sir," that blue worthy answered in immediate recognition. "He surely is sir. In the bullpen sir. Go right on back sir."

26

I think if he would have fired off one more overeager "sir," I would have slammed my walking stick down on his desk in protest. *Even the Peelers read Dickens*, I thought, with my usual dose of petty envy.

Dickens swept past the obliging constable into the inner sanctum of the Bow Street Station. The Bullpen was a larger open room filled with desks, bookcases, wide message boards on each side wall, with layers of notices on white paper pinned atop one another so thickly that the boards looked like ruffled chickens, a large metal cage (bars from ceiling to floor) filling one corner, a smaller barred holding cell filling the other corner, both cages occupied, the small one by a quiet woman with a child at her breast, the larger with an octopus of tattered rags which turned out to be three drunken tramps sleeping loudly in a pile, a fireplace built into the opposite corner, and four cushioned wooden rockers pulled up to the dancing blaze.

Two of the rockers were occupied. At our unannounced entrance, the two men turned quickly to identify us, on alert. One was a constable in blue uniform. The other, in his sharp black coat and sharp inquiring eyes, was unmistakably Inspector Field, whom I had met only once some fifteen months before. He seemed to recognize Dickens immediately and his face broke into a cordial smile as he rose to greet us.

"Dickens, a welcome surprise, good to see you again."

"This is my friend, Wilkie Collins," Dickens said, presenting me.

"Of course, Mister Collins," Field said, as he extended his oversized hand. "I remember you well. You were one of the party at 'Orsemonger Lane when the Mannings 'ad their last dance. I remember the large pocketwatch you wore on a chain and kept in the front pocket of your brocade vest that evening. I remember thinking 'ow you would be a lucky man to go away from that crowd with such a 'andsome watch still in your possession."

We shook hands heartily. Needless to say I was stunned at the unerring accuracy of his memory.

His eyes took on a mischievous glint: "You don't seem to be

wearin' your elegant pocket watch this evenin'. It must be a 'eavy trinket to carry around everyday?"

"Interesting you should ask," I said, as I walked, unsuspecting, into his trap. "I seem to have lost it. About a month ago, it just disappeared. I awoke one morning, and as I dressed I realized that I had misplaced it somewhere. Strange, never did turn up."

"Been out the evenin' before?" Field inquired sharply.

Dickens stood with an aggravating grin of amusement on his face.

"Why, yes?" My answer was really a question. *What business is it of yours, Mister Policeman?*

"Where to, if I might inquire?"

"Why, I had attended an excellent *George Barnwell* at Drury Lane."

"Crush in the aisles and exitways to the street on the way out?"

"Of course, as always. It was a well attended play."

With a sharp movement, Inspector Field administered a light, comradely tap to my chest with the forefinger of his right hand and declared, "Not lost or misplaced, Wilkie. Picked off right there in the crowd at the theatre. The Doncaster Swell Mob was workin' the West End about that time. We actually nabbed two of 'em outside Covent Garden Opera 'Ouse but all of the others got away. I'll wager the rest of this month's wages your watch is for sale right now in a fence's store in Calais or Edinburgh or Dublin."

I stood mouth agape in amazement. Not only had the man remembered me, my watch, and my person from a single meeting fifteen months before, but he had just convinced me with utter certainty to the time and place when my watch was stolen, and of its probable thief.

"Good show, Field," Dickens smiled broadly.

"You remember Rogers," Field addressed Dickens, presenting the constable who had been standing silently by his side throughout my interrogation.

"Of course, of course," Dickens said, shaking hands jovially.

I had no recollection of Rogers being with Field at the hanging in Horsemonger Lane, yet Dickens and he were shaking hands like old friends. Then it dawned on me. This wasn't the first time he had visited this stationhouse, as he had led me to believe.

Dickens and I were graciously tendered the two remaining easy chairs before the fire, and Field supplied us each with a steaming cup of ferocious black coffee brewed in a hanging pot on the hearth. We sat warming by that fire for more than an hour while Dickens plied Field with questions. That worthy talked earnestly of his work, described the cases he was pursuing at the moment. It was the intellectual exercises that Field performed on the track of a criminal that Dickens wanted to understand.

Myself and most of the rest of London would be allowed to share Dickens's interest in the subject over the course of that year. By midsummer, Dickens's series of articles on the Metropolitan Protectives would begin appearing in *Household Words*. The third of those articles, titled "The Science of Detecting," would be a composite account of Dickens's conversations with Field that very night. Another, titled "A Night At the Stationhouse," would describe the premises and procedures of the Bow Street Station. But, as we sat by that cozy fire, those articles were still some five months in the future. For Dickens's part, it was no secret that he was pumping Field for information, and, on Field's own part, it was clear that he was willingly allowing himself to be pumped. I don't think Field ever envisioned how famous he would become when Dickens put his pen to work later that year in the *Household Words* articles, and then still later when Dickens used Field as the template for the first full-fledged professional detective in English fiction.

"Inspector Field." The desk constable opened the door and interrupted our congenial host. "She's entered Rats' Castle no more than ten minutes past. Looks to be spendin' the night."

"Thank you, Bush." Field sent the Constable back to his post.

"What is it?" Dickens inquired.

"A break in a case we are presently pursuin'. A woman we want to talk with 'as been spotted enterin' one of 'er regular 'aunts."

Whether it was the fire of curiosity in Dickens's eye or Dickens's almost extra-sensory ability to transfer his own thoughts into the minds of others, Field immediately proffered the invitation which Dickens craved.

"Gentlemen, would you be interested in accompanyin' us? It is a raw night, but you might find this interestin'."

"On the contrary, it is a fine night!" Dickens laughed, as he literally bounded to his coat and hat and walking stick.

Field and Rogers secreted truncheons in the inner pockets of their greatcoats, and Rogers took a large bull's-eye down off its shelf. He tested the light once to make sure, and then led us out into a cold, heavy fog.

"The one we are after is a master thief, 'eyewayman and 'ousebreaker named Tally Ho Thompson," Field explained. "'E got 'is name from 'is fancy 'orsemanship when 'ee was workin' the roads up 'round Shooter's 'Ill. 'Ee's been in and out of our grasp three times in recent weeks, and now 'ee seems to 'ave disappeared off the face of the earth. But 'ee's a reg'lar rogue with the ladies, and one of 'is favorites, one Scarlet Bess, 'as just checked into Rats' Castle for the night. If we press 'er 'ard, mayhap she'll tell where 'ee is. I doubt it. She's an old 'and. Not easily tricked is Scarlet Bess Nisbet."

Somewhere above us and to the right, in the grey blanket of fog, a church clock struck eleven.

"Saint Giles Church," Field informed us with a certainty which the darkness of the night, the thickness of the fog, and the labyrinthine confusion of the streets immediately called into question. *How can he know that's Saint Giles*, I scoffed.

"Aye, Saint Giles," Rogers, swinging his bull's-eye, agreed, "we're almost to the rookery. Look sharp!"

Though one could barely see, the streets seemed narrower, more tortuous. Turning and stopping and turning again, we ascended small inclines, and then edged gingerly downhill, always moving relentlessly to our left as if the world had started to list in that direction. Suddenly, jabbing back with his bull's-eye, Rogers brought us to a halt.

Only then did we get the opportunity to savour the particular attractions of the neighborhood. Sickening smells hung in the air of the labyrinthine cavern formed by the narrow streets and twisting alleyways of the rookery. The creaking sounds of houses getting ready to tumble down moaned softly in the foggy night.

A voice attached to a shambling rat-like creature materialized out of the fog, and addressed Rogers and Inspector Field. "She's in there, Guv, she is," it said, and it stuck out its filthy hand.

"You've earned it tonight, Mike Slater," Field said, filling that emaciated claw with a brown coin. The man's rodent face, startled in the light of the bull's-eye, opened into a toothless death's-head grin.

"'ook it, Mike," Rogers ordered our informant, and the man scurried back to his hole.

"I must warn you Mister Dickens, Mister Collins," Field's voice was almost fatherly, "you may see and 'ear things 'ere which will disgust you or frighten you or cause you to look with despair on the reality of man's fallen state. This is an ugly, evil place peopled with thieves, murderers, prostitutes, and the worst coves in the city of London. The men are animals, and the women are perversions of all that is chaste and respectable. We must go amongst these women. They will make lewd overtures and propositions. They may even take liberties in order to influence us. You may find this encounter 'eyely offensive."

"Let us push on. Reality is something from which no writer should ever shrink," Dickens asserted gamely. I personally wondered whether we were in for a rather heavier dose of reality than ordered, as had been the case at the Manning hanging.

Rogers led the way with his bull's-eye.

31

"Close up now, gentlemen," Field ordered. "Keep together. We are going down. 'Eads!"

We stopped as we descended a flight of rickety steps into a black, foul-smelling underworld. At the bottom of this filthy cistern, Rogers kicked in a locked door. We entered a dim, close cellar lit by a smoky fire and a few random candles set in waxen pools on dirty tables. The cellar was full of dangerous-looking people, chiefly young men in various conditions of raggedness. There were also women present.

When Inspector Field stepped through the doorway, the whole company went silent.

"'Ow are you tonight, lads? I've brought some company to see you tonight, ladies. Rats' Castle is indeed busy this evenin'." Field was not laughing as he moved between the tables. His sharp eyes noted every grimace of guilt and hate and fear on the face of every cringing felon in the room.

Though they were upwards of thirty and he but one, they cowered before him, laughed at his jokes, answered when he spoke.

As he passed among them, a large woman in a black dress laced loosely across her breasts, bolder than the others, rose to joke with Field. She pointed a finger at Dickens and myself. "Ye've brought us some juicy gentlemen, 'aven't ye Inspector, sir?" the harlot taunted.

He smiled benignly, but with a quick sideways movement clasped the arm of another young woman.

"Ah, Scarlet Bess, I thought that was you. You're the one I've come to see tonight."

When he made his swift move and pulled the woman to her feet in the center of that crowd of ruffians, they could easily have overpowered him. But no one resisted his movement with Scarlet Bess in tow across the room. All present in Rats' Castle were relieved that Inspector Field hadn't come for them.

Bess struggled, but in Field's firm grasp she was quickly subdued.

"Hi've done nothink," she protested. "Lamme go. You canna take *me*. Hi've done nothink."

32

Field ignored her whining cries.

"Please, please doan let 'im take me," she pleaded to the others as Field led her up to where we waited, with our backs to the door.

At closer view, Scarlet Bess proved a surprisingly handsome as well as exotic speciman, albeit dirty and rough. Her hair was long and brown and splashed in an unruly cascade about her face and neck. Her eyes, also brown and large, were somewhat reddened by drink. A sullen look of hate and fear twisted her full mouth. I hesitate to describe her appearance in more detail, but, heeding the dictum of Dickens my mentor that a true writer should not shrink from reality, I must go on. The one aspect of her appearance which could not be overlooked were the two capacious mounds straining at the laces of her bodice.

Field seemed to have her and the whole room, down to the scuttling rats, under his control. Yet, her calm was only momentary. In one last desperate spasm, she fell to her knees, clutching at Field's legs and pleading for his mercy. Field remained unmoved by her histrionics. Twisting up hard on her wrist, he yanked her to her feet and thrust her through the opening left by the absence of the door which Rogers had shattered off its pegs.

I am sure that Dickens was as relieved as I to escape that pit of cutthroats. The taciturn Rogers, giving one final flash of his bull's-eye across the restless surface of the room as a warning for its occupants to stay put, formed our rear guard.

Field, with his prize, led us up out of that underworld to a narrow black street which ultimately surfaced into a wider thoroughfare. There, he pulled up beneath the hazy light of a solitary streetlamp and confronted the woman.

"It's Thompson I want, not you Bess," Field said, facing her, still keeping firm hold of her wrist. "Where is your cove? Tell me and you're free to 'ook it."

"Aven't seen 'im in a fortnight." Her voice was strange as she answered, no longer angry or desperate, but seductive. "You've taken me afore, Mister Field. 'Ee's not my cove no more. What is it *you* want?"

"It's Thompson I want," Field repeated calmly.

With her free hand, the harlot suddenly clawed at the laces of her bodice. "No, hit's this you want," the creature crooned obscenely, as the top of her dress dropped to her waist. In the same motion, she pressed her body hard against Field's chest.

With a swift punitive decisiveness, Field slapped her hard.

The creature recoiled away from him, the whiteness of her exposed breasts undulating in the saffron light of the fog-bound gaslamp.

He dragged her into the shadows of a wall some yards away from us. "It's Thompson I want, you little 'ore!" His voice was raised, slightly out of control. The disembodied murmuring of their lowered voices floated toward us out of the darkness.

The woman's actions convinced both Dickens and myself that she was capable of any conceivable lewdness for the purposes of her criminal lover's preservation. We agreed, as Lord Tennyson had said it in the violent rhythms of his great masterpiece, that she was indeed "Nature red in tooth and claw." And yet, recollecting that scene later, we could not but feel pity and even responsibility for this woman and so many more like her who come up to London looking for a life and find instead only degradation. Our society, then and no less now, seems able to view women in only two widely separate ways, as respectable matrons or as whores. There should be some middle ground, some synthesis (as that curious German exile, Marx, who haunted the British Museum, might put it) of these opposing and limiting views of women. But in eighteen hundred fifty-one there were thousands of Scarlet Besses in London proper, and more arriving every day.

Field's handling of this whole indelicate situation bespoke his mastery over this fallen world. He was rough with her because he understood her motives, but he never lost control of his temper, never tried to hurt her. It was as if he could identify with her hopeless plight. We learned later that Field was a bachelor who lived alone in Great Russell Street near the

British Museum. Another time, he actually said in reference to a criminal bearing the odd name of John Butt: "'Ee's not so different from me, I from 'im. I found 'im because I know 'ow 'ee thinks." Having obtained what information he needed, Field and his prisoner emerged from the darkness. He dismissed her under our streetlamp, and the London night swallowed her up in an instant.

With Rogers and his bull's-eye once again in the lead, we retraced our steps to the Bow Street Stationhouse. The fog had not relinquished its grip on the city. Beneath another lone streetlamp, Field paused to light a cigar. Quietly he apologized for the woman's shocking behavior. He stated that he had obtained and would obtain more information from the woman, which would guarantee that Tally Ho Thompson would be run to ground. And then, he said a rather strange thing.

"The women of these rookeries are the 'ardest to deal with," Field said, "the 'ardest by a stretch. There's much more to them than the men. The men are often slow an' 'ard an' don't 'ave no 'ooman feelin's, live like animals. But the women still seem to believe in love, 'old on to that chance. Too bad. They learn ta lie, steal, do anythin' for love. 'Ats 'ow the men turn 'em into 'ores."

We bid Inspector Field "good night" at the stationhouse door. He protested that Rogers should light us back to our lodgings, but Dickens steadfastly refused that courtesy. "These are my streets. I walk them every night," Dickens insisted. Field only chuckled at that bit of braggadocio as if thinking, *They are my streets, an' I could teach you much about 'em.* Dickens extracted a promise that, when on some future evening some particularly interesting case or bit of detective work arose, Field would summon him to another evening of observation.

WE ARE OFF!

(April 12, 1851)

One week later to the day, I was working late with Dickens in the Wellington Street offices, when a sharp knocking at the street door interrupted us. The knock was quiet insistent and authoritative. It was well after dark.

"Ah, the knocking at the gate," Dickens joked. "MacCready would make much of this. He is doing *Macbeth* this very night."

I peeked out through the small porthole window in the door and was blinded as if by the headlight of a train bearing down upon me in a tunnel.

"Bright light . . ." I stammered as Dickens boldly peered out.

"It's Constable Rogers and his bull's-eye," Dickens announced as he hastened to unbolt the door.

"There's been a report of a murder. Before dawn this morning. Near Blackfriars Bridge." Rogers spoke in haste.

"A murder!" Curiosity and excitement vibrated in Dickens's voice.

"Aye, murder allright. Thought to be a gentlemen, stabbed and 'elped into the Thames. Whether dead or alive, we don't know, but our nets are out."

"Dead or alive! Heigh-ho Wilkie, did you hear that?"

How could I not have heard it.

"Inspector Field sent me to fetch ye, as promised." Rogers could barely mask his enmity toward us as the cause of his being sent on this menial errand, and thus exiled from the eye of a murder investigation. "Please gentlemen, we must 'urry to get back before they leave for the river."

Dickens and I dashed back up the stairs to extinguish the gaslights and pull on our greatcoats while Rogers champed in the lower hallway.

"Wilkie, this takes me back fifteen years to when I was a young reporter on the *Mirror of Parliament* and the *True Sun*. This is truly something to get the blood up."

On foot, Rogers led us at a stiff gallop through the dark maze of West London's streets. We passed through Covent Garden just at the moment when the crowd was the thickest, choking the narrow street as they waited for the doors to open at that famous theater, but Rogers paid the crowd no attention. There was bigger game abroad this night. Breathless, we arrived at the detectives' door of the Bow Street Station.

Inside the bullpen, Field rose from his pillowed rocker and shook our hands heartily. "So glad you could make it, gentlemen," he said (quite comically, I thought—as if he had invited us for tea and crumpets, rather than crime and murder). I noticed a woman in a deep maroon dress warming herself by the fire. I'm sure that Dickens noticed her as well. He missed nothing. In the blaze of the fire, her appearance— the low cut of the top of her gown, the chaos of her hair—revealed why the niceties of social etiquette did not immediately apply. Yet, it was impossible to keep one's eyes from her as she sat, unintroduced, like a threat, across the room.

"We're waitin' for word from the river. A body, rumored a gentleman's, went in off the steps above Blackfriars Bridge when the tide was goin' up."

"Extraordinary," Dickens exclaimed. "I can't tell you how pleased I am that you summoned us."

"The body will come down on the tide tonight, unless its gotten 'ung up on something. But they're pretty good about that. They normally stick to the middle of the river where the current runs fastest."

"What are we waiting upon?" I inquired politely. "Constable

Rogers implied great urgency." Had Rogers not left the bullpen, I probably wouldn't have posed the question.

Field, scratching the side of his eye with that crook'd forefinger, said in a lowered voice: "Rogers 'as a tendency to exaggerate when 'ee gets a bit excited, you know—the subordinate's eagerness not to miss out. 'Ee probably gave you a devil of a run to get back 'ere," Field chuckled.

I wasn't nearly as amused by Rogers's officiousness.

Continuing, Field leaned conspiratorially into us. "It's a little game we play with the watermen. The body should come down on the tide if our informant 'as got the times right," he said, and glanced eloquently to the woman by the fire. "A waterside prostitute. Says she saw it all. Says body went in off the stairs above Blackfriars. We figure the Thames river rats will save us the price of a dredger. One in particular we keep in our pay. We're waitin' for word of 'im."

"How did it go in?" Dickens asked eagerly. No detail could be too insignificant for his novelist's curiosity.

For my part, I was captured by the woman. Her neck was white and her full breasts almost completely exposed by the low-cut, loosely laced bosom of her dark, blood-coloured dress. She stared fixedly at the flames as if contemplating throwing herself into them. The shimmering blaze sent flickering shadows across her face which softened her mien, and ripples of orange light sparked in her thick mob of ungoverned curls.

From across the room, she seemed beautiful to me. Dickens has frequently cautioned me about my tendency to idealize.*

"She saw it all," Field answered Dickens's question.

He led us across the bullpen to hold audience with the fire-woman.

---

*Years later, in a cautionary letter, when Collins was caught in the throes of his obsession with the real "Women In White," Dickens would remind his friend of his tendency "to be carried away like a paper boat on the tide."

"This is Meggy Sheehey, also known as Irish Meg," Field introduced the woman, who raised her eyes from the fire with disdain. "This is Mister Dickens and Mister Collins."

"Aye . . . Mister Dickens, eh? Oy've 'eard o' you, allright, oy 'ave."

"We're lucky to 'ave Meg this time." Field played to his audience. "We've got ourselves a reg'lar eyewitness come for'ard voluntarily."

"The bloody bastards did'na pay me. That's the only reason I follered 'em. To make 'em pay. Fieldsy knows that. All's for a price, Fieldsy. For a price. Don't forget."

Field frowned at her familiarity. "We're not so sure Meg didn't 'ave something to do with this man's goin' in, are we Meg? That scene's still possible. You're goin' to watch your langwidge, ain't you Meg?"

Her lips clamped tight, and she slumped back in the chair, subdued.

"Now," Field ordered, bending down and crooking his forefinger lightly under her defiant chin, "tell your story from start to the throwin' in."

"Oy wos workin' the street outsoyd the door o' *The Snug Harbor* verry late las' night. On a suddin, five swells, all drunk, climb out o' a 'ansom cab. They muss'a bin piled atop each other. Wos a strange sight. Five swells in that place near the river at that time o' night. *The Snug*, she's a sailors' pub, she is. But there wos five fine 'uns, standin' there in the street big as life. Wos a strange sight, allright."

As if the strangeness of it all had suddenly parched her whole being, the fire-woman reached for her glass, which was sitting on the small deal table at her right hand. Field caught her meaning immediately, and produced a half-full bottle of gin out of a cabinet. Her glass filled, Irish Meg returned to her tale.

"The five swells didna go inta *The Snug*. Smart o' 'em. Instead they spotted me. I gave 'em me terms. They walked me to a bench near the river. Two o' 'em used me. The other three jus' watched. Two o' 'em used me but only one paid proper.

39

The others, the one wi' the fat, curlin' nosebrush, laughed and spit on me as I knelt there. They were an ugly crew, all drunk, and at each other the 'ole time. They staggered away along the river. I follered 'em, keepin' my distance."

At this point in her narrative, Rogers stuck his head in and called Inspector Field from the room to consult. The woman seized the occasion to take a long pull from her gin glass. Satisfied, she grinned slyly up at us and dropped all pretension. "Wot are you gents?" she asked boldly. "Swells come to sniff about in London's dustbin? Swells brought round to watch the animals perform? You know, gents, for a price you can perform with the animals." With a wink, she brazenly threw back her shoulders to display the full white expanse of her breasts and with both hands she formed the most indecent of gestures. With the thumb and forefinger of her left she formed a circle through which she drove her straightened right forefinger with a pumping motion. She was the second prostitute to whom Field had introduced us, yet she was utterly different from Scarlet Bess. This one seemed to have an ironic sense of humor, seemed to enjoy taunting these two voyeurist swells, whose witness to her degradation she obviously resented. When Field came back into the room, Irish Meg gave a short laugh at our discomfiture, and dove back into her story.

"I follered all the way to Blackfriars Bridge. They moved slow—a couple stopped to piss in the shadows. Then they started yellin' at each other. 'Bout some girl. The little man yappin' her name. Helen, I think it was, or somethin' like. Right before Blackfriars Bridge a fight broke out between the big man with the whiskers and the little man. Two others grabbed the big man, but the little man had a big knife. 'Ee stabbed the big man in the belly while t'others 'eld 'im. T'other man just watched, then sicked-up all over the ground."

"You say you can identify the men," Field pressed.

"Oh, I knows 'em allright. I sees the whole thing. 'Ow the big man falls on the ground and don' move. 'Ow the rest on 'em gather roun' him pokin' and rollin' 'im over. 'Ow they whisper together. 'Ow they pick 'im up, carry 'im to the steps and push 'im in. Oh, I sees it all, allright."

"And you're sure you can recognize all of their faces?"

To my great surprise it was Dickens's voice which had taken up the interrogation. In the excitement of her story, his curiosity had made him blurt out the question without thinking.

"Theer faces ain't all I'd rekernize o' 'em," Irish Meg laughed at her vulgar joke. Dickens couldn't suppress his own grin. Field laughed out loud.

"Remarkable," Dickens exclaimed.

"With gin and a promise of good pay, Meg can, at times, be remarkable indeed," Field flattered her.

"Oh, oy'm a pricey 'ore, oy am," Irish Meg saluted us.

At that very moment Rogers poked his head back in, and announced that the signal had arrived from the river.

Dickens's eyes flashed with anticipation.

"Now Dickens, Mister Collins, Meggy girl," Field jabbed his forefinger at each of us in turn, "we are off!"

UNDER BLACKFRIARS BRIDGE

(April 12, 1851)

We marched in Rogers's tow through the dark labyrinth of streets, until the sour smell of the Thames and the dark shapes of warehouses, skeletal docks, and the naked masts of ships signaled our arrival in the shadowy waterside neighborhood.

Out of one of those shadows suddenly stepped an apparition. Inspector Field confronted it. "Good evenin' to you, Mister Marcus," he said. "Ben keepin' the watch as directed?"

"Lor', if it ain't Insperrer Field hirrselferrer." This Marcus seemed overwhelmed either by the great honor of being greeted by that personage or by the heavy cargo of gin he had already taken on that evening.

Rogers immediately thrust forward his flaming eye and illuminated this spectral figure. His clothes were all rags and he shook uncontrollably from the cut of the sharp river wind or, perhaps, from the effects of the gin. His head was wrapped in a sailor's knit cap which, pulled down tight around his face, caused him to resemble a grinning skull. "Yee're quite the loose rogue tonight, ain't ye, Mister Marcus?" Rogers threatened.

Field, impatient, moved between Rogers and this riverside skull. "Loose rogue perhaps, but on the watch, right Mister Marcus?"

"Yetherrer. Onna watcherrer all night. Irs arful colderrer, Mirrer Insperrer. Need my money, shurr. Need to girr waarrrmmerrer."

At the mention of money, Field's forefinger became unfriendly and began tapping the sepulchral Marcus on the chest. "You've been skulkin' 'ere all evenin', Marcus. What 'ave you done ta earn your gin?"

"I dorrn spend ir on gin," the skull, abashed, protested.

"It's all you spend it on, wretch," Rogers spat.

"Give us your report," Field ordered.

I watched Dickens as he hung on every word and I could tell that he was recording it down to the very sound and inflection of the drunken informant's slurred speech. I could see Dickens sitting at his desk later, and opening a lock in his mind, and all of it flowing out to become characters and scenes in one or another of his novels. As for me, I watched it all from the background in the company of Irish Meg.

"'Orrible ain't 'ee," she moved closer and whispered to me. When I looked at her in the dim backlight of Rogers's bull's-eye, her eyes were sad, as if she were seeing something in a mirror that frightened her. She was no longer taunting me with obscene gestures; rather, she seemed to want someone to

42

talk with, and for some reason she had chosen me. I didn't answer her overture.

"Ee's bin out morrer 'an an arrerrer," Marcus slobbered. "Ee's orrerdrue, orrerdrue. I'rr take yerrer ter wherrer he'rr purt in."

We followed our guide's unsteady lead down through the darkness to the river. A sliver of moon cast dim shadows across its surface. Its current crept, deathly black, between its low jagged shores. To me it seemed a river of death, full of pathetic suicides and drowned bodies, a graveyard for the city's lost.

Marcus led us to a jumble of small boats pulled up in the mud within view of the towering iron scaffold of Blackfriars Bridge. "Ee'll purr in 'ere, 'Umphry wirrll," he assured us.

Field grabbed a handful of Marcus and escorted him away out of our hearing. In a minute or two Field returned alone and Marcus, that grinning skull, had returned to his grave-hole in the city.

We all moved into the lee of an overturned boat to escape the wind. Dickens and Field conversed in low tones. Rogers stood lookout. Irish Meg moved so close to me that I could smell the gin on her breath, feel the voluptuous rise and fall of her breathing beneath her slight wrap. I removed my long woolen scarf which had been wrapped across my chest beneath my greatcoat and placed it around Irish Meg's neck. The shivering woman accepted it without protest, but in doing so fixed me with the strangest of looks, eyes startled. She said not a word as she wrapped the scarf around her white neck, but her eyes forced mine to retreat back to the silent, black expanse of that infernal river.

We waited twenty minutes beneath that overturned boat. Rogers's bull's-eye paced back and forth along the river's edge like the eye of some huge prowling hound. Twice he returned to report the obvious to Inspector Field: "No sign o' 'im 'ere yet sir."

"'Ee knows the body's out there. 'Ee should've snagged it by now," Field spat the words toward the river.

"Ee's a sure waterman," Rogers consoled his governor, "and you know 'ee's too afeerd to ever cross us."

"Aye, but we can't wait 'ere all night," Field said, glancing at Dickens and myself. "Let's give these fine gentlemen a real adventure, Rogers." He grinned at us in the light of the bull's-eye. "Give the signal with your light, and fetch our man of the Thames Police."

Rogers marched off to the dark river bank, and swung his bull's-eye over his head three times. Within moments his signal was answered by the sound of oars slapping the thick water. After another moment or two, a low dark shape slid into shore.

We heard voices. Gruff greetings were exchanged as Field joined Rogers at the river's edge. Dickens, the woman and myself quickly left our temporary shelter and followed. Without hesitation, at Field's brusque "Go on, get in," we climbed into the launch and found ourselves propelled out into the grasp of that black current. The oarsmen leaned to their work. We moved steadily upstream against the tide toward the towering iron hulk that is Blackfriars Bridge. Dickens and Field conversed. I could only catch snatches of their conversation.

"We'll find 'im. 'Ee'll not get by us in the dark of midriver now."

Dickens nodded vigorously and said something which I could not overhear. Irish Meg Sheehey huddled at my side. "This is passin' stoopid, this is," she muttered as the boat rocked against the current and we were swallowed into the dark maw of shadow that is the underbridge.

That is how Dickens and I found ourselves in a four-oared Thames Police Galley lying in the deep shadow of Blackfriars Bridge. The massive iron skeleton quartered the lowering sky above us, and, below us, its hulking black shadow seemed to penetrate all the way to the bottom of the stream.

"We're lookin' for a small boat with one man at the sculls. If 'ee's got wot we want 'ee'll be low in the water or else 'ee'll 'ave our goods in tow," Field instructed us. We floated on the flood. The Thames policeman in the bow held fast to one of the bridge pilings. The river rushed swiftly by.

We didn't have to wait long. Field, of course, saw it first, no more than a small moving shadow on the water, but enough for Field's forefinger to point and Field's brusque voice to order: "There. There's our man. Bend to 'em, lads."

We shot out of the deep shadow of the underbridge and caught the current, which sent us swiftly toward our target. The man, bent to the oars of the small boat for the purpose of steering, not rowing (for the rushing tide carried the boat firmly in its grasp), did not seem to notice us as we bore down upon him. To the rear of his mongrel boat, something split the water in tow. With one last strong pull, our oarsmen shipped their sculls and we intercepted him.

It looked like a boat which had barely survived a shipwreck. It was patched and braced with bits of the rejected garbage of the Thames, the most slapped together of boats, a boat of many colors, a patchwork boat with more crazy boards and dashes of pitch than could be found on a countrywoman's quilt.

At the boat's sculls sat a block of a man. His hulking shoulders conjured the African gorillas I had so recently seen with Dickens in the Zoological Gardens in Hyde Park. We floated alongside and Constable Rogers clamped onto the waterman's ragged gunwale. A mean-looking hooked and pointed boatman's gaff rested in the bottom of this waterman's boat. However, when he spoke, his voice was amiable enough.

"'Iss un's a reel swell, 'spector," the waterman nodded to the cargo in tow behind his makeshift boat. "More lace an' muttonchops than yer damn Prince Regent."

For a long moment, Field stared at him without saying a word, but I noticed that intimidating forefinger make a contemplative scratch at the corner of his eyebrow. Meanwhile, the waterman's dark cargo floated and bounced merrily on the flood, arms and legs rolling crazily like some comic marionette at each tug of its rope.

"Where 'ave you been 'idin' all evenin'?" Field demanded. "We've been waitin' almost an 'our for you to deliver our package, and it's no night for waitin' under bridges."

"Yer mustachioed friend," the waterman said, jerking a thumb toward his cargo, "got detained 'mongst the keels an' anchor ropes of the hupstream shippin'. Found hisself in an orful tangle, 'ee did. I hackchoohally 'ad to tie hup an go ho-ver the side jus' to cut 'im loose. Sorry, guv'ner, but theese blokes don't always jus' swim up an' hook themselves to yer line like yer reg'lar little fishes do."

"Did you search the body? Was there identification on it?" Field's voice sounded as if he wasn't really interested in his own question, as if he already knew its answer, as if this were a familiar game.

"Pleese guv'nor," the man's voice evidenced great dismay. "I nivver teched nothink. I knows the rules. The searchin' is the job o' the dirtective. All I did wos wot you said," he protested. "Find the body. 'Ats all. 'Ats all."

Seemingly satisfied with the man's protestations, Field, with a jerk of his forefinger, ordered the man to follow the police galley to shore.

"'Ee was out so long because 'ee searched the body, stripped it of its valuables and 'id them somewhere upstream," Field explained. "It will take us days, maybe weeks, to identify the body. That corpse won't 'ave a shillin' or a scrap of identification. It'll be lucky if its got the gold in its teeth!"

Within minutes, the waterman beached his mongrel boat in the mud next to ours. We watched with morbid curiosity, as, pulling hand over hand, he dragged his grisly cargo ashore. The rope was noosed beneath the dead man's armpits. The body was coatless and bootless. A huge dark stain covered the whole back of what, by the hint of its muddy sleeves, must have been a white evening shirt. The corpse came to rest face down at our feet.

I watched Dickens as the waterman pulled his grisly piece of salvage to us. He stared hard at the hole ripped in the center of that dark stain.

"My God, how could this happen?" he said in a low voice.

"'Appens once, sometimes twice each week," Rogers replied, brusque and unfeeling. "Man's been stabbed," he diagnosed the body's ailment.

46

"Stabbed indeed," Field said, taking up the diagnosis as impersonally as if describing a large river trout recently fileted for his supper, "and, from the looks of that wound, by a large, flat, quite pointed blade. Not your usual waterside robber's blade, eh Rogers?"

"No sir. Not at all, sir."

"Who are these fine gennulmen?" the waterman demanded of Field.

Field introduced us. "This is the famous Mister Charles Dickens," he said, grinning as if enjoying some private joke, "and Mister Wilkie Collins."

"Famous fer wot?"

"For books."

"Don't know nothink 'bout books."

The man faced Dickens and me down, and, congenially enough in his rough way, introduced himself: "I be 'Umphry 'Owse. If I worked on land they'd call me a resurrection man, but since I works the river they calls me a fisher o' men." He howled at his own joke.

Rogers quickly stooped to the corpse, showing no squeamishness as he rifled its pockets. "Nothin'," he informed Field.

"You've done your usual thorough job," Field muttered.

Humphrey House, the waterman, flinched perceptibly and shrank backwards.

At that moment, Rogers rolled the body over to continue his search. The corpse's gaunt dead eyes stared up at us. Drops of moisture and smears of mud distorted that sightless face.

Dickens started back, his face twisting in shock and recognition.

"What is it?" Inspector Field, who missed nothing, and certainly not such a dramatic change of expression, asked immediately.

I had never seen the "Inimitable" so discomposed. No one, not even Macready, could have imitated that startled look.

"I . . . I know that face," Dickens stammered.

47

THE BODY WILL TELL US!

(April 13, 1851)

It was midnight by the bells atop Saint Paul's, but not for the spirit which once inhabited that sodden corpse staring up from its bed in the mud of the Victoria embankment.

"I know that face," Dickens repeated, his voice shaking.

"Well, who is it?" Rogers's impatience showed.

"What ho, identified on the spot," Field took a lighter tack.

"Yes . . . Yes . . . I know the man," Dickens uttered the words slowly as if in a daze.

Inspector Field became positively festive.

The corpse lay silent like some shipwrecked seaman washed ashore on an alien beach.

"It is Lawyer Partlow of Lincoln's Inn Fields. He is an acquaintance of Forster's. In fact, one of Forster's close neighbours." Dickens's voice gained strength with each word. "Forster lives at fifty-eight Lincoln's Inn Fields and Partlow at sixty-two. We shared a hansom back from the theatre one evening. Their addresses were a subject of the conversation."

Both Field and Rogers were impressed by Dickens's novelist's memory.

"You 'ave no idea 'ow much better than a 'FOUND DEAD' notice posted on boards across the city your identification is," Field gushed.

"We wouldn't 'ave identified this bloke for days," Rogers nodded.

"Partlow is well known among the players at Covent Garden Theatre. He is one of the most visible patrons and the theatre's

48

solicitor, said to be an expert in angel contracts and private fund raising. He has even taken his turn in the crowd scenes of some of the more populous productions." Dickens's voice had gradually become clinical and detached. "Macready dislikes him, but then Macready dislikes everyone," Dickens finished with a quip, the procession of facts from his capacious memory having dispelled his initial shock at being acquainted with such a brutally murdered corpse.

"Excellent work, Mister Dickens," Inspector Field complimented him. "You 'ave saved me days of work with your identification."

Dickens bowed and smiled.

A lorry clattered up on the street; the horse stood snorting in the cold wind. Two Bow Street constables placed the body in a winding sheet, the sheet in the lorry and drove off. Field directed us to wait, which occasioned Dickens and me to retreat once again into the shelter of the same overturned boat we had employed earlier. From that protected vantage we watched as Inspector Field tied up the loose ends of the evening.

First he summoned his water rat, honest Humphrey, and lectured him at some length. Through it all, the dredger repeatedly shook his head in denial, and held out his hands in shrugs of the sort the guilty make when their good character is being impugned. Finally, Field threw up his hands and, with a curse, paid the man with one large coin. With that, the water rat scurried to his mongrel boat, pushed off the mud, clambered aboard and was carried off by the flood.

Field next turned to Irish Meg Sheehey. He moved her off toward the river out of our hearing. I could barely make out their shadows standing close together against the gray-black of the river. I imagine that Field was outlining her responsibilities as the chief witness in the case. I am also certain that money was exchanged. Their private colloquy ended, they moved back toward our point of vantage.

As they approached up that beach of oily mud, without really knowing why, I stepped toward her. Actually, Inspector

Field was somewhat startled when I suddenly popped out from under that overturned boat. I stopped short. I had nothing to say, especially with Dickens and Field standing by. My sudden impulsive movement toward this fallen creature made me feel quite foolish indeed.

Meg Sheehey did a strange thing, however. She smiled as if she understood.

"Mind your manners, Meggy," Inspector Field snapped. He missed nothing. "Be gone," he ordered with a harsh jab of his frightening forefinger.

Her face twisted into a sudden look of disdain for all of us. She turned and ran off into the night.

I was, of course, embarrassed by my impulsiveness, embarrassed by my romantic idealization of this common street harlot, but most of all I was embarrassed that Dickens and Field had seen my attraction to the woman. Yet, the woman had cast a strange spell over me. She had an independence about her atypical of her sex in our age. When she disappeared into the night, all that was left was that image of her gazing raptly into the fire in her blood red dress back at the stationhouse. I was convinced that Meggy Sheehey, the fire-woman, was different from all the others. I felt a strange sadness that our brief intercourse had been forced to end so abruptly. I never expected to meet her again. Little did I know then about the fickleness of expectations.

Field quickly dispatched Rogers with orders to oversee the cleaning and scrutinizing of Lawyer Partlow's corpse, ending with a directive to report the results to him at "the usual place."

Then Field turned to us: "Gentlemen, it 'as been an eventful evenin'. If you are like me, you are chilled to the bone. There is only one remedy. You must allow me to stand you a 'ot gin. I'm sure you want to see this affair through. It will be an 'our until the surgeon's scrutiny of the deceased is completed."

We accepted his invitation without hesitation.

Inspector Field led us back through narrow airless streets to the Bow Street neighbourhood. We passed by the bright lamps burning on the facade of the Police Station where, we presumed, the shell of what had been Lawyer Partlow was being scrutinized. A few abrupt turns brought us to a closed alley and a pub sign that read "THE LORD GORDON ARMS." This was clearly Field's "usual place." The public house was warm and hospitable. The Inspector was well-known there. The publican, who in this case proved an ample and jovial lady of the ruddy persuasion, came out from behind the tap and personally escorted us to a private room down a short rear hallway.

"They will warm us a flavorful gin 'ere, gentlemen," Field assured us, "and tease it with the flavor of nutmeg and lemon if you so desire."

He gave his order to the woman with a curt nod, and she, in turn, dispatched a blank-looking boy of fifteen or sixteen who had followed us down the hallway. With quick facility, she stoked and lit the fire, and, with an energetic pumping of a large antique bellows, it was soon blazing away.

"Miss Katie Tillotson, Proprietress," Field introduced our hostess after she had vacated the room. "Inherited the Lord Gordon from 'er first 'usband thirty years ago and 'as gone through two more since; first two dead, natural, third driven away for stealin' from 'er till and drinkin' up 'er profits. Fine woman, Miss Katie. Keeps a clean, well-lit 'ouse."

Neither Dickens nor I had any argument with that. Within moments, the dull boy returned with a large steaming jug from which, to our frozen senses, emanated the most fragrant odor of spiced gin we had ever sniffed. He poured us each a steaming mug, and withdrew. For long minutes, we warmed ourselves by the welcome hearth, and sipped gratefully from our smoking cups. It was a reflective Dickens who finally broke the silence.

"It seems hard to believe what I have seen this evening, Inspector Field. Reality is indeed a shocking thing."

"What's shockin'," Field answered slowly, "is that this reality 'appens every week. People take to murder as easy and reg'lar as if it were a darts game or a dust disposal."

"One can't help but wonder why that man was so brutally murdered."

"The 'why' of it is the last thing to make itself known in most o' these cases. We can find the ''ow' and the 'where' and the 'when' and even the 'who,' but the 'why?' Even the murderers sometimes don't know 'why.'"

"Ah, but to me, the 'why' is the most interesting."

I could see that Dickens was hooked.

"Not to me," Field disagreed. He and Dickens had fallen into a debate which reminded me of two scholars of different disciplines presenting their opposing views of the same case. "To me, the real game is the readin' of the signs, the gatherin' of the clues, the puttin' together of the puzzle. My satisfactions come in catchin' my man. Let the magistrates worry about catchin' 'is reasons."

"But aren't you curious about them? After you catch them don't you talk to them to find out 'why?'"

"Not atall. Not atall. After I get 'em cuffed, I don't even think on 'em anymore. I've done my job and there is always another waitin'."

Dickens had no further argument for that and we sipped our gin in silence for a minute or two.

"How could something like what we witnessed this evening happen in a civilized society?" Dickens mused aloud. "This man was a gentleman, accepted in the highest, most respectable circles."

"Because it ain't a civilized society," Field was enjoying himself, "otherwise there'd be no need for my kind. As to 'ow it 'appened . . ."

"Yes, how?"

"The body will tell us."

That cryptic statement left both Dickens and myself at sea.

"'Ow did it 'appen," Field repeated, seeing Dickens and I befuddled at his pronouncement. "A drunken argument, the woman says. The body will tell us more."

At that very moment, Rogers entered our snug retreat bearing a folded paper, the Police Surgeon's report on the corpse. Field took the report from his lieutenant but, before looking at it, called for the dull-eyed boy to bring another mug and, when delivered, poured his second-in-command a steaming draught. Only when Rogers was settled amongst us did Field turn to see what indeed "the body would tell us."

"Well?" Dickens couldn't wait. "What does it say?"

"Yes," I added, paraphrasing Inspector Field ironically, "just what is it that Lawyer Partlow's body has to tell us?"

He smiled patronizingly, the professional briefing the amateurs: "As one might expect, 'is clothes were expensively tailored. 'Is waistcoat was missin', probably appropriated along with all money and identifyin' papers by 'Umphrey the waterman. 'Is 'ands were still gloved. 'Eavy bruises on the face and 'ead, but, because they contain splinters of creosoted wood, they probably were caused by the tides throwin' 'im against the 'ulls of ships after 'ee was put in the water. 'Ee was stabbed from behind by a long, quite wide, flat blade, long enough to go all the way through the body and emerge from the chest. Blade was withdrawn with a downward wrench which split the whole back open. Shape of wound and exit wound suggest some kind of medieval sword, very 'eavy, skin around the wound totally crushed. That's what the body of our friend Partlow 'as to say tonight, gentlemen."

We were visibly impressed.

"Oh, one more thing. Surgical opinion says death by stabbin', not death by drownin'. That's important."

"Why?" I asked.

"Makes a difference as to whether we're lookin' for just one murderer or whether all four of the men present are to be charged. Meg said they either 'elped carry the body to the stairs and threw it in, or they stood by and watched while it was done without interferin'. But if the stab wound killed him, the others get off free."

With that, we were even more impressed.

"What does it all mean?" Dickens asked.

"What it means," Inspector Field said, glancing quickly at Rogers, who sipped at his steaming gin and looked out from beneath his fierce black eyebrows, "is that this is planned murder. No drunken argument as Meggy thought. Murder plain and simple."

"For God's sake, why do you say that?" Dickens exploded.

Field smiled benignly, "Isn't it obvious? Don't you see it?"

Neither Dickens nor I saw it at all.

Inspector Field finally decided that he had tantalized us quite enough: "Gentlemen on a drunken spree don't carry antique weapons like that which made this wound. Perhaps they carry a walkin' stick or a small truncheon secreted in an inner pocket. But this murderer was carryin' a 'eavy sword brought along for the purpose of murder and none other."

"So what is your next step?" Dickens asked Field.

"The same as yours," Field answered unblinking.

Dickens, puzzled, took the bait: "And what is that?"

"To go 'ome and get some sleep."

We all smiled.

"I quite agree," Dickens stood up. "It has been a long and eventful evening."

"Your assistance 'as been greatly appreciated, sir," Rogers spoke up.

"Yes, indeed." Field's animation was genuine.

"We would very much like to continue to follow this case, to give any assistance that we can, of course, but mainly for curiosity's sake," Dickens addressed Field cautiously. "You have drawn us right into the middle of one of your mysteries, and, I feel I speak for Mister Collins as well, I found the evening exciting and fascinating. Will you keep us informed? May we continue to observe your investigation at first hand?"

Inspector Field smiled openly at Dickens and answered, without the slightest hesitation, "You've identified our murdered man. Meg says there are four others involved. Who knows, perhaps you can identify 'em too. It is my thinkin' that these swells are from your part of town, rather than mine. Before this is done your 'elp may be even more useful than it 'as already been 'ere at the start."

With Field's assurances that he would keep us informed,

and, in fact, summon us at any crucial point in the case, we parted company.

It was nearing two in the morning. As we walked back through those deserted streets, I began to understand Dickens's great affection for them. He walked his beloved streets out of restlessness, but one could not help but see those streets' potential for this kind of shocking reality which Field had guided us down into this night. I am convinced that those night streets were Dickens's greatest inspiration.

DEATH CLOSING ALL
AROUND ME

(April 14, 1851)

If this were one of my novels, this chapter would not exist. It digresses. As a memoir, not a novel, however, I am bound to tell what happened when it happened. Historians and biographers may some day refer to this manuscript, probably to learn about him, not me.

This particular date, April fourteenth, eighteen hundred fifty-one, proved one of the most important in Dickens's personal history. Only one day after looking into the dead eyes of that murdered man, Dickens on this day was forced to confront an event which darkened his view of life. After the events of this day, he was never the same again, either in life or in fiction.

I slept late the morning after our nocturnal adventure in the company of Inspector Field. I had business in the City, so I did not look in at the *Household Words* office that afternoon. Forster later told me that Dickens rose late at Wellington

Street, and immediately called for a coach to take him to Malvern to visit his wife. The following day, the fourteenth, he returned early to the city but did not go to Wellington Street. Instead, he went to his city house in Devonshire Terrace. Mrs. Dickens was in Malvern, recuperating from one of her frequent undiagnosable illnesses, but the children were quartered in Devonshire Terrace in the care of a nurse and three trusted family servants. Forster looked in there late in the afternoon, and found Dickens in the nursery playing with the youngest, Dora Annie, who within the week had recovered from a stiff bout with the chicken pox. As Forster described it, she was skipping about the room and perching on her father's lap like a bird newly freed from its cage. Dickens had spent the afternoon preparing the evening's speech and playing with the children. He and Forster rode in a cab into town at six.

I met Dickens as he was climbing out of the hansom outside The London Tavern at number five Bishopsgate Street. There was a crush of people at the door, those waiting to get in, plus the inevitable Grub Streeters who seemed to appear whenever it was publicized that Dickens would be in attendance at any public function. He looked tired, but he was jovial upon coming in. When his good friend Macready inquired after Mrs. Dickens's health, I saw Dickens wink, and overheard him answer with an evil grin, "I fear my wife is once again in the early stages of her anti-Malthusian state." It was an unkind thing to say about his wife in her absence, but the all-male company could not help chuckling at his wit. I, however, knew that his joke was nothing but a joke. Mrs. Dickens had been in the throes of an elusive and unsettling illness for more than four months, and had been recuperating at the spa at Malvern for the last two. During all of that time Dickens had been working full time and sleeping most nights in the *Household Words* offices at Wellington Street.

That night of the fourteenth, Dickens was in the Chair presiding over the annual dinner of the General Theatrical Fund. We peopled every table that had been brought in for the occasion and the tap of The London Tavern was filled to overflowing with those unfortunates who had made their pledge to the fund either too late or too usurously to assure them a good table for the festivities. I was sitting at a table with Sala and Egg and Phillip Collins, immediately behind the most prominent of the satellite tables peopled with Dickens's oldest friends: Forster, Wills, Macready, Bulwar, Trevor Blount and Talfourd, a lawyer who lived his whole life under the illusion that he was really a literary man.

Immediately following the serving of the wine and the first course of meat pie and French potatoes served on clam shells, Sir John Falstaff held court, to the delight of all. Dickens introduced that worthy from the Chair. Falstaff entered from a small anteroom on the right, all whiskers and belly. He wore a capacious jerkin that was part short cape and part large-buttoned doublet. Around his bulging waist was a thick leather belt from which hung a pointy dagger of the Italian mode and a heavy broad-bladed hand sword. His loose leather trousers were rolled at his boottops and large, mean-looking riding spurs were strapped to his heels. As he entered, he brandished an oversized drinking tankard.

It was, of course, Mark Lemon, one of Dickens's closest friends and perhaps *the* most enthusiastic of the collaborators and actors in Dickens's frequent amateur theatricals. Lemon, indeed, seemed born to the part of Falstaff. He possessed the great girth, the jolly eye, the booming voice, the bristling whiskers, and the tipsy rolling gait that were all impeccable credentials for the part. Macready had even asked him to play the part professionally a few years before, when Covent Garden was getting up a *Henry IV, Part One,* but Lemon refused, protesting that "once an amateur always an amateur." Covent Garden settled for Alexander Welsh, but even Macready, in private, agreed that his portrayal did not at all come up to Lemon's.

Upon entering, Falstaff stood in a small cleared space immediately in front of the Chair, where Dickens sat applauding happily. As befit the fat drunkard and ruffian that he was, Falstaff glared around belligerently, then took a long draught from his tankard and sat down. He arranged himself comfortably in the chair, comically adjusting his swords so that they didn't poke his bulging stomach, took another look around, another deep draught, and began:

> "For, Harry, I do not speak to thee in
> drink . . ."

With that Lemon rolled his eyes and gazed at his huge tankard.

> "And yet there is a virtuous man whom I have
> often noted in thy company, but I know not
> his name . . ."

We all recognized the speech immediately, the tavern scene from Act II. What could be more appropriate for this tavern scene?

> "A good portly man, i' faith, and a
> corpulent . . ."

"You bloated barrel of sack!" It was Macready who barked this insult from the table immediately in front of the stage.

The whole company burst out laughing as Falstaff paused a brief moment to frown with disdain upon this groundling heckler before continuing on:

> "of a cheerful look, a pleasing eye, and a most
> noble carriage."

"A fat drunkard and whoremonger!" This insult came from Dickens in the Chair and suddenly the scenario was clear. Macready and Dickens were intentionally inciting the crowd as a way of involving them in this small exercise in theatre. We were expected to be part of the cast.

Falstaff paid no attention but rode straight on with his argument:

"and, as I think, his age some fifty, or, by'r
Lady, inclining to threescore; and now I
remember me, his name is Falstaff."

"Falstaff, you big-bellied varlet!" came a laughing taunt from
the midst of the mob in the tap. I recognized Garis the actor's
voice.
"You fat bag of wind!" Another tapster gleefully took up the
game.
Falstaff went on, undaunted:

"If that man should be lewdly given, he
deceiveth me; for, Harry, I see virtue in his
looks."

"Virtue in his drunken red nose!"
"Virtue in his bouncing belly!"

The insults flew fast and furious. Falstaff, ignoring their jibes,
his booming voice rising above the crowd, continued to flatter
himself shamelessly:

"If then the tree may be known by the fruit, as
the fruit by the tree, then, peremptorily I
speak of it, there is virtue in that Falstaff. Him
keep with, the rest banish."

"You obese bucket of beer!" High spirits flowed as freely as the
wine, and I found myself shouting insults right along with the
others. We tried to outdo each other in the alliterative quality
of our catcalls.
"You jiggling jerkin of flesh!"
"You farting fricassee of mutton *merde!*"
"You mountainous mound of meat!"
The insults only spurred Falstaff forward faster and more
fiercely on his flight of fatuous self-flattery:

59

"No, my good lord: banish Peto, banish
Bardolph, banish Poins; but for sweet Jack
Falstaff, kind Jack Falstaff, true Jack
Falstaff . . ."

"Fat Jack Falstaff!"

". . . valiant Jack Falstaff, and therefore
more valiant being as he is old Jack Falstaff,
banish not him thy Harry's company, banish
not him thy Harry's company. Banish plump
Jack, and banish all the world!"

With a flourish of his crushed hat and a clinking of his spurs,
Falstaff swept off the stage to a deafening round of applause and
cheers.

Everyone was entertained by Lemon's Falstaff and merri-
ment buzzed through the dining room and the tap as the
second course, a hearty roast in natural brown gravy, was
served with cooked carrots. As we ate and drank, anticipation
built for Dickens's speech.

The coffee was being served by the tavern's scullery maids.
In mere moments, the glass would be tapped for silence, the
introduction would be made, and Dickens would rise to speak.
I was lighting my cigar in anticipation, when an unusual flurry
of activity at the table immediately in front caught my
attention.

First, the Serjeant-At-Arms, a large actor named George
Ford, whom I had seen in supporting roles at both Covent
Garden and Drury Lane, approached Forster, whispered in his
ear and escorted him from his table.

My eyes followed as they repaired to the rear of the tavern
near the door. Forster quickly entered into deep conversation
with a young man who appeared out of breath and rather red
in the face. Almost immediately, Forster became very agitated
and actually reached out, grabbed the young man by the

shoulders, and shook him. The young man replied by shaking his head violently up and down, signifying affirmation of whatever had so greatly agitated Forster. Without another word, Forster turned and hurried back to his table.

Sitting down, Forster immediately leaned close, first to Macready and then to Lemon, who, after uncostuming himself, had joined the party of Dickens's oldest friends, and spoke excitedly in a lowered voice.

"Good lord!" I overheard Lemon exclaim in shock. Macready controlled his reaction better, but his eyes went wide.

At the very moment that I was leaning forward to eavesdrop on that trio so deep in mysterious conversation, Dickens was introduced. He arose at the center of the double-winged head table, smiled out at the gathering and raised his glass to toast the General Theatrical Fund. His smile set in motion a wave of applause, which drowned out all other sounds. Forster, Macready, and Lemon were startled, looked furtively around and then at each other. There was panic and indecision in their faces.

Dickens began with an acknowledgment of the usefulness of the Theatrical Fund. I must admit that I didn't really hear his opening words due to my curious observation of the agitation at the table directly in front of me. I was convinced that something quite unusual was up.

Dickens's booming voice exerted its control over the room. Forster sank back in his chair as if defeated. With the palms of his hands held up to the other two, he gestured for them to wait.

"Although the General Theatrical Fund,
unlike some similar public institutions, is
represented by no fabric of stone, or brick, or
glass—like that wonderful achievement of my
ingenious friend Mr. Paxton, of which the
great demerit, as we learn from the best
authorities, is, that it ought to have fallen
down before it was quite built, and would by
no means consent to do it."

Great peels of laughter accompanied this comment with everyone joining in except Forster and Lemon and Macready who each looked as if they were in the midst of choking.

> "Although, I say, the General Theatrical Fund
> is represented by no great architectural edifice,
> it is nevertheless as plain a fact, rests upon as
> solid a foundation, and carries as erect a front
> as any building in the world."

Thus Dickens began his speech, but, much to my own surprise, I wasn't paying full attention. He was the best after-dinner speaker I had ever heard, yet this night I was distracted. Forster was so nervous that his hand shook as he lit his cigar. Macready sat scowling, his bushy eyebrows stretched taut. Lemon's eyes darted everywhere, with a delicate nervousness unbefitting of Good Jack Falstaff.

Dickens had gotten up steam and his speech was speeding along its track with clear direction and the full exercise of his whimsical powers of description:

> "It is a society which says to the actor, you
> may do the light business, or the heavy
> business, or the comic business, or the serious
> business, or the eccentric business; you may
> be the captain who courts the young lady; you
> may be the Baron who gives the *fete*, and who
> sits on the sofa under the canopy, with the
> Baroness, to behold the *fete*; or you may be
> the peasant who swells the drinking chorus at
> the *fete*, and who may usually be observed to
> turn his glass upside-down immediately before
> drinking the Baron's health; or, to come to the
> actresses, she may be the Fairy, residing

forever in a revolving star; or you may even
be a Witch in *Macbeth*, bearing a striking
resemblance to Malcolm or Donalbain of
the previous scenes with his wig of the hind-
side before."

It was one of his usual lively performances, yet it left me
standing at the station. Finally, his voice began to rise as it
always did when he drew near to finishing with his usual
flourish:

". . . the actor sometimes comes from scenes
of affliction and misfortune—even from death
itself—to play his part before us; all men must
do that violence to their feelings, in passing
on to the fulfillment of their duties in the
great strife and fight of life."

When he heard Dickens utter those words, Forster turned
white, and looked at Macready as if he had just seen the ghost
of Banquo sit down at the table.

With a final toast to the Fund, Dickens smiled over the
whole room, gave a small courteous bow and sat down. The
applause was thunderous, and lasted long minutes. My eyes
never left Forster's face. His eyes were riveted upon Dickens in
the Chair. Finally, the room restored itself to the normality of
smoking and drinking. It was then that Forster and Lemon
moved quickly from their seats to the Organizer's table. Forster
bent across and spoke briefly to Dickens. For a long moment,
a paralysis seemed to lock that midsection of the head table in
its grip.

Then, with a sudden though quite unsteady movement,
Dickens was up and clearly taking flight. When he reached the
end of the table, Forster and Lemon immediately flanked him.
As they crossed the crowded room, they resembled two bailiffs
escorting a prisoner into custody. All the excitement and
animation which had enlivened Dickens's face as he spoke to

the assembly had drained from his countenance. His lips had gone white and a sickly grey cast had descended over his face. People at the tables rose to shake Dickens's hand and compliment him on his speech as he passed through the crowd, but Forster shoved them violently away.

I could no longer contain my curiosity or my concern for my friend. I rushed to Dickens's side as Forster and Lemon guided him between tables toward the door.

"What is it? Charles, what is it?" Though unintended, my voice had clearly caught the urgency of the scene.

Forster glared at me.

"Bad news. Bad news indeed," Lemon said, recognizing me.

Charles could barely speak. He was badly shaken, seemed near fainting. He was not the vigorous, willful strider of the night streets with whom I was accustomed to keeping company. "It's, it's Dora, Wilkie. Oh God!" he stammered, a look of utter despair crippling his countenance.

Forster and Lemon, each with a hand on one of his elbows, continued to pilot him toward the door.

With a look of panic flooding his countenance, Dickens swivelled his head backwards even as he was moving away from me: "Wilkie, please follow us. We will need you tonight. Devonshire Terrace." It was a plea in the voice of a man who has been washed overboard and is crying out in the night for someone to throw him a rope.

With that, Forster and Lemon rushed him through the door and into a waiting carriage. I was left standing befuddled in the street before the tavern door. Two or three of the Grub Streeters were still loitering in attendance. They had, of course, recognized Dickens when he came out. Now, they looked to me for some explanation. I hailed a passing hansom and escaped.

Upon arriving at the house in Devonshire Terrace, I found out what had happened. The words are hard to write even at a safe distance from the reality of the event. The child, Dickens's youngest, was dead.

Great sadness had replaced violence in Forster's face. His

voice cracked. I never liked the man, but that night I realized what a true friend of Dickens he was. He grieved the death of Dickens's child as if the child had been his own. He felt his closest friend's pain as if he were suffering it himself.

It seems that all had thought little Dora Annie brilliantly recovered from a brain congestion and the chicken pox. When Dickens and Forster had left the house, she had been smiling and happy. No more than an hour later, the child's illness mysteriously returned, convulsions set in, and, before the doctor could be summoned, she was dead. *

We sat in uneasy silence in a small downstairs parlor for perhaps fifteen minutes before Dickens reappeared. His face was ashen, but he was steady on his feet. He summoned Forster from the room and they held private consultation. I learned later that Mrs. Dickens was the subject of their discussion. Dickens had designated Forster for the delicate assignment of bringing Kate Dickens back from the spa at Malvern. He wrote a letter to his wife which Forster was to hand-deliver. It did not reveal the terrible truth of the child's death but, nevertheless, prepared the poor mother, herself in quite delicate health, for the receiving of the cold reality upon her arrival. Forster departed immediately in a new carriage with fresh horses which had been summoned by the servants. Dickens, Lemon and I met in the foyer to see Forster off. We started to follow him out to the carriage, but he quickly motioned us back.

"Stay inside," he ordered through clenched teeth. "The sharks are beginning to gather."

A small crowd of reporters were already milling in the street before the house and more were arriving in hansom cabs each minute. At least ten or twelve were loitering around the front gate looking expectantly up at the house as if getting ready to

---

*She probably died of what is now known as Reye's Syndrome, a mysterious disease, possibly liver connected, which follows recovery from a virus or a chicken pox.

storm it. Dickens looked at these sensation mongers, but who they were and the reason for their presence did not seem to register in his rational thoughts.

"Charlie, Charlie, why don't you get some sleep? Kate won't be here until morning." It was Lemon coaxing him as he stood in a paralyzed daze at the bottom of the stairway in the foyer.

"I must be with little Dora. I must stay with her. She is so alone on her journey. I must keep the vigil. She is so alone." Dickens spoke the words in a slow, drugged voice as if he wasn't really there.

"Yes, of course. We'll stay with her, Charlie, that's the thing," Lemon consoled him.

Our eyes met. "I'll take care of things down here," I whispered, as Lemon, with his arm around Charles's shoulder, led Dickens up the stairs.

When they had disappeared into the upper reaches of the house, I turned to my task. Half of Grub Street, it seemed, was clamoring at the gate. The unruly mob of reporters, knowing that Dickens had been called from the Chair of the General Theatrical Fund Dinner on some emergency, was understandably restless. They were beginning to raise a din which was disturbing the neighborhood, and which would disturb Dickens in his mourning if not dealt with quickly. I took a few moments to assemble my thoughts and steel myself to the task, then marched out to face them.

As I looked down from the front steps at the crowd of them, I remembered Inspector Field striding fearlessly into the midst of that mob of cutthroats in that Rats' Castle. That image decided me against standing safely on the steps behind the closed gate to address them. Instead, I walked right down, opened the gate, closed it tight behind me, and strode into their very midst. It was the first time that the press had ever clamored for my opinion as they did for Dickens's every time he appeared in public. I must admit I relished being the center of their attention even though they hadn't the slightest idea who I was.

"I am Wilkie Collins," the reporters, to my exhilaration, all bent to scribble my name, "a colleague of Mister Dickens." I paused, trying to compose what I was next going to say.

"Well Guv, get on wi' it. Wha' 'as 'appened?" one of the more impatient of the Grub Street veterans badgered me.

"A family tragedy," I blurted out. "Mister Dickens's youngest child, Dora Annie, died this evening. She suffered a relapse of an ongoing sickness which resulted in convulsions and caused her death."

I stopped for breath as the madding crowd closed in tight. Questions rained down. "Mister Dickens is himself a member of the press," I pleaded, "all pertinent information will be made available to you." The crowd of reporters had grown to some twenty or thirty. "You must not cause a disturbance here in the street," I cautioned them. "All information will be made available to you," I assured them as I made a temporary escape back into the house.

I made three different forays out to converse with those insensitive vultures camped in the street. New arrivals arrived, those who had been there from the beginning hung on, and hired messengers came and went with the frequency of foreign armies in Belgium. Indeed, as the sole answerer of all their questions, I felt quite the celebrity. The night raced by for me. It passed much more slowly, however, for Charles and Mark Lemon.

Twice I looked in on them, carrying a tray of hot coffee. The small dead body, dressed all in white, lay on its back on what I thought was a rather large bed for such a small child. The two men kept the vigil, one on each side of the bed. The first time that I entered, Dickens sat slumped in silence, his head resting against the velvet side of his high-backed chair, his empty eyes staring in disbelief at the motionless white corpse before him. Lemon sat warily across from him, tilted forward on the edge of his hard wooden seat. No longer did he resemble jolly Jack Falstaff. Now he watched Dickens carefully as if trying to anticipate his every movement, thought, need. They were a dejected Robinson Crusoe and his attentive man Friday cast totally adrift, trying to stay afloat. The second time I entered,

Dickens was up and pacing. He was speaking rapidly in a low hoarse whisper. As I poured the coffee, I listened to his distraught ramblings. I don't think he even realized that I was in the room.

"Nothing is more inexplicable than the sudden death of a small child. This is my punishment. For Nell. For Paul. For my treatment of my father. For my other Dora, David's Dora. Oh yes, God surely has a wickedly ironic sense! He unleashes this hound of hell to plague me for my exploitation of children. Dora's death is a judgement on me and my creations."

As he constructed the plots of his novels, he was constructing the edifice of his own responsibility and guilt for the unfortunate child's death. Lemon motioned me from the room. I left willingly. I prayed that Lemon would find the words to soothe our poor driven and tortured Dickens. For me, entering that room where those two shipwrecked souls kept their midnight vigil was like descending into some underground tomb.

I was nodding, barely awake, in a chair in the foyer, when Dickens and Lemon came down the steps at seven in the morning. The sun was up and it was a glorious new day, yet Dickens looked like some aged debauchee. His face was haggard and twisted by the tension of his grief. His rich brown hair was thoroughly disheveled and his eyes were dim and empty.

"Ah, Wilkie, my companion of my evening walks, I am glad that you are here." His voice was sad but he seemed lucid and rational.

I led Dickens into the small parlor and we sat down. Lemon excused himself to freshen up. One of the servants entered and informed Dickens that the morticians, Peyrouten and Polhemus, had been summoned. We were left alone. I was terrified. I knew not what to say.

Dickens broke the awkward silence.

"Death seems to be closing in all around me, Wilkie.

Horrible! Everywhere I look there are dead eyes, and I can identify them all."

I thought for a moment that he was referring to the man that Field had fished out of the Thames two nights before, but he was referring to no particular corpse, no particular eyes. He was referring to all the ghosts who plagued his imagination.

"I wish there were some way I could lessen the burden of your grief," I leaned to him and whispered lamely.

"It is better that you don't start writing novels, Wilkie," he stared wildly into my face. "Novels try to deal with reality and reality is a sick thing, a diseased bleak house where no one should be forced to live."

There was a clamor out in the street, and it drew his attention.

"The reporters, Charles," I prompted. "They've been out there all night."

He looked at me bewildered: "Why?"

"Because you are news."

Panic gripped his countenance: "Wilkie, you must drive them away before Kate arrives. They will unsettle her."

I felt helpless in the face of his plea. For the briefest moment I considered getting my hands somehow on a gun and firing on those Grub Street vultures. Yet I knew that I had to tell him the truth.

"There is only one way that they will be persuaded to retire."

His tired eyes looked at me uncomprehending.

"They must have a statement from you. You are the reason they are here. You are the only one who can satisfy them. If you ask them to leave, they will go. They have been out there all night, waiting."

"For me?" he spoke the words as if he hadn't slept in weeks.

"For you." *The Inimitable*, that cruel sarcastic phrase crossed my mind.

Lemon returned. "What is it?" he asked me upon observing Dickens's new agitation.

Dickens's eyes darted back and forth between the two of us. "I feel like a ship that has hit a rock," he finally said, "stove in and at the mercy of the storm." He stopped and gazed at us for long seconds. "You surely are the best of friends," he finally said. "I shall never forget how you have sat up with me this night."

With that, he stepped into the foyer and moved to the door. "We must get rid of them before Kate arrives," he turned and reiterated. With Lemon on one side and myself on the other, he walked slowly out to meet his voracious public.

"IT TAKES A GENTLEMAN TO CATCH A GENTLEMAN"

(April 31, 1851—late afternoon)

Two weeks after his youngest child was buried in Highgate Cemetery, Dickens returned to London. He had resided during that too brief time of mourning at the spa at Great Malvern where Kate was recuperating. I dined with Forster and Wills at the Garrick Club on the twenty-sixth of April. Dickens was, of course, our sole topic of conversation. Wills, myself and Sala had held the fort at Wellington Street. Forster had relayed instructions from Dickens concerning business at the magazine. As we sat at the table over brandy and cigars following dinner, Forster was uncharacteristically expansive in his description of Dickens's state of mind.

"He appears to be acting very inconsistently," Forster harrumphed, "almost, I hesitate to say it, yet I know it will go no further, almost . . . unstable."

"Unstable?" I said, encouraging him to continue.

"Yes, his moods fluctuate wildly. One moment he may be laughing and joking, yet a short time later he will suddenly become morose and distant. I spent the night in the guest quarters. All evening Charles was lively with the children, attentive to Kate, jocular with me. About ten I said goodnight and withdrew to my room on the second floor. Just prior to retiring, I looked out of my window at the moon and, to my surprise, observed Dickens setting out across the moors. His long striding gait is unmistakable. I inquired the next morning of the servants and found out that he walked out like that every night. 'Long wild walks on the heath' as one of the older serving people described it. Now doesn't that seem unstable to you?"

I could barely keep from laughing aloud. The evidence for Forster's great concern about Dickens's mental instability was the single act which Dickens undertook more consistently than any other (except, of course, his writing). On the contrary, his fierce walks across the Malvern moors were nothing more nor less than a sign of his return to his normal exercise of both the legs and the imagination. The city streets, the Malvern moors, the Thames at midnight—they were all nothing more than the landscape of his imagination which he needed to visit regularly.

Forster did tell one story which alarmed me, because it echoed a guilty sentiment which Dickens had expressed during that long night of the child's death watch. Forster described how Dickens came to him with a copy of a letter he had written in August of the previous year.

"He read me one line of the letter." Forster recalled, "and, when he was done, he laughed insanely for a long moment. 'And you scoff when I tell you that I am psychic!' he said."

"Well, what did the letter say?" I had to prod Forster.

"The letter read: 'I have still to kill Dora—I mean the Copperfield's Dora—'" Forster intoned.

"It was a novelist's joke thrown off more than eight months ago." I objected to Forster's gravity. "Surely, he couldn't believe that his own ill-considered words could have any meaning eight months later."

"He brought the letter to me, and, in a very distraught state, read me that one line aloud," Forster insisted.

"He is a man who believes in the power of words," Wills said, entering the fray on Forster's side.

"It was a bad joke, nothing more," I said, scoffing at their old-maid superstition. But things were connecting in my mind. On the night the child died, Dickens had paced the room expressing his own guilt and seeing Dora's death as a punishment inflicted upon him by a literary God, who did not like the way he treated his characters. Indeed, maybe that was a sign of insanity, mixing up real people with fictional characters. If it was, however, then all of us—Dickens, Thackeray, even myself—belonged in Bedlam, rather than out walking the streets, sharpening our pens.

Within four days of that concerned dinner, Dickens was back in London. The house in Devonshire Terrace held such painful recent memories that from the evening of his return he took up permanent bachelor residence at the *Household Words* offices in Wellington Street. To my great surprise, when I entered the offices the next morning, he was sitting at his desk.

"Wilkie," he said, rising and shaking my hand enthusiastically, "you and Wills have kept the ship from sinking, held her steady while the Captain was indisposed." Quite pleased with his sailing metaphor, he beamed and shook my hand some more. Yet, as the day went on, I could not help but observe the very inconsistency which Forster had described. He would work with great intensity for a time, but then he would simply stop and sit looking off into space. By the middle of the afternoon, I had come to the conclusion that Forster's theories carried more weight than I had allotted them. Dickens was, indeed, not himself. He was a man struggling against the spectres haunting his mind. Something new was needed to distract him from this now restless, now lethargic state of mental anguish. As if by a miracle, that something walked in the door at precisely five o'clock on the afternoon of April thirty-first. To our surprise, it was none other than Inspector Field of Bow Street Station.

"Mister Dickens, sir. And Mister Collins, sir." Field stepped out of the stairwell. "Please forgive this sudden intrusion. Doubtless, I am the person you least expected to see disruptin' the center of your lit'rary offices. Yet 'ere I am, and, believe it or not, I'm 'ere on business." He punctuated his last assertion with a sharp tap of his demonstrative forefinger on Dickens's desk.

"Inspector Field, what a pleasant surprise," Dickens was veritably beaming as he leapt up from his chair.

I too rose and circumnavigated my desk to greet and shake hands with Field. It was only then that I noticed the everpresent Rogers lurking at the top of the stairwell.

Field was substantially encouraged by the heartiness of Dickens's greeting. He scratched the side of his mouth with his crook'd forefinger, thus summoning a sly grin of renewed conspiracy. Dickens quickly pulled two wooden chairs up between our two desks and all four of us took our seats in a rough circle. Inspector Field's momentary grin of conspiracy was replaced by an intense gravity, out of which the personal condolences of the man, and of the whole force of the Metropolitan Protectives were tendered. Dickens accepted his condolences with a sad up-and-down nodding of the head, a ritual gesture I had already seen him perform a number of times. I was beginning to recognize it as a piece of stage business, which Dickens-the-actor had improvised and polished as a stock reaction to this particular scene.

"You said that you're here on business?" Dickens said, breaking the silence.

"I am indeed."

"It couldn't involve our mutual acquaintance, Lawyer Partlow, so recently encountered on the peaceful banks of the Thames, could it?"

"It could indeed." Field took up his coy game.

How Field knew that Dickens had returned to London, I do not venture to guess. He seemed to know everything.

"I'm intrigued. What is it?"

73

"I want you and Mister Collins to become spies in my employ," Field put it bluntly.

"Spies?" The word had caught Dickens's attention just as it had mine.

"Yes, spies."

Dickens and I exchanged equally puzzled looks.

"Upon whom do you propose we commit this act of spying?" I asked.

"On whoever is available at The Player's Club located at number thirty-six King Street in the West End," Field replied in deadly seriousness.

Dickens and I looked at each other in surprise.

Dickens was, of course, an honorary member of The Player's Club as he was of all the various London actors' establishments, but he rarely went there, The Garrick Club being the regular meeting place of his particular theatrical circle. I had no doubts, however, that he could enter The Player's Club at any time and be greeted with every courtesy of the house.

"The Player's Club? Why?" he asked, posing the natural question.

"I need information concernin' the identities of the four men in company with Solicitor Partlow the night 'ee was murdered. We are makin' little progress on this partic'lar case. The man lived alone, 'ad no relatives. 'Is landlady says 'ee went out every evenin', when not otherwise engaged, to dine at The Player's Club. Yet, and 'ere's the rub, 'ee rarely returned to 'is rooms before three or four in the mornin'. Player's Club closes doors at eleven-thirty, says I. Landlady 'as no further explanation."

At this juncture of his narrative, Field pulled in on the reins and stopped for a short breather.

"We 'ave traced 'is movements of that evenin' to The Player's Club where we 'ave been brought up rather short."

"Brought up short? How's that?" Dickens glanced at me.

"Blokes won't talk to us," Rogers admitted.

"No one on the premises seems inclined to discuss the dead

club member," Field said, taking up the narrative with equanimity. "It is almost as if the 'elp at The Player's Club 'olds some irrational fear of 'im. Or perhaps they 'ave been instructed not to give out information concernin' any club member. We could, of course, get a writ from the Queen's Bench and break in there and accost the members present concernin' their dealin's with Partlow and their whereabouts on the night that our dead friend went for 'is fatal swim, but we would probably not obtain much useful information, it almost always bein' the case that gentlemen intensely dislike bein' disturbed in the private environs of their club rooms."

"That certainly is the case," Dickens agreed.

"It ain't like trampin' into some Rats' Castle and 'aulin' out our man for questionin'," Rogers interjected. "Gennelmen is a diff'rent problem."

"Indeed they are," Inspector Field said. "Gentlemen require much more subtlety, discretion, and delicate persuasion in order to get 'em to peach on their fellow gentlemen. In other words, gentlemen, it takes a gentleman to catch a gentleman."

"Precisely." Dickens's eyes were sparkling.

"Therefore, I concluded that if I just 'ad a friendly ear mixin' with the unsuspectin' members some busy club night, such as tonight, say, and if the conversation perchance turned to the gruesome death of Lawyer Partlow, that somethin' perhaps might be learned. And then I said to myself . . . didn't I Rogers?" (Rogers nodded emphatically) ". . . I said, our friend Mister Dickens 'as many connections in the theatre, was an acquaintance of the deceased, would be welcomed at The Player's Club. And there you are."

"And there you are!" Rogers repeated for emphasis.

"Well," Field pressed our decision, "will you do it?"

"Spies, Wilkie," Dickens said excitedly, "what do you think of that?"

"Well, really . . ."

"Splendid! We'll do it," he replied to Field.

Field immediately was up and shaking both of our hands

enthusiastically. "Welcome to the Protectives, gentlemen," he said with great relish.

"We are yours, Inspector Field, but how are we to proceed? What are we to do?" Dickens inquired, turning to the more practical aspects of the undertaking.

"We need to know where Partlow went, what 'ee did, in whose company 'ee did it. If you could go there, converse with the members, it would be quite 'elpful. Rogers." He turned to his faithful shadow, who was rummaging in the pouch which he carried slung over his shoulder.

"Yes sir," Rogers answered, handing over a folded newspaper.

Field immediately unfolded it to reveal the sensational headline: "PROMINENT WEST END SOLICITOR MURDERED." It was a two-week-old *Times*.

"You carry this," Field directed Dickens, as if he were some playwright blocking out the movements of his actors. "You let it be known that you 'ave been out of the city an' 'ave been catchin' up on the news. You've been readin' about Partlow's murder. Terrible thing. That's the tack. It is our 'ope that this ruse will loosen some gossip's tongue. Who knows, it may even flush our killer." With that, Field turned to me. "And you, Mister Collins, are very important to this scheme. While Mister Dickens is entertainin' 'is audience and tryin' to draw 'em out, you remain in the background carefully observin' the crowd, notin' every reaction, eye peeled for any suspicious movement, 'urried flight or nervous tick."

"Spies indeed," I scoffed. "What you want is the net of Hapheastus."

"Don't know the gentleman," Field's face was deadly serious, "but if 'is net will catch us a murderer, tell 'im to bring it along."

"Your plan is excellent," Dickens said, taking the newspaper. "I can't wait to set it in motion." He didn't bother to ask me if I would accompany him. Like any bold knight, he simply took for granted that his faithful squire, his Sancho, would be at his side. Of course, he was right!

All of the sadness, the loss of his power of concentration was gone from Dickens's mien. He was animated, trembling to act. He could have been a character in one of his own novels. "It takes a gentleman to catch a gentleman," Field had said, and Dickens was in the process of inventing a gentleman detective to work side by side with the professional detective.

"SPIES!"

(April 31, 1851—evening)

The *maitre'd* at The Player's Club, with his thin pencil moustache and black frock coat, gushed like a Parisian fountain when Dickens entered: "Oh Meestair Deekens, welcome back to zee Player's Club. Eet has bean a long time, Meestair Deekens. Welcome back." The person nodded to me in total non-recognition and said "Zanck you, sir" when he took my hat and gloves. *Someday*, I thought, *they will recognize me as well as him.*

Upon entering the dining room, we created quite a stir. No one disturbed our dinner, but a low hubbub of gawking and pointing took possession of the room. When we had finished, Dickens suggested we retire to the smoking lounge for our brandy and cigars. While retrieving his prop newspaper from the cloakroom, Dickens whispered, "Now let us join the rabble!"

"The rabble" were more than eager to close ranks around us. Within seconds upon entering the smoking lounge, we were surrounded by greeters, professed acquaintances, devoted readers, and all manner of actors, writers and theatre patrons. Dickens recognized a few, pretended to recognize many, made new and fervent acquaintance with a multitude, and smiled and shook hands with all. All the while, he kept on prominent display his copy of the *Times* with its gory headline. Men bowed in and bowed out after shaking the great man's hand but a few, who felt, because of prior acquaintance, that they held a greater claim to his company, lingered. Ultimately, we were invited by two well-known actors, Mister Grahame Storey of the Adelphi and Mister Earle Davis of Drury Lane, to join their group.

We were ushered to chairs of honor in a circle of six near one of the three glowing fireplaces. Without question, Dickens was the center of attention, and the newspaper trumpeting the murder of Lawyer Partlow lay prominently displayed on his lap as the snifters arrived and the cigars were lit. It could only be a matter of time before someone in this doting circle noticed it and commented upon it. We were not disappointed.

"I see you are reading about the unfortunate affair of Solicitor Partlow's death," Storey of the Adelphi gravely intoned, right on cue.

"Yes," Dickens replied, tapping the newspaper in his lap with the back of his cigar hand. "I've been out of town two weeks. Was wading through the backed-up papers at the *Household Words* office before coming out tonight, and this one caught my eye. First I'd heard of it. Terrible thing!"

"Quite, quite," Davis of Drury Lane said, nodding through the blue smoke of a Turkish cigarette.

"Great surprise to all of us," another agreed.

"Indeed," assented other voices.

"Poor man was an acquaintance of mine," Dickens announced sadly. "Met him with the Covent Garden crowd."

"Poor man indeed," Storey harrumphed with a sarcastic tone.

Consulting his newspaper, Dickens pushed the point: "Says he was here drinking the night of his death." Dickens cocked a mischievous eye and remarked with an evil grin, "Why, any one of you here might have been the last to see him alive." He paused for effect. "Perhaps the murderer is in this room right now."

They stared at Dickens, aghast.

"Really, Charles," I said, stepping in to lighten the mood, "you've been reading too many of your own novels."

At that, everyone laughed, but he had succeeded in planting the seed of suspicion which made them think back to their own comings and goings that evening.

"Besides," Dickens raised his brandy snifter, "no actor could have done this. Actors only murder people on stage. Theirs is the act of murder which makes no allowance for the reality of murder."

"Oh, yes, I quite agree," said a rather precious middle-aged gent of delicate stature and features, an actor—as evidenced by the way he flourished his cigar—wearing black polished leather pumps. "No actor could have done it. Smacks too much of common robbery if you ask me."

"I remember he was sitting right over there by the card tables," added another actor, Cazamian by name, who was either a Hungarian or a specialist in singing roles, clearly evidenced by the blue and green silk scarf meticulously wrapped about his precious vocal chords.

"Yes." Storey, with a rather petulant edge on his voice, continued the reconstruction. "With a whole group of Covent Garden people, if memory serves me. The new *Macbeth* was all they could bear to discuss. You'd think Macready was the only actor in London."

"It was the Covent Garden crowd alright," Cazamian affirmed, "Partlow and Paroissien the stage manager, and some of the minor actors."

"Yes, and as the night went on it became a rather drunken and ugly scene," Davis (who I finally placed as having acted an excellent George Barnwell, which I had seen some weeks before at Drury Lane) remembered.

"Quite true. They ended up with their own private corner, because their abusiveness drove everyone who remained over to the far side of the room," Storey recalled, showing little sympathy for the deceased.

I exchanged a quick glance with Dickens. I nodded toward Storey and Dickens assented with a small return nod.

"Shocking, isn't it?" Dickens's voice was low and contemplative. "That the excesses of drunkenness would lead to the murder of a gentleman."

Mister Storey frowned. He tried to control himself but he could not. "Gentleman indeed!" he barked.

To our surprise, a number of the others nodded in assent of this indignant slur on the deceased Partlow's membership in that privileged class.

Dickens merely raised an eyebrow and stared hard at Storey, waiting.

"Referring to Partlow as a gentleman is severely stretching the margins of the class, if you ask me," Storey explained.

"Hear, hear," Silk Scarf supported that statement.

"Man partook of every vice available within the confines of London," Davis interjected gruffly. "Frequented establishments so low that no gentleman would ever enter them, yet he bragged of his profligacy when in his cups. Not surprised at all that someone murdered him."

"If you ask me it wasn't drink which led him to his murderer." Storey was clearly the head surgeon in this vivisection of Partlow's character.

"What then?" There was mischief in Dickens's voice. "Bad manners?"

"Too much of the evil smoke, I would venture," Storey intoned.

"Evil smoke?" Dickens inquired.

"Known opium addict," Davis explained, sarcasm lacing his voice. "One of his large coterie of 'gentleman's' vices."

Dickens was conducting this forum masterfully. They were revealing information without gaining the slightest knowledge of his purposes.

"Opium? My word!" Dickens the actor projected his surprise and chagrin. "You feel that murder lurked inevitably, then, in the depths to which Solicitor Partlow had sunk?"

"Well put, sir." A new voice, belonging to a tall, strikingly handsome, richly dressed gentleman, intruded upon the gossipy circle around the hearth. All that marred the tall gentleman's appearance was the twist of a sneer which remained on his mouth even after he had removed his cigar from its center. "No one in England has written more eloquently of the depths to which a gentleman can sink than yourself, sir. Ah, Sir Mulberry Hawk, the evil Steerforth, Ralph Nickleby. Well put indeed, sir!"

I could see that Dickens was pleased at this well-read intruder's knowledgeable flattery. The man pressed between chairs into the center of our circle. Dickens rose graciously to meet him.

"I was leaving after a dinner in one of the private dining rooms, and Sylvere, the *maitre'd*, apprised me of your presence in the club. I could not pass up the opportunity to make the acquaintance of the finest novelist in England. Mister Dickens, I am Henry Ashbee. I wish that I could write as you do." The man was a whirlwind.

"Thank you, Mister Ashbee. Meeting a reader as knowledgeable as yourself would be a distinct pleasure for any writer. Will you join us?" I could see that Dickens was struck with the man.

"I'm sorry but I have an engagement. Gentlemen," he said, as he gave his sneering smile all around, "I apologize for intruding on your conversation, but I could not leave the house without meeting Mister Dickens. I am an amateur writer, and I could not let pass the opportunity of meeting a true professional. Please excuse me." And with that, he was gone.

"Bright chap, Ashbee," Davis's words fought their way through another cloud of thick blue Turkish smoke, "bit mysterious, though. No one seems to know much about him. He is a Lord, yet he is known to be interested in business. Travels often to Hamburg and Paris. Fancies self a connoisseur of the arts. Ahhh . . ." (this drawn out meaningfully) "They say Ashbee is a great collector, ahhh . . . of exotic things, you know." Davis's economical characterization seemed to

81

satisfy the assembled company, as evidenced by grave nods all around. As for me, I didn't have the slightest idea what the man was talking about. Exotic things indeed?

"Collects books, they say," Storey said, having to have the last word. "I've heard his rare editions of Cervantes are priceless."

"Well," Dickens said, extinguishing his cigar in the burnt-orange glass dish atop the three-footed, bear-toed ash receptacle, which stood at attention like a dwarf orderly in the command of Dickens's ranking leather armchair, "Wilkie, we too must excuse ourselves and move on. It is getting late and I must work tomorrow."

"Gentlemen," I prefaced my handshakes, "it has been my pleasure to make each of your acquaintance." As these exchanges were proceeding, I observed Dickens lean across to Storey. I moved closer and overheard Charles's request.

"Might I have a word with you in private? I say, I need your help."

"Of course. Of course," Storey stammered, reeling from the honor.

As the others reseated themselves, we withdrew with Mister Storey of the Adelphi in tow. We crossed the marble floor of the foyer beneath the crystal chandelier and occupied a small anteroom near the front door which was furnished for the purpose of writing and dispatching messages via the street porter whom the *maitre'd* kept on call.

"I must tell you that I have not been completely straightforward in my conversations here this evening," Dickens confided. "I feel I have exploited you, and I fear I would like to continue to do so."

Mister Storey of the Adelphi stared.

"I apologize for not being more candid," Dickens went on, "but I certainly could use your help."

"Of course, of course, more than happy to assist," Storey mumbled.

I was somewhat taken aback by Dickens's forthrightness. I didn't feel it wise to reveal that we were spying for Inspector

Field here in this private gentlemen's retreat. I feared that Dickens was about to betray our ungentlemanly conduct, yet what could I say? He had taken charge of the charade from the moment we had entered the club.

"By the most bizarre of coincidences," Dickens explained to Mister Storey of the Adelphi, "I am writing a novel set in the world of actors and the London theatres which involves just such a murder. For that reason, the murder of Solicitor Partlow arouses my curiosity. Could you fill in some of the detail for me?"

On Storey's countenance, weak and unwelcome suspicion contended with a strong desire to please and show himself to advantage with Dickens.

I let out my breath in a subdued expression of relief at Dickens's novel subterfuge. I assumed that Mister Storey would have refused us as spies but could never withhold mere information which could assist in the alchemic act of turning life into art. Dickens's invention carried the day.

"You were here that night and observed the deceased gentleman in question. What is your true opinion of his state?" Dickens probed.

"I observed Partlow the whole evening," Storey replied with some heat. "He is, was, one of the most insufferable boors, one of the most disagreeable of the Club's members. He was very drunk, loud, even obscene."

"Obscene?"

"As I remember, just before they left, a loud and obscene argument, terrible graphic language, concerning some tart some members of the group had shared, broke out. Partlow and Paroissien, the stage manager at Covent Garden, actually leapt to their feet in anger. But someone settled it all. Actually, I think that chap Ashbee was one of the party."

"Do you remember who else was in the group?"

"Certainly Paroissien. He and Partlow were frequently in company together. Word has it they shared the same vices."

"Such as?" Dickens coolly extracted a small pad and pencil

from his inside coat pocket as if prepared to note down Storey's every word.

"All of the usual ones—strong drink, prostitutes, gaming—but it is rumored that he also partakes of the more unusual. He is said to be an opium addict and I have heard that he hires women to flagellate him and that he fancies young boys. I must caution you, however, that I am only repeating rumour, though widely dispersed rumour."

Dickens slowly shook his head in quiet moral indignation.

"You said there were others besides those two. Do you know who they were?"

"No. Though I vaguely remember someone saying that they looked like two of the supporting cast of the new *Macbeth*. One was a thin, sallow-looking chap, the other large and loud and with a beard."

"You don't know their names?"

"No, I don't." Storey of the Adelphi said this last somewhat slowly as if a sudden suspicion began to seep into his consciousness.

Dickens sensed this sudden drawing back on the part of his auditor. "No matter," he smiled, lightly dismissing their whole discussion. "Could hardly put all this opium taking and these exotic appetites in one of my novels anyway. There would be a public outcry."

Dickens's replacing of his small notepad (with nothing written on it) into his coat pocket seemed to put Mister Storey back at ease. After a short silence, Dickens extended his hand with an affectionate "Grahame, I can't thank you enough. Your insights will help me create my characters."

Storey of the Adelphi beamed.

We parted with Mister Storey in the foyer and retrieved our hats and gloves from the shelf in the cloak closet. Yet Dickens lingered. He was waiting for Sylvere, the *maitre'd*, to free himself from bidding "Adieu" to a group at the door. When the man turned and realized that Dickens was waiting to speak to him, he beamed and hurried to attend upon us.

Dickens prefaced his discussion with "Excellent meal and

fine cigars, Sylvere," and a hearty handshake punctuated by the soft scratching of two or more coins changing hands.

"Zank you vayrree much, Meestair Deekens," he fawned, his right hand disappearing into the depository of his trouser pocket.

"Sylvere, you can satisfy my curiosity. Solicitor Partlow was here the night he was so brutally murdered. I have been told that he left in a group. Can you tell me who he was with?"

"Ah, zee Poeleece Inspectair ask mee zee same questeeoun," the sly foreigner grinned at Dickens.

Unexpectedly Dickens shook hands with the creature again.

Not unexpectedly, the creature's hand again immediately sought out his right trouser pocket.

"But I am not the police," Dickens reassured him. "I am a writer with a fascination for crime."

"Certainemont. Of course. But you must understand, zee membairs, zay do not like mee to talk of zair private affairs."

Dickens seemed positively obsessed with shaking this oily imported servant's hand: "Who did he leave with?" There was a slight edge of impatience in Dickens's voice.

Efficient Sylvere spoke only after making his deposit in his trouser pocket: "Meestair Partlow wass een a party of five ven ee left. Zair wass ees friend Meestair Pairosseean and two guests ooze names I don know." At that, the Frenchman stopped, a rapid wave of caution washing over his face.

"And the fifth?" Dickens commanded without benefit of handshake.

The man's caution suddenly turned to a brief flash of fear. But that fear passed as the man jingled his pocket once for reassurance. "Zee fifth man," he finally volunteered, "wass Meestair Henry Ashbee."

The smiling Sylvere bowed us out of The Player's Club into a gaslit London night. I suggested that, since it was such a pleasant night, we ought to walk, knowing that walking in London at night was Dickens's favorite pastime. To my surprise, he ignored my suggestion.

He stopped on the stone steps of the club, staring down at

the street where three gentlemen, who had exited short minutes before us, were entering their cab. The street porter, dressed in a worn black morning suit and a top hat, dented on both sides, the upper half leaning forward precariously over his bushy eyebrows, held the hansom's door for them. I could see why the man had caught Dickens's attention: he was comical in his threadbare, crazily tilted mimicry of gentility. Dickens pounced on this street porter as if he wanted to lift him up with both hands and set him down whole within the pages of his next novel. I quickly found, however, that Dickens had no aesthetic designs upon this precariously hatted denizen of the London night. His designs were involved with life (and death) rather than art. Inspector Dickens was buying more information.

No handshakes this time. No punctilio. Two coins opened their conversation. The man in the broken backed hat actually bit on each coin as Dickens spoke to him concerning the night of the murder. When Dickens finished, the man silently scratched his head, then brazenly stuck out his hand. He was a grizzled Oliver Twist asking for "More!" His outstretched hand occasioned a rather simple exchange. Dickens filled it with a gleaming half-crown and the man began to talk animatedly.

Yes, he remembered the evening well.

Yes, all were drunk.

Yes, Mister Ashbee seemed to be in charge of the group.

"Do you know where they went after they left here?" Dickens asked eagerly. "Did you overhear?"

Suddenly the man's well of information seemed to dry up and his Oliver Twist hand began to sidle up toward us to ask for more.

The creature's mercenary inclination triggered one of the rare outbursts of anger which I observed in my friend Charles Dickens during the full twenty-three years of our association. With a quick swipe, Dickens knocked the man's crazy hat off.

The creature dove down and grovelled in the gutter after it as if his head were still inside. As he readjusted it to its precarious lean atop his head, Dickens screamed at him without raising his voice.

"You've told me nothing, you greedy wretch. Tell all or I'll take back what I've already given. I'll see that you lose your lowly place here. I'll thrash you within an inch of your life. Tell me, for I know that you know. Where did they go?"

Dickens's voice was hard and relentless. It sounded like Inspector Field threatening some squirming felon in some forsaken cellar in some condemned Rats' Castle in some depraved rookery in the lower depths of London's worst neighbourhood.

The man was visibly shaken by Dickens's threats.

"'Ee ordered 'is driver to Lady Godiva's 'Ouse of Gentlemen's Entertainments in Upper Grosvenor Street, Mayfair."

"LADY GODIVA'S HOUSE OF GENTLEMEN'S ENTERTAINMENTS"

(April 31, 1851—late evening)

We entered one of the hansom cabs queued up outside of The Player's Club. Dickens directed the driver to deliver us to Wellington Street, Strand, the intersection closest both to the *Household Words* office and to my digs near St. Martin's Lane. That was the corner where we bid each other goodnight at the conclusion of our late evening walks.

As the hansom rolled slowly away, I sank back into the seat somewhat relieved that the intrigues of the evening had been survived. Dickens, however, sat restless, on the edge of the upholstered bench, like some watchful bird of prey. It was not yet ten o'clock, and the streets remained busily populated. Gentlemen with canes, smoking cigars, strolled the sidewalks. Women materialized out of dark doorways to either be immediately rebuffed or to engage in commercial conversations with the ambulating gentlemen. Carriages, cabs, handcarts, and pedestrians entered the left side of the window and were propelled out of the right. Something was percolating inside Dickens's imagination.

"Wilkie," he said, darting his head at me, "Wilkie, are you game for more excitement tonight, for a new species of nocturnal adventure?"

In my relaxed posture, it took me a moment to divine his intention.

"Really Charles, you're not thinking . . ."

"Yes, I certainly am."

"This is not well-considered," I protested. "We will be recognized."

"We have nothing to be ashamed of," he snapped. "We are on a case."

"A case," I sputtered. "A case!"

Simultaneously we burst into subdued laughter.

"Dickens and Collins of the Metropolitan Protectives, eh?" I tipped him a wink.

"Young Wilkie," he said, grinning mischievously, "if you are going to be a novelist, and if I am going to be a detective, we must pursue reality and experience like two hounds on the scent."

With that he pounded up on the roof of the hansom with the butt of his open palm, and the conveyance lurched to a sudden halt.

"Turn around, and take us to Upper Grosvenor Street in Mayfair. Do you know the location of Lady Godiva's House of Gentlemen's Entertainments?" Dickens asked the question without the slightest hint of embarrassment.

"Yassir. Knows the 'ouse wellsir," came the hospitable answer.

88

There was no fog, and the moon scudded amongst stringy clouds. The hansom clattered along the Hyde Park railings before lurching to the right into the narrow crowded streets of Mayfair. Ah, Mayfair, the gentleman's playground. Little has changed in that district in the twenty years since I visited it with Dickens that night.

Flower girls and trinket vendors arrayed in colored scarves and ribbons hawked their wares on the street corners. Victuallers with their pots and grilles cooked loudly. Beggars and streetsweepers and dancing boskers and street musicians and dog trainers were all busily vying for the attention of the strolling pedestrians. The houses were all large and high and, almost without exception, brightly lit and beckoning. Some houses promised the more exotic of entertainments by the use of bright gaslight behind striking blue or red or orange curtains, thus projecting a prurient glow. Legions of gentlemen strolled the streets. By far the most fully represented of the various commercial species were the prostitutes, all gaily scarved and boldly painted, and either cascading with snakelike curls, or saucily tressed in the twirling French style, all low-cut, creamy white-necked, and seductively postured. Gentlemen engaged them in conversation on the walkway, or drew them to the windows of their coaches with a mere tap of their walking sticks upon lamppost or window edge.

"'Air's Godiva's casino over 'air," the cabman hollered down over the side of the box as he reined in. Our cab stopped in front of a high mansion brightly lit in white, angelic light.

"Here we are," Dickens said with more than a trace of uncertainty.

"Yes, aren't we," I answered with sarcasm. Yet, I must admit that I was excited. Fantasies of the illicit entertainments within Lady Godiva's establishment had been slinking within my secret mind since the moment Dickens ordered our hansom to turn around.

"Let's get on with it," Dickens motioned me to follow as he boldly struck out for the high iron gate to Lady Godiva's impressive house.

89

A black man of more than six and a half feet in height guarded the gateway entrance. He looked us both up and down for a long moment before opening the gate and inviting us to enter.

"Good evening, gentlemen," he greeted us in a polite West Indian accent, which signified that we had qualified by social class to enter Lady Godiva's notorious accommodations house, well known as one of the most opulent casinos and brothels in all of London. When our towering black Cerberus smiled, a diamond star inset in his white front tooth flashed.

It was a gaming and drinking, as well as whoring, establishment, and its different functions were neatly compartmentalized. The largest room at the front was the casino. The long table with the wheel sunken in its center formed the hub while the lesser tables radiated from it. The casino seemed desultory and bored. A few players gathered around the central table. All seemed to be just passing time as they waited for some more engaging entertainment to begin. All the players were men, dressed in evening clothes. Two women, dressed opulently in floor length gowns and gleaming tastefully with jewels, circulated, serving drinks and lighting the gentlemen's cigars. All but a few of the smaller tables were unoccupied. At one, a male employee of the house was dealing the French game *chemin de fer* out of a boot; at another, a drunken man of some sixty years, whom Dickens felt he recognized as a long standing M.P., was playing the Spanish game of Fan-Tan with a female dealer. As we passed, he suddenly lurched to his feet, threw his cards angrily down and cursed his luck with an epithet which sounded something like "Goreddammdevilsgorm."

Dickens smiled disarmingly as the suspected M.P., laden with a heavy cargo of drink, lugged into him heavily.

"Owrr, beggrrpradden. Cmmumsy er me," the man half-belched.

"Quite alright. No harm done," Dickens actually had caught the man and straightened him somewhat to arrest his falling down on the floor.

The man stared at Dickens with that dumb, eternally

grateful look of puppies being sold out of sacks in the street. To my surprise, Dickens did not immediately move out of range of the drunkard's fiery breath. By all indications he was preparing to engage the sot in conversation.

"I say, this is our first time here," Dickens said, smiling gamely. "Could you give us some idea of the attractions of the house?"

The man swayed with his eyes blinking. He squinted as if he wasn't sure that Dickens was real.

"Doan pray fanny ithher," he pointed back at the woman sitting demurely at the now-vacant card table. "Britch arrays 'ins."

With that, our drunken friend staggered off to the bar. We found out later that he was one Sir Frederick Capalan, M.P. for a section of West Devon.

"Excuse me, sir," the woman Fan-Tan dealer said politely after Sir M.P. had reeled out of earshot. "I could not help overhearing your inquiry, and I would be quite happy to describe the working of the house to you."

"Thank you. Please do," Dickens answered. I think he was a bit surprised that a woman would speak up so boldly without being asked.

"As I am certain you have observed, this is the casino room where all of the games of chance are offered. It is early yet." She paused. "Later, after the gentlemen have partaken of the ladies of the house, this room will fill up, and play will be heavy and quite heated."

She next pointed past our friend the M.P. leaning against the bar, toward the large curved portal at the bottom of the spacious room: "Through that arched doorway is our amphi-theatre, gentlemen. The entertainments will begin in just a few minutes. That is where the auctions are held. The upper two floors of the house are taken up completely by the girls' private bedrooms. Might I suggest that you get some cham-pagne at the bar and join the other gentlemen below the stage? You will not want to miss your chance to bid on the lady of your choice."

This whole description of the lurid act of buying human flesh for sexual purposes was communicated in a most demure and respectful style, as if she were directing us to some white-curtained parlor for the serving of high tea. Dickens tipped her a shilling, then made boldly for the bar. My imagination was suddenly glutted with images so perverse, that I could not help but hang back a bit until I had regained my equilibrium. What disoriented me was that, in the center of those perverse scenarios of my imagination, there moved a gentleman who greatly resembled myself.

"Sssharrmpayerrn," the M.P. from Devon growled at the barman. The sparkling white wine was served to him, and, at a silent gesture from Dickens, to us as well. Sir M.P. turned and squinted hard at us. "Harrmenntt arr met urr troo bleefrore," he waved his champagne glass with such abandon, that when he put it to his lips he drank nothing but air. He immediately held the empty glass out to the attentive barman with a look of honest bewilderment on his face.

The barman refilled his glass, and he downed it immediately in one long pull. His arm, like the mechanical appendage of some automaton at the great Crystal Palace Science Exhibit, came up for another refill. This time, however, he took only a dainty sip.

"Gemmellmammellmum," he said, there being some question whether that word would ever escape its grapple with his tongue, "troo the treeayturrr," and he pointed drunkenly into the darkness through the Moorish portal, thus signifying the way to the theatre. He took another sip of champagne, turned unsteadily, then, swivelling the upper extremity of his besotted body back toward us, made a rather eloquent motion for us to follow. When he reached the arch of the portal, he stopped for another foray into his champagne glass. For some inexplicable reason, this long sip seemed to momentarily steady our Parliamentary guide. He actually became capable of addressing us with a near coherence: "Heere's weere ye takes yeere pick," he pointed into the darkness. "Shee arkshuns off the cunts."

Dickens looked at me with nervous amusement and we followed the M.P. in. The darkness, the closeness of the room, the proximity of a rather thick crowd of drinking, cigar-smoking gentlemen, made me momentarily uncomfortable. Dickens, however, was committing the feel, the smell, the sounds of that prurient sexual darkness to his novelist's memory.

We took a place close and just to the right of the small stage. On the stage, the gaslamps went slowly up, spreading a circle of jaundiced yellow light in front of a hanging scarlet curtain. The gentlemen quieted expectantly.

I looked guiltily at Dickens. At that moment, I felt that our imaginations were in no manner up to the task of envisioning the reality of what would soon occur on that stage.

Suddenly, our reticence was exploded by the striking up of a gay chord on a piano and the parting of the scarlet curtain. A large blonde woman, all paints around the eyes and heavy rouge on her cheeks, took center stage. Her scarlet gown failed miserably (and intentionally, I am sure) to enclose her voluminous breasts. She swept forward and burst into a doggerel song.

The time has come, Derri Da, Derri Da, Derri Da,
To buy a girl, Derri Da, Derri Derri Derri Da.
A gay girl,
A play girl,
A fey girl, Derri Da, Derri Da.
Buy a girl,
For a toy,
And she will not be coy,
When she plays with your Derri Derri Derri Derri Da!

She sang lustily, like a provincial music hall performer, and, tucking her breasts temporarily back into her gown, called for the auction to begin.

"Who is she?" Dickens asked, tugging at the sleeve of a shadowed gentleman standing beside us in the darkness.

The gentleman, with a mocking laugh, apprised us that the scarlet singer was the mistress of the house, Lady Godiva herself.

The words of the novelist in eighteen seventy are not adequate to describe what next occurred on that stage. Yet, I am not really writing a novel. I am a clandestine Boswell for Dickens. This memoir is not meant to be published. It can't be published now, because our readers would never believe it, and, besides, one doesn't use real people in one's novels. No one knows about these events, not even Forster who insists that only he shall write "the Inimitable's" biography. Yet, as Dickens said, we must learn to deal with reality—and what was taking place on that stage was reality with a vengeance. I feel that I must somehow find the words to describe it. It is my fervent hope that if anyone reads this document, long after I am gone, that what follows will not prove overly offensive, though offensive, I am sure, to many it must ultimately be.

The blonde woman pranced about the stage as, one by one, she brought forward her merchandise for sale. Displaying each object placed on the auction block, she called for bids and directed each successful purchaser to the cashier for the collecting of his evening's prize.

Each of the women, when summoned from behind the curtain, put on a brief display of their various charms and accomplishments. The stage was raised about three feet above the floor. As we stood below, looking up, our eyes were on a precise line just below the waist level of those women who in succession occupied the stage. As the auction progressed, we found ourselves looking into a succession of exposed and, in fact, proffered Mounts of Venus.

The women were dressed either in some exotic costume, such as that of a French sailor, an Egyptian princess, an Amazon warrior, or in some seductive state of *deshabille* formed out of lascivious black or red stockings, lacy garter belts and diaphanous *peignoirs*. On stage, they proceeded slowly to discard, piece by piece, every article of their costumes until they stood entirely naked before us, except perhaps for some small trinket of jewelry.

Thus unencumbered, these women proceeded to expose themselves by every imaginable contortion of their supple young bodies. They fully displayed, against a backdrop of their meticulously powdered white skins, their pink and brown secret aureoles and their richly forested nether labia. A description of the performance of one auction lot will suffice.

She came in the costume of a French cabaret dancer, and when she kicked high and bent over, throwing her skirt up behind, it was revealed that she wore nothing beneath her voluminous petticoats. At commands from Mistress Godiva, she seductively unwrapped her skirt and, one by one, dropped her petticoats to a total of three until she stood naked from the waist. At the command of some gentleman's voice, she unfastened her tightly laced corset thus freeing her breasts and leaving her standing totally naked before the company. Other voices from beneath the stage commanded her to expose herself in different ways. She took a wide stance and at each gutteral command from the dark pit displayed herself in a series of slow archings of her back and bendings of her hips. With her fingers she caressed herself on command and opened and closed the labia of her Mount of Venus. Turning and bending at the waist until her palms lay flat upon the boards of the stage, she exhibited her full *derriere*; placing her hands on her hips she spread its creamy globes upon orders from the voices in the darkness.

We had known that rituals of this sort took place beneath the surface of our society, but, I am sure, neither of us considered how perverse and dehumanizing these sexual rituals could be. And yet, there was a fascination about the scene. Dickens stared directly ahead, unflinching, at the sub-human display unfolding on the stage. He later told me that it was more base than a slave auction he had once observed in Virginia.

The sex auction continued. As the whores' clothes fell with a gathering monotony, I thought of many things. These women were degraded marionettes, dancing on the strings of the perverse male imaginations gathered in the darkness. I remembered the murderess, Mrs. Manning, dancing on her string and hissing back at the crowd as the noose was tightened around her white neck. Each winning bid in this flesh auction bound each naked wretch in an evening's net of submission. I remembered Field's hand clamping Scarlet Bess's fragile white wrist in its relentless grasp, and Irish Meg smiling nervously and reaching forth her glass for more gin. Scarlet Bess and Irish Meg, both whores, yet somehow still human. They still clung, perhaps hopelessly, to some small, fragile remnants of their womanhood, their humanity—but not these wretches. They were like the dead child I had glimpsed in horror only a fortnight before. They looked as if they were still alive, but they were dead inside. Their only existence was in the minds of these sick men who bought their bodies.

Some men construct their fantasies of women in their imaginations, and then attempt to bring those fantasies to life in configurations of words. Through the ages (except in this age), sexuality and writing have been great allies. David's songs, Sappho's hymns, Boccaccio's wry stories of men and women joined in joy, Cleland's epic obscenities. Words can turn sex into magic. Sex, in its real state, as it was now appearing before us, was tortuous and artificial. I felt trapped within this "real life" text, which Dickens was composing as we pursued Inspector Field's "real life" murder mystery. We had all become characters in some yet unwritten novel. I had voluntarily allowed Dickens to imprison me in his imaginary text. But, as those women struck their naked poses, I desired only to escape this prisonhouse of words within which Dickens had enclosed me. Reality is the stage upon which all men commit their crimes, but writing about reality is the prison where the novelist serves his sentence. I watched him in the yellow-tinged darkness. He could not take his eyes off of the women on the stage. What will he do with them, I wondered? Will he attempt to capture their degradation in words?

The auction came to an end. Only a few voyeurs who had

not participated in the bidding loitered in the room when the lights went up. One, the drunken M.P. from Devon, sat on the floor with his back against the wall, snoring loudly. All the others had withdrawn with their prizes to the private bedrooms in the upper reaches of the house. I felt somewhat embarrassed, either because of the light coming up and taking away my anonymity, or, strangely, because I was empty-handed, as if some judgment on my manhood might be handed down. Dickens, however, was on the watch. When Lady Godiva re-entered from behind the scarlet curtain, he approached her straightaway. She received us quizzically, as if expecting to deal with some complaint.

"Gentlemen," she said, not recognizing Dickens, "were you unable to fit any of the ladies of my house to your liking?" She paused, and then, cocking her head as she studied us, continued "Or was there something special you required?"

"No, not at all," Dickens assured her. "We are not here to partake of the excellent entertainments of your house."

"You are not?" Her look positively overflowed with disdain.

When Dickens introduced himself, and then me, her recognition overcame her suspicion and she visibly relaxed toward us.

"Am I and my girls to appear in your next novel, sir?" she laughed.

"One can never know," Dickens said, taking up her playful tone, "perhaps in some form. I fear my audience would be quite unable to take you all neat."

"No, you don't write *that* kind of books, do you sir? I've looked into one or two of yours, and they are decidedly not *that* kind."

"We are here in search of information," Dickens said, rather sharply changing the subject, "and I hoped that you could help us."

She was immediately suspicious. But Dickens was well prepared to deal with her reticence. Reaching out, he took her right hand in both of his own, saying, "It could be quite profitable for both of us."

As she drew her hand from his grasp, it closed around the dull yellow shine of a gold sovereign.

"Yes, I am sure it can be," she said, her suspicion superseded by her greed. "Would you gentlemen care to join me in my private salon?"

Settled there, Dickens revealed the true reason for our visit to Lady Godiva's House of Gentlemen's Entertainments.

"A fortnight ago a group of revellers came to your house. Lawyer Partlow, who was subsequently murdered and cast into the Thames that very night, after leaving your premises, was a member of that group. Is there anything you can tell us about them?"

"I read about that murder. I've been expecting the police. You're a surprise."

"Yes, well," Dickens was improvising, "Partlow was of interest to me."

"I remember that party well." She leaned conspiratorially toward us. "They are all pretty reg'lar attendants upon my girls, especially Lord Ashbee. He attends here several nights each week."

I was somewhat surprised at her openness. She seemed to feel no responsibility to protect in any way the reputations of her regular clients.

"Ashbee?" Dickens sounded somewhat startled.

"Yes, he brought them in, drunk. Theatre people. The kind who only come here when someone like Ashbee or Partlow is paying."

"How many were there in the party?"

"Five, I would say," she answered, after some consideration. "Three bought women, but afterwards they all sat together in the casino playing cards and drinking champagne. Five, I am sure of it." She paused to reflect. "Strange, now that I think of it, one left for a time. Struck me because I was talking to Lord Ashbee and Solicitor Partlow when this one got up and left. He was someone important backstage at Covent Garden. The other two were railing him about something. He walked right out the door. Later, he was back, in the company of the others."

"Do you remember how long he was gone?"

She shook her head in the negative.

"He may have just needed air," the woman offered. "They were all quite drunk."

"Yes. Of course," Dickens agreed. "Can you remember anything else?"

"They left about two or three in the morning, quite loud and very, very drunk. Henry Ashbee did not leave with them."

"Where did he go?" he finally asked.

"Nowhere."

"I beg your pardon?"

"He did not leave at all that night. You see, Mister Dickens, I entertained him myself. It is a courtesy I extend to special customers. It involves out of the ordinary entertainments."

"Such as the smoking of opium?"

She raised her eyebrows at his question. "Perhaps."

"I understand."

"Mister Dickens, I would be happy to entertain you and Mister Collins in such a manner this evening. A number of my employees of different types are now free. It is a courtesy I extend only to special customers."

"Yes. Of course. I do quite understand." Dickens's face was flushed. He was, perhaps, beginning to feel the same overwhelming need to escape which had infected me back in that smoky darkness during that obscene performance. "But we must go now. You have been very helpful indeed," he saluted her with a hypocritical smile and another golden handshake.

With that, we fled like housebreakers from an alarum. The casino was filled as we made our exit. The men, just come from the beds of their whores, crowded around the tables. The Mayfair streets were deserted (all the street whores having retired to the dark reaches of Hyde Park, knowing that the gentlemen leaving the fancy houses of Mayfair at this hour would be sated, and show no interest in them) as we contemplated in silence all that we had experienced that night.

"Paroissien, that is his name!" Dickens broke our silent march.

"Whose name?" I inquired.

"Why, the stage manager, of course. At Covent Garden. I have been trying to remember his name ever since that fat pander described him. He is the one who left and then returned that night. Why did he leave?"

"For any number of reasons," I must have seemed incredibly dull then, "all of which we have already rehearsed."

"Not at all," he argued in a calculating voice. "We haven't rehearsed the most important and obvious one of all."

"We haven't?"

"He left to procure the murder weapon. He left Godiva's House, took a cab to Covent Garden, and secreted Macbeth's handsword on his person."

I stared wide-eyed at Dickens. He was constructing the whole plot, chapter by chapter, right there in the middle of the gaslit street.

"No, that is how it happened, I'm certain," he said.

With a lurch, he took off walking.

"Wilkie," he said, with excitement in his voice, "we have almost reconstructed the night of the murder, but we must follow it to its violent end."

His pace quickened. At Hyde Park Corner he hailed a passing hansom. "Take me to the embankment side of Black-friar's Bridge," he ordered.

"Rawht, sir," the cabman signified with an accompanying flick of his long whip to his business partner's rump, which gave off a sharp click as if it were a form of terminal punctuation.

It had been a long and disturbing night. I had expected to proceed directly home to my warm bed, and now we were off once again on some wild flight of Dickens's nocturnal imagination. As I often had before, I felt like some character in one of his novels.

I thought I knew what he was doing. He had become the murderer. He was imagining what this Paroissien might have been thinking. Imagining his hand clutching the murder weapon concealed beneath his cloak. Imagining his hatred for the lawyer sitting across from him.

When the cab bumped to a halt, he instructed the cabman to wait.

We walked to the head of the stairs which descended into the fast-moving black river. Dickens started down, but stopped as if he had decided that he had gone far enough.

"Wilkie," his voice was sad, "we have retraced the steps of a murderer. We have witnessed what he witnessed, heard what he heard, and yet what do we know? How much of it do we really understand?"

"Very little I would think," I spoke truthfully for myself. "We don't know why he did it."

"Precisely, but do you know what really bothers me?"

"What?"

"We never will understand because we cannot go inside of him, because we cannot write the truth of it. No one will really know why he committed the murder or what the true reality of London was in our time, because none of us, the writers, are allowed to use our words!"

The trip back to Wellington Street was accomplished with dispatch.

He climbed out of the cab in front of the *Household Words* offices. I decided to take the cab on to my digs. As it drew away, I looked back. He was standing alone on the curbstone, and two dark figures were materializing out of the shadows to intercept him before he went in.

"IS THIS A DAGGER WHICH I SEE BEFORE ME?"

(May 1, 1851)

I arrived at the Wellington Street offices at eleven the following morning. To my surprise, "the Inimitable" was still in his nightshirt. He was brewing a can of coffee on the hearth, which he had stoked to a hearty blaze.

"We stayed up half the night planning, Wilkie," Dickens explained with enthusiasm. Field and Rogers had been waiting when he returned after midnight, and had listened eagerly to his report. Though bleary-eyed, he was excited: "We're going to Covent Garden tonight, Wilkie, to identify them. That done," he was positively trembling with the adventure of it, "we will install an elaborate spy network within the very theatre itself to gather the evidence against them."

He passed me a steaming cup of coffee distractedly.

"Field is a genius," he burbled on. "He has all his players ready, their roles written, and the curtain waiting to go up."

"He must be," I commented wryly, "if his drama is good enough to open *sans* rehearsal at Covent Garden."

Dickens tipped me the sly wink of a co-conspirator.

"Just what is our role in our genius's little drama?" I asked with more than a hint of sarcasm in my tone.

"He needs our help to get him and his witness into the theatre."

"Meg? The prostitute?" My pulse suddenly quickened. She was a common harlot with a fondness for gin, yet the prospect of seeing her again made my blood rush. I cannot explain why.

All I know is that since the night of our only meeting the woman had been in my mind, her surprised look as I gave her my scarf against the river wind haunting me like a fond memory from childhood.

"Yes, only she can identify the men who were present when Solicitor Partlow was murdered. But there is more."

"How much more?"

"Field needs us to gather information. We are to mingle backstage with the cast and ask questions. I will arrange it with Macready."

"Spies once again, is it?"

Dickens sensed my discomfort with our roles: "Yes, I suppose so. But Field is right. I am known there. They will trust us, and will think nothing of us asking questions which Field himself could never ask. In fact, we are even hoping, perhaps, to find the murder weapon there." Field may not have been a genius but, in Dickens, he had recruited a highly enthusiastic ally.

We put in a cursory day at the *Household Words* office and I left Dickens at five to prepare for the adventures of the evening. I dined alone at a public house—meat pie, French potatoes, and a hearty tankard of ale—then returned to my flat to dress for the theatre. Our roles were those of the gentlemen swells paying a visit backstage. I hired a cab, collected Dickens at Wellington Street, and we arrived at Covent Garden shortly after seven. The curtain was scheduled to rise at seven-thirty.

We descended into the usual flood of humanity which coursed around Covent Garden on play nights. The cobbled thoroughfares beneath the towering stone walls of the theatre were choked with stalls and tents and handcarts and trestles for the offering of goods to the crowd. The coaches of the rich lined up as Lords and Ladies, Merchants and Matrons, Milliners, Serving Girls, Clerks, and Apprentices passed by. The theatre was one of the few places where all of the classes of London society gathered to partake of the same entertainment. Though the street was dense with people, there was no jostling or bumping, no strong sense that the pickpockets were about. It was a leisurely shopping crowd taking in the evening's sights and sounds and smells before entering the theatre for the night's formal entertainment (very different from a crowd of the sort that might gather for a public hanging at Horsemonger Lane Gaol). Small groups gathered around street buskers who danced or sang or fiddled or juggled or made grotesque faces at the curious. Inspector Field suddenly materialized from behind a huge pot of bright yellow country flowers.

"Gentlemen," he greeted us, his darting eyes scanning the crowd to see if our meeting was in any way observed. Satisfied, he drew us, with a silent flex of his forefinger, behind the huge pot of yellow flowers, and announced, "Rogers and our witness are ready. We will await your signal from directly hopposite the stage door," and with that he disappeared as abruptly as he had materialized.

"Well," Dickens said to me.

"Indeed," I said to him.

With that, we struck out in the direction of the stage door.

We had taken no more than a few steps when a young Fleet Street man, notepad at the ready (Gads, they seemed to be everywhere he went in those days), accosted us.

"Mister Dickens, isn't it? Oh yes, I would recognize you anywhere, Mister Dickens." The young man never paused. "Could you give *Putnam's Morning Express* a few words concerning Mister Macready's *Macbeth*?" The interview was underway as if he had harpooned Dickens and was reeling in his catch.

"I haven't seen it yet!" Dickens tried to push past him.

"No matter, you are here, you must be eager to see it, yes, eager to see it," and he scribbled that last phrase on his notepad. I followed closely, screening Dickens off from further pursuit from the young Fleet Streeter who had just conducted a successful interview with himself. We gained the stage door without further incident.

Dickens tapped politely with his cane. The door guard opened it cautiously. Aged, bespectacled, stooped and droopily mustachioed, he was about to launch into his set speech about no one being allowed backstage within ten minutes of curtain when Dickens cut him off: "Good evening Mister Spilka. I trust you remember me. I am Charles Dickens, and I believe that Mister Macready left explicit directions concerning my admittance." Dickens delivered his speech with charm and great familiarity, and it worked with the immediate success that Ali Baba's "Open Sesame" had upon the cave of the forty thieves.

According to plan, we entered the backstage area to reconnoitre before signaling for Field and Irish Meg to come forward. It was twenty-five minutes after seven. The backstage was chaotic. Every member of the company seemed running hither and thither, half-dressed. Scenery—huge stretches of painted cloth, and bulkier objects such as trees, great rocks made of wood and paper, castle battlements—was going up and down on ropes as if controlled by some gigantic puppeteer. Workmen were furiously fanning smoke onto the stage from smudge pots to create the ghostly mist of the battlefield. All around us, actors were pacing, posing, making gestures.

I observed the gleam enter Dickens's countenance as soon as we passed through the stage door. It always appeared whenever he got around actors.

Three soldiers immediately before us flourished their swords in the air. Later, Inspector Field would apprise us of his interest in these "prop swords."

"Not props at all!" Dickens would quickly disabuse him of that misconception. "The real thing. Fencing classes conducted twice weekly in the morning onstage. Fight master requires attendance of all, both principals and cast actors."

As Dickens stood gawking at the chaotic flurry of activity, a wiry clean-shaven man with jet black hair and piercing dark eyes (whom Dickens recognized, and whom immediately acknowledged Dickens with a tight smile and hurried nod), moved through that chaos biting off short sharp orders.

This was Pariossien.

We were only brief minutes from the curtain. Dickens was carefully surveying the whole backstage area, slowly executing a three hundred and sixty degree turn on the balls of his feet.

"There," he whispered, pointing with his walking stick at a rather dark corner where a heavy stage curtain hung in front of what appeared to be an unornamented brick wall. "There," Dickens hissed, "the perfect place."

With that, he turned abruptly on his heel and marched directly to old man Spilka at the stage door. Field and Irish Meg must have been waiting just outside, because they materialized immediately upon the door being opened. Spilka stared wide-eyed at Meg's vulgar harlot's dress, but, at a glance from Dickens, looked the other way. In the confusion before the curtain, no one noticed them enter. Dickens secreted them behind the aforementioned curtain.

The three weird sisters, their hair grotesquely tangled about their faces, large artificial wens and warts raised on their foreheads and chins, black lines of charcoal stick slashing out of their eyes and down across their cheeks, stood primping before us in the wings. Martial sound effects and the metallic clashings of an approaching storm rose moodily from the far side of the stage. The three witches scurried out and took their places. Paroissien, the stage manager, raised his arm and pointed with one finger. Ah, the power of the man! Every eye was upon him. A drum began a quiet measured beat. Paroissien dropped his arm, and the curtain rose to the eerie chant of the three weird sisters rising out of the hanging smoke.

With a slight tug on my sleeve, Dickens pulled me behind the curtain where Field and Irish Meg had secreted themselves. Meg was leaning back against the brick wall, visibly shaken, as if she had, indeed, as Macbeth would later in the evening, seen a ghost. I considered taking her hand and saying something comforting.

"He's our man, the stage manager," Field whispered excitedly to Dickens. "She pointed him out straight off."

Field didn't hesitate in giving Dickens direction: "Leave us. Your presence is too conspicuous. Now we must identify the two others. When that is done we will leave by the way we came. Leave us."

The play was well underway. We stood in the wings and watched the light play through the smoke on the armor of sword-carrying men. The metallic thunder crashed.

"Hallo Charles, Wilkie," a gruff voice suddenly whispered beside us in the darkness of the wings. It was Macready, all bushy eyebrows and wide scowling mouth. "Can't talk now. Have to palaver with the witches."

He turned to his dresser, a weasely little man named Freddy Leavis, for a final check of his makeup and costume. Another actor joined Macready. The witches on stage chanted their devil's litany. A drum sounded, and Macbeth and Banquo swept solemnly onstage.

Macready was truly a commanding presence. When he stationed himself at center stage, every eye locked upon him. His voice shook the theatre, or seemed to. When he walked to the front of the stage, he controlled every eye and ear and imagination in the house.

"If chance will have me king, why, chance may crown me . . ." From beneath his deep brows Macready's eyes burned down into the darkness.

I glanced sideways at Dickens. He was not looking at the stage.

"Time and the hour runs through the roughest day," Macready solemnly intoned.

Dickens's back was turned to the stage. His whole attention was on the curtain behind which Field and Irish Meg were secreted. I watched as Field moved out from behind that curtain and circulated about the backstage area. He talked to no one, yet observed everything. After a complete circuit, he returned to his concealment. His presence went unnoticed. What had been unregulated chaos before the curtain rose had subsided into quiet order. Actors came and went with subdued concentration. Paroissien, the object of Field's greatest interest, stood in the wings close to the stage with a sheaf of papers in one hand and a look of fierce concentration on his dark face. Every two or three minutes, as a scene was about to change or an entrance was to be made or some offstage effect was to be sounded, he gave sharp pointed signals, wordlessly, with his prepossessing forefinger.

"I have no spur/To prick the sides of my intent, but only/Vaulting ambition, which o'erleaps itself . . ." Macbeth paced the stage.

Dickens, too, was restless. He kept glancing at the curtain behind which Field and Meg were secreted. I, too, was curious. However, my thoughts were upon the emotions of Irish Meg. I wanted to say something to her, I know not what, before she returned to the night streets, where I could never, honestly, pursue her.

"False face must hide what the false heart doth know."

Dickens moved away from me. But, to my surprise, he did not approach the curtain where our co-conspirators stood concealed. Instead, he crossed the wings to a wooden stairway which led up to some enclosed dressing cubicles used by the female actors. At the foot of those stairs stood a young woman with her hand to her face. She seemed just an actress silently rehearsing her part. I followed after Dickens out of curiosity. I don't think Dickens even realized that I was behind him. When we drew near to the young actress, it became clear that she was weeping, the hand to her face an unsuccessful attempt to hide her tears.

When she took her hand away, the young lady proved quite young indeed. She could not have been older than fifteen years. It was strange to encounter one so young in such a distinguished theatre company. Her face was childlike, yet she was also a woman. Her full figure, even in the loose servant's costume in which she was attired, betrayed her deceptive maturity. Her hair was a shiny shade of light brown, with dancing gold highlights becoming visible whenever the slightest ray of light reflected off of it. But the dominant, most compelling, aspect of her appearance was her eyes. They were large and round and brown and so innocent, that one wanted to protect her without her even being threatened. But when Dickens first looked into those eyes, they were brimming with tears, and she seemed very threatened indeed. No wonder, then, that he fell in love the first moment he saw her.

"Look like th' innocent flower,/But be the serpent under 't . . ." Lady Macbeth had taken the stage to converse with Macready.

"Excuse me, Miss, but might I be of some assistance?" Dickens did not hesitate. A handkerchief had materialized out of his sleeve. She took it, and buried her face in it. Her shoulders shook with her sobs.

"Please, young lady, nothing can be so frightening. Please tell me what is wrong. I would like very much to help." I had never heard Dickens speak in a voice so gentle and concerned.

The young actress's sobs slowly subsided. She wiped the tears from her cheeks, and daintily blew her nose, then looked up at Dickens with those doe eyes. For Dickens, the mystery of Partlow's murder and all else—me, Inspector Field, *Macbeth*—was forgotten.

"Oh sir, I am so ashamed. Why would they force me to do this so suddenly?" Her voice still quaked as she spoke.

Dickens reached out his hands toward her shoulders to calm her, but quickly drew them back as if thinking better of the idea.

"Is this a dagger which I see before me,/The handle toward my hand? Come, let me clutch thee!" Macready's great voice rent the charged air.

"Who is forcing you to do what?" Dickens asked quietly.

"Only tonight, after the play had begun, and my mother was already onstage, he brought me this new costume. He ordered me to play the whole scene with both hands at my sides, as if I was too dumbstruck by the appearance of Lady Macbeth to notice my own indecency."

"Indecency?" Dickens said it with a slight catch in his voice.

My eyes followed Dickens's eyes as they tried to solve the mystery of her costume, which she was holding bunched at the neck with that hand not occupied with Dickens's handkerchief. With the silent eloquence that only a natural actress could accomplish, she let both of her hands fall to her sides. The coarse brown peasant's smock fell open. Its neck hole had been slashed downward and the front was almost completely undone to her waist. She stood there helplessly, tears brimming in her eyes, her white shoulders and the tops of her breasts almost fully revealed.

"Yes, I see," Dickens delicately averted his eyes which, of course, caused me to avert my own. When I turned back, the young woman had turned her back to us, buried her head in the rising stairs, and recommenced her sobbing.

"A dagger of the mind," Macready's soliloquy continued onstage, "a false creation,/Proceeding from the heat-oppressed brain?"

Dickens ascertained, after a brief questioning, that her role in the play was that of a wanton serving girl interrupted in the midst of a nocturnal assignation by Lady Macbeth, as that murderous worthy stalks the battlements, wringing her hands. The young actress's role was to suddenly start up out of the darkness in the company of a half-dressed young man, and, having startled everyone, flee in disarray from the stage.

"The manager, sir, he says no one knows what I'm doing there in the middle of that dark night unless I wear my blouse all undone, sir. It is indecent, sir, and I feel like a harlot. He says if I do not wear this new costume, and allow the light to fall on my open laces, that he will serve me notice, sir, and my mother also. Oh sir, I do not know what to do."

We found out later that the girl's mother was a professional actress initiating her daughter into her profession by cadging a minor role in the plays in which she contracted to perform, and that, at the very moment, she was onstage in the part of none other than Lady Macbeth. This opportunity at Covent Garden was the daughter's first major theatre role.

"Oh sir, this play has been running for four weeks. Why must he suddenly change my costume? It is such a small part." She was an actress, but I do not feel that she was experienced enough or talented enough to feign the childlike innocence which she had fallen into before Dickens.

"Mister Paroissien, the stage manager, made this change?" I could sense Dickens's mind churning for the solution.

"Yes sir, the manager," she said, a small spark of hope flashing in her voice. "You know him, sir?"

"Oh yes, I know him allright," Dickens answered, grimly remembering why he had come to this theatre this night.

"Sleep no more!/Macbeth does murder sleep!"

The two stood looking at each other in silence. She was truly a vision of innocence and beauty in that scanty costume. I am not surprised that Charles was drawn to her. There was a magnetic intensity in her eyes. That look, as if words were no longer necessary, sealed my friend Charles's doom. That look was the beginning and the end, and bound them forever like Paulo and Francesca.

"I see what your part calls for and its reason," Dickens said, breaking the silence of that mesmerizing look.

The young woman's face, full of expectancy, streaked with tears, fell.

"But," Dickens went on, and that writer's gleam came into his eye, "I also think I know a way to suggest sexuality, without being at all indecent. You must trust me. I am an expert at such matters."

When his head swivelled in search of Paroissien, I knew that he was going to intercede for this child-woman, like that knight errant out of *Eliduc*.

"O Banquo, Banquo,/Our royal master's murder'd!"

"Wilkie," he ordered, as if I were his faithful squire, "stay with her. This will only take a moment."

To my great surprise, within short minutes he returned with Paroissien in tow. I could only imagine what Inspector Field, observing this conversation from behind his arras yet unable to overhear, must have been imagining. He told us later that, when he saw Dickens confronting Paroissien, he cursed himself for ever considering the cooperation of amateur detectives.

"Poor girl is terrified of appearing indecent," Dickens was saying as they came up. "I know the scene. I helped Macready compose it. There is a stylish and suggestive way to play her small part."

When the stage manager and the young actress faced each other, the girl lowered her eyes as if cowed in his presence.

"Now, what is the problem?" Paroissien did not raise his voice and the inquiry was not made unkindly, yet the young woman's eyes, when she raised her face to answer, were terror-stricken.

"It is the blouse, sir. It is indecent. I cannot just stand there with my hands at my sides and let the whole audience stare at me."

"Let's briefly put on manly readiness," Macready's voice seemed to taunt us from the stage.

Paroissien's lips compressed into a tight line.

"If I might make a suggestion?" Dickens, who had been simply waiting for the appropriate moment to intrude, did so. "If the scene is altered ever so slightly, if she is but allowed to use her hands in an expressive way, the comic sexuality can be suggested, while at the same time avoiding the tasteless immodesty of such a sensational costume." Dickens delivered his little speech in his most diplomatic and accommodating voice.

There was something in Paroissien's eyes, in the tension on the muscles of his neck, that gave me the sudden intuition that he was enraged. Yet, on the surface, he never lost his equanimity. "I am, of course," he said, "open to suggestion, especially from such an eminent friend of the theatre, if that suggestion is reasonable."

"Oh, most reasonable, most reasonable." Dickens, who, with his acute talent for reading people's emotions, had, I'm certain, detected the rage smoldering beneath the stage manager's facade of politeness, assured him.

"What is it, then?" Pariossien could barely conceal his anger.

"Why don't you do it this way," Dickens's voice changed to one of command and intimidation. Beneath what seemed to be a straightforward narration of how the girl could play the scene was the clear threat that if this advice was not taken, further steps would be. "In seconds, your stage seamstress could sew some laces into that smock. When the serving girl pops up out of the darkness, her dress will indeed be all unlaced. The light will catch a brief glimpse of her white skin and the fact that she has been surprised in the midst of a sexual encounter will be immediately apparent. But then, she will guiltily begin to lace herself up as Lady Macbeth addresses her in distraction. *Voila!* The necessary hint of sexuality is present, and" he turned back to the girl, "your time on stage is spent in the protection of your modesty."

Paroissien did not say anything right off. Perhaps he was struggling to keep from strangling Dickens on the spot.

"It wouldn't be natural," Dickens pressed him. "No woman, even the most debased, would just stand there with herself all *unlaced*, and make no attempt to cover up."

Paroissien buckled. "Yes, of course, I do see your point, more natural, yes, let us try it that way," he said, nodding to the young actress. Without another word, he turned on his heel, and returned to his post in the front wings.

"Oh, thank you, sir, thank you," she said, beaming at Dickens before scurrying off to find the seamstress, for her scene was fast approaching.

"Naught's had, all 's spent./Where our desire is got without content . . ." Lady Macbeth commented from the stage as her daughter fled.

Dickens led me back to our prior vantage point in the wings. Lady Macbeth, the young actress's mother, was not known to Charles or myself by name, though Dickens expressed a vague memory of having seen her onstage before. When the famous sleepwalking scene commenced, Dickens focused his concentration fiercely upon the stage. When the girl jumped to her feet out of the black shadows into the white-hot moonlight, he was the only person in the whole theatre who was not startled. His eyes burned with excitement as she played her tiny role just as he had scripted it, and fled into the darkness at the far side of the stage.

"Out, damned spot! out, I say!" Lady Macbeth delivered her lines.

"Would it not be to our advantage if the blood were still on their hands?" a voice inquired, startling us from immediately behind. It was Field. I glanced around quickly to see if we were being observed. Paroissien was well in front of us at the edge of the stage.

"Yes, that would certainly simplify things," Dickens smiled.

"Listen. I don't have much time. Meg and I will slip out at the first opportunity. Our work is done." (I am afraid that a man as perceptive as Inspector Field could not miss the disappointment in my face. Could he imagine that, in my secret mind, I had hoped for an opportunity to converse with Irish Meg?) "Banquo and Macduff are the other two. Even with the wigs and the powder, Meg is sure. Could you find out their names, perhaps engage them in conversation?" With that, he was gone, sliding like a piece of the scenery back behind his arras.

"To-morrow, and to-morrow, and to-morrow,/Creeps in this petty pace from day to day."

We never saw Field and his witness make their exit. Macready's voice held every eye and heart and mind in that theatre in its thrall.

> "Life's but a walking shadow, a poor player
> That struts and frets his hour upon the stage
> And then is heard no more: it is a tale
> Told by an idiot, full of sound and fury,
> Signifying nothing."

Field and Irish Meg must have slipped out of the stage door sometime during the emotion and confusion of the final scene. When I finally realized that they were gone, I felt as if I had lost her forever.

Even as the "BRAVO's" were growing to a crescendo, Dickens was dispatching old Spilka to the public house across the way for champagne. The effervescent bottles arrived before the numerous curtain calls and final bows of the principals were taken. Dickens arranged the bottles on a makeshift trestle just off the wings, while old Spilka gathered as many odd drinking receptacles as he could find, and when the players came off the stage, pulling off their wigs and false beards, loosening their stays, unstrapping their swords, elated at the enthusiasm of the audience still applauding in the stalls even though the gas was coming up, there stood Dickens with a champagne bottle in one hand and his cup upraised in a toast to the company. It was the kind of flourish which Dickens gloried in.

"Never has a company of *Macbeth* fretted its hour upon the stage with more accomplished sound and fury. Fellow actors, I salute you," he said, and he toasted them, one and all, with a sweep of his arm. "Please join me in a small impromptu toast to the finest acting company in London." With that invitation, they descended upon the champagne with the same rabid appetite with which the inhabitants of Saint Antoine would descend upon that broken cask of wine eight years later in *A Tale of Two Cities*. Macready, still in full make-up, joined Dickens, pumping his hand. Macready raised his mailed arm, and every member of the company paused to listen.

Macready proclaimed: "The Inimitable." All of the members of the company in unison echoed Dickens's favorite appellation. "An actor. One of us," Macready intoned solemnly before drinking off his toast.

As that crowd of actors raised their glasses, emptied them, then raised them once again, Dickens leaned close to me, and directed my attention to our friend Paroissien standing scowling in the wings, without a glass in his hand. "Seems we have a Methodistical presence to frown upon the proceedings," Dickens quipped, as he moved away from me in the direction of Macduff and Banquo, who stood drinking from the same bottle, passing it back and forth with two of the three weird sisters. Dickens opened his remarks with compliments upon their executions of their roles, and soon was engaged in easy conversation with Field's two unsuspecting suspects. Macduff was a fairly tall (about Dickens's height) but spare man, who had padded his body for his warlike role, while Banquo was a man of much more ample girth and broad shoulders, who looked and carried himself like a soldier.

I shook hands with Macready, who, in the exuberation of the moment, engaged me in some uncharacteristic raillery. "Young Wilkie," he said knitting those burly brows in mock sternness, "when will you be presenting us with a play that we can perform?" I must smile as I think of it now, because five years later, after the first public performance of *The Frozen Deep*, Macready, in retirement then, would be the first to congratulate me with the gruff admission that "a modern part like that could tempt me to take the stage once again."

When my attention returned to detached observation of the festivities, I noticed that Paroissien, the stage manager, had disappeared, and that Dickens had broken off his jovial conversation with Macduff and Banquo, and was standing by himself, indecisively, as if momentarily suspended on the brink of some precipitous act. He was gazing across the room at the young woman in the serving girl's blouse. Even as he stared at her from that distance, her face came up and their eyes met. They held each other's gaze for a long moment, and then Dickens moved decisively.

For some inexplicable reason, I felt compelled to follow. I joined the two of them in time to overhear their fateful introductions.

"My name is Charles Dickens."

There was a slight flutter in his voice as he said it.

Her eyes were wide with excitement as she looked up into his.

"I am Ellen Ternan."*

---

*There is some confusion amongst Dickens scholars as to the appearance in Dickens's life of Miss Ellen Ternan. According to the researches of Ada Nisbet and Edgar Johnson, Dickens did not meet

Miss Ternan until five years later, in 1856. Professor Robert Altman, however, in his monograph, *The Mystery of Ellen Ternan*, asserts that Dickens met Miss Ternan as much as five years earlier, and supports that contention by comparing the stage productions in which Mrs. Ternan and her daughter appeared between 1852 and 1856 with the plays which Dickens himself attended during those years. Professor Altman's comparisons show that during that time period Dickens never missed a theatrical production in which Miss Ternan performed. In fact, during that period Dickens developed the habit of returning to see some of these performances two, three, and, in the instance of the 1854 *George Barnwell* at the Covent Garden theatre, four documented times. It is, therefore, quite possible that the romantic backstage meeting of Dickens and Miss Ternan in 1856 was staged for the purpose of intentionally starting a string of events which would eventually thrust their long-standing relationship out into the open, thus giving Dickens the seeming motivation to separate from his afflicted wife, Kate. In other words, when Dickens finally decided that he wanted to go public with his affair with Miss Ternan, he re-orchestrated their dramatic meeting of five years earlier.

Further, Dickens scholars disagree as to whether Ellen Ternan was 19 or 20 years old when she and Dickens allegedly first met in 1856. However, Stanford Whitmore, who agrees with Altman that Dickens met the young actress much earlier, argues that she was only sixteen years old in 1852 when Dickens had developed a correspondence with her family employing a code name.

Collins's manuscript supports that theory that Dickens met her in her fifteenth year, served as her guardian for almost five years, and then, when she was of age, allowed her to surface and their connection to become public when he could no longer tolerate life with his wife. This scenario, for example, explains the episode of the bracelet in 1857 which precipitated the separation of Charles and Kate Dickens. Scholars have always taken this episode on face value, yet it is too obvious a blunder, especially for a man of the meticulous attention to detail and obsession for organization of Charles Dickens. How then did it happen? If Dickens had maintained a relationship, of whatever nature, with the girl for five years prior to the bracelet episode in 1857, then perhaps he intentionally orchestrated that

INSPECTOR FIELD, PLAYWRIGHT,
OR "BAITING THE TRAP"

(May 4, 1851—evening)

Following that evening of *Macbeth* at Covent Garden, where
so much had transpired both on and off the case, Dickens
seemed to rally and return to his vocations and avocations with
a renewed enthusiasm. Before the sudden death of little Dora,
Dickens had been tyrannically rehearsing his amateur troupe
for a benefit performance of Bulwar Lytton's new comedy, *Not
So Bad As We Seem*. The Duke of Devonshire had graciously
offered his residence, Devonshire House, in Picadilly, as the
site of its opening benefit performance before Her Majesty and
the Court. Rehearsals had only commenced, when first

---

episode to bring the situation out into the open. He wanted Kate to
cut the cord of marriage.

Finally, the obviousness and the attention-drawing quality of the
oft-documented public displays associated with the Ellen Ternan
legend of 1856–57—the backstage meeting, the bracelet episode, the
notice in the *Times*, the highly publicized feud with Thackeray—can
all be read as an elaborate smokescreen thrown up by Dickens the
novelist to camouflage Ellen's past, her residence in Miss Coutts's
Urania Cottage. Thackeray may very well have been a part of the
whole plot with Dickens and Collins since he certainly, as evidenced
by his feelings for Jane Brookfield, would be sympathetic to such an
extramarital relationship. This Collins manuscript proves the capa-
bility of Dickens to turn his own life into an elaborate fiction, to plot
and structure his and Ellen's real life as if it were one of his novels: life
(1851) becomes art (1856–57) to serve life.

Dickens's father, and then his younger child, had died so suddenly. With Dickens unable to continue, the date for the performance before the Queen had been tentatively reset for May twenty-second in hopes that, after a time of mourning, Dickens might feel inclined to take up the reins, and resume his seat on the box as both manager and actor. Now, to the joy and relief of all, that seemed to be exactly his intention.

He ordered rehearsals to resume on May third in Devonshire House (the Duke having hospitably offered his manse, not only for the benefit performance itself, but for the getting up of the whole production). I had a small part in the piece, that of valet to Lord Wilmot, which was Charles's lead role. Douglas Jerrold had another of the major roles, as did Augustus Egg. Wills had declined a part, in fact the part which was given to me, because he felt it might distract him from his duties at the *Household Words* office. Forster, in a masterful bit of casting, played a dour and inflexible Magistrate. Though much caught up in the rush of the rehearsals, neither Dickens nor myself had forgotten about Inspector Field's murder investigation, which we had left backstage at Covent Garden Theatre. I was sure that the murder case was not all that Dickens had left backstage at Covent Garden.

Three full days passed before Field once again summoned us. It was early evening, and rehearsal was drawing to a close at Devonshire House, when the taciturn Rogers materialized in the doorway. He saluted Dickens respectfully, and delivered Field's summons to Bow Street Station. Dickens drew that rehearsal to a precipitate close, and we soon joined Field in the bullpen.

First off, Inspector Field sat us down before the fire to give us a full report. Teasing, he began: "I've been keepin' an eye on you two, I 'ave" (eyes a-twinkle) "and Rogers tells me you've been rehearsin' a play the last two nights. Well, I'm proud to say, I've been workin' on my own little play these three days past, since our night at Covent Garden."

But Field did not choose to elaborate on his theatrical metaphor. Instead, he announced the results of our little

Covent Garden fishing expedition. "Meggy spotted all three of 'em, she did. Your Mister Paroissien, the stage manager, was the primary object, to be sure. With absolute certainty, 'ee is the man who stabbed Solicitor Partlow. The gatherin' of the proper evidence is all that delays 'is takin' up."

"What evidence need be gathered?" I pressed him. "Isn't Irish Meg's identification enough?"

Field turned to me with the look one would give a small child who doesn't understand the intricacies of an adult game. "Lincoln's Inn lawyers make a 'abit of destroyin' the testimonies of girls like Meggy." Field spoke slowly. "She is not a person in a court of law. She is not 'ooman. She 'as no moral right to testify. For the lawyers and the 'onorable judges, she does not exist. She is no more than a low-class common criminal, a piece of garbage off the streets, a perversion of 'oomanity who sells 'erself every night to whoever can pay 'er modest price. No, we cannot take your Mister Paroissien to the dock on Meggy's word alone. We need corroboration from some more 'respectable' members of society." Field delivered this speech with a moral indignation and contempt for "Lincoln's Inn lawyers" that bespoke a strong sympathy for Meg and those women like her, and indeed all members, whether male or female, of her disenfranchised class of the streets.

"'Respectable'?" Dickens echoed.

"Yes," Field grinned evilly at us, "from the two respectable gentlemen who helped Paroissien murder the esteemed 'oremongerin' Solicitor Partlow."

For some reason, my pulse began to race, and the firelit world of the stationhouse began to blur and waver crazily before my eyes, as Field spoke of Irish Meg. My blood was up in indignation, but I held my tongue, not wishing to reveal my weakness for the woman to Dickens and Field. I could no more deny her identity as a human being, than I could ignore that devil inside myself which longed desperately to see her again.

"She picked out the other two as well," Field said, continuing with his report. "Banquo and Macduff," he laughed, using their character names. "Minor actors whom Partlow seems to 'ave regularly patronized. Banquo is a Mister Kenley Jones Fielding, and Macduff answers to the name of Martin Price. Both are middle-aged drunkards and 'orechasers whose propensities for the seekin' out of every possible vice match up well with our reports of Solicitor Partlow. Meggy and I 'ad to wait until they removed their wigs, but then she was quite positive in 'er identification."

"But how do you propose to entice or force these two to offer evidence against Paroissien, to confess to their part in the murder?" Dickens asked.

"Ah," Field said, "why 'the play's the thing.'"

Dickens looked at me: *What ho! A detective who quotes Shakespeare?*

Inspector Field was a natural storyteller.

"That night, after leavin' Covent Garden Theatre, after payin' Meggy for 'er trouble, Rogers and myself retired to our usual place down the 'all in The Lord Gordon Arms.

"'Mister Rogers,' says I after we're comfortably seated with our steamin' cups of burnt gin, 'we've got to draw 'em out. We've got to trap 'em before we can properly threaten 'em.'

"'Yessir,' says he (and Field nods to Rogers who has joined us), 'draw 'em out we must. Meggy is the ticket,' says he after some consideration, 'she's the only witness, the only one who can put a scare into 'em.'

"'Very good, Mister Rogers,' says I, 'very good. But two of 'em are a bit much, even for an old trooper like Meggy Sheehey, to 'andle.'"

"'Two indeed might be too much,' says 'ee.

"And then it was that the idea came to me," Field continued. "'The play's the thing.' says I, 'the play's the thing!'"

Dickens was quicker than I in intuiting Inspector Field's meaning.

"So you organized your own little play within the play, I take it," Dickens spoke up.

"There you are," Field answered, "there you are!" He rubbed his hands together in anticipation. "Right there in The Lord Gordon's back room, Rogers and I put together our own little actin' troupe, composed the parts they were to play. Subtle stuff it 'ad to be. We didn't want to spook our Mister Paroissien." He reined in, took a sip of his gin, then galloped on.

"Rogers and I decided that we would work on our two corroboratin' witnesses independently. We decided on some-one on the inside and someone on the outside. Meggy would be our outside bait. But who for Mister Inside?

"'I think I've got just the man,' finally says I.

"'And who might that be sir?' says 'ee.

"'Why none other than our old and dear friend Mister Tally Ho Thompson,' says I, waitin' to see if Mister Rogers is goin' to burst into volleys of laughter. There was, indeed, a long interval of quite contemplative silence as Rogers gave the depths of 'is gin glass 'is fullest attention.

"'No better choice in the city of London,' finally says 'ee."

I could tell that Dickens was not only engaged, but fully entertained by Field's playful narrative. "Man's got an extraor-dinary gift for dialogue," Dickens said later.

"Well," Field went on, "that settled, we 'ad our actors. All we 'ad left was to figure out what to do with 'em. It took another round of burnt gin to write our script."

"How did you know that Thompson and Irish Meg would consent to act in your little play?" Dickens interrupted.

Field's eyes narrowed somewhat as if he was trying to decide just how he was going to answer. When he did answer, he was brutal in his straightforwardness (and reinstated our view of the hardness of the man which had been temporarily softened by his playful narrative).

"No choice for 'em. I own 'em and they know it. They play my game by my rules, or I put 'em where they can't play any games at all." He punctuated his cold statement of underworld reality with a brisk tap of his heretofore passive forefinger upon the wooden arm of his easy chair. For someone who had shown such indignation toward "Lincoln's Inn lawyers," he showed his own utterly pragmatic and ruthless side as well. In those days, there always seemed to be two sides to everything and everyone.

"I take it then that this Thompson and our friend Irish Meg readily agreed to take their parts in your play," Dickens pursued.

"Oh, not at all," Field grinned. "They fought like cornered rats to escape the ignominy of workin', for a change, on my side of the law. Thompson pleaded professional ethics. Said a gentleman of 'is profession could not afford such an unsavory association. 'Why, if it ever got out,' 'ee said, 'worse than peachin'.' Meggy just whined and cursed and spat to the end of drivin' up the price. Shrewd businesswoman of the Moll Flanders school that Meggy."

"But in the end, they went along, became your actors?" Dickens was thoroughly enjoying gathering this underworld material. I fully expected to encounter a highwayman-turned-actor in his next novel. I also wondered if a harlot working for the police would be the subject of my first.

"Indeed they did. Once they saw the light, they fell into the project with 'eye enthusiasm, and with a talent which surprised even Sergeant Rogers and myself. It took me all of the next mornin' to extract Tally Ho from Newgate. The man 'as a worldly sort of 'onor about 'im. I knew 'ee'd do the job because 'ee knew that doin' the job would get 'im a clean slate. Rogers already 'ad Meggy waitin' at Bow Street when I arrived with Thompson. They waited there for me while I negotiated with your friend Mister Macready the final detail of our little play within a play."

Once again, Dickens's raised eyebrows betrayed his surprise.

"I used your name. 'Ope you don't mind?" Field said, countering Dickens's eyebrows with a slight bending forward and a quick tap of his forefinger to Dickens's left knee. "Soon as I mentioned you were on the case, Macready gave me 'is full attention. Needless to say, 'ee was a bit skeptical, but after I assured 'im that Thompson was a born actor and an excellent swordsman, 'ee took 'im on. 'Ee shall be one of the murderers in Act III,' 'ee said, and that was that. Inspired bit of type castin', wouldn't you say? I, of course, 'ad no proof whatsoever upon which to base my claims for Thompson's talents, yet two night's performances 'ave proven me a prophet. In fact, your friend Macready is so pleased with Tally Ho's antics that 'ee 'as actually asked 'im to stay on in the role."

Dickens chuckled, and shook his head at Field's inventiveness.

"Thompson's part in my play was to ingratiate 'imself with Fielding who is well known for 'is 'abit of drinkin' in late-hours clubs. Price was to be Meggy's lookout. 'Ee is known to 'ave an eye for ladies of the professional sort. Neither of my actors seem to be 'avin' any trouble in the playin' of their roles. Last night Thompson drank late at The Blue Welkin Club with Fielding, and Meggy and Price retired to a backstairs room at The 'Addon Inn." Field was pleased with his actors. I could not share his enthusiasm for Irish Meg's part in his little play. Field was using her as a paid sexual performer. Perhaps he felt that her getting paid twice for a single performance justified her role. "She is a sharp businesswoman," Field assured us.

"It is interesting, is it not Inspector Field? You've brought the worlds of St. Giles rookery and Covent Garden together on the same stage." Dickens was setting off on one of his philosophical flights, and I was just not in the mood for it. All I could imagine was Meg Sheehey seducing some stranger capable of strangling her. "A world of thieves and whores and highwaymen intermingling with the rich, supposedly civilized world of artists, lawyers, and even titled gentlemen. What no one realizes is that they are both the same world. The same fog blankets both. The same mud coats the boots of the gentleman, the actor, and the thief."

"Quite so. Quite so," agreed Field. Dickens's sociological ramble seemed to be working as a powerful soporific upon Inspector Field who was compelled to snap himself back to alertness. "Yes. Well. The curtain on *Macbeth* will be comin' down, and the curtain on *Field's Folly* or *St. Giles Meets the West End* or *Rookeries and Kings*, what you wish, will be goin' up quite soon. Would you and Mister Collins wish to join Rogers and me in the stalls? Tonight we plan to tighten the noose a bit around both of 'em."

Field's police carriage set us down a short distance from Covent Garden. The four of us, in a tight phalanx, found a sheltered point of vantage in the dark mouth of a narrow alley opposite the stage entrance. Field's timing was precise. Within minutes after taking up our concealed position, *Macbeth* let out, and the streets were flooded with theatre-goers. The flood soon slowed to a mere trickle and Field turned to us: "Our actors shall be emergin' soon. Look alive. There's Meggy."

All my senses pricked at the mention of her name.

Her prey did not keep her waiting. A large bewhiskered man in greatcoat and rakish rounded hat soon strode out of the stage door and offered her his arm. As they moved off, Field nodded sharply to Rogers, and that worthy followed them. Vile images tortured my imagination, and I realized how absurd these impulsive feelings for this common harlot were, and how impossible it was getting for me to drive them away.

"There they are!" Field's sharp whisper broke my unwholesome reverie.

Two men had emerged from the stage door, and paused in the street under a gaslamp to light their cigars.

"Thompson's the one on the left," Field directed us. "Looks like a real actor, don't 'ee? Other one's Fielding."

The man whom Field pointed out seemed a bit taller than medium English height, but looked a rather remarkable physical specimen possessed of wide shoulders and longish wiry-looking legs. He wore a short cape, which came to just below his hips, a long wool scarf looped around his neck, and a double-billed deerstalker upon his head. In the flash of his lucifer, I could see that he was clean-shaven. The other man, Fielding, was large, swollen of girth, heavy of jowl, with a full beard topped by a beret.

"Let us follow these two," Field whispered, "and see where they choose to imbibe tonight. Then, I'll stand a warm gin at the Lord Gordon while we wait for the curtain to go up on Act Two of tonight's performance."

To my surprise, Dickens checked us. "I will join you in The Lord Gordon Arms," he whispered hurriedly, for Thompson and Fielding were already beginning to amble off into the darkness. "There is some business I need to discuss with Macready. It will not take long. I will join you." With that he hurried off toward the theatre.

There was no time to argue with him. Field simply nodded and set off (with me, puzzled, following) after our two cigar-puffing actors. I was slow to comprehend. A *rather strange time to discuss business*, I thought. I was not even sure that Macready would welcome such a discussion after a strenuous performance of *Macbeth*. But then the light filtered through. Dickens wasn't entering the stage door to see Macready.

We followed the two smoking men at a healthy distance, since it was a fairly clear night, for London. They strolled at a leisurely pace up Gower Street until they reached a cellar club frequented by the acting fraternity called The Green Room. They went down, and, within minutes, Field had posted one of his underlings on watch. With that, we escaped the damp chill into the snug comfort of The Lord Gordon Arms.

"We will give our principals some time to work on their projects, before we tighten the noose," Field chuckled.

Once seated, I asked him directly: "Just how do you plan to tighten your noose around these men?"

"Blackmail, of course." Field smiled without the least compunction. "Tonight, at exactly twelve-thirty in the mornin' for Meg and one-thirty for Thompson, our actors are goin' to mention to their respective charges that the murder of Solicitor Partlow 'as been witnessed, and, unless prevented, could become a well-known fact."

"Thus, all we have to do is wait to see what they do?"

"That's it," Field grinned. "We're on a fishin' expedition."

Our tankards of burnt gin arrived.

"I take it that you expect them to confess to their own presence at the murder, and to give the evidence which will seal your case against Paroissien," said I.

"Very good," Inspector Field replied. "That's it exactly. Our only fear is that they might not feel so inclined to go along; that they might feel inclined to vent their anger on the bearer of the blackmail threat."

"In other words, you're afraid they might kill the messengers?"

"Possibly," Field certainly didn't show much concern, "but Tally Ho and Meggy can certainly take care of themselves. Nothin' to fear."

But fear for Meggy's safety I did nevertheless.

A brief period of contemplative silence had settled between Field and myself, when Dickens suddenly appeared. He was all flushed animation and enthusiasm. "Hope I haven't missed anything," he began, as he took his seat and waved for a gin.

"Not a thing," Field assured him with a dramatic yawn. "Essence of detective work. Five percent triumph, ninety-five percent waitin'."

As we partook of a rather lengthy dose of that ninety-five percent essence, Field enumerated the physical evidence of the case. "The other evenin', while Meggy was makin' 'er identifications backstage, I was on the lookout for our murder weapon. There are some twenty long swords among the props of the play. All are made of wood but for those of Macbeth and Macduff, which must ring of steel when they clash. There are, 'owever, four 'andswords of a 'eavy antique type which would do quite nicely for our Mister Paroissien's murder weapon. I interviewed the people who clean up after the actors. Interestin' enough, one of the daggers *was* missin' the mornin' after Solicitor Partlow was killed," Dickens leaned intently over the table, hanging on Field's every word, "but that missin' dagger mysteriously reappeared by the time the curtain went up that evenin'."

"So it was the murder weapon?" Dickens stated the obvious.

127

"It appears so," Field displayed great patience. "At The Player's Club, Paroissien and Lawyer Partlow 'ave a violent argument. Later, when the subject is raised again at the brothel, Paroissien disappears for a time then rejoins the group, and later that evenin' Partlow is murdered."

"He returned to the theatre to get the dagger." Dickens was quite proud of himself.

"Precisely," Field said, punctuating his agreement with a sip from his gin glass. "The next day, after cleanin' all traces of the murder from the 'andsword, 'ee returns it to the theatre in time for that evenin's performance. Unfortunately, for Paroissien, one of the cleanin' people noticed that the 'andsword was missin' before 'ee 'ad a chance to replace it. Backstage man searches for missin' 'andsword, can't find it, waits for the stage manager to come in, reports 'andsword missin', is told to search for it once again, and lo, finds missin' 'andsword in place which 'ee is sure 'ee 'ad already searched that mornin'. Needless to say, prop man goes off shakin' 'is 'ead. Promptly forgets the whole affair until I start askin' 'andsword questions. That story will bear some weight in court, I would say."

"What is our next step?" Dickens asked. I could not help but notice his automatic inclusion of himself as equal partner with Field in the case.

Inspector Field consulted his watch and drained his gin. "Twelve of the clock, time to check in on Meggy and Mister Martin Price," he said.

In a blur of settling up, hailing a cab, and clattering through the streets, we soon found ourselves in the shadows of yet another damp, narrow mews. With his usual dispatch, Rogers gave his report. "Back room, second floor, 'aven't stirred," he said, pointing to a rusty looking building of four sparsely windowed storeys dimly lit and poorly painted. The faded sign over the door read "THE HADDON INN, LODGINGS BY THE DAY OR WEEK."

Inspector Field once again consulted his gold pocket watch. "In about one more minute, Meggy will be breakin' the bad news to our friend Price. We'll give it a few minutes to sink in, and then we'll observe its effect."

"What are we going to do?" It was my voice, somewhat faltering.

"Apply the screw, what else?" Field replied.

Two, three minutes passed. I felt panic rising within me. Meg was closed in that room with a man twice her size, who had already participated in one murder, and whom she had just threatened to blackmail. I envisaged him beating her to death, slashing her with a razor, strangling her. Sikes and Nancy all over again, only this time for real.

"Why are we waiting?" I blurted out. "Good God, he could have killed her by now!"

Dickens, Field, Rogers, all stared at me in surprise.

"Yes, it is time to go," Field gave his order soberly, and moved quickly across the street to the door of the rusty hotel.

We did not pause in the foyer. A man behind a high counter used for the signing in of guests stood up when we entered.

"Stay!" Field pointed his forefinger at the man. The man sat back down on his stool without so much as a word.

We climbed one short flight of steps at a run, and, slowing at a hard-sign from Rogers, traversed a narrow hallway to the back of the building. The door had a wooden numeral 14 on its top panel.

Rogers tried the door knob and found it locked.

Without the slightest hesitation, Inspector Field stepped forward and kicked the door in.

What we encountered, when we flooded through that splintered door, was more the material of comedy than of the bloody tragedy I had been envisaging. Meg stood wearing only her skirt and boots. Kneeling at her feet, stark naked except for his black stockings and garters, his face streaming with tears, was Mister Price. When we entered, he screamed and comically attempted to cover himself—first his nakedness, then his tear-stained face, then, indecisive, the former with one hand, while he tried to erase the evidence of his tears with his other guilty paw. All that I could think of was that comical scene in

Mister Fielding's novel in which young Tom surprises his first love Molly *in flagrante* with Parson Square.

Field charitably allowed Price to dress before the interrogation.

"'Ee hadmits 'ee was there," Meggy reported to Field. "I told 'im I saw it all, right to 'is 'elpin' throw the body in the river. All 'ee's done is blubber ever since."

"Mister Price," Field began, "we know you were an accessory to the murder of Solicitor Partlow. You can swing for what you did just as Paroissien is goin' to swing for the actual killin'. But you can save yourself. You can be my witness in court. What'll it be?"

"I have no choice. I'll d-do anything you want. Anything." The man broke down, covering his face with his hands and quaking with sobs.

"Tell me exactly what 'appened," Field's voice showed no pity.

"Par-r-r-roissien and Partlow," his speech was a weak and nervous stammer, "had b-b-been arguing all evening about the girl. He killed him over the girl."

"What girl? 'Er name," Field cut him off.

"Young actress, Ellen Ternan. Old Peggy Ternan's youngest."

Dickens's countenance went completely white, as if some embalmer had drained off all his blood. He reached out and gripped the mantlepiece over the hearth to steady himself. He didn't, however, say a word.

"What about the girl? Why were they so angry?" Field continued.

"The lawyer was b-b-boasting that the girl was a virgin and that he'd bought her maidenhead from the mother. That's when our pinch-faced stage manager lost his head. At The Player's Club. He started screamin' at Partlow. We were all drunk. We laughed at him. Only made him wilder. Then later, at the river, Paroissien taunts him about the girl, like he was baitin' him, and Partlow says again that he's bought her virginity and he means to 'ave 'er. That's when the stage

130

manager pulls out the knife and sticks it right in Partlow's belly. It happened so fast, so unexpected."

"None of you knew of the sword until you saw 'im use it to take the lawyer's life?"

"No. He took it from under his coat. None of us knew that he had it." Fear now dominated the actor's face.

"Meg says that you 'elped Paroissien dispose of the body. Is that true? Be careful 'ere. Watch what you say." Stab of sharp forefinger.

"It's true. We had no choice. He threatened us," the man's voice was racing. "He's standing there with blood dripping off that sword in his hand and he tells us to help him put the body in the river and we do it. I d-d-did it without even thinking. Everything was happening so fast. I was drunk. I wanted it to end."

Field abruptly turned away from him to Dickens and myself. "You 'ave 'eard all, gentlemen. Bear witness."

He turned sharply back to Price: "You will be summoned to tell this story in court." Firm tap of the forefinger to the cowed actor's chest. "Do not change it at all or these gentlemen will bear witness to your perjury." Another decisive tap. "Mention this conversation tonight to no one if you wish to save yourself." Tap number three, intimidating forefinger withdrawn. With finality, Field turned on his heel. "Meggy. Gentlemen." He motioned with a slight bob of his head that it was time to follow him out. We left the man Price alone and cowering in the room.

Outside of that disreputable hotel, Field took Irish Meg aside. He stood with his hand on Meg's shoulder in an almost fatherly tableau. I assumed that he was complimenting her on a job well done. Money clearly was exchanged. Then Meggy was gone—gone out of my life once again, without even a word exchanged. I was sorely tempted to break off as Dickens had done earlier in the evening, to go after her, but I hadn't the courage.

"Now, gentlemen," Field said, "let us see 'ow our other little character group is farin'."

It was almost one o'clock. Field's play was unfolding precisely on schedule. Field's man intercepted us outside of The Green Room. "'Aven't budged," he reported. "Been drinkin' steadily these two 'ours past."

"Let's 'ope Fielding can still comprehend what our fellow is about to tell 'im," Field grinned.

"Will he tell him in there, or bring him outside to break the bad news that he is caught?" Dickens asked.

"Inside. I directed 'im to do it in the public room, to forestall any inclinations to drunken violence which Fielding might consider."

"Tally Ho can certainly handle 'im, I would think," Rogers added.

"To be sure," Field agreed. "But there is no tellin' what a man will do, when backed into a corner."

"I would like to see the look on the man's face when Thompson accuses him," Dickens said equivocally, half wishing, half requesting permission.

"Go inside, and observe if you wish," Field said, giving that permission. "Rogers and I will wait out 'ere, in case there is an attempt to flee."

I followed Dickens into the cellar club. It was a capacious room, with perhaps a dozen tables down its length to where a large hearth blazed. The majority of the tables were occupied. Groups of four or five gathered around single tables, drinking. One group of ten, including three women, had pulled two tables together near the fire. A couple of tables were occupied by solitary drinkers, reading newspapers or studying scripts.

Fielding and Thompson sat by themselves in the rear corner near the large group, which had consolidated its tables in front of the hearth. We took an empty table near a door to what, I presumed, was the establishment's kitchen. Our drinks were ordered, and promptly arrived. I consulted my timepiece, and nodded to Dickens. "It is almost time," I said. We were too far away to overhear, but we followed the scene as it played out in dumb show before us. When Thompson began to speak, Fielding had been bent over, staring morosely into his gin glass. As Thompson spoke, Fielding's head rose slowly, and his mouth dropped open in amazement. He stared into Thompson's face, then questioned him sharply. "What are you saying? What is this?" These, perhaps, were the questions his lips formed. Thompson glared across the table at him.

Suddenly, Fielding leapt to his feet, and screamed out, "Who are you?" Every eye turned on the two men arguing in the corner. They stood facing each other, anger flashing between them.

Fielding made the first move. He lunged for Thompson's throat with both hands, but Thompson was much too quick. With a sharp bob of his head and a ducking of his shoulder, Thompson easily evaded his antagonist's grasp, and sidestepped the big man's lunge. With his weight committed almost completely forward, Fielding tottered on the edge of losing his balance. With some effort, he righted himself, and turned on Thompson once again. Fielding was quite drunk, as well as enraged. Thompson's hands, palms out in a placating gesture, attempted to calm Fielding. Fielding picked up a gin tankard from the table, and threw it at Thompson, who ducked. The tankard shattered against the stone face of the hearth.

Everyone in the room was now on their feet. The large group near the hearth had already abandoned their tables, and were fleeing down the room. Others were edging away from the two antagonists, moving toward the door.

Once again, the hulking Fielding lunged at Thompson. Once again, the quicksilver Thompson evaded that charge, and, as Fielding toppled past him, struck him with a sharp upward-angled punch to the kidneys. Fielding howled in pain, and turned on his tormentor. This time, however, Thompson didn't wait. With a quick motion, he dipped his shoulder, and ran at full speed into Fielding's belly, bowling the big man over backwards into the two tables run together, which the large group had abandoned. Glassware and crockery shattered, as the flimsy tables splintered beneath the weight of the two catapulting men. Thompson landed on top of Fielding, and, with a quick backward leap of wondrous agility, bounced up onto his feet. Fielding groped forward on his hands and knees. Thompson took one step backwards, and then, with all his strength, stepped forward and kicked Fielding square in the face. So much for the Marquess of Queensberry Rules.

That ended it. The actor crumbled in a drunken heap as Field and Rogers burst through the door with their cudgels at the ready. Peace was quickly restored, as Rogers and Thompson led the semi-conscious Fielding out to the street. Inspector Field identified himself to, and tried to mollify, the landlord, whose tables and crockery had taken such a thrashing. Dickens wore the most angelic of smiles, as if he had just witnessed the championship match between the Tewksbury Duck and Chelsea Smalls.*

When we joined Rogers and Tally Ho Thompson outside, they had Fielding sitting in the gutter propped against a lamppost. The actor's face was a bloody mess, and he seemed to be teetering in a daze.

"A bit rough in there, eh?" Inspector Field remarked to Thompson.

"No worse than Shooters Hill," Thompson grinned. "People tend not to take me seriously enough."

"Yes. Quite true," Field said, tapping him affectionately on the shoulder with his forefinger, "but I will never underestimate you, lad."

Tally Ho Thompson grinned and said, "I'm sure you won't, not you."

It was as if they were playing a game, adversaries, yet somehow comrades. Dickens was fascinated by this relationship between the detective and the criminal.

---

*These evidently were the public names of two of the more popular boxing personalities of the Victorian age. Whether Collins was drawing upon boxers of the 1850's or the 1860's could not be determined.

Our attention reverted to Fielding, who seemed to be coming around.

"Why don't you call it a night's work?" Inspector Field forcefully suggested to Tally Ho Thompson. "You've played your part well. We can now press our advantage with Mister Fielding."

"Any objections to my continuing in the role of murderer at Covent Garden?" Thompson asked.

Field's eyebrows went up. "Don't tell me you're thinkin' of takin' up a life of 'onest labor," he said.

"I've sort of taken a fancy to the actor's game," Thompson grinned, "and I certainly wouldn't call it honest labor. Takes half the effort as my former line of work."

"Better ye be a murderer on Dunsinane than on Shooters 'Ill, I would say," Field said, answering wit with wit.

"Who are you? How dare you?" Fielding's pitiful wounded howl brought an end to Thompson and Field's conversing. With a quick nod, Tally Ho Thompson faded back into the shadows.

"Interesting fellow, this Tally Ho Thompson," Dickens, leaning close to me, whispered. "I must talk with him again." I was now certain that Dickens's next novel would feature a highwayman-turned-actor.

"Inspector Field of the Metropolitan Protectives," the policeman said. The interrogation of the helpless Fielding was begun. "We know all about your involvement in the murder of Solicitor Partlow, sir, and you are goin' to be one of our prime witnesses at the Queen's Bench."

"Witness?" he repeated—drunken, befuddled, yet grasping enough of what was being said for fear to show itself in his voice.

"You're a part of this murder," Field said, dogging the man mercilessly. "Answer our questions and you might be able to save yourself. Answer."

"Answer," the actor repeated dully.

"Why did Paroissien kill Lawyer Partlow?"

"It was the wench. Peggy Ternan's stupid little wench."

"How was it the wench?"

"Stage manager flew into a rage when Lawyer said he'd bought her."

"What was said?" Field asked, showing extraordinary patience.

"Screaming. Curses. Stage manager said again and again 'She's mine! She's mine!'" The sodden actor seemed to be gaining in coherence.

"And? What did Partlow do?"

Fielding's face twisted in a bit of sick mirth. "Laughed at him, he did. Laughed right in his face."

"Where was this?"

"At The Player's Club."

"And later? At the river?"

"The two of 'em took it up again."

"Over the girl?"

"The same," he said, his head lolling, "the little whore. Her own mother panders for her."

I felt Dickens starting to move beside me, and, instinctively, I reached out and grasped his arm. When I looked into his face, I saw that he was caught in a tide of mad anger. With my restraining hand on his arm, the violent tension of his body relaxed. Our eyes met but he quickly turned away. In embarrassment? Shame? Not a word exchanged between us, but so much revealed. We were gentlemen. Our secrets, those weaknesses revealed, were always held in the strictest confidence.

"You saw Paroissien stab the Lawyer?" Field was losing his witness.

Fielding nodded drunkenly in assent.

"And you 'elped throw the body in the river?"

The actor nodded again, his head lolling wildly at the finish.

Field bent down, grasped Fielding by both lapels, and yanked him to his unsteady feet with his back still against the lamppost. Field shook him hard once, banging his head against the post. Field's face pressed within an inch of his victim's bloody countenance. "I own you now," Field hissed

136

into his face. "In court you will answer every question just as you 'ave answered it this evenin'. If you try to run, to the Continent, to the ends of the earth, I will find you. One lie, and I will 'ang you just as 'eye as I am goin' to 'ang the murderer. Do you understand my meanin'?"

We left this unfortunate victim of Inspector Field's terrible wrath propped precariously against that lamppost.

"When will you arrest Paroissien?" Dickens asked.

"Not right away. I want to observe 'im a bit longer. There is one more witness I wish to interview."

"Who would that be?" I asked.

"Lord 'Enry Ashbee, of course," Field answered as if I was a dolt.

"Of course."

"You are going to drag a titled gentleman into such a sordid affair?" Dickens seemed startled.

Again Field's face revealed surprise and not a little impatience. "Murder 'as no class consciousness," he finally answered.

"Might we be present to observe the arrest of Paroissien?"

"You 'ave been on this case from its very beginnin'," Field smiled, "you shall be present at its end. I will send Rogers for you."

INSPECTOR FIELD, NOVELIST; OR, "THE MURDERER'S ROOM"

(May 8, 1851—evening)

The night Inspector Field chose for the arrest of Paroissien was the coldest of the English spring. The sky shone clear, but the wind slicing up the Thames was exceedingly sharp. The stars hung in the black sky. Four days had passed since our last foray out with Field to coerce his witnesses. We were leaving Devonshire House after rehearsal of *Not So Bad As We Seem* (the benefit performance for Her Majesty being less than two weeks away), when Serjeant Rogers clattered up in a hansom. Since we were in a group with a number of the other members of the amateur troupe, Rogers hung back. He stood on the step of the cab staring at us, until he caught Dickens's eye. With that, he gave a sharp nod, and climbed back in.

Of course, Dickens and myself disengaged as quickly as possible from the others, and joined Rogers in the cab. I am sure that Forster observed our hasty withdrawal. I am sure he huffed and puffed about us after we drove away. "'Ee sent me for you. Tonight's the night, mates. Tonight's the night we take 'im," Rogers announced.

Field was waiting in the bullpen when we arrived at Bow Street Station.

"Don't remove your coats, gentlemen," he ordered right off as he fetched his own greatcoat and that square, sharp hat from the pegs on the wall. "We are goin' out without delay to take up Mister Paroissien for the murder of Solicitor Partlow."

"What has happened?" Dickens was curious. "Has there been any change in the stage manager's circumstances? Is he preparing to flee?"

"Not at all," Field answered. "Quite the opposite. The man is secure. 'Ee is re-establishin' 'is former liasons. 'Ee thinks 'ee's gotten away with it and it is forgotten."

"Liasons?" Dickens asked.

"Yes," Rogers said, showing no reticence (he missed little, yet it occurred to me that he had not yet observed Dickens's attraction to the Ternan girl, though I was certain he was fully cognizant of mine toward Irish Meg Sheehey), "'ee pursues once again the girl who was the cause of it all."

Dickens blanched—went white as a French potato. For some strange reason, Dickens's pallid, strained face made me remember the night of his daughter's death. That night he had warned me against the perils of writing novels. "Reality is a sick thing," he had said, "a diseased, bleak house where no one should be forced to live." This threat to Miss Ternan was like the death of another of his children. It was the childlike qualities of the girl which had initially attracted him to her. Was it not ironic that those same qualities aroused the sexual appetites of both Partlow and Paroissien? How sickening that the girl's own mother was auctioning off her childhood.

"The Ternan woman and 'er daughter. 'Ee dined with the two of 'em this evenin'. We must go," Field said, moving toward the back door of the stationhouse. "A problem 'as arisen with the surveillance."

"What problem?" It was Rogers asking. His voice betrayed his impatience at having missed out on some event in the case. I am sure he blamed Dickens and me for this loss.

"Constable Gatewood 'as lost contact with Paroissien and the two women." Alarm again spread like a white death across Dickens's face.

A post-chaise waited for us in the narrow mews behind the station. We mounted it in haste, and, at Field's order to the postilion, set off. The horses picked up speed and we seemed to be catapulting across London.

"There was no performance of *Macbeth* this night." Field, at another "What 'appened?" from Rogers, took up the narrative. "Nevertheless, our Mister Paroissien went to the theatre. There, as if by plan, 'ee met the woman Ternan and the daughter. They supped together at a nearby public 'ouse. When they left the pub, Constable Gatewood was close. They set out walkin', and Gatewood followed. 'Owever, without warnin', Paroissien 'ailed a passin' cab. Gatewood, unable to find a similar conveyance, was left at a disadvantage. 'Ee attempted to pursue the 'ansom on foot but, due to the sparsity of traffic and the speed of the 'orse, 'ee could not keep up."

"Man's an incompetent idiot!" Rogers spat.

"When was this?" Dickens said, taking up the questioning.

"No more than an hour and a half ago," Field answered. "Constable Gatewood immediately returned to Bow Street Station, and, though quite winded, gave his report."

139

"Ought to be cashiered," Rogers groused openly.

"From the direction the cab took, Paroissien could 'ave been takin' the two women to 'is lodgin's, but that is only the flimsiest of speculation. I 'ad already decided to take 'im up tonight, and 'ad sent Rogers to find the two of you when Gatewood arrived with 'is unfortunate report. This break in our surveillance convinced me that it was time to drop the net over Paroissien before 'ee made a more permanent escape."

"What do you mean 'a more permanent escape'?" It was the first time I had opened my mouth since we had entered the carriage.

"Out of London. To the Continent. To America."

"Good God, why have we waited this long to apprehend this monster? He is dangerous to society, to . . . to . . ." Dickens's voice was distraught. Field could not help but mark it. His forefinger, crook'd, came up and speculatively scratched at the side of his eye.

"I chose to 'old off on 'is arrest," Field said, breaking the short pause, "because for the last three days I 'ave been attemptin', to no avail, to attain an interview with Lord 'Enry Ashbee. I 'ave been repeatedly informed upon callin' at 'is 'ome that 'ee is out of the city. I 'ave reason, 'owever, to think otherwise. It is possible 'ee 'as a secret entrance to 'is 'ouse which allows 'im to come and go undetected."

Dickens could not have asked for a fuller explanation of Field's methods and motives, yet the tension in his face did not abate.

Our post-chaise galloped headlong through the dark thoroughfares and only slowed as we entered an area of lofty dark tenements arranged in a labyrinth of crazy narrow streets off Charing Cross, in a mongrel section of public houses, boarding houses, gentlemen's hotels, and private lodging establishments commonly known as Soho.

"There!" Field shouted, with a lunge of his ubiquitous forefinger. "That is the 'ouse. Stop the coach!"

The postilion reined in as ordered, and we came to a stop in front of a high brooding stone building, blackened by a century of London soot.

"'Is rooms is on the third floor, in the back," Rogers informed us.

"You lead," Field nodded.

We followed Rogers into the dark lodging house in a tight file, Field immediately behind him, Dickens next, and myself bringing up the nervous rear. Inside the front entrance was a squalid, narrow foyer. It was clearly a house partitioned in such a manner, that there was little wasted space. Three paces into this cramped entranceway a narrow flight of stairs reared abruptly and steeply up.

Maintaining our rigid file behind Rogers, who had lit his bull's-eye in a not-wholly-successful attempt to penetrate the thick darkness, we began our ascent. Rogers's light wavered weakly above, as we climbed two storeys into a narrow corridor. A gaslight flickered down this corridor, but it offered only the weakest resistance against the crush of the building's darkness. Tiny cracks of flickering light seeped out from beneath the doors, signaling that some species of troglodytic life might possibly exist in the depths of this dark cavern.

We walked slowly, almost groping our way despite Rogers's bull's-eye in the lead. It was a frightening place. The wavering light cast devilish shadows upon the walls, as if we had entered some decrepit inferno. Abruptly, Rogers stood before a closed door, nodding to Field, and pronouncing, "This is 'is," with a professional certainty. No light seeped out from beneath the door. No sound emanated from within.

"Open it," Inspector Field ordered in a low whisper.

I braced myself for the crack of splintering wood, as Rogers kicked the door in, but he tried the brass knob first, and the door floated silently open.

Rogers turned quickly to Field. "Not only unlocked but not even closed," he whispered.

"Yes, strange," Field answered.

No one moved.

"Well," Field finally broke the silence, "perhaps we ought to go in. You two stay back, behind me and Rogers," Field ordered in a whisper to Dickens. "If there is a fight, it's our fight, not yours."

Field moved in front of Rogers, drawing a small cudgel out of an inside pocket of his greatcoat, and, with a waggle of his singular forefinger, directed his eager Serjeant to follow. As we had done all evening, Dickens and your humble servant brought up the rear. Thus, we entered the murderer's rooms.

It was dark as pitch inside. Rogers had extinguished his bull's-eye, so that the advantage of surprise and the cover of darkness would be ours. Yet, with every step I took into that dark circle of violent possibility, my nerves stretched tighter. Was the murderer there, lurking in the dark, his weapon primed and ready to fire, as we came within range of his ambush? Every possibility raced and tumbled in my frightened mind, yet I followed Dickens and Field blindly.

We stopped when a silent touch of a hand passed quickly from one to another along the file. I sensed that Field was listening.

"Raise a light," he ordered Rogers, "there is no one 'ere."

The task of relighting his bull's-eye in the all-encompassing darkness of those silent rooms took Serjeant Rogers only a moment. How he could accomplish the delicate task so quickly in the utter dark attests to his professionalism. The light flared, sending lank shadows up the walls. We stood in the doorway of an inner chamber, and watched as the light groped its way around the interior walls. It was Paroissien's bedchamber. Two chairs sat against the wall, with clothes draped casually over their straight backs. A large pier glass hung above a commodious dry sink cluttered with male utensils for shaving and daily hygiene. The glass reflected back the light of Rogers's bull's-eye, reflected the disheveled bedstead that filled the greater part of the room, reflected the glass cylinder of the oil lamp sitting next to the leather razor strop on the dry sink, reflected the white porcelain of the wash basin, reflected the bluish milkglass of the water pitcher, reflected a large and disturbing dark shadow on the floor at the foot of the impassive bed.

Inspector Field was not often wrong in his analytic perceptions, but in this case he was in error. There *was* someone in that bedchamber. Upon closer inspection, there was someone, but it was someone who was only formerly someone. Field's igniting of the oil lamp on the dry sink set the chamber ablaze with light, and revealed the body of Paroissien face downward on the floor with arms outspread, his ankles pointing through the doorway to the kitchen, his open vacant eyes staring into the dust beneath the tousled bed. In the middle of the white shirt, which covered his back and which was soaked brown in blood, were six jagged stab wounds. The blood-soaked shirt was the only clothing that Paroissien wore. His corpse was naked from the waist down, the deep brownish-red pool spreading in a dark halo beneath him.

I looked away from that terrible sight, but I could not escape it. The pier glass impassively reflected the bloody corpse. Rogers and Field also stared down in shock. Mister Paroissien, the guilty murderer of Solicitor Partlow, was, without question, himself murdered, and murdered very thoroughly.

"Good God!" It was Dickens's voice.

"Stay clear. Don't touch anythin' yet," Field ordered.

Dickens and I stepped back into the doorway from the front chamber. Field dispatched Rogers to call reinforcements to the scene for the purpose of securing the building from the intrusions of sensation-mongers. Then, standing next to the corpse at the foot of the bed, Field slowly turned in a complete circle, his deep-set black eyes burning into every corner of the room.

When he finally stirred, he startled us. With a quick decisiveness he moved closer to the bed, bent to examine the rumpled blood-stained sheet.

What does he see that interests him? I thought. *What is he looking for? What has he found?*

From the bed, Field moved quickly to the dry sink. One drawer of the two in the face of the wooden stand was pulled open. The drawer contained household necessities. Field left it as it was, and I stole a look into it moments later. It was filled with the necessaries for boot polishing and sewing, and the small tools for such common household affairs as picture-hanging and fabric cleaning. Field seemed quite interested in this drawer, but when I looked into it, I saw nothing threatening or out of the ordinary.

Next Field moved to the doorway of the adjoining chamber (which, upon later inspection, proved to be the entrance to a small kitchen and water closet, which held a large chamber-pot), and stood facing in toward the bed almost treading on the stiffening feet of the corpse. He was leaning so precariously forward, that I thought that he was going to lose his balance, and pitch headlong down on top of the bloody body. Instead, he bent down, and examined the soles of the late Paroissien's bare feet. Then, he was up and moving along the wall to a position approximately half the distance between the dry sink with its open drawer and the doorway through which Parois-sien had entered, prior to receiving his first stab wound in the back.

On the move again, he stepped to the chairs against the wall near where we stood. With one professional hand, he inven-toried the clothes—one pair white cotton underbreeches, one pair tweed trousers, one tweed jacket, one pair grey gloves, one pair black stockings with garters, one pair leather pumps. We later found a greatcoat and hat, on a chair near the door in the front parlor. One other wooden straight-backed chair was pulled up to the side of the bed, but it held no clothes nor anything else, just stood there empty, seemingly out of place. Nevertheless, Inspector Field bent to study this chair, reached down, and removed some small tatter of something from the wood of the chair's seat. He placed whatever this clue was in one of his many inside pockets before I could distinguish its color or texture or meaning.

For more long minutes, Field prowled that room. He bent this and poked at that, his crook'd forefinger scratching lightly at the side of his eye. "He was recreating the scene," Dickens speculated later, "writing it exactly as a novelist would."

The last thing Field bent to examine was the corpse itself. I glanced at Dickens but, to my surprise, Dickens was not looking at Inspector Field. Dickens was watching the scene unfold in the large mirror. The pier glass over the dry sink reproduced every move of Inspector Field's detective investigation: his precise measurement, with a small ruler extracted from one of his many inner pockets, of the length and width of each stab wound, and the recording of those measurements in his small notebook; his sketching of a diagram of the configuration of the stab wounds, and his placing the numbers one through six next to each wound in that configuration; his insertion of his formidable forefinger into each wound testing no doubt for its depth; his frozen pondering over the body as he rested on one knee beside it. I must admit that I too became fascinated by this angle of view which Dickens had chosen. Watching it all take place in the mirror somehow made it seem not so real or terrible or brutal.

Later, when we were alone, I asked Dickens why he had been watching so intently in the mirror rather than looking directly upon Field. "Mirroring life, that is what I do," Dickens answered almost wistfully. "Perhaps I didn't want to look too closely because I was afraid I would see too much. Perhaps I am like the famous inhabitants of Plato's cave, content to watch the mere shadows of reality."

I watched through Dickens's mirror for a brief time but when Inspector Field rose from his contemplation of the stab wounds in the corpse's back, he regained my full and direct attention. He shot a quick glance at Dickens and myself, and he too caught Dickens looking in the mirror, because he then glanced quickly into the glass startling Dickens.

Gingerly, with his right foot, Inspector Field rolled the corpse over onto its back. My mind immediately recalled the dead eyes of Solicitor Partlow, staring up into the Thames night. Paroissien's mouth was twisted into a silent gasp of surprise, as if he had made a sudden drawing in of breath to cry out or curse, but then froze in the midst of that aborted act.

After a momentary hesitation, Field once again stooped to inspect the corpse. First he examined closely the face, neck and hands. Next, however, Field did one of the most distasteful things I have ever seen a gentleman do. He took the dead man's sexual appendage in his hand and squeezed it twice with an upward movement toward the head, with the intent, I presume, to force any liquid which might have pooled within to flow out. Whether or not he was successful neither Dickens nor I could see. Then, carefully, he stretched and examined the skin of the member, concerning which he made a number of notes in his small black book. The indecorousness of this episode brought to Dickens's countenance a look of chagrin so severe that it verged upon pain. I found it a bizarre and mildly revolting procedure, but I was not nearly so strongly affected. When Field finished, he rubbed his hand twice on his trouser leg and rose to his feet. With one quick step he moved to the foot of the bed. For a long moment he stared down at the wrinkled and blood stained sheets, then a quick glance down at the dead body, then a glance to the doorway from the kitchen, then a glance into the pier glass, then another glance into the kitchen's doorway, then another glance to the corpse, then his eyes returned to contemplation of the tousled bed.

"That is all there is to be done 'ere, gentlemen," he announced, startling both Dickens and myself when he broke the silence which had reigned over the chamber. "Let us return to Bow Street. My constables will clean up 'ere."

I was ready to leave. I actually took an immediate step backward to the door. Dickens, however, did exactly the opposite. He stepped into the room, moved directly to the corpse. Field did not object. Dickens bent to the dead body and, with the thumb and forefinger of his right hand, closed the man's vacant staring eyes. With that, Dickens turned and led us from that chamber.

"What did you learn in there?" Dickens timidly inquired in the coach.

Inspector Field deflated the entire evening with the grim resignation of his profound verdict: "The young woman killed 'im, I'm afraid."

Dickens slumped back against the cushions as if he had received a sharp blow to the chest.

READING THE BOOK OF THE DEAD; OR, "OUT, OUT DAMNED SPOT"

(May 8, 1851—almost midnight)

Novel writing, this compulsive attempt to mirror reality, is much like detectiving, yet different. In writing a novel, the author must construct a credible plot, even if, in reality, the events upon which that plot is modeled take irrational turns. What the detective undertakes is precisely the opposite. The detective looks at the events and furnishings of the world, studies them, and constructs the plot of his story. A novelist is, from the onset, lord of the whole, and his talent for words and structures serves as a valet to the parts. A detective begins as valet to the parts, but by his ingenuity and hard work rises to become lord of the whole. There lies the difference between art and reality.

Though this is but a secret journal, it nonetheless poses all of the novelist's problems. I am a novelist, yet this is not a novel. I am forced to play the role of the greenest of apprentice detectives. I cannot see where this tale is going. Perhaps Dickens could see further. Yet, that cold night at Bow Street Station, newly returned from that grisly scene in the murderer's lodgings, I felt that Dickens was as far adrift as was I.

Dickens once said, on one of our night walks, "We should be able to read the world as we would read a book." Should not I, then, have been able to read this vision of the world, which had been thrust upon us that night? The scene of that grisly crime was a text, a veritable three-decker, yet I was fully incapable of reading past page one. Thank the Lord that Inspector Field was an expert at reading the book of the dead.

"What makes you believe that Miss Ternan killed the stage manager?" Dickens was already arguing in the young woman's defense. "I saw no evidences . . ."

"I cannot yet prove it," Field answered, trying to hide his surprise at the emotional strain detectable in Dickens's manner. "Yet, in my own mind, she is the one. All the signs were there, in the room, all pointin' to 'er."

"What signs?" It was my voice, the faithful bulldog.

Field smiled benignly, giving two nervous little scratches to the side of his eye with his crook'd forefinger. "The signs were there, posted all about that room. You gentlemen just did not know 'ow to read 'em."

Both Dickens and I waited for him to explain.

"Tho' it's neither 'ere nor there until we catch up with the principals in our little drama, this is what I am certain 'appened. We all know that Paroissien killed Solicitor Partlow over the girl. That night Partlow 'ad struck a bargain with the girl's mother for the sale for sexual purposes of 'er *virgin* daughter." For some unexplained reason he gave particular emphasis to that word "virgin" by a quick tap on the wooden arm of his chair with his formidable forefinger.

How could he know she was a virgin? The thought darted through my consciousness no sooner than Inspector Field enunciated it.

As if reading my mind, Field continued with his narrative.

"Rakes of wealth and power, of the order of Lawyer Partlow and Lord Ashbee, take great satisfaction in the deflowerin' of such an innocent. They coveted 'er because she was young and beautiful, but especially unspoiled."

"They?" my voice challenged him again.

"No. Partlow is the only one of whom I can be certain. I simply suspect that Ashbee is of that type. No . . . I meant Partlow."

Dickens sat like a stone idol.

"The night of the first murder, Partlow, in 'is cups and feelin' secure in the company of other rakes and drunkards, boasted of 'is purchase of the girl's virtue, perhaps even went so far as to describe when and where 'ee planned to force 'imself upon 'er. That night, as 'is tongue ran loose, Partlow either did not suspect, or was too drunk to care, that Paroissien also coveted the young woman, and could not stand to 'ear another man boastin' of the ownership of that which 'ee so passionately longed to possess. In an uncontrolled passion of lust and 'ate, Paroissien killed Partlow, and, with the 'elp of the others, threw his mortal remains into the Thames."

He paused and glanced in Dickens's direction, as if to check a barometer. *Steady there*, his eyes seemed to say.

"You both know the details of our investigation. Paroissien 'angs back until 'ee feels 'ee 'as put the bloodhounds off the scent. 'Ee feels 'ee 'as gotten away with it, and, in 'is false security, allows 'is lust for the Ternan girl to rise up out of its dormant state. Rememberin' Partlow's boasts, 'ee is convinced that 'ee can buy the girl. 'Ee approaches the maternal bawd. The deal is struck. Paroissien's dinner this evenin' with the mother and the girl was the scene of the final transaction. Paroissien, by payin' money or by offerin' the promise of favor, possessed himself of the prize he had so long lusted after and even killed to possess. Since the girl herself would probably be innocent to all that was afoot, the scenario most likely followed the conventional rake's progress. Paroissien pays the Ternan woman, mother lures daughter to Paroissien's lodgin's, then abandons 'er. Perhaps they drug 'er. Thus, the scene is set. Yet, when the script is played out, the result is murder."

"But all of this is sheer speculation," Dickens sputtered.

"Quite right. Quite so." Field tapped the arm of his chair

with his forefinger. "Yet it is true and real, I am certain. What 'appened next is not speculation, and verifies this whole scenario."

Dickens subsided back into a wounded silence. Field softened his voice as if he sensed that there was more at stake in this case for Dickens than the gathering of authentic material for his next novel.

"It is from this point in the night's events that the signs posted in that dead man's bedchamber present a much clearer picture."

The man stood unwavering in his sense of his own rightness.

"Aye, the signs," Rogers nodded in iteration of his superior's authority and credibility.

"The stage manager took 'er by force in that bed. She put up a struggle. The actual rentin' and drivin' of the bedclothes to the floor signal 'er futile resistance. 'Ee deflowered 'er. 'Er virgin blood mixed with 'is spendin's pooled in one spot on the foundation sheet, a bright red stain laced with dirty yellow streaks. It formed an almost perfect 'eart-shaped sign. That is the shape formed by the female body lyin' on its back. Perhaps she was unconscious for some time after 'ee finished with 'er, for she did not move as these fluids drained from 'er body. Perhaps 'ee remained atop 'er body preventin' motion or flight."

Field described it as if the girl was no more than a prop which he could maneuver across his stage at whim.

Dickens's face remained dead and impassive throughout.

"Paroissien left the room, threatenin' to return and resume 'is perverse attentions. No doubt 'ee proceeded to the water closet to relieve 'imself. 'Ee did not, 'owever, clean 'imself. 'Ee did not wash the virgin blood from 'is sexual member."

I remembered the distasteful thoroughness of Field's inspection of that appendage.

"Terrified by the threat of 'is return, the Ternan girl 'urriedly searches the room for a weapon to defend 'erself. She finds 'er weapon and waits beside the doorway, through which 'ee must

150

re-enter. The weapon, a large pair of sewin' shears, is ready in 'er 'ands. Paroissien, wearin' only 'is shirt, returns through the door, realizes the girl is not in the bed, 'alts puzzled. In 'er panic, she does not 'esitate. With both 'ands she stabs into the man's back. 'Ee never saw 'is killer. 'Ee pitched face forward on the floor. 'Ee may 'ave been killed instantly by the first thrust. It may 'ave pierced 'is 'eart. Nevertheless, she was on 'im as 'ee fell, stabbin', stabbin', in a frenzy of fear, stabbin' 'im five more times."

Dickens simply could not maintain his unnatural detachment any longer. "That's absurd." He was attempting to speak forcefully, but his voice wavered out of control. Field and Rogers stared at him in surprise. His voice was a thin rasp: "She could not have done this evil thing. She is too young and innocent. She hasn't the strength. You cannot be serious."

Field's face rarely betrayed any emotion, yet I thought I detected a softening around Field's mouth and eyes, an understanding. I feel that at that moment Field realized that Dickens was in love with the girl.

"You cannot know this, all of this," Dickens struggled on. "That room was splashed with blood. You cannot prove that he had his way with her. There was no such murder weapon in that room, no sewing shears."

Field spoke softly: "True. There was no murder weapon in the room when we arrived. She took it away with 'er. Do you remember the drawer that 'ung open in the washstand? Sometimes it is not so important what *is* in an opened drawer as what *is not* and ought to be. There were needles, spools of thread, fabric patches, swatches of dark wool, but no shears for the cuttin' of these 'ousehold fabrics. Those shears were the murder weapon. The wounds were not made by a knife. Those wounds were too large, too wide. They were made by a thick, blunt, pointed object. The doubled blade of a pair of sewin' shears."

"No. No. I can't believe it. She is but a child," Dickens said in a low distraught whisper. "How do you know that she

151

was the only one there? Could not someone else have been there?"

"There are, of course, other possibilities," Field said calmly. "Another person or persons could 'ave been in the room with 'em."

"What do you mean? Who?" Dickens strained forward in the chair.

"Or, they could 'ave been surprised in the act of love."

"What do you mean?" Dickens sank back. "Why would others be there?"

Field stared levelly at him.

Dickens slowly lowered his eyes, shaking his head in disbelief, and murmuring "no, no," beneath the threshold of hearing. After a long moment, his head came back up, his eyes still struggling with that disbelief.

"Watching?" It was more a plea than a question.

"Yes, possibly, or . . ." Field's voice was quiet, level, cold.

"Oh God, Wilkie, what a perverse dose of reality we have walked into this night." He was turning to me for relief from the relentless truths that Inspector Field sent raining down upon his sensibilities. "Who could possibly make up such a godless party?"

"Perhaps the old bawd who sold her daughter. Perhaps Ashbee. Perhaps someone of whom we have no information at all. Anythin' is possible." Field, I feel, was simply musing aloud, with no real conviction in his voice, yet Dickens seized that straw.

"Ashbee?" Dickens pressed him. "Why Ashbee?"

"No one else is involved in this case."

"You feel Ashbee, a gentleman, would stoop to this?"

"I have unearthed some rather unsettlin' rumors concernin' Milord Ashbee," Field replied.

"Then, if he or the old witch were there, they could have killed Paroissien. She may be innocent."

"No . . . ," Field replied sadly, "I fear she is no longer innocent."

Dickens glared. Field met his eyes with a steady gaze.

"Unless Paroissien left the front door open by some prior arrangement, they were not surprised. There were no marks of forced entry. Unless the mother, the others, entered with Paroissien and the girl, there was no one else there. There is no sign of any other person 'avin' ever been in that bedchamber." Field spoke with quiet decisiveness.

Dickens's eyes were dead.

"I am certain that Miss Ternan killed Paroissien. But, I am not certain that a crime 'as been committed 'ere. She could well 'ave been defendin' 'erself against further violence."

Hope fluttered feebly in Dickens's countenance. "Yes, could not Paroissien have been killed after the girl left the rooms, if, indeed, she ever entered them? Could it not have been one of those actors? He was universally disliked at the theatre."

"I would be surprised if that were the case," Field replied. "Both Fielding and Price were being followed tonight. If they went anywhere near Paroissien's rooms, I will know it. The girl was there, and 'er virginity was taken. That 'eart-shaped spot of blood on the bed sheet can only be 'ers. The dead man's blood never reached the bed."

As strenuously as he was trying to control them, all of Dickens's emotions of horror, of loss, of love and pity and hate and fear and utter repulsion plagued his countenance. I looked upon Dickens's face, and a dark thought cast a jagged shadow across my imagination. Was Dickens so stricken because the girl was no longer a virgin? Did he mourn the loss of a lustful dream no different from that of the two murdered men who preceeded him in their fascination with this Medusa child?

"Are you a'right, Mister Dickens?" Field addressed his stationhouse guest with genuine concern.

"Yes," Dickens replied slowly. "Yes. I am simply shaken by this evening's events. It is all so . . . so shocking."

Suddenly, he started up and faced Inspector Field and Sergeant Rogers with an intense air of supplication in both his posture and his voice.

"I . . . we . . . we must find her, save her!"

MILORD IN THE AFTERNOON

(May 9, 1851—late morning)

Events progressed in a rush following the murder of Paroissien. Field could not afford to allow the trail of the Ternan women, the suspected murderess and her pandering mother, to grow cold. He had to find the girl before she could flee the country. Sentinels were dispatched to monitor the railway carriages and the ports of departure for America and the Continent. Field, like a great spider, was putting out his threads, spinning a complex web of surveillances, spies, informers. Dickens—driven by a tempest in his soul, driven perhaps by a paternal desire to protect his innocent child-woman; or perhaps by guile, by lust, by shame for his whole gender, driven by myriad confused motives—also needed to find her; needed, in his romantic imagination, to ride out like some latter-day Saint George to slay the dragons and rescue her.

By pre-arrangement, I arrived at the *Household Words* office in Wellington Street shortly after nine that next morning. Dickens, by all evidence, had been up and at work for some time. He seemed quite busy, yet I soon realized that he was an actor in a role. We had been instructed by Inspector Field to wait, but, for Dickens, waiting was clearly (as indicated by his heated pacing of the room, as if he were some caged animal) intolerable. In midstride, he burst out: "There is no time to lose." His voice was stretched taut with emotion. "We must find that old bawd and the child before they flee the city. We must awaken Macready. We must find out where they live and go to their lodgings."

It was all that I could do to persuade him that Inspector Field was doing exactly that. I must confess, however, that I wondered if we would ever be given entry back into the case. It was in the hands of the professionals now. Was Dickens not already suspect in Field's eyes due to his passionate outbursts on behalf of the young woman?

Yet, he had told us to wait . . . and wait we did through a long morning of pretending to ready the next number of *Household Words* for the printer. The sound of a clattering post-chaise reining in below the bow-window jolted us out of an awkward preoccupation with our own secret thoughts. We looked directly down as Inspector Field and Serjeant Rogers disembarked. Our eyes met in a look of relief, of rekindled excitement that we were still actors in the play.

In a torrent of words Field apprised us of his morning's machinations. He had been hard at work spinning out his web, but with little success. The paths of escape by rail, by coach, by sea had been sealed. Macready had been awakened, informed of the death of his stage manager, and consulted as to the lodgings of the formidable Peggy Ternan and her *ingénue* daughter. Both Price and Fielding had been fully interrogated as to the habits, companions, and frequentings of the deceased Paroissien.

"The two women 'ave temporarily disappeared," Field declared, "but they are still in the city. They shall resurface soon."

Inspector Field, however, had not clattered up Wellington Street merely out of professional courtesy. No, he was not the kind of man who wasted his time in gestures of meaningless *politesse*.

"All along there 'as been one gapin' 'ole in this case," he began.

"What hole?" It was my voice which posed the obvious question.

"Everyone involved in this affair 'as been interviewed, 'as been placed under surveillance, except for one man, Lord 'Enry Ashbee."

155

"Are you sure that Ashbee is a part of this case at all?" Dickens seemed calm. "He is, from reputation and all appearances, a gentleman of wealth and influence."

"No. Not sure," Field answered.

"Then why does he arouse your suspicions?"

"Because 'ee refuses to talk with me," he hesitated effectively, "and because of the rumors about, concernin' milordship."

"What rumors?" I jumped in with another obvious question. Only Rogers, who I am sure was contemplating the uselessness of consorting with such rank amateurs as Dickens and myself, chose to hold his tongue.

"Ashbee certainly is a gentleman of wealth and influence," Field said patiently, "but my information suggests 'ee is also a notorious rake, a man of many identities who samples all of the perversions of the city under cover of darkness. 'Ee was of the group the night that Solicitor Partlow was killed. And . . ." Inspector Field tapped his emphatic forefinger sharply upon Dickens's desktop. "And 'ee refuses to grant me access to 'is person for the posin' of the most routine of questions. We must get at Lord Ashbee now. I 'ave tripled the surveillance around 'is 'ouse at Nottin' 'Ill Gate. Though 'is servants deny it, I am sure that 'ee is in the city."

I looked at Dickens.

Dickens, a small grin pursing his lips, returned my glance. We both instinctively knew what was coming next.

Noting our reactions, Field decided to forego the formality of asking.

"Well, sirs, what'll it be?" He had a sly grin on his face. "Are you ready to go back on duty for Inspector Field?"

"To be sure."

"Yes, certainly."

"Yes. I knew you would," he said, smiling with genuine approval of our eagerness. "You've been bitten just as I 'ave. You are too far in, now, to go aturnin' back."

"Quite right." Dickens, in an overflow of enthusiasm, clapped Inspector Field on the shoulder. "We want to follow this to the very end. We'll do anything we can to help, won't we, Wilkie?"

Like a puppet whose strings had been pulled, I, of course, nodded my assent, though I must admit that Dickens was much more sanguine about the dangers involved than was I.

"Well, you want us to pay a call upon Lord Ashbee, I take it." Dickens was completely reanimated.

"Exactly."

"We were introduced briefly that night at The Players Club," Dickens said, turning to me for corroboration, "and he expressed the desire of furthering our acquaintance, did he not, Wilkie?"

"Yes, quite emphatically," I answered. "I am certain we will be welcomed if we call upon him."

Inspector Field fairly beamed.

Rogers, I noticed, sulked silently in the background.

Dickens, however, was all business. For him this was no longer mere novelist's research. He was in deadly earnest, and the girl was the reason.

"How do you want us to play this scene?" Dickens-the-actor asked.

"Very carefully. We do not want to scare 'im off. It will be enough to know that 'ee is still in the city. If you can gain access to 'is lordship's person, that will be more than I 'ave been able to accomplish. I simply want you to observe 'im. Perhaps mention the death of Partlow, the turmoil surroundin' the Covent Garden company. Of course, you must use your own judgment as to what will be appropriate."

"I could suggest that I would like to interview him as an active patron of the arts for an article in *Household Words*."

"Yes, that might catch 'is interest, open 'im up a bit."

"Open him up about what?" I was puzzled. "You have just cautioned us, Inspector, not to scare him away and yet you want us to 'open him up'?"

"Simply observe 'is reactions, Mister Collins. 'Ee will not reveal 'imself in 'is conversation. You can be sure of that. But 'is face will react. 'Ee may exhibit nervousness in 'is gestures.

You must be closely observant, and perhaps you will come away with some sense of the man, of whether 'ee is involved in this case or not. That is all. Simply observe. It is the little things, the twitches that give 'em away. Those twitches carry no weight in the court of the land, but for the true detective they are everythin'."

Dickens smiled. Field's oration came to be known among the three of us in later years as his "Simply observe" speech. Field was charging Dickens to go out and function as a novelist in the real world, to write a character from the observation of real life. In a way, it was a challenge from the detective to the novelist, as if Field was saying "Are you really the genius of characterization that all of England acknowledges you to be? Then be deuced certain you get this character right."

"Well, then, when do we make our little social call?" Dickens asked.

"This very afternoon if possible. Right away if convenient."

"Done!" Dickens cried, and both Field and he broke out in a short laugh.

I looked at Rogers. Even his dour countenance could not help but surrender to a timid and momentary grin.

A hansom cab was called. Our coats were buttoned against the gusting wind, and we embarked upon our latest assignment of deception.

Lord Henry Ashbee's mansion of white stone with wooden gables sprawled at the head of a long drive. The house was composed of two wings with a small fountained garden in the middle, and rose to a height of four storeys, including the gabled attics. It sat in the middle of a heavily wooded park. In the summer, with the trees fully clothed in foliage, it would be totally invisible from the high-road.

Recognized immediately as gentlemen by the servant who answered the bell, we were admitted to the foyer. The servant took away Dickens's card on a silver tray. The hallway was dominated by a wide grey marble staircase which rose to a capacious second-floor balcony.

Ashbee fairly exploded out of one of the side doorways, descending upon us hand outstretched.

"Mister Dickens. Mister Collins. What a genuine and pleasant surprise. I am most pleased that you remember me from our brief meeting. I can honestly say that it is for me a genuine honor to welcome into my home a writer whom I so admire, and who has provided me with so much reading pleasure." As he spoke, he pumped our hands with unbridled enthusiasm, but his words were in no way fawning. He delivered the speech of welcome with a quiet sincerity mixed with enthusiasm, which put Dickens and myself at ease. What I observed was either a man genuinely delighted to receive us, or an extremely competent actor.

Ashbee ushered us into his parlor, and, when we politely refused his offer of brandy (it being too early in the day), he dispatched his manservant for chocolate coffee. He offered us cigars, which we accepted. "Freshly imported from the West Indies," he assured us. What I observed was a man intent upon every touch of hospitality.

Ashbee cut an impressive figure. He was between thirty and forty years of age, tall, slim, handsome of face, noble of carriage, with rich, wavy brown hair brushed carefully around the edges of his face. Unlike the vast majority of men of the age, Ashbee chose to face the world cleanshaven. His dress and carriage marked him as a gentleman. His was a noble, youthful figure. Only his eyes and the cruel twist to the side of his mouth seemed flaws in his congenial appearance.

"Gentlemen, I am pleased to welcome you. Might I ask what occasions this surprise visit?" Lord Ashbee began.

"Two reasons, really," Dickens answered. "A desire, since our initial meeting of the other evening, to further pursue our acquaintance. A novelist does not often meet a reader who can quote chapter and verse. Secondly, I wish, only with your consent of course, to exploit you as a source in an article which Mister Collins and myself are preparing for *Household Words*, an article on the survival of the arts—painting, the theatre, literature—in modern London, the conflict of patronage with the demands and growing power of the popular audience . . . that sort of thing. I was hoping you might offer your views of the modern art scene."

I marvelled at the smoothness and forthrightness with which Dickens lied. I had been rehearsing with him as an actor for nearly six weeks, but I had never observed him in such mastery of his part.

"Ah, the arts," Lord Ashbee said, slouching contemplatively in his chair and bringing his hands together in front of his face, the thumbs meeting on his lips, and the fingertips forming the effigy of a Gothic cathedral.

"May I be frank?" he continued. "I am sure that you would not place my comments in an embarrassing light."

"I assure you, sir," Dickens leaned forward, "you will be quoted accurately and with no editorial manipulation. You have my word."

"That is enough," Ashbee smiled, but that twist at the right corner of his mouth distorted the trust which that smile should have expressed. "My view of the arts is a quite simple one. I am a sensualist."

He must have noted the surprise pass over both Dickens's and my countenance at his use of that word. A "sensualist" was not something that a respectable gentleman at mid-century readily admitted to being.

"Ah, I see I shock you," he said, his twisted grin dancing. "I don't mean to shock. I don't use that word in its vulgar sense. I am a sensualist in that I live for the stimulation which beauty can bring to all of my senses. It was on the Continent—in Paris, in Rome—that I learned the sensual pleasures of surrounding oneself with beauty. No, not vulgar sensuality, but the joy of possessing and looking at sublime paintings and works of sculpture, of reading and hearing the most elevated language in the hands of the finest writers and actors. I have no motives for my artistic patronage other than personal pleasure. I am a collector of beauty: that which is lasting, like my Greek and Roman statues; that which is entertaining and thoughtful, such as your novels; that which stirs the emotions of an evening, such as Macready's plays."

It was, it seemed, an honest and heartfelt speech.

"Yes, of course, I understand you now." Dickens was too acquiescent. "You govern your life by your aesthetic sense?"

"Yes. Well put. That is it indeed. I feel that London offers a variety of opportunity for such aesthetic appetites."

"What would you say are the most attractive aesthetic opportunities which London offers?"

"*You* certainly are one, sir," he smiled with a sudden grotesque animation, his handsome face marred by that cruel twist. "English literature, your novels, the marvelous poetry of Wordsworth and Byron, and Lord Tennyson, is at its highest point since Shakespeare. The English theatre is, to my mind, the best in all of Europe. Even English painting is beginning to show the daring, the fire, of the French. A painter like Turner could not have come to prominence in the last century—too radical. Yet now he carries the day. Have you seen his latest seascapes? Striking. If only the English could learn to paint the nude as the French can."

It was a *tour de force*.

Dickens returned his notebook to his pocket. "Exactly the sort of comments I was looking for," he assured Lord Ashbee. "Art is indeed a touching of the personal passion. The theatre, that is where my sensual stimulation is found. I hold our London stage in that same high regard which you have expressed."

It was conversation of a high caliber among gentlemen of rank and education and aesthetic taste. I held my tongue and tried to observe closely, but I found myself being carried away in the ideas and idealism. Dickens, however, with patient cunning, was steering the conversation toward the theatre and the murders.

"Macready's company at Covent Garden carries the field right now, I believe," I said, making my first clumsy foray into the conversation. "Have you seen his *Macbeth*, sir?"

"Yes," Ashbee said, turning to me, "a quite authentic and moving interpretation but for the sensationalism of the final act. Playing a bit too much to the stalls, there, I felt."

"Shocking, the events of last evening. I have heard that Covent Garden is to be closed temporarily, performances suspended," Dickens followed up, and I sank gratefully back into my chair.

"What events?" I felt that a slowing of his voice, a quick moving of his cigar to his mouth before his question, revealed a slight discomfiture.

"Oh, you haven't heard?" I spoke up again. I was becoming positively garrulous. "Last night, Macready's stage manager, a Mister Paroissien, was brutally murdered in his lodgings. Terrible thing!"

"Yes," Dickens said, stepping right in. "I will do an article on it for the *Household Narrative*, our news tabloid. I plan to call it 'A Death Offstage.'"

"My God, Paroissien." Either Ashbee was a very good actor or he was genuinely shocked by the news. "The man was an acquaintance of mine."

"I've heard he was a real taskmaster backstage," Dickens carried right on, "but stabbing him six times in the back is a bit extreme even for an actor's bruised ego."

Like vultures, we all laughed at Dickens's morbid wit, but Lord Ashbee's heart didn't seem to be in this conversation.

"The police feel that it was some angry member of the cast of *Macbeth* who did it," I spoke up again. "They are looking for any irregularities at the theatre, interviewing the actors and backstage people."

"Curious, is it not?" Dickens struck a philosophic note. "Murder onstage and murder off. Real life imitating art. Isn't it supposed to be the other way around?"

"Yes, curious indeed," Ashbee agreed, but he said no more.

"My friend Macready is really quite upset about it," Dickens feebly tried to keep this topic of conversation alive.

Suddenly, I cannot define exactly what it was, perhaps a tensing of his person, a change in the openness of his face, Ashbee was on his guard. I could hear Inspector Field's words—"We don't want to scare him off"—echoing in my mind. Dickens also must have sensed it. He immediately changed the subject.

"If memory serves," Dickens began (and Ashbee visibly tensed), "you mentioned at our first brief meeting that you were also a writer" (Ashbee relaxed as he realized that Dickens no longer wished to discuss Paroissien's murder).

"You have an excellent memory, sir," Ashbee was again his congenial self. "Yes, perhaps I did mention my amateur scribbling."

"Perhaps I could read some of your best work sometime," Dickens tendered the polite offer which sooner or later every writer tenders to every other writer. It is an offer which never means what it purports to mean. It is not really an offer to read your competitor's work. Rather, it is a challenge. "Are you good enough to let me see your work? Are you confident enough to know that I will not be laughing hysterically at you as I read?" are the real questions hidden in that seemingly innocuous offer to read another writer's work.

"I would be honored," Ashbee answered guardedly, "although I cannot predict if the subjects of my writing will be congenial to your tastes. My book is unusual, often unsettling in its realistic descriptions."

"Oh, no fear of that," Dickens laughed. "I have eclectic tastes."

That strange, grotesque grin once again twisted Ashbee's face. It was as if he were enjoying some ironic private joke.

"When I get a substantial piece of my work in order, I should be pleased to have you read it. I would value your opinion."

"What is the nature of your work?" Dickens politely probed.

"It is an extended analysis of London life. For lack of a better title, I am calling it *The Memoirs of a Victorian Gentleman*." Again, that quirky grin, as if some joke were being played at our expense.

"Aha, sounds quite interesting," Dickens responded.

I could tell immediately that his enthusiasm was feigned. From the title it sounded like a very conventional sort of book, the kind of thing that Thackeray and the lace-curtain crowd of Berkeley Square novelists might assay. I could tell that Dickens found the title boring, because he dropped the subject in the subterfuge of relighting his already-lit cigar.

"Well," Dickens emerged from a veritable cloud of blue smoke which he had puffed up around his head as a diversion, "we do not want to monopolize your whole afternoon with our intrusion, but I do have one more request, Lord Ashbee, which I hope you will see fit to grant."

"Please, my friends call me Henry. What is it? I am at your service," Ashbee answered graciously.

"Henry," Dickens picked up his invitation to familiarity, "could you give us a brief tour of your house and collections? One hears rumours of the treasures you have collected. I am sure Mister Collins shares my aesthetic curiosity."

"Yes, absolutely," I immediately assured our host.

"Of course, nothing easier," he arose with a certain arrogance and pride in this opportunity to display his wealth and taste.

The following thirty minutes were a feast of unrivalled splendor. Each painting, each statue, each sculpted marble fragment, each tapestry captured our senses in a new and exciting way. Seeing such exquisite pieces exhibited in the warmth and richness of his sumptuously appointed rooms was an experience so much more personal than viewing similar works in the cold public rooms of the British Museum or the National Gallery. And his collection rivalled those collections. The paintings on the walls were signed by Poussin, Claude, Van der Veldes, Ruisdael, Hobbema, and the English painters West, Copley, Stanfield and Gainsborough. There were two priceless Canalettos, a striking Titian, a Watteau. The sculpture and statues must have been the spoils of every temple and palace in Ancient Greece and Imperial Rome. He saved his most interesting (and perhaps revealing) gallery room for last. It was a small room with every inch of wall space taken over by small (none larger than twelve inches square) pictures and miniatures—oils, watercolors, sketches, line drawings, cartoons. "I call this my grotesque room," he announced. "It is like walking into an opium dream." It was, indeed, a room of turmoil, violence and horror. The room was dominated by the work of his favorite English painter, J. M. W. Turner. There must have been eight or ten small oils or watercolors of fires, tigers, storms and roiling seas. The rest of the room was hung with the grotesque representations of real and mythic monsters of painters like Hogarth, Daumier, Blake.

The last room into which he led us was the library. Its shelves were lined with a wealth of richly bound volumes in leather, green baize and gold leaf representing the greatest works of English and Continental literature. Ashbee proudly directed our attention to his complete set of the works of Charles Dickens occupying a prominent portion of a shelf right at eye level, a prestigious location in any library. "I hope, Mister Collins, that your work will soon accompany those of Mister Dickens on my library shelves," Ashbee politely declared.

Yet, I could not help but feel that something was wrong about this room. It felt crowded. Throughout the house, Ashbee's priceless art collection was displayed in spacious, well-lit rooms, yet the library was small and dark. And there was no desk, no reading chairs. But something else had captured my attention when we entered.

Ashbee had led us on a leisurely tour of his house and art collection with evident delight and pride in exhibiting each treasure. When we entered the library, however, he did a strange thing. He fairly leapt from the doorway to the opposite wall to straighten a small picture. As we entered behind this spasm of sudden movement, he was turning to us with a somewhat embarrassed smile which twisted off into his directing of our eyes to Dickens's novels in their place of honor. He pointed with pride to the rare collectors' volumes in his library, editions of Cervantes and Voltaire and Galileo and Pascal, a Gutenberg Bible, and an enormous three-decker of Richardson's *Clarissa*. In a more modern vein, he owned full collections of the works of Rabelais and Sir Walter Scott.

After savouring the delights of his library, he ushered us out, carefully closing and locking the door behind. "The servants, you know," he explained. "They are not allowed in there. Books are too small and portable, too much of a temptation."

In the large entrance foyer he once again assured us of how much our surprise visit had pleased him. A cab was summoned from the high-road and we made our escape.

As we left the Ashbee estate, I sensed that Inspector Field and his surveillance minions were somewhere nearby. I surveyed the passing landscape, but, if they were there, it was beyond my powers to detect their presence. There was some sporadic traffic on the high-road, but no sign of Field's black post-chaise.

"Seems a nice enough chap," I remarked to Charles as our cab started down the high-road toward the city. "Quite hospitable. Certainly serious about his art collecting, is he not?"

Dickens turned to me with a look of utter amazement on his face as if I were some barking idiot newly escaped from Bedlam.

"You did not, for one moment, believe all that twaddle about transcending the vulgar and the everyday through art, did you?" he scoffed.

"Why, I . . ."

"The man is hiding something," Dickens said, slapping the padded seat for emphasis. "No sensualist, as he deems himself, exists for purely aesthetic motives. Man's lower appetites are much stronger than his aesthetic sense. Aesthete indeed! He protests too much."

I was, needless to say, shocked at Dickens's vehement denunciation. I saw no grounds for it. I wondered if Dickens had taken a personal dislike to the man. My brief ruminations were abruptly terminated in a pounding of galloping hooves, a rush of black bulk and a harsh shouted order—"REIN IN!"—to our cabman.

Inspector Field intercepted us in his speeding post-chaise about two miles from Lord Ashbee's estate. He waved our cabman to the side of the high-road, and we made our report right there.

"Well," Field began jovially, "'ow did you find Milord this afternoon?"

Rogers loitered dourly at his side.

"We found him at home, quite pleased to accept our call, expansive and gracious in giving us a tour of his house. Quite hospitable," Dickens answered Field's opening foray.

Disappointment momentarily darkened Field's face. I must admit that, after what Dickens had only moments before stated to me, I was somewhat surprised at the positive evaluation which Dickens gave. I had failed to catch the irony in Dickens's voice, the teasing look in his eye.

"All of which leads me to believe," Dickens went on after that brief pause for effect, "that the man is guilty as Thackeray's Jesuit."*

At this sudden pronouncement, Field's equanimity returned: "Oh, I see, the literary man must 'ave 'is fun with the poor servant of 'is Majesty. That's your game, eh?"

Dickens laughed. There was a rapport between them.

"I do not know what occasions my doubts," Dickens said, turning serious, "but I am certain that we only saw the surface of that house, of the man. He is deeper. There is something going on there, behind the aesthetic facade."

"What do you mean?" Field quietly drew him further up the intuitive path, whose gate he had opened.

"I am convinced that Ashbee was hiding something, that there were things which he did not wish Wilkie and me to observe, subjects he did not want us to pursue in our conversation."

"'Idin' what? What subjects?"

---

*This is probably a reference to a character in Thackeray's *Henry Esmond*, which was not yet published but parts of which Dickens might well have recently seen in manuscript form.

"I don't rightly know. He seemed somewhat nervous when we mentioned Paroissien's murder."

"Did you notice anythin' specifically amiss," Field probed, "out of place, unusual?" He was keenly interested now, on the scent.

I waited. Charles was managing this show. I must admit that I honestly felt that I had nothing to say.

"He said he was a writer," Dickens began. "He said he was writing a book, yet how strange that we saw no place where a writer would work—no desk, no study, no place in his library."

Field looked blankly at Dickens as if to say, "That is all?" I feel that it was almost out of desperation that he turned to me. "Did you 'ave this same feelin', Mister Collins?" he asked. "Did you notice anythin' out of the ordinary?"

"Not really," I said, disappointing him. He shot a quick glance at Rogers, which I interpreted as meaning *what a waste of time these two are!*, but to my own surprise, I did not subside into my hitherto silent state. "There was this somewhat strange business with a crooked picture frame in the library. It was probably nothing. And the library, it seemed so small and cramped," I finished lamely, "so unlike the rest of the house."

"What strange business? What did 'ee do?" Field's animation had temporarily returned.

"He virtually raced to straighten it as we entered," Dickens cut in.

Inspector Field's forefinger, emphatically crook'd, jumped to the corner of his eyebrow and scratched once, twice, thrice.

"What did 'ee do when you mentioned Paroissien's murder?" Field asked with relish.

"He exhibited surprise, even shock," Dickens answered. "Freely admitted that he knew the man. Acted as if our announcement of the murder was the first he had heard of it."

"Acted?" Field's forefinger scratched once more.

"It was as if his reaction was being held under tight rein," I ventured my agreement with Dickens's observation. "I sensed that he did not wish to talk about the murder."

Dickens nodded his assent to my characterization.

Field and Rogers listened hungrily, like two birds of prey.

"In other words," Field said, staring at us so hard you would have thought he was trying to look right through us, "you think 'ee's in it? You think 'ee was 'idin' somethin'? You think 'ee was lyin'?"

Dickens and I looked at each other. It was as if the man was interrogating *us*.

"Why yes, I suppose so," I said, "but I cannot be certain."

"I am more certain!" Charles said with a decisiveness which surprised me. We had been together during the whole visit to Ashbee's manse, and he had seen and heard no more than I. "I sensed from the moment Paroissien's name was mentioned that Lord Ashbee was uneasy, suspicious."

"That's it then!" Field said. "You two gentlemen 'ave done yeoman service for the Protectives. We will pursue this further. I will maintain my surveillance upon the Ashbee estate."

"And," Dickens said, interrupting Field's retreat toward the post-chaise, "you will keep us informed? If possible you will summon us to continue as observers of the actual unfolding of the case?"

"Yes," I added, "we are so deep into it now that you must allow us to follow it through to the end."

Field hesitated.

Rogers scowled.

"Yes, of course," Field finally consented.

With a curt farewell, Field and Rogers remounted their dark police carriage, and were carried off at a gallop. Dickens and I re-entered our cab, and enjoyed a more leisurely ride into the city.

As we drew near our respective lodgings, Charles ordered the cabman to drop me first. As I began to step out, Dickens stopped me with a gentle hand on my arm. He was quite serious, even contemplative.

"Wilkie," he said, "she was there. I could sense her presence."

His almost obsessive gaze disconcerted me.

"Do not be deceived by Ashbee," he warned. "That man is not what he seems. We must save her from him."

He had conjured himself into St. George all right, preparing to ride forth with his lance at the ready.

A VOICE FROM THE SHADOWS

(May 9, 1851—late afternoon)

What immediately follows has no relevance to the Partlow/Paroissien case. The meeting I am about to describe was never brought to the attention of either Charles or Inspector Field, but, I must admit, it has great relevance to my participation in that case. Since I never mentioned it to either Dickens or Field, I suppose it might be construed as a clandestine meeting. Nothing could be further from the truth. I neither planned nor sought this meeting, but I did acquiesce to it (thus, I am not altogether blameless). In fact, if I am honest, I must confess that I secretly hoped for just such a meeting. To put the clearest possible light upon it, I chose not to mention this meeting to either Dickens or Field, because I was not proud of it at all, and if it occurred again, I am sure that I would handle the whole affair quite differently.

I probably would not report this meeting at all, if it did not ultimately have relevance to the story I am trying to record in this memoir. Perhaps, when this story finds its audience in another time and place, it and I will not be judged so harshly as I feared I would be, if this meeting came to light under the censorious gaze of my own age.

As I write this secret memoir, I cannot help but feel that it should be as meticulously plotted as a novel. But real life doesn't happen like a novel. Sometimes things which are not part of the plot occur in the midst of heated plot development. What is the writer to do? Simply forget some events and only emphasize others? Or, report the events of reality as they occur? That is why I am writing of this meeting, because it helps me to understand what my story is all about, and why I am writing it down after all these years.

That afternoon of Dickens's and my visit to Lord Ashbee's impressive collections, I stepped down from our hired cab at the end of my narrow street, and waved as St. George clattered away. I was pleasantly drained yet exhilarated at our afternoon's adventure as I walked to my lodgings at number seventeen. I lived in two small rooms with a pantry, off Longacre on West Dickson Street, a cozy suite of bachelor digs. The afternoon was closing fast, the sun blinking feebly through the grey overcast.

"Mister Collins, sir?" came a voice from the shadows of a crevasse between two stone buildings.

It was Irish Meg Sheehey's voice. When she stepped out into the waning light, she was like a luminous apparition painted on some sensual Renaissance canvas. Her fiery hair, her dark eyes, her dusky skin, the heave of her bosom, caused by the low cut of her dress and her careless laces, all contributed to an impression which for days had haunted my heated imagination.

"Mister Collins," she repeated. "I must speak with you."

"Why Meg, hello, yes, it is almost dark, speak to me, of course, yes, I'm surprised to see you, Meg," I stammered on like a flustered twit.

We stood there in the street in silence for a long moment, our eyes meeting. All I could see was the soft heave of her chest against the taut laces of her dress, the seductive invitation in her eyes, the bold cock of her head. What I failed to see was the fear and pain behind her eyes, her desperation. It was a long and riveting look. When it was finished, we both knew that it was no longer possible for either of us to lie to the other. It was as if in that long, penetrating look we had stripped each other naked. The normal hypocrisy of everyday life somehow seemed out of place in that quiet street with those soft shadows gathering around us like bedclothes.

"Yes, Meggy," it seemed so proper to call her that as if we had become chums, "what can I do for you? What is it? Are you in distress?" And I have called Dickens St. George!

"No sir, but can I 'ave a few words with you, sir?" she answered quietly. "I needs to talk to someone."

"Yes?" I was too confused by my own emotions to realize that she had not yet stated her business, because she was waiting for me to invite her in out of the public censure of the street. "What is it?" I repeated, and I stood there, thoroughly insensible to the look of the whole affair to whatever passers-by there might be.

"'Ere, sir?" she prompted me.

My neck swivelled here and there, looking about, as her meaning suddenly pricked my consciousness of where we were, and how it must look. "No, yes, of course, let us go in," I blurted out. "We can talk in the privacy of my rooms."

Even as I said it, I saw the door to my rooms closing behind Meggy and my other self; I saw Meggy and that dark self clasped in each other's arms; I saw Meggy and myself in bed in my rooms, naked, primal, damned.

We made the entrance to my building without being seen, and climbed the stairs undetected. The wooden door swung silently closed behind us and we were alone.

Suddenly, standing facing her in the fading light of my sitting room, terror burned like a hot wire straight through me. *What was I doing?* I was a gentleman, and I had admitted a common woman of the streets into my private lodgings. I was already compromised. *What a prig you are!* some other voice croaked.

"What is it I can do for you, Meg?" I asked. "Is it about the murder case? Have you been threatened?"

"No sir, no. I needs to talk to someone. 'Bout me. That's all."

"I am afraid I don't understand. If you are in some kind of

trouble, would it not be better to discuss it with Inspector Field?"

"Inspector Field don't care 'bout me." The words virtually exploded from her. "In 'is book I'm just a street 'ore, an animal like all the other creetures 'ee pushes an' pulls an' dangles aloft for 'is amusement an' uses for 'is purposes. 'Ee don't care for me. 'Ee summons me to 'is rooms an' 'as me. If 'ee knew I'd told you that 'ee'd 'ave me taken up, 'ee would. If I die 'ee'd just git summat else for 'is informer. Wouldn't even remember my name in a fortnight."

Though she never raised her voice, there was a violent despair in her words, a desperation and bitterness that frightened me.

"I don't want to die that way," her voice quickened. "Not in the streets. Not in a 'ole in the water. Not like Mister Dickens's Nancy, beat to death. Not from the pox or consumption. I want to be a normal person, not a gin-soaked old 'ag. I needs 'elp to be so, to change. Please, I needs 'elp."

It was such an impassioned plea, so elegant in its way. She was so sure and clearsighted in her perception of her self, her world, her terrible future. For a woman of her class in our age in the city of London, there were so few alternatives. She was very perceptive about what her future would be if she remained on the streets.

"But Meg," I said, the uncertainty quavering in my voice, "why me?"

"I comes to you because you're a gentleman an I sees the way you look at me."

I stared at her.

"You're my only chance, Mister Collins," she went on, warming to her performance. "You look at me different from all the others."

She is using all of her feminine wiles to entrap me. I considered my position, but I could not take my eyes from her breasts rising against the flimsy top of her dress. I remembered the first time I had seen Irish Meg, my immediate attraction, which I had, just as immediately, driven down into hiding in the underworld of myself.

"What? How do I . . ." I stammered, then pulled up short. She perceived my confusion, and it gave her courage.

"You want me, I can tell, but you also look at me like I was somebody, a 'ooman bein', not just a thing to be bought an' used an' thrown out after. Not just a dirty street 'ore," she spat that epithet. "I'm not that to you, am I, Mister Collins, am I?" She was not begging. Her question was more a challenge than a plea for approval.

"No, Meg, of course not," I said, looking levelly at her, and (to my own consternation) realizing that I meant it. Yet, I did not wholly mean it. I wanted her as a whore. I could not avoid the fact that her being so readily available was the genesis of my attraction for her.

"I see 'ow you looks at me. You're lookin' at me that way now. Like you want me, but you don't know what to do with me."

"Yes, I do look at you, think of you." I realized that we were in a contest for control. Suddenly, that other room from the night before intruded itself upon my fantasy; a man alone with a woman in his lodgings, the door closed, it had ended in murder. What *was* Irish Meg doing in my rooms? Had she come to seduce, and then blackmail me? To murder and rob me? Was her accomplice, Tally Ho Thompson perhaps, waiting outside? *What a nervous twit you are!* I thought, trying to mock away my misgivings.

"The very first night, I seen the way you looked at me," she repeated more boldly, "an' I said to myself 'this one's interested, 'ee is, this one's all eyes 'ee is,' an' I couldn't help but laugh. You want to buy me, don't you? Try me? It's easy. All it takes is coin. Or power, the kind that Field 'olds over me." She said the last bitterly, and then repented mentioning his name. "Oh, sir, on your 'onner as a gentleman, you must never say that I spoke 'is name 'ere. 'Ee'd 'ave me taken up."

"Inspector Field? He uses you . . . in *that* way?"

"'Ee does." She said it boldly, with no reticence or guilt.

"An' I ain't the only one. 'Is wife died, you know, couple of years ago, of a fever. 'Ee doted on 'er. 'Ee is very gentle with me when we're in that way. Oh, God, 'ee must never know I said any of this."

"He will never know from me. I do not want to buy you, to have you that way." Her eyes fixed upon mine, and flayed away all the hypocrisy of my surface life as a proper gentleman, accused me, charged me, sentenced me, and pardoned me, all in one fierce, riveting look.

"Yes, I want you," I heard myself confessing aloud. I could not believe that I was allowing my private dreams to see the light of reality. "I cannot deny it."

Her eyes never wavered from mine, but her face relaxed, lightened around the corners of the eyes and mouth, as if a cloud had suddenly passed across the face of the sun.

". . . yet I could never bring myself to buy you for an hour or a night," I finished.

"You can be anythin' you want to be, do anythin' you want," she said, breaking her spellbinding silence. "You can think what you want to be, an' then you can make your thoughts come alive. You could make yourself fall in love with me, Mister Collins, if you thought about it long enough."

She moved closer, her face tilted up to be kissed, her eyes mesmerizing me. Now, twenty years since Irish Meg looked at me in that way, I realize that what she was defining was the power of invention of the novelist, that I had been pursuing under the mentorship of Dickens. What Irish Meg was saying was, that a person (or a writer) need not be bound only to private dreams (or fictions), that he could venture out into the world, and invent a life in reality as well—invent a life, and then live it, a life born out of art. *That is why Dickens goes out to walk the streets late at night*, I realized. *That is why Dickens so enjoys taking such risks in the real world*. A writer could take a single image—a London fog or a moonlit woman in a white dress—and turn it into an elaborate fiction, then he could follow that fiction wherever it might take him.

"Yes, we can be anything we want to be," I agreed. "We can change, make ourselves better than we are."

"You can . . . because you're a man. A woman ain't that lucky. I'm a woman in a world where wimmin are nothin', worse than nothin' if they're alone. Maybe in novels wimmin can change, be on their own, find jobs as governesses an' the like, but it ain't that way in real life on the streets."

"What is it, Meg? Tell what you want of me. I desire to help you." I wanted to reach out to her, take her in my arms, but I could not move.

"I wants to leave the streets, sir. I can read an' write. I wants to work for a gentleman like yourself or Mister Dickens. Could you 'elp me, sir? I would do all your bidding. I would be off the streets an' yours for only your private purposes."

Slowly, I began to feel the heat rising in my blood. Irish Meg stood before me, willing, petitioning, and I knew that I could simply reach out and touch those dusky breasts rising to each voluptuous breath she drew. I knew that she would counterfeit love for me, employing all of the oft-rehearsed gestures and roles of an accomplished actress. How ironic that both Dickens and I should be captivated by such adept actresses. Some sentiment within my confused, divided self made me hang back, because I knew that I would possess only art, not life.

Her eyes never wavered. They challenged me. It was as if her eyes were asking me out of a street-worn curiosity: "You know you 'ave me, my fine young gentleman, now just what is it you propose to do with me? Use me an' pay me, as one pays a cabman for the convenience of 'is 'orse?"

"You want me," she said once again (yet there was a quiver of fearful desperation in her voice). "I can see it when you looks at me. You wants to love me. But can you? Could you love one 'oose bin a 'ore? Or do you just wants to own me?" She paused to draw a breath which drew my eyes to her rising breasts. "I wants ta be loved, I do. But men can't love the likes o' me. I've seen lies told in the name o' love. I've seen hexploitation passed off as love. Love don't come ta 'ores. Only the river comes. I'm runnin' from the river. I don't care 'ow it's done. I just want to escape the streets before I die. That's why I come ta you."

My voice, my words, yet I knew not what I was saying. She had carried me away as if on a tide. "Yes, I want you," I said. "I want you as all the others want you, yet I cannot buy you. Ours is an attraction of bodies, yet we are still beings with hearts. You are here because your heart still retains some shred of its humanity; your heart can still hope for some real life despite all the falseness which has imprisoned it."

As the words tumbled from me, her eyes widened as if surprised, like that night on the river when I gave her my scarf. I could not pull my eyes from hers.

"Can't buy me?" she seemed puzzled.

"No," I said, though I wanted to.

"Why not? Anyone kin buy me."

Now, the desperation was in my voice. For some reason, it was suddenly important that I make her understand. "Do you think that all men are incapable of love?" I did not wait for an answer, but rushed headlong on. "Do you believe that all men simply want to buy and own women? If you believe that, then there can be no love because you will not allow it."

When she spoke again, her words came slowly as if she was on an unfamiliar stage playing an unrehearsed part.

"A girl can't be poor in London an' stay clean," she said quietly. "You can't live by that dirty river nor walk those dirty streets without gettin' dirty yourself." Her eyes came up, and reasserted their hold upon me. "But maybe, I thought, if you try, if you can find 'elp, you might wash the dust off, or some of it."

I could stand her intense gaze no longer. I had to turn away, to walk to the window, to light the lamp on my writing desk, yet not to light it, to somehow collect myself there in the gathering darkness. I returned down the room to stand before her. Her closeness made the fire blaze up within me once again. Yet, I had thought of something to say. And she had thought of something to do which eased the shadowed gravity of our discomfort.

177

She smiled . . . an open innocent nervous smile that a farm lass in Devon might bestow upon her awkward beau. Her self-conscious smile, for an instant, made me feel that indeed I could love her.

"Mister Dickens and myself, we know a woman," I began. I had regained my gentleman's formality, my pretentious superiority. I felt a great power over her, yet the heated attraction of my other self gave that power the lie. "We know a woman who . . ."

"Is she a bawd? A rich folks' bawd?" she asked, and I felt I detected (but perhaps I only imagined) a faint undertone of disappointment in her voice.

"A bawd? Miss Coutts?" I was at a loss. Laughter beyond my control began welling up in my throat, and burst forth in a half-strangulated chuckle.

"Wot the 'ell's so funny?" Meggy demanded, planting her hands firmly on her hips, her Irish eyes flashing.

"Oh, no, nothing," I answered. "She does keep a house full of prostitutes, but somehow I feel that Miss Coutts would be somewhat at a loss if she knew she was being characterized as a bawd."

"I know that name," Meg was serious, "an' I've 'eard of that 'ouse. It's Miss Burdett-Coutts of the stone bank at Trafalgar Square, ain't it? We calls it the 'ouse for runaway 'ores."

"Yes, that is the place. We could get you into that house. Is that what you had in mind?"

"I don't think so," Irish Meg seemed genuinely confused. "I don't know right now what I 'ad in mind." Her voice sank to barely a whisper: "I 'ad you in mind, that's all."

Then it was her turn to flee, to gather herself. She crossed to the window where the last light was fading behind the wispy curtains.

"I don't want savin'," Meg moved toward me, not much more than a voice in the shadows, "all I wants is to survive, to live like a reg'lar 'ooman bein'. That's all."

There was a silent pause but, when she began again, her soft voice was within reach of my arms. I could almost feel her seductive breathing.

"I thought maybe with a man like you . . . a man who looks at me that way . . . who wants me for wot I am, not for wot 'ee can make me be. That's it. Still a 'ore but a legal 'ore like all those fancy married tarts with their prams in 'Eyde Park."

"What do you mean?" I understood her proposal perfectly but, as a stall, I pretended incomprehension.

"I'd 'oped that you'd keep me. Not to marry, I didn't mean that, though it sounded that way. Wouldn't 'ope for that. But dress me, an' teach me to fit into your gentleman's company. I'd do what you pleased to escape the streets."

Her's was a blatant offer of her wares, if I was man enough to buy. My protective coloration, the formality and stiffness of the proper Victorian gentleman, instinctively (and quite pompously) groused to my defense: "Why, I can't imagine . . ."

"Can you imagine livin' out every dark dream of what you ever wanted to do with a woman? Wot if I says to you that *not* touchin' me now is a lie? Wot if I says to you that your whole life is a lie? Listen to me," she said, and her hand touched my chest, "I can make it real."

She must have sensed the disarray, which my silence signalled. Gently, she taunted me toward action. "You want to be like 'im, don't you?" she whispered from the shadows. "Mister Dickens wouldn't be afraid to touch me . . . to fuck me. 'Ee'd do what 'ee wanted, then, somehow, 'ee'd write about it. I sees the way 'ee looks at me too. Like I'm some spessman under glass in some museum for study."

As I write this, as I look back upon that pivotal moment in my life, I cannot help but think of how many times in his books Dickens arranged just such situations, where the lower classes, the poor, the criminal element, bump up against and confront the upper classes, gentlemen and gentlewomen. His scenes are much less passionate, his language less accurate, less vulgar, less real, yet they are this same scene.

Darkness had completely filled the room. We were but the

voices of two shadows. I had to touch her, to verify her reality, no . . . my reality. I gathered her into my arms as one pulls a quilt close on a bitter night. I felt her softness, her warmth. Her hands like smooth fabric caressed my face. Her arms glided around by neck, closing out all the world.

We kissed.

A first kiss, like a feint, then a hard long kiss that neither wished ever to end. We gasped for breath. Her body moved urgently against mine. Our lips searched out each other once again.

Three sharp knocks sounded, like an axe biting into the wood of the door.

I recoiled from Meg, as if those startling sounds were nails being driven into a cross of guilt, upon which I suddenly found myself hung.

Three more knuckle raps fell upon my flimsy door.

"Who's there?" I called out. "One moment."

"It is Charles, Wilkie, with Inspector Field."

"Oh, God, 'ee must not find me 'ere," Irish Meg begged in a whisper.

"One moment, Charles," I repeated.

I pushed her into my bedroom and closed the door. My mind was racing. Since I had come in only a short time before, all that I needed to go out, my hat, gloves, walking stick, were conveniently deposited on a chair in my sitting room. There would be no necessity for me going back into my bedroom, for opening the bedroom door behind which Meg was secreted.

I opened the door without further hesitation, and Inspector Field entered, followed by Dickens.

"Charles," I said, counterfeiting acute surprise, "I just left you no more than thirty minutes past. What has happened?"

Dickens never got the opportunity to respond to my inquiry.

"We 'ave no time to lose, Mister Collins," Inspector Field gruffly informed me. "We must pursue them, before we lose the trail. Will you accompany us? Now?"

"Why . . . of course," I said, looking at Dickens. He was grinning with eagerness. "Pursue whom? What trail?"

I must admit that, in the excitement of their bursting in, I actually forgot that Meg was concealed in the next room. My heated desire to have her, fanned to such a wild flame in our embrace of only moments before, had subsided into cold ash.

"Your questions will be answered on the way," Inspector Field assured me. "Are you ready? Let us go."

As we exited my rooms, Field hesitated a brief instant on the threshold, turned back before closing the door.

"Strange," he said, as we descended the stairs.

"What is it?" I inquired.

"There was a smell of scent in your parlor." He had that searching look on his face of a man trying to remember an old comrade's name.

"Woman who cleans up," I replied, surprising myself at the facility with which the lie leapt to my lips, "must drench herself in it." I felt certain that that lie kept Irish Meg out of it, but with a sharper like Field, one can never be sure. He let the subject drop easily enough. Irish Meg, I am sure, made her own way out of my rooms, and, to my knowledge, never stole a thing.

In the coach, Field briefed me on the developments in the case.

"Your visit this afternoon seems to 'ave, with certainty, flushed our friend Ashbee," he began.

"There has been a flurry of suspicious activity at the Ashbee estate since we left there this afternoon," Dickens interrupted.

I listened intently as we clattered through the night streets. We had been scheduled to rehearse *Not So Bad As We Seem* later that evening, but Dickens quickly informed me that, through Wills, he had cancelled the rehearsal.

"Immediately after you left the estate," Field continued, "all but one of the servants, a butler who lives on the premises, departed the 'ouse, dismissed through the weekend. One, under questionin', described preparations for Milord's departure for somewhere. No idea where. The country, perhaps. Perhaps the Continent. None could say for certain." Field stopped but a moment to draw breath.

"Only moments after," he proceeded on, "a closed coach, its top fully loaded with baggage, which gives one to suspect that the sudden withdrawal was not so sudden after all; at any rate, this coach, springs 'eavy against the road, galloped away from the vicinity of the Ashbee estate." Again he paused for breath.

"Vicinity?" I had the temerity to interject.

"We are not sure where it left from," Field continued, "though its 'aste was too suspicious to overlook. Gatewood was not caught up short this time. 'Ee followed. 'Ee 'as not yet reported in. It did not come from the carriage 'ouse behind Ashbee's main 'ouse. It may 'ave come from the back reaches of the estate, perhaps some concealed outbuilding in the wooded park. Its curtains were drawn. We 'ave no idea who was inside. It 'it the 'eye-road at full gallop."

"You feel it was Ashbee, yes?"

"Ah, but there is more," he said, pausing for effect. "This afternoon, while we were watchin' the Ashbee estate, Mrs. Peggy Ternan was picked up attemptin' to sneak back into 'er temporary lodgin's near Covent Garden Theatre. At first, she vows that nothin' 'as 'appened. 'Where's your daughter Ellen?' our man says. 'Gone to visit relatives,' the old bawd answers. 'Not good enough,' our man presses. The result, under rigorous questionin', the old 'ore takes a fright, and admits that 'er daughter 'as, in 'er words, 'left the city in the protection of a gentleman.'"

"That 'gentleman' being Ashbee." There was pain in Dickens's voice as he placed this *coda* upon Field's narrative.

With that, the coach horses reined in at the Bow Street Station.

"Keep your seats, gentlemen. This won't take long. Rogers!" Field sent his lieutenant into the building with a jab of his omnipotent forefinger.

"What do you propose to do?" I asked, with an outsider's timidity.

"We must go back to Ashbee's house, and see if she is there," Dickens's voice was stretched taut.

"She is not there," Inspector Field answered decisively, "but you are right. We must search the premises now. No time to attain permission from the Queen's Bench. A search might tell us where she 'as been taken."

In mere minutes, Sergeant Rogers returned, accompanied by the redoubtable Mister Tally Ho Thompson, who climbed into the coach, and, with a jaunty wave and a grinning "Gents," seated himself.

"If we're goin' ta be breakin' an' enterin', might as well 'ave an expert along," Field grinned across at us. Rogers climbed dourly up on the box.

MILORD'S SECRET LIBRARY

(May 9, 1851—evening)

We rattled over the cobbled streets, and soon emerged onto the moonswept high-road. Tally Ho Thompson seemed unable to suppress the singular bemusement, which kept twisting his face into a quite remarkable series of Pickwickian smirks.

"Mister Thompson is 'ere purely in an advisory capacity," Inspector Field announced some minutes after the ne'er-do-well had taken his place in the coach. "You will gain our entry into the 'ouse," Field said, giving Thompson his marching orders, "and then you will do your best imitation of Lot's biblical wife." Field punctuated that last with a stab of his forefinger into Thompson's greatcoat, and seemed quite pleased with his little metaphor. "You will not remove any negotiable objects from the premises."

"In other words," Thompson smirked, "make the crack, and turn to salt."

"Ah, a quick study," Field approved.

The coach bounced and lurched with each rut and curve in

the highroad. The night was clear, and the moon was full and white. Light pooled like fog in the open spaces. It was not a very good night for housebreaking.

"An' wot 'appens if we get caught, Cap'n? If the country sheriffs descend on us from Shooters 'Ill with pistols an' blunderbusses? They don't never go habroad without their barking persuaders. Wot will my hadvisory capacity be then, eh?" Thompson brought up the possibility calmly, fighting off his irrepressible grin of bemusement. He was clearly enjoying the discomfiture of Field at having to treat him as an equal.

Field's forefinger came up for a familiar scratch at the side of his eye. "You are under my protection," he assured Tally Ho Thompson.

"Sure I am, but just for fancy's sake, ain't it possible I'm present 'ere as a convenient way for all you gents to hedge your bets?"

With studied sarcasm, Field said: "Why, what, pray tell, can you mean?"

"I mean, Cap'n, you brought me along so that if you get caught breakin' into this posh bloke's digs, you can say it wos me, and you wos on my trail, and you come out sharp as nails, and I come out prime for a dance with Jack Ketch. That's wot *I* mean."

Field smiled a benevolent smile. "Why, Mister Thompson, you are *too* suspicious. You are on the right side of the law now." Suddenly Field's face went hard. "You are storin' up favors in 'eaven, Thompson," he said, as the forefinger scratched threateningly at the lower lip. "Don't forget that I am the Father who bestows those favors."

I was somewhat taken aback at Field's blasphemous analogy, but the redoubtable Inspector just chuckled at his own extravagance. The coach pulled up in a back lane, sheltered from view of the Ashbee estate, and from the relentless moonlight, by an overhanging arch of ancient elm trees.

The moonlight filtered through the branches of the trees, as we five housebreakers, in faith to Field's lead, traversed the forested park toward the Ashbee manse. Field led, with

184

Thompson immediately behind; Dickens and I came next, with Rogers serving as our rearguard.

Thoughts of alarm and apprehension raced through my mind. I wondered if Field and Rogers were armed with pistols, or "barkers," as Thompson called them. As we moved through the trees, I seemed surrounded by a tumult of sounds—the noises of scurrying animals, the wind, the moving branches of the trees overhead, the pounding of my own heart. I had to stop, and take a deep breath to compose myself. When I stopped, Rogers coughed a short sharp signal, and the others paused also.

"What is it?" Field whispered back at his sergeant.

"Mister Collins is blowed," Rogers whispered, with what I imagined to be a great relish. Indeed, he was right. I felt as if we had been rushing headlong. I later realized that it was the anxiety I was feeling, not the exercise, which had so winded me. We went on at a slower pace, until abruptly the forest park ended, and we reached the edge of the rolling lawns. We stopped inside the shadows of the treeline.

Tally Ho Thompson stepped forward. "When I get it open, I'll show a glim. You come straight to the light. No 'esitation. Got it?" He took great pleasure in giving orders to Field and Rogers. "Well, gennulmen, and you, too, Inspector Field," he said, his face convulsed with mischieviousness, "success to the crack." He saluted us and was gone.

We waited. The house, white in the moonlight, loomed fifty meters away across an expanse of carefully manicured lawn. *Surely we will be seen approaching the house*, my nervous mind speculated. *Surely we will make exemplary targets for the "barkers" when we attempt to cross that lawn.*

I did not have long to brood on those threatening possibilities. Thompson's light popped up almost immediately in the deep shadows of the verandah. Behind Dickens and Field, we started across that open moonlit expanse at a full run.

Only the crunch of the grass beneath the quick pad of our feet marred the marble silence of the moment. We reached the shelter of the verandah, and flattened ourselves against the wall of the house. My eyes were riveted upon Dickens and Field. Neither seemed the least bit ill at ease. As I think back upon it, both would probably have made excellent cracksmen or highwaymen, if they had not already taken up law-abiding professions. As for me, there could have been no worse cracksman in all of England. My imagination burned with images of alarm and flight and capture and public humiliation, if not death or wounding.

Yet all was perfectly quiet and serene.

"Child's play," an elfin voice chuckled out of the darkness. "No bars. Small matter of pickin' one quite undistinguished lock, an' we are in, gennulmen and public servants."

Thompson was waiting for us, calmly smoking in the darkness. The beacon light he had struck was nothing else but a Lucifer off of which he lit the stub of his cigar. "I've already been inside," he whispered. "No sign of anybody on this side of the 'ouse. Step lightly, though. You never know when they are goin' to step out of the woodwork." With a flourish he ushered us through an open door and a set of flimsy curtains into Ashbee's house. Field ordered Rogers to remain at our point of entry as a rearguard and lookout.

We stole in through a large sitting room with rugs covering the floors. Away from the windows and the moonlight, all was dark as pitch. We were forced to proceed slowly, feeling our way across that room populated with heavy malicious furniture. I barked my shin sharply upon a small table, but I did not cry out, though I cursed inwardly.

Thompson led us to the door of the room. "It opens onto the main entrance 'all of the 'ouse," he whispered. With that, he withdrew as if to say, "I've done my part, gents, now we'll see 'ow game you are."

"I know where we are. I can find the way from here," Dickens assured Inspector Field in a whisper.

What am I doing here in someone else's house in the middle of the night with these two madmen, was the unsettling thought which rooted itself in my frightened consciousness. Nevertheless, I was there, and those two seemed bent upon proceeding with this insane misadventure. It had been a terribly unsettling day for me—first Irish Meg, and now, my first felony.

We moved slowly across the foyer, boots scraping softly on the marble floor.

"Very quiet now," Field imprecated in a fierce whisper. "No stumblin' up against each other." He motioned for Dickens to take the lead down into a black tunnel, the long passageway off of which opened the rooms through which Ashbee had conducted us that afternoon. The library, if my memory served, stood at the very end of this passage. "The library," Field directed Dickens. "Both of you remarked it. We'll start there."

At the end of the hallway, Field stepped in front of Dickens, and tried the door to the library. It opened silently, and we plunged into the sort of deep blackness that exists only in windowless rooms. For a long moment, the three of us simply stood still in the silent dark immediately inside the library door. Field was probably trying to decide whether or not to strike a light. I heard a quiet movement in front of me. My eyes had not yet accustomed themselves to the impenetrable darkness. I presumed it was Field on the move.

"The picture you remarked," he whispered with some urgency. "Where?"

Neither Dickens nor I knew whom he was addressing. You could not see a thing. Consequently, we both answered almost in unison.

"Straight in from the door at eye-level," Dickens answered.

"There," I pointed stupidly, realizing, even as I did so, that Field could not see my upraised arm.

I heard Field moving again—a Lucifer struck—tiny halo of light casting monstrous shadows on the wall of books—light moves to the solitary picture hung amongst the shelves—light circles the picture—Field's hand touches the picture, moves tentatively around its edges, finally grasps the frame and pulls—picture, much to Dickens's and my surprise, tilts sideways like a lever—then something occurred for which none of us were prepared.

The whole wall began to move, and artificial light spilled into the room in which we stood. A gasp of surprise accompanied by a "Wot the bloody 'ell!" and a "Ooo in 'ell har . . . ?" greeted us as the wall pulled back to reveal a quite large book-strewn room, and an equally large startled footman staring at us. He was sitting on a large overstuffed settee, with a large oversized book on his knee. We had, evidently, surprised him in the perusal of this book.

Surprised him indeed! When he leapt to his feet, the book dropping to the oriental rug, his trousers were seen to be bunched around his ankles and his sexual member stood rampant in the grasp of his large right hand.

I must admit that my first impulse was to laughter. I am sure that Dickens and Field were equally surprised. My eyes darted from the hulking man with the drooping moustache, standing there so *in flagrante,* to the book discarded on the floor, to the bottle of Scots whiskey next to the book. We had evidently surprised this worthy in the act of amusing himself in the private perusal of one of his master's books.

This footman, whom we later assumed to be the sole remaining caretaker of the premises, was clearly startled. Yet, he kept his wits about him. He was not so startled that he was unable to reach to a nearby deal table, from whence a loaded pistol leapt into his quivering hand. To our great good fortune, he also maintained the presence of mind to only point it in our direction, not to immediately fire it wildly at us. The man, indeed, made a bizarre, quite laughable, figure standing there with a look of panic on his face, his trousers bunched around his ankles, and both hands on a duelling pistol which was jumping and jerking like a Punch and Judy puppet.

"Now." It was Inspector Field's voice. "Be calm with that," he spoke soothingly. "This is not what it seems to be. We mean you no 'arm. Please do not shoot. We are not 'ousebreakers. No bloodshed is necessary 'ere. I am Inspector Field of the Metropolitan Protectives."

"Hin huh pig's heye, you har," the moustachioed man barked as the pistol quivered precariously. Its barrel, as it bounced from Field to Dickens to myself, seemed as large and black as the new Hammersmith railway tunnel.

"Now, don't shoot. It's true. We are the detectives authorized to investigate Lord Ashbee's 'ouse," Field cajoled the man, whose half-naked state was becoming somewhat of a greater embarrassment with each passing moment.

"Master don't like no one hin 'is room," the man said, waving the cocked pistol wildly.

"Why don't you escort us out, then?" Inspector Field suggested.

With one hand, the man stooped, and pulled his trousers up. With a snap, he got one of his braces over a shoulder.

"Just escort us out, and no 'arm will be done." Somehow Field had talked himself into a negotiating position with this dolt. "Your master need never know that we got in without your knowledge, or that we found you in 'is private room."

The burly footman thought long and hard on that. It looked as if his deliberations were causing him great pain about the lips and eyebrows.

"Don't nobody move." He kept the gun pointed at us as he edged toward the door. "Cuntstables har hown the heyeroad. They'll do you!"

From this gibberish, I deduced that he meant to lock us in, and summon the local authorities to arrest us. Field darted a glance at Dickens and myself, which I found very reassuring. He seemed to be saying "Don't worry; all that this can be now is an embarrassment." I almost felt as if I were the one who had been caught with my pants down.

Ashbee's servant circled around us, the firearm still shaking in his hands, as if he were afflicted with some palsy. "Don't ye move a whit," he ordered, without conviction, as he edged toward the doorway. Field slowly nodded his head in acquiescence.

As the man with the pistol slowly backed through the doorway, his eyebrows suddenly shot up, his eyes went wide, he uttered a low, gutteral grunt, and proceeded to collapse face forward onto the oriental carpet. The pistol dropped from his hand as he fell, and bounced weakly to the side on the ornate rug. Dickens, Field, and myself stared stupidly at our fallen antagonist. Tally Ho Thompson, the source of our sudden deliverance, stepped grinning through the doorway thwacking a black gutta percha equalizer against the meat of his palm.

"Just a slight tap in the right spot behind the ear does surely relax one, wouldn't you say, gents? 'Ee'll just 'ave a good 'eadache in the mornin'," he assured us with a puckish wink.

"'Ee must not be loose in the mornin' to warn 'is master," Field was thinking aloud, nothing more. "The man knows who we are, and if Ashbee finds out we've been 'ere, 'ee'll be all the more skitterish. We must take this idiot into custody. Thompson, fetch Rogers."

Before Thompson left, he turned to Field and said, "I've checked the whole 'ouse. 'Ee" (nodding to the unconscious man) "must be the only one 'ere."

"Well," Dickens said to Field, as we all turned our attention to Ashbee's secret library, "what do you make of this?"

Ah, dear reader, how do I tell this part? There were surprises in that secret room much more startling than a frightened footman caught perusing his master's books. This memoir shall never be published in our time; thus, I should not hesitate to write candidly of what we found; and yet, by habit and instinct, I do hesitate: our age shrinks from the sort of realism which Henry Ashbee had collected there in his secret library. I was repelled by it, yet strongly attracted, let us say "fascinated," by what we found therein. It was much like my own fascination for Meggy Sheehey. I could not admit to it, yet neither could I deny it.

Within a few brief moments it was perfectly clear why Lord Ashbee chose to keep his library a secret. All the books collected there dwelt upon but one subject: 'Lust' in every conceivable perversion, in every possible locale, social class and human relationship. That library portrayed 'Lust' as the new Leviathan of our century, which would replace Hobbes's ruling passion of self-interest with the more bestial urges of man's sexuality.

You must pardon my bluntness, dear reader. I simply cannot, due possibly to lack of invention, conceive of any more tactful, less brutish, manner to describe the contents of Lord Henry Ashbee's secret library. *Memoirs of a Victorian Gentleman* indeed! His books were the memoirs, both true and clearly fictitious, of Victorian rakes, sodomists, pederasts, flagellants, ravishers, and supposed gentlemen indulging in every possible sexual perversion known to man or beast alike. Those books—illustrated, hand-copied, privately printed, mass-produced, bound in every size, every folio variation, stiff of cover as well as soft—those books were all there, some yellowed with centuries of age, some as new as the Parliamentary Blue Books or the green monthly numbers of Dickens's latest novel. There was no denying their existence, and yet, to my own utter amazement, I felt the impulse, the temptation, to deny them, to transform that infamous collection of books into something else, a collection about boats, or horses, or gentlemen's fashion. Yet, I cannot transform this reality. It is a text which cannot be undermined.

Like the outer library, the walls of this secret library were lined with shelves filled with books. But the books were not of uniform sizes bound in the standard gilt and leathers of our day, and did not form themselves into ordered symmetrical groups upon the shelves. No, these shelves were a chaos of sizes, shapes, colors, books stacked, leaned, upright, on their backs, on their sides, upside down, books coverless, spineless, books old, books brand new, books opulently bound, books tawdry in dog-eared disarray, books that were not even books, but only loose manuscript pages piled and strewn about like leaves. Other books lay in piles, some ten or fifteen volumes high, all about on the floor.

The only furniture in the room was the large settee and deal lamp table, and a quite oversized writing desk commanding the center of the room, and surrounded by the piles of books on the floor. The wide expanse of desktop was strewn with bound volumes pressed open, and loose manuscript pages scribbled upon in what seemed a hurried, perhaps fevered, hand.

Dickens and I moved immediately to the shelves, and silently studied the lascivious titles of the volumes strewn so negligently about.

"Look at this," Dickens pushed a volume at me. "My God, Wilkie, these hacks are stealing my characters for their dirty little novels."

The title of the book was *The Amorous Adventures of Sir Mulberry Hawke*.

Other titles caught my eye as I scanned those shelves: *Eveline: The Amorous Adventures of a Victorian Lady, Twemlow's Fetishes, The Birch in the Boudoir, Sub-Umbra or Sport Among the She-Noodles, Lady Pokingham, The Sultan's Pleasure Chamber, A Man with a Maid, A Season Amongst The Haycocks* and *La Rose d'Amour or the Convent of Lust*. The titles themselves were enough to bring a blush to the cheek of one perusing them.

Glancing over, I noticed Dickens reading fixedly in one of those volumes, so I, too, procured one from an immediate shelf in order to comprehend more fully the subject matter of this provocative collection. The book which came to my hand was rather cynically titled *They All Do It*, and consisted of a narrative of the events of an amorous weekend at the country estate of His Scots Lordship, Sir James Dil-Dough. If you choose, though I do not advise it, you may read along with me a brief excerpt:

> The ladies were now also divested of everything, till the complete party were in a state of buff, excepting the pretty boots and stockings, which I always think look far sweeter than naked legs and feet.
>
> The interest centred in the engagement between Bertha and Charles, as the others were all

anxious to see the working of his fine prick in her splendid cunt. He was in a very rampant state of anticipation, so she laid him at full length on his back on a soft springy sofa, then stretching across his legs she first bent down her head to kiss and lubricate the fine prick with her mouth, then placing herself right over him gradually sheathed his grand instrument within her longing cunt, pressing down upon him, with her lips glued to his, as she seemed to enjoy the sense of possessing it all. I motioned to her bottom with my finger, and Fanny, understanding my ideas, at once mounted up behind her mistress and brought the head of her well-cold-creamed dildoe to the charge against her brown-wrinkled bottom-hole, at the same time clasping her hands round Bertha, one hand feeling Charlie's fine prick, whilst the fingers of her other were tickling the fine clitoris of our mistress of ceremonies. It was a delightful tableau, and it awfully excited us all when they at once plunged into a course of most delicious fucking.

What a singular piece of writing, and what a singular use of language! I had never read a passage quite like that. Yet there it was in my hand; that scurrilous passage actually existed and there were hundreds, nay, thousands more collected there in that secret room. I returned that book to its shelf as if it were hot. Dickens, evidently possessing a greater tolerance than I for the debased use of language displayed in these books, was still reading with obvious interest. Inspector Field was not. In fact, he displayed no interest in the books whatsoever. He was prowling the room, moving the furniture, and turning things over as if they were rocks, and something might crawl out from beneath them.*

Suddenly he dove to one knee on the rug, and plucked a ball of pinkish fluff from out of the thick pile. Reaching inside his coat with his other hand, he extracted from some inner pocket a similar rag of fabric pinned to a paper card. Rising to his feet, he moved quickly to the light. Dickens joined me in staring at Inspector Field.

"She 'as been 'ere," Field declared.

"Miss Ternan? Are you certain?" Dickens asked excitedly.

"'Er red dress lay on that chair in Paroissien's room, and she sat on the couch in that same dress." He held the two tiny pieces of fabric fluff triumphantly up before Dickens's nose. "They're a perfect match!"

"I see," Dickens answered with a thorough lack of enthusiasm. "You have matched whatever you have found here on this floor to that which you found on the chair in the dead man's room, have you not?"

"Indeed I 'ave. By George, you are learnin', sir, to keep your eyes open and read the world. Wot a good detective you could be, sir."

Dickens and Field stood together, looking hard around the room for a long moment.

"Well?" Field addressed Dickens as a mentor would his student.

---

*In Steven Marcus's *The Other Victorians*, Henry Ashbee is identified as the biggest collector of pornography in nineteenth-century England. This came to light after Ashbee's death when his estate was being inventoried. Marcus even speculates that Ashbee is the author of *My Secret Life*, the 4000-page sexual autobiography of a prominent Victorian gentleman. None of the Dickens biographies examine the possibility that these two very different kinds of mid-Victorian writers knew of each other or could possibly have influenced each other. The greatest novelist and the greatest pornographer of the Victorian age in close proximity could point to a mode of influence no Dickens scholar has yet explored.

"The key to his and her whereabouts is in this room, if we can only find it and interpret it properly," Dickens answered.

"That's it!" Field assented.

"But where would he take the girl, and why, and for what purpose?" It was my voice suddenly come to life. "He was not involved in either of the murders. He does not need to protect himself."

"Or does he?" Dickens leapt upon my questions. "Is there yet some other secret hidden within this room in which both Ashbee and Miss Ternan are involved?"

"Or, perhaps, not even 'idden," Field said, joining in our wild speculations, "perhaps just sittin' 'ere before us in plain sight."

Taking that cue, we joined Field in his prowling of the room. Dickens soon discovered a door, set two steps downward, in a dark back corner among the shelves. Field tried it once but it was locked from without, so he temporarily abandoned the effort with a shrug: "Could be 'is private entrance and exit. Could go to the basement. Could go anywhere."

We prowled along each row of shelves, and stepped over each pile of books upon the floor, but there seemed no order to their arrangement. Ultimately, it was only natural that we converge upon Ashbee's writing desk. Spread out on its top were the pages, some piled neatly in an obvious order, others strewn about at random, of a handwritten manuscript.

Atop one of the ordered piles was an almost blank leaf with the manuscript's title scrawled across it: *My Secret Life: Memoirs of a Victorian Gentleman.*

Of a sudden I remembered what Ashbee had said earlier in the day, "I too am a writer, but what I write is very different from your work." The title he had given us earlier was really only the subtitle of his *magnum opus.*

"It is Ashbee's manuscript," Dickens informed Field. "I'll wager it is all written in his own hand, because it is too private to trust to the prying eyes of a secretary. I will also wager that, when finished, it will deserve its place among the others of its type upon these shelves."

"'Ee is a writer of scurrilous books, then." Field puzzled over it. "That could be a thing to wish kept 'idden."

"No," Dickens disagreed, "being the writer of this text is not what he wishes to hide, but being the man who has lived this text, now that is a secret he could not well allow to be revealed."

Dickens gathered a handful of the loose leaves spread across the desk, and began to read. Inspector Field followed suit. Not wishing to seem unobservant, I did so as well.

"Extraordinary," Dickens exclaimed after finishing only a few pages. "Extraordinary," he repeated a few more pages along. "It will never be published," Dickens finally put it down after some ten minutes of feverish reading, "but the man can write, and write well. He almost makes his own perversion seem palatable. These pages are nothing more than detailed diaries of his own sexual exploits. It appears that our friend Ashbee is an obsessive rake with a twisted literary bent."

I remember afterwards how I inquired of Dickens what he meant by the repetition of that term "extraordinary" as he read Ashbee's manuscript.

"I said that?" he seemed surprised at my question.

"Yes," I assured him.

"I could not stop reading. It was as if his narrative, his succession of sexual atrocities, drove me forward from one page to the next. As I read, I could not help but feel that the man behind those words, the man doing all of those things to those women whom he seduced or bought or simply forced, could well be me or you, Wilkie."

"The man is a pig!" Field pronounced, as the critical evaluation of his reading of the manuscript. "Tha's all this tells us. We need some facts, not these fictions."

Inwardly, I had to chuckle at Field's self-righteousness, given what Irish Meg had let slip about the Inspector's own sexual proclivities. But he shall never see this, so my joke shall remain my own.

We seemed at a temporary impasse as we stood around that large desk, fingering the loose pages of Ashbee's scurrilous manuscript. Dickens, always the curious one, began to fiddle with a quaint mechanical contraption which sat upon the cluttered desk. This common species of machine is often displayed for sale in the ruder street fairs of Petticoat Lane or St. Giles Circus. It was a model of a young girl on a swing, her skirts raised, being rudely accosted by a quite erect bear standing on its hind legs. Dickens seemed bent on making it work, but the comical machine seemed to be broken. He wound it tightly, but it refused to perform. He attempted to pick it up for a closer examination, and found it anchored to the desk top. He was about to abandon his interest when, accidentally pressing upon the bear's head, he was startled by the sudden swinging open of a concealed panel in the side of Ashbee's desk. Indeed, that small door popped open so sharply that it administered a firm slap to the fronts of Dickens's legs. That panel concealed a secret compartment. All Inspector Field could do was laugh, and shake his head at the continuous good fortune of Dickens, the amateur detective.

Secreted within this hiding place were three diary-size books bound in green leather. Field pounced eagerly upon them. "Perhaps these are the facts we 'ave been lookin' for."

The first and second of these volumes seemed nothing more than address books, listing names and places of residence. From a quick perusal of the first, the three of us decided that it was a listing of prominent procurers, bawds, whoremasters and houses of licentious entertainment. Many of the names and locations were familiar to Inspector Field, but he read with relish new names and addresses toward which his sharp hat and intimidating forefinger might point. What also surprised, however, was that this first book contained names of quite prominent London gentlemen, whom Dickens recognized right off.

"Brother rakes?" Field speculated.

The second small volume contained only the names and places of residence of women, more than two hundred, some only noted by first names, some carrying full names, some given full names plus titles or place of occupation or professional practice. Again, some very prominent and recognizable names were included therein. We all surmised the nature of this list; it could be none other than the ubiquitous Ashbee's many conquests. Field displayed little interest in this listing, while Dickens chuckled rather merrily at some of the more prominent names. Later, he would remark that it was like reading Valmont's account book in La Clos's lascivious novel.

The third miniature volume was a true diary, and it was this one which gained and held our attention. Each entry was a narrative description of a meeting of a group called the Dionysian Circle. Each entry was dated and included the names of each of the members in attendance. The number of participants varied from five or six to as many as fifteen gentlemen, and some very prominent gentlemen indeed, their places of occupation stretching from the Houses of Parliament to Lincoln's Inn to the City to the richest estates in the suburbs of London. The purpose of their meetings was presented quite straightforwardly and graphically. Their society was an organization founded for the sole purpose of staging and participating in the most elaborate sexual orgies imaginable.

"We must take these and study them," Field had found his facts. "Every name, every place of residence 'ere, is a link to Ashbee and the girl's whereabouts."

Dickens's nose was buried in the third diary. "Extraordinary," he muttered once again, "positively extraordinary!" It was unlike Charles. He was not given to flights of fulsome hyperbole. "Look at this!" He veritably leaped at us with his discovery. "Read it. It is the key."

Field took the book from Dickens and began reading where directed. "There," Dickens said, "that is what they plan for Ellen." In his excitement he forgot the formal mode of address he had previously used whenever he referred to Miss Ternan in conversation.

Following a long description of the initiation of two supposedly virgin sisters into the rites of the Circle, and the orgy

which expanded out of that brutal ceremony at the penulti-
mate meeting, appeared this passage, the final entry in the
diary:

> The Circle convened on the twenty-fifth day of
> March, 1851, at eight of the evening. Lord
> Edgeley had contrived to kidnap the young
> woman who had been discussed in our previous
> meeting and promptly convened the meeting of
> the Circle as he held her against her will in the
> basement of his city house near St. James Park.
> Twelve members accepted his invitation upon
> the assurance that she was but fifteen years of
> age, fresh from the country and exquisitely
> endowed with virgin charms as well. Full access
> to each of her different virginities was promised
> by the usual method of the drawing of lots. I
> was fortunate enough to draw her mouth and
> the number one. The girl was terrified but the
> continuous assaults upon her charms soon sub-
> dued her.

What followed was a meticulous account of the group rape of
this kidnap victim by the assembled membership of the
Dionysian Circle. Dickens, however, quickly pointed to the
final paragraph:

> The lot has fallen to me as the convener of the
> next meeting of the Circle. I have been in-
> structed to procure the delicacies for the satis-
> faction of each of our various appetites and to
> appropriately plan and choreograph the enter-
> tainments of the evening. I have in mind a play,
> a play in which the members of the Circle are
> both audience and actors, a theatre of the lewd,

with the actresses playing their roles and the
male members of the Circle taking the stage as
actors, a theatre of the real where the purely
physical drama is not simulated but is actually
performed for an audience, where art meets the
fever of the hidden life. I must choose the
proper location for my stage. There must be
room for the audience and abundant light so
that the actors' motions can be closely observed.
The Notting Hill Gate estate would be the best
but the Kensington house would also serve
quite well as would the rented apartments in
Soho if they are still available. Those details
shall be attended to after my cast is obtained and
I have written my script.

With that prefiguration of the next meeting, the diary runs out.

"The names of some of the most powerful men of the realm
are mentioned in this book," Inspector Field observed.

"This is indeed a very exclusive and aristocratic circle of
pleasure seekers, and the richness of their tastes in entertainment is matched only by the richness of their purses," Dickens
assented.

"'Tis a delicate group to deal with," Field seemed almost
hesitant.

"He means her to be the actress in his play. We must find
her, before they do to her what they have done to all of these
women before," Dickens said, and slammed the small green
leather book down on the desk. "Partlow, Paroissien, this
Dionysian Circle of rakes, they seek women out, force them to
play their parts, and when a woman refuses to follow the script,
they bend her to their will. Ellen is innocent of that murder.
That is clear to me. She was defending her honor, refusing to
play their lewd part."

Field glanced quickly at me, a look of rather strained
tolerance on his face.

"Yes, we must find 'er," Field finally assented, "but we must also be careful in 'ow we go about it. We are dealing with very powerful men. Our first charge must be to locate and place under twenty-four 'our watch each of Ashbee's residences."

Inspector Field deposited into the inner recesses of his capacious greatcoat the three small diaries. That done, I fully expected the order to break off our little experiment in housebreaking and withdraw, but one other avenue yet remained to be explored.

Field moved quickly across the secret library to the door in the back corner. "We must 'ave you open, we must," he muttered. With that he reached into the mysterious recesses of his magical greatcoat and extracted a shiny object which resembled a teaspoon with the exception that half of its bowl was cut away and the remaining edge was triply notched. Inserting this into the keyhole of the locked door, he turned it slowly backward and forth until, with a tinny snap, the spring gave and the final secret of Lord Henry Ashbee's house opened unto us. Field gave the door one small push with his massive forefinger and it swung silently open on well-oiled hinges to reveal . . . a pit of darkness.

What that pit of darkness turned out to be, was an extremely narrow stairway descending into the bowels of Ashbee's house. We needed Rogers and his trusty bull's-eye, but Inspector Field chose not to summon him. Instead, he made for the desk, and pulled three candles and a box of Lucifers out of a small side drawer. "Saw 'em when I searched the desk," he explained. "Wondered why one drawer was filled with candles."

We each in turn lit a candle, and, with Field in the lead, began our descent. As I took my first timorous step down into that dark stairwell behind the fearless Inspector and Dickens, my hand was shaking so badly that the light on the walls fluttered and flapped like public school boys at their morning exercises.

The stairway led downward beneath the house exactly twenty-two steps. We descended slowly, alert for man-traps which may have been rigged for intruders. At the bottom opened outwards an underground passageway, floored in stone with walls and ceiling of packed dirt buttressed by thick beams, rocks and heavy wooden planks. There was moisture on the rocks of the side walls, but the stone floor was dry. The tunnel appeared rather well engineered. It was a narrow passage, and barely high enough for a man to traverse without bending. Dickens had to stoop the whole way. We proceeded with our candles fluttering ever so slightly in the soft underground air currents.

The tunnel led from the house, beneath the back garden to the carriage house, a rather spacious (since Lord Ashbee had three coaches of different sizes and shapes) outbuilding which opened onto a tree-lined carriage path. A narrow stairway ascended to this carriage house. The underground passageway, however, continued on. When we reached this juncture, Field decided to ascend the steps, and inspect the carriage house.

It was an expansive functional building. Completely open within, its four roof support pillars effectively partitioned off the three carriage stalls (the stables were immediately adjacent). As we emerged from the stairwell, we first, before passing on to the open gravel carriage floor, were obliged to pass through the harness room which exuded a heavy musk of leather, saddle soap and neat's-foot oil. Passing through that spider's web of hanging reins, drying tack and harness of varying sizes and functions, we emerged on the carriage house floor. A racy black phaeton crouched in the area against the right wall. To our left, a more sedate private hansom sat patiently, an intimate closed carriage suitable for quiet evening rides through the suburban parks. The widest of the three stalls, in the center, was empty. Inspector Field went to one knee to examine the ruts in the gravel of this empty berth.

"A large and 'eavy coach rested 'ere," Field decided. "When it was pulled out, it was much 'eavier still. We are lookin' for a Brighton stage, I think, drawn by four 'orses, a vehicle suitable for long journeys.

"They departed from here then?" Dickens asked.

"So it seems," Field answered. "Shut up so that no one could observe."

"It was she, the Ternan girl, he was hiding," Dickens's voice was grim with the certainty of it.

Field nodded in agreement. His forefinger flicked at the side of his eye.

"Nothing else 'ere," he finally declared. "We must follow that tunnel to its end."

With that he turned decisively, marched to the head of the stairwell, Dickens and myself in close pursuit, and paused to relight his candle, before descending once again into the darkness.

The underground passage continued further to a terminus in another flight of narrow stairs. The door at the top of the steps contained an elaborate hinged peek-hole. The door was unlocked and gave entrance to a circular room (upon stepping outside through the building's only door we found that it was a shuttered gazebo set in the midst of a heavily wooded, totally secluded forest glade). The room was furnished with rounded couches which fit precisely the contours of the walls, small tables to hold refreshments, and a large circular bed precisely in its center.

"A place for secret sport," Field speculated, glancing at Dickens.

"The bed is almost like a stage," Dickens rasped, "a place for performances to be viewed by an audience seated all around."

"This special room, the underground passageway, it is a place specially built for arrivin' and leavin' without bein' seen. Ashbee 'eld 'is more exotic affairs in this room," Inspector Field ruminated aloud. "Milord certainly goes to great lengths to keep 'is peculiar lifestyle secret, don't 'ee?" Field finished with a cynical chuckle that said *'is secrets won't be secret for long if I've got any say in it.*

"He's an inhuman fiend," Dickens spoke with slow intense heat. "He must be stopped."

Lord Ashbee's secret life had, indeed, been unearthed, but the man himself, and the girl Ellen Ternan, had flown. That house had given up all its secrets. Now, if those secrets could be properly decoded, they could lead us to the nobleman-rake and the actress-murderess who was either his prisoner, or his willing whore. We made our way back through the woods to our secreted coach. To our great surprise, another coach had pulled up beside ours. Constable Rogers and Tally Ho Thompson leaned against this second coach, smoking and whispering to another black-coated, stiff-hatted Constable. The Ashbee butler, still blissfully unconscious, lay cuffed to a wheel on the ground.

"Well, Gatewood," Field barked. "Well, where are they? Where did the coach go?"

The man, Constable Gatewood, faced Inspector Field with the look of a man facing the guillotine. "We lost 'im, sir," he admitted.

A look of inexpressible loss and despair tore at Dickens's eyes, drew his lips backward in a painful gasp of fear.

"We was blocked by a wagon driven by one of 'is 'irelings." Gatewood described it, though no one but me seemed to be listening. "On the 'eye-road into London. We searched but we could not pick up the trail."

"We'll pick up the trail, don't you worry," Field said, patting the purloined notebooks in his greatcoat pocket.

NOT SO GOOD AS WE SEEM

(May 10, 1851—evening)

This memoir now begins to move apace. Events tumbled so rapidly upon one another, that neither Dickens nor myself had time for cool deliberation upon our roles in the drama. Dickens's responsibilities, to *Household Words*, to his play in rehearsal for the Queen's benefit, to his family, pressed upon him while, simultaneously, Inspector Field pressed the hunt for the young woman, who was, I greatly suspected, the one responsibility which, for Dickens, overshadowed all of the others.

As for me, thoughts of Irish Meg preyed upon my mind. She was not at my flat when I returned from our little adventure in house burglary. She had let herself out, leaving no message. I had great difficulty sleeping that night. She danced in my waking dreams, threatening to expose every flaw in my hypocritical "gentleman's" disguise.

Tossing upon that barren bed across that long night, I realized that both Dickens and myself were pursuing our darker selves, in the forms of these elusive women. Both Dickens and myself were attempting to prove our courage (I as lover? he as protector?). We were attempting to express those inexpressible desires, which our very age refused to acknowledge as even existing. The revelations offered up by Milord's secret library had been shocking and profound. They tortured my faculties that long and sleepless night. How different in our longings after our Ellens and our Meggys were Dickens and myself from Ashbee? How different in wanting to act out exalted romantic fantasies, or stage much darker dramas?

I did not come to my senses until the lights went up on our makeshift stage in the music room at Devonshire House that evening. The rehearsal of *Not So Bad As We Seem* went well. Dickens conducted it briskly. He acted his scenes with a grim intent, as if he felt some relief at being able to lose himself in his other stage selves: the demanding stage manager, the actor, the character in Bulwar's play, a Lord of the Realm caught in somewhat embarrassing circumstances. Yet, he moved through the rehearsal without his usual humor, his quick and cutting wit. It was as if he were suppressing a restless agitation of the soul which longed for some resolution.

Forster was his usual dour self, sleepwalking through his part. Mark Lemon did his usual cutting up (falling to his knees and pleading in the terms of Falstaff's "Banish" speech when he forgot or misremembered his lines). Dickens, however, seemed oddly unaffected, aloof from all the little nuances which make life on the stage a worthwhile lark. It was as if we were all apparitions in one of his dreams, and he was waiting for the moment when he would awaken from us, and reenter the real world.

It was she who was on his mind. All the rest was merely social duty. I must confess that when I thought of Dickens possessing his Ellen Ternan, I envisioned a great man undone; a Lear perhaps, or an Agamemnon; a strong, powerful man reduced to nothing by *la belle dame sans merci*.

At the end of the rehearsal, as the cast, in high spirits, was breaking up, he took me aside, his co-conspirator.

"I must see the girl's mother. She is in the custody of Inspector Field for questioning this night at Bow Street," he said with that breathless excitement of the hunter in his voice. "I must observe her. That old whore is responsible for these attempts to debase her daughter; I am sure of it. Let us postpone our dinner. Let us take a cab to Bow Street directly. Let us hear the old bawd's story for ourselves."

He offered this agenda without the slightest doubt that I, as ever, would immediately assent, and that we two amateur detectives would hail a cab, and set off once again for another evening of underworld reality.

Thus, dear reader, you can only imagine how taken aback Dickens was when I declined his offer!

"I will not accompany you tonight." Dickens's eyebrows raised. "I am exhausted. I have barely slept in the last three days," I lied. "Beyond that," I continued in a weaseling way, "I am, temporarily, heartily sick of the sordidness of this affair, and, for this night at least, it is my desire to avoid hearing the protestations of that corrupt old whore. I need a respite from it, Charles. Tomorrow I will be a new man, your faithful bulldog, and we will walk out wherever you choose, but tonight I must decline."

He shrugged, trying to hide his disappointment.

I must digress. I made feeble excuses because I could no

longer stand the torments of my own fantasies. In truth, I did not accompany Charles to Bow Street because I had to see Irish Meg again.

Yet, I had no idea what I wanted to say. In no way had I been able to subdue my desire for her (yet no gentleman could allow himself to articulate such feelings for one of her debased station in life). Conversely, I had been totally unsuccessful in convincing myself to put her off. Rejecting her became a rejection of myself, of whatever potential for becoming a true novelist I entertained. I remembered Lemon's favorite speech: *Banish Lemon, Banish Forster, Banish Dickens, Banish Field, but Banish Irish Meg Sheehey was something I could not do.*

The disappointment showed on Dickens's face. He had come to take for granted that I would always consent to accompany him on whatever nocturnal adventure he chose. Yet, he was gracious: "You must come to *Household Words* tomorrow morning, and I will recount the old bawd's story to you."

"I'll be there." We shook hands resolutely upon it.

Despite my protestations of fatigue, I did not return to my empty flat. I set off at a brisk pace, hoping to collect my thoughts as I walked, toward Covent Garden.

The night air was damp and the streets were foggy. Ill-smelling winds blew off the Thames sending waste paper and biting clouds of dirt hurtling through the atmosphere. I had gotten so familiar with the West End streets from accompanying Dickens upon his night walks that I did not even have to think in my progress toward Covent Garden. The walk allowed me total preoccupation with my thoughts, yet when I arrived, I had made no progress whatsoever. I had learned to move with ease through the landscape of my outer world, but my inner world was like a labyrinth in which I felt irretrievably lost.

I felt confident that Irish Meg would be plying her trade in the vicinity of Covent Garden this night, either as an agent of Inspector Field or as a testament to her higher status due to Field's sponsorship.

I took up a post in the deep black shadows of the mouth of

a small mews opening into the wide back carriage court of the Covent Garden Theatre. Other whores strolled about. Horses coughed and stamped in the damp night air. Coachmen and postilions loitered about smoking and laughing to pass the time. *What if she has already enticed a rich customer*, the thought festered. A gnarled flowerwoman scuttled across the court, singing "Derry Derry Da, Derry Da, Derry Da," in a mad wavering voice.

As I watched from the darkness, I could not help but think of how I was creating a kind of fiction. I had often felt I was a character in one of Dickens's novels, but this night I was no longer Dickens's character; I had become my own. Yet, I was still but a character in a fiction, not yet real.

Three gaslamps in a line down the middle of the court struggled against the blackness of the sky, and the shifting clouds of fog. The haloed light dropped bright cones of illumination to the bases of the posts upon which they were mounted. Only the aimless whores and the loitering servants moved in and out of these tiny islands of artificial light. I stepped for a moment out of the shadows, and consulted my new gold repeater. Back in the shelter of the dark, I calculated that *Macbeth* was still in the fourth act.

And then she was there.

I had glanced away for but a brief moment and somehow she had materialized beneath the center lamppost. She leaned, with her back to the post, as if that narrow cone of light was her enchanted circle. She wore her usual exceedingly low-cut gown. The whiteness of the tops of her breasts reflected like a pool upon which the tigerish beauty of her face floated. The gaslight caught her hair and set it aflame. She posed, motionless, the stuff of men's dark dreams. My eyes were drawn to her as a ship to the Lodestone Rock, or a sailor to a siren's song.

Things never work out in reality the way one envisions them in dreams. I started forward out of the shadows of my place of concealment to greet her. However, as I moved toward her in the fog, she straightened and greeted a figure emerging from the backstage door of the theatre. I recognized Tally Ho

Thompson as he sauntered languidly into Meg's lamp light, and lit a cigar by means of a Lucifer struck upon the post.

Since I wished to speak to Meg alone, I quickly withdrew once again into the shadows. I remembered that Thompson's character died violently in Act Three; thus, his evening's work was completed. They engaged in quite natural-looking conversation. I wondered if they were both still on duty for Inspector Field. The only hint of intimacy occurred when she reached for Thompson's cigar, took it from his hand, and drew deeply upon it. They both laughed as she exhaled a large puff of grey smoke.

Impatient, I abandon my safe shadows, and once again started for Meg's charmed circle of light. My intention was to lure her away from her conversation with Thompson by means of some pretext. Before I had advanced more than five steps, the whole composition of the scene changed.

A tall buxom woman suddenly stepped out of the shadows to stand glaring at the two of them. She pointed at Thompson, and began to scream in short violent bursts.

"Oi've 'eerd yee're han hactor on stage. 'At makes yew too good for the likes o' me, don' it now?"

The heads of both Thompson and Irish Meg snapped around to look at the screaming woman. I stopped in my tracks, half in shadow, half out.

"Or mebbe yew like yee're fine uptown 'ores better, his that hit?" The woman, her face livid, spat her accusing question at Thompson.

"Bess, wot's wrong?" Thompson tried to placate this flaming virago. "I'm workin' for Fieldsy. I 'aven't been able to drop in at Rats' Castle because I'm on a job for Fieldsy. Hit was this or Newgate, you see."

"Yee belong in Newgate for talkin' to the likes o' this slut."

Irish Meg recoiled at the insult, but quickly recovered. "You dirty 'ore," Meg hissed back, "you smell of the scum of the river where yee'll end up, floatin' with the other dust."

At that, in blind jealousy and rage, Scarlet Bess, screaming vile words, which I cannot reproduce even in this private memoir, advanced upon Irish Meg, as one might imagine the Yorkshire Ripper vaulting out of the mist upon his unsuspecting victim.

There was madness, but there was also something exotic and strangely comic about her headlong charge. Thompson took a placating stance in front of Irish Meg, both hands upraised. Scarlet Bess launched herself at him from a yard or two away, and the speed of her charge took them both to the ground, where she proceeded to flail wildly at his head and shoulders with both her small fists.

I stood, mouth agape, a motionless spectator.

Thompson, wrestling her roughly across his body, extricated himself from her fists.

Meggy, inadvisedly, grabbed handfuls of Scarlet Bess's blazing hair, and dragged that virago across the stones away from Tally Ho Thompson, who righted himself, displaying the most inexplicable reaction that I could imagine.

He arose laughing, gasping out great shouts of hilarity, as the two whores rolled on the ground, pummelling each other and tearing at each other's hair. Curiously, Thompson made no motion to intervene. He simply stepped back, and watched them fight.

Irish Meg got in the first yanks and chops, but Scarlet Bess was much taller and stronger, and, when she righted herself after Meg's initial mastery from behind, proved more than a formidable foe. When she got to her feet, and turned to fight, her face was so twisted with pain and jealousy and rage, that she looked like one of the damned in Scarlatti's disturbing illustrations of Hall's English translation of Dante's *Inferno*.

She descended upon Irish Meg like some rabid animal, clawing, tearing, flailing her fists madly. Meg was not prepared for so fierce an onslaught, and was driven to the ground. She did, however, manage to grasp her attacker about the legs, and drag her down to the paving stones as well.

I advanced upon the two women rolling about on the ground. Each was struggling to regain her feet. As Scarlet Bess got to her knees, Irish Meg lunged up, and managed a rather stiff handful of the front of Bess's gown. The whole top of the larger woman's dress came away in Meg's hand and, when released, fluttered in tatters at Scarlet Bess's waist. The result was the complete exposure of Scarlet Bess's more than impressive breasts. Thompson's eyes went wide, and an angelic grin spread across his face. I, once again, felt anchored in my boots, knowing not what to do.

Instinctively (out of a momentary modesty), Scarlet Bess hugged herself, all arms and elbows, in the attempt to cover the rolling milky expanse of her exposed breasts. With Bess's arms thus involved, Irish Meg seized the opportunity to scramble to her feet, and, standing over the other, drew back and hit her in the face with her closed fist.

Scarlet Bess reeled backward, her arms splaying out as if she were being mounted on a cross. She shook her head once, twice, and then, much to Meg's surprise, struggled to her feet, bare breasts gloriously unattended, to once again square off. Now her face was no longer twisted in jealousy and hate, but had gone cold and murderous. She advanced upon Irish Meg, claws crooked before her, fangs bared.

Meg, wisely, decided to retreat. She turned to run, but was not quick enough. With a wild dive, Scarlet Bess grasped two handfuls of the back of Irish Meg's skirts and dragged her to the ground.

In a frantic effort to escape the mad virago's grasp, Meg attempted to crawl away on her hands and knees, but succeeded only in causing the whole bottom portion of her gown to tear away. Since, as befits her profession, she typically wore few, if any, fitted underclothes (and this being an "if any" evening), there she was crawling away across the stones gloriously naked from the waist down. I must admit that an irresistible heat began to gather in my body as I observed these two women, their clothes in such total disarray. A crowd began to gather, coachmen, postilions, the other whores. No one seemed in the least inclined to intervene.

Cockney yells of "The big 'un 'ull taker 'er!" and "The Irish wench fights for her life!" and "A bob says hits the one with the bouncin' bubs!" and "tuppence on that bare white arse!" They were actually placing wagers on the outcome of this catfight.

I looked at Tally Ho Thompson.

He grinned back stupidly at me.

"We must do something!" I shouted above the din of the crowd. "This is barbaric."

"What ho, barbaric!" he pushed through the crowd to my side.

"We must stop them," I persisted. "They'll kill each other."

"No such chance," Thompson talked through his ever-present smug grin. "Wenches only kill their men and their 'usbands."

He seemed quite proud of this observation. My amazed silence evidently persuaded him to continue to wax philosophical.

"There can't be" he continued, "no better show than two mad 'ores in a good fight. Hit 'as ev'rything! Sex. Violence. Flesh. Blood. Where else can you see a broad white arse like that 'un" (as Irish Meg careened by on her hands and knees) "stickin' out with its owner payin' no attention to hit (or to yew)? This is just where it really gits good," he protested, "when they start pullin' each other's bubs, an' slappin' each other's bums, an' tearin' out great swatches of 'air."

I glared at him in disbelief. I considered shaking that stupid unconcerned grin off his face. He must have caught the displeasure in my look, because he quickly changed his careless stance.

"Seems a shame we're goin' to 'ave to step in," he admitted grudgingly, "but I guess we will."

At that very moment, Irish Meg lunged at Scarlet Bess's face with the probable intention of clawing out her eyes. She missed her mark but her sharp nails raked down across her adversary's neck and bared breasts, leaving long reddening welts which turned almost immediately to scarlet lines of blood. Driven to madness by the sight of her own bleeding breasts, Bess struck out at Meg with a downward chop of her closed fist which caught that worthy on the side of the neck and drove her with great force into the cobbled ground.

Irish Meg, much the smaller of the two, was stunned, able to rise only to one knee.

Scarlet Bess, blood streaming from her raked breasts, fell upon her, pummelling with both fists.

It was then that Thompson and myself made the mistake of stepping in.

We first attempted to pull Bess off of the seemingly dazed and defenseless Irish Meg. No sooner had we disentangled the two, than Irish Meg leapt to her feet and, in complete control of her physical powers yet carried away by blind rage and pain, vaulted onto Tally Ho Thompson's back. Feeling this mad beast clawing at him from behind, and afraid for his sight, my ally Thompson immediately abandoned his hold upon Scarlet Bess, and swung sharply away in the attempt to throw his tormentor from her position of dominance astride his back. In so doing, however, he left me at the mercy of his raging mistress. In but a moment, I found myself outmanned. Bess was a full head taller, and every bit as strong as I.

I attempted to maintain my hold on her arm, but she swung me around as a bargeman swings his bowline. I held on tenaciously, but the violent centrifugal force spun us both to the ground. She landed heavily atop me in a most indecorous manner. The fact of the matter is that as we tumbled both of her arms surrounded my head and crushed it to her naked chest. As a consequence, I was pummelled about the ears by the unrestrained mounds of her wildly swinging breasts.

Thompson was faring no better. Unable to shake off the enraged Meg clinging to his back and clawing blindly at his face, he was dancing as if on fire. Slapping frantically behind him with one hand at the white flesh of his tormentor's bare *derriere,* and desperately fending off with his other her attempts to claw out his eyes, he resembled a berserk windmill.

Ultimately, the blind violence of these initial grapples gave way to a brief surcease. All four of us wrestled out of each other's grasps, and struggled to our feet. Scarlet Bess glared down at me from what seemed a quite imposing height. Letting loose a volley of curses, the two enraged whores renewed their hostilities. For some reason they had forgotten their hatred for each other, and made Thompson and myself the fresh objects of their rage.

Bess charged down upon me. I backed away, raising my hands in an attempt to placate her. Moving close upon me, she stopped abruptly, and, giving a slight feint with her hands, which caused me to raise my arms to ward off the expected blow, she suddenly kicked out with her right foot, landing an excruciatingly sharp blow to a most vulnerable area of my lower abdomen. Her kick doubled me over with pain, and I felt my knees buckling irretrievably beneath me. I collapsed to the ground with an instinctive movement in which my knees sought my chest as a means of protecting my already bruised vulnerability. At last, Scarlet Bess did not hesitate to kick me once again sharply and ignominiously in the backside.

As I looked up from my humiliating position amongst the paving stones, I saw Thompson sparring with Irish Meg a few feet away. He was attempting to hold her off with a series of sharp pushes to her shoulders. Yet, even as he seemed to be gaining a toehold against Meg's mad rushes, unbeknownst to him Scarlet Bess was descending fiercely upon him from his blind side.

The force of her rush carried all three to the ground in a heap of flailing arms, kicking legs and scandalously cursing female tongues. I righted myself, and hobbled to Thompson's aid. The two women were atop him. For some unexplainable reason, Thompson was laughing maniacally. I bent to pull Irish Meg off, sharp pains shooting upward all the way to my chest as I did so, when the whole fiasco took an unpredicted turn.

The police arrived.

Two constables of the Protectives, in their black hats and brass-buttoned black coats, rushed in through the crowd with their truncheons drawn in preparation for the worst specimen in street violence, public mayhem and murder. What they

214

found was two half-naked whores purposefully assaulting two rather badly disheveled gentlemen.

"Halt!" shouted the larger, plumper of the two constables, brandishing his truncheon. We stopped our fighting, and faced the two constables.

"Cover thyselves, women!" the thin, long-faced constable, staring wide-eyed at Meg and Bess in all their fleshly glory, ordered haltingly.

"With what, you bloody poof?" Irish Meg spat back as she stood, wearing nothing below her waist, save her short stockings and pumps.

The two constables were struck dumb by her outburst. With the most comical looks on their faces they stared first at us, then at the crowd. One of the whores from the crowd of on-lookers retrieved Meg's tattered skirt and tossed it over the heads of the two Protectives to her. Without ceremony, before everyone, she wriggled into it. In the meantime, Bess was hugging the tatters of her bodice around her wounded breasts.

The fat constable looked at the thin constable. The thin, lantern-jawed constable shrugged helplessly. Without even attempting to gather any explanations, the two constables, brandishing their truncheons to cut a path through the harmlessly curious crowd, marched all four of us off to—where else?—Bow Street Station.

Proceeding at a brisk march under the prodding of constables Lomas and Hovde, as I later ascertained their names, we arrived at Bow Street with little delay. So quickly, indeed, that I barely had opportunity to marshal my wits, and consider how I was going to explain myself to Dickens and Field, whom I knew would be there, though hardly expecting my arrival in custody.

There was little need for concern on my part, however. When the four of us entered the station, Rogers was on the desk. When our two dutiful escorts began to announce us, Rogers, with a smug look of triumph on his insufferable face, abruptly arose and disappeared into the bullpen. Inspector

Field and Charles returned with him immediately to confront the four of us lined up in our various degrees of disarray.

Field looked at Dickens.

Dickens looked at Field.

They both looked at that super-efficient monster, Serjeant Rogers.

And, in a moment, they all three burst into uproarious laughter.

Thompson, whose insolent grin had never been subdued throughout any of these proceedings, was, to my amazement, laughing right along with them.

At this turn of events, Meg and Bess, glancing toward each other as if for permission, began to emit small giggles.

I alone found the situation no laughing matter. The unmentionable pain inflicted by Scarlet Bess's kick was just beginning to subside. I knew I would be sore for days. I was thoroughly embarrassed at having been arrested in such low company. And now my closest friend and patron was laughing at my discomfiture. Worst of all, I was forced to observe the satisfaction that puppet, Rogers, was taking in my humiliation.

"Why Wilkie, I thought you were returning to your rooms for a quiet evening with a book and a glass of sherry," Dickens taunted.

"You seem to 'ave become tangled up in one of London's nighttime adventures, Mister Collins," Inspector Field added.

"I was but an innocent stander-by when this whole misunderstanding occurred," I protested much too soberly for their giddy mood.

At that, Meg burst out with a mocking laugh and a garbled comment of derision that sounded like "insentmybloodywhitearseewas!"

Field dismissed Constables Lomas and Hovde with a "well 'andled, men," which seemed to satisfy their curiosity as to their superior's strange reaction to their prisoners. Then Field quickly reinstituted the businesslike atmosphere of the stationhouse which had been usurped by the intrusion of this French farce.

"Thompson," Field barked, without ever raising his voice, "explain the situation to your meddlesome mistress. Make it clear I'll brook no more interference from 'er. Then send 'er 'ome."

"Meg, sit on that bench!" he ordered *sotto voce* with a quick stab of his decisive forefinger.

Thompson took the thoroughly intimidated Scarlet Bess aside.

"Mister Collins," Inspector Field said, turning lastly to me, "no doubt you will wish to join Mister Dickens and myself. We were just about to dive down into a most interestin' document."

I followed him and Dickens sheepishly through the door to the bullpen. As I was leaving that front room of the station-house I could not help, like Lot's wife, but glanced backward at my fellow partners in crime. Thompson and Scarlet Bess were kissing tenderly in the far corner. Irish Meg, her head lowered, sat like an abandoned waif on a bench against the front wall.

Inside the door, Field stopped as if having a second thought. I was the last of us through the door, and when he turned to address me, I felt like one of his criminals about to be accused. But his face broke into a mischievous grin, and he said, "Mister Collins, would you please ask your accomplice, Mister Thompson, to step in with us?"

I turned quickly back to the duty room, quite willing to take orders from Inspector Field now that I had gotten a brief taste of the criminal life. I motioned to Thompson who was still standing against the wall with Scarlet Bess, and waited for him in the doorway. Strangely, we had become comrades in crime, and a new ease of association and communication had developed between us, the gentleman-writer and the highwayman-actor. As he moved to join me in the doorway, he guided Scarlet Bess to the bench, and sat her down next to Irish Meg, who had been sitting there forlornly the whole time. When we left the room to join Dickens and Field by the hearth, the two women were deposited next to each other in apparent peace.

Dickens was already seated when we arrived, a small sheaf of papers resting on his crossed knees. Field was standing with his back to the fire, warming himself.

"Mister Dickens and myself were just beginnin' to examine the testimonies of Missus Peggy Ternan, the mother of our suspicioned murderess, when you gentlemen arrived so cleverly. What did occasion your arrival in custody, might I ask?" Field's insatiable curiosity had certainly gotten the better of his discretionary impulses.

"The two 'ores got in a 'air-puller," Thompson answered without the slightest hesitation. "Over me, I suppose," he added with the insolence that always governed his facial expression.

"Oh, two 'ores in love, is it now?" Field mocked him. "Fightin' over a grand gentleman like yourself?"

"That's it, guv," Thompson remained totally unbowed.

Field, seeing that he could not intimidate Thompson, glanced quickly to me. For some reason, whether out of continuing curiosity or spite, he decided to pursue the subject in this new quarter. "And you, Mister Collins, 'ow were you mistaken for a member of this ring of criminals?"

I laughed nervously. "I happened to be passing by at the very moment the two women fell upon one another," I said, trying to control the tremor in my voice. "It was barbarous. Thompson and I were merely trying to pull them apart when the Constables mistook us for participants in the riot."

"Yes, of course," Field, realizing that he was going to get no worthwhile entertainment from either of us, said dourly.

"You know 'ow it is, sir. 'Ores in love, you know," Thompson got in one last taunt at his master.

"Sit down, Thompson," Inspector Field ordered. "I want you to 'ear what Mister Dickens is about to read. I still may be able to use you in this affair."

It was then that Dickens said a strange thing, which, as I look back upon it, may have been directed toward my ears only. "A harlot in love," he said it in a soft, contemplative tone. "Have you gentlemen ever considered a harlot capable of love? Have you ever considered a harlot human?"

THE BAWD'S TESTIMONY

(May 10, 1851—mid-evening)

If there was one skill for which Dickens had a marvelous facility, it was his continuing ability to read (and I am sure, write) shorthand or "law scribble" as the clerks and reporters in Chancery Lane had called it for centuries. It had been fifteen years since Dickens had been one of their number, yet he had not forgotten one single cipher. In the hour that followed my embarrassing arrival at Bow Street, Dickens read us aloud a dialogue narrative out of a Protectives constable's transcript, a narrative of venality and degradation and falsehood that made the savageries of Mister Lyell's prehistoric animal packs pale by comparison.

Field had conducted the interrogation of Mrs. Peggy Ternan, but he called Rogers in and charged us all to listen to Dickens's reading, to evaluate the information dragged out of the creature, and to ready any suggestions as to our next move in the case.

"We might's well 'ave everyone 'ere for this," Field interjected just before Dickens was about to step off with his reading. "Rogers," he ordered, "bring in Irish Meg. She's in this up to 'er bubs. If Thompson's tall lass is still out there, send 'er 'ome."

The door opened. I caught a glimpse of Meg and Bess sitting like sisters on the bench. Meg was ushered in, but I dared not look at her. I wondered if all the others in the room had noticed my agitation in her presence, and were secretly laughing at me behind their hands.

"This testermoney is the old bawd's own words as best we

could get 'em down," Field said, introducing the entertainment. "She is bein' 'eld in custody, as is the butler we surprised in Lord Ashbee's private library. They'll not 'ave the oppertunity to warn any of our principals in this case. Mister Dickens 'as kindly consented to read 'em out for us, my voice bein' summat tired from 'agglin' with the old 'ore all day."

With that, Dickens stood and commenced. After only a few questions and answers, his voice began to take on the opposed characters of the two antagonists in the dialogue. His rendition of Field's dominance and contempt and bullying power was consistent and relentless and measured. His characterization of the creature's answers was quirky and fluctuating, coy and fearful, full of the chameleon postures of an accomplished actress. I had heard Dickens give speeches in his own persona to full rooms, but this was the first time I had ever heard him read aloud in any sort of dramatic circumstance. Since then—is it not ironic?—this sort of dramatic reading became almost his life. Countless times in the years before his death I sat spellbound as he read aloud *The Christmas Carol* or the murder of Nancy to halls jammed with people as motionless and straining to catch every word as was I that evening.

What follows in its entirety, including some of Dickens-the-actor's gestures and voice inflections, is the old bawd's testimony which he read that night:

> Q: To begin, state your name, missus.
> A: I am Margaret Ternan, abandoned wife of Patrick John Ternan, run off to Australia now these twelve years since.
> Q: You are called Peggy by your familiars?
> A: I am.
> Q: State your place of occupation.
> A: Presently, Covent Garden Theatre in the

company of Mister William Macready.
(haughtily) I am an actress.

Q: (clearly losing or pretending to lose his
temper) You are an old whore who will do
anything for money!

A: That's a lie! You have no right . . .

Q: Quiet, woman! You are under oath. You
can be taken up and placed in prison
under no charge for an indefinite time for
lying to me in this room.

A: (sullen silence)

Q: (Dickens paused, as if he were Inspector
Field gathering his temper in the face of
the old bawd's insolence. When he resumed, it was in a very measured yet harsh
tone of voice. He was truly becoming the
role he was reading; he was feeling all of
Field's anger in the face of the woman's
sullenness.) Madam, you have a daughter,
one Ellen, who also works in Mister Macready's company?

A: Yes, I do.

Q: What is your daughter's age?

A: Sixteen years this July next.

Q: Is she not rather young to be working
nightly in the theatre?

A: She is very talented and wise for her age,
and Mister Macready has marked her skill.

Q: (The creature had been lulled into a false
ease of conversation by Field's subdued
line of questioning.) Madam, where is
your daughter right now?

A: (He virtually spat the words into her up-
turned face and she recoiled from the clear
evidence of his harnessed hatred.)

Q: Where is the girl? (He pressed the
woman.)

A: I do not know. At home, in our rooms, for all I know. (The professional actress was finding difficulty in carrying off her role in the face of both Dickens's/Field's vehemence.)

Q: Speak, you lying old slut. Where is she? You know and you shall tell or you will never step upon a stage again but for the high stage at Horsemonger Lane Gaol as a member of Jack Ketch's company. Where is she? (Dickens pronounced the last almost tenderly with a break in his voice and lapse from his part.)

A: (The woman cowers before his anger. Her voice shakes.) She is safe.

Q: Do not toy with us. Your daughter is suspected of murder. You are taken up as an accomplice to that crime.

A: I know nothing of what you speak.

Q: You know everything, and you will tell me all, or I will personally see that you rot in Newgate until the day that you swing at the end of a rope.

Dickens's reading had taken on a life of its own. I could not help but recoil from the violence in the Field character's voice, as, in my imagination, he towered over the cowering woman character. Yet, the woman, if she can be characterized by that supposedly gentle term, persisted in her lies, her unpacking of all her actress's tricks.

A: Your threats are empty. I have done nothing.

Q: You have done everything.

A: I and my daughter are innocent.

Q: You are as innocent as the whore of

Babylon, you lying wretch. Where is the girl?

A: She is safe. She has a protector.

Q: Lord Ashbee?

A: (At the mention of that name, Dickens's woman character is startled. She answers haltingly.) Yes, Milord is our patron. (The old whore stares at Inspector Field with a new-found respect and fear. He knows more than she suspected. He has trapped her. She is not ready for his next question. Field stabs hard where she is unguarded.)

Q: Did your daughter Ellen kill Paroissien the stage manager?

A: (The woman goes white. *He knows all. How can I escape? He truly means to hang us both.* Yet, she hangs tenuously to her role, her actress's mask.) No. (She begins weakly.) No, never. Ellen is but a child. (Her voice trembles at the maternal guise it struggles to assume.)

Q: A child whom you sell to whoever is willing to pay?

A: Sell? My own child? (She is all actress now.)

Q: Did you sell your child to Lawyer Partlow who was murdered?

Q: Did you sell your child to Paroissien for increased favor on the stage?

Q: Did you sell your child as a love slave to Lord Henry Ashbee?

Q: Did you, you foul whoremonger?

Q: Did you? Did you sell her?

(Field screams each question at the woman. She sits cowering. *He knows all.* She breaks. Tears flow, not stage tears induced by astringents rubbed across the

223

eyes, tears of fear of Field who stands over her in a rage.)

A: They vowed to protect her, to use her well, never to turn her out.

Q: (in soft cajoling voice) They gave you money to protect her?

A: They did.

Q: You took her to them—Partlow, Paroissien, Ashbee—left her with them, and they gave you money?

A: Only Milord Ashbee. (The woman still retains some faint hope of escape, still contrives to lie. This is a grievous error in the world of Inspector Field.)

Q: Only Milord Ashbee?

A: Yes, Lawyer Partlow died, God rest, before he ever became my daughter's protector.

Q: Paroissien? Did he not threaten you with dismissal from the Covent Garden company? Did he not offer you a plum role in Mister Macready's next play? Did he not promise your daughter's advancement as an actress?

A: We had no dealings with Stage Manager Paroissien. The man was a pig. The world is better for his death.

Q: Did you or your daughter kill Mister Paroissien?

A: No. No. We had no dealings with Paroissien.

Q: (Field steps back. His forefinger goes slowly to scratch at the side of his eye. A triumphant grin spreads menacingly across his face. He speaks softly.) You never saw Paroissien the night he was murdered.

A: We surely saw him at the theatre.

Q: After the play was done?

A: No. I went nowhere near the man.

Q: And your daughter?

A: No. I do not know. (Confusion was upon her.) We did not leave the theatre together that night.

Q: (Field pounces.) You lie, wretch! Don't you ever lie to William Field again! (His voice slowed, became almost rational.) You were seen and followed, the three of you, Paroissien, your daughter, your miserable self. You were both with the man. He was murdered later that evening.

A: (The woman stared blankly at Field. Dickens made it so real, timed each pause, mastered each emotional inflection of voice, that I felt I was there.)

Q: Did Paroissien offer you money for her also? Were you double dealing? Selling your daughter secretly to Paroissien for one night's use before selling her permanently to Ashbee?

A: No. Yes. Yes, we were with him. He gave me money over dinner when Ellen retired to make water. We took a hackney coach to his lodgings. I left Ellen there with him.

Q: Did you go up to his rooms?

A: No, I pretended I was late for an engagement. I left them in the cab, and hailed another. She protested being left in his protection. He vowed to see her home. She returned to our lodgings alone. She had been running in her stage slippers.

Q: How was she dressed? As you had left her?

A: No.

Q: How, woman?

A: She wore only her cape and slippers.

Q: She was naked beneath her wrap?

A: Yes.

At that Field paused, to contemplate his next question, I am sure.

Q: Did you go back to Paroissien's?
A: Yes. In a cab.
Q: Did you go up to his rooms?
A: Yes. (The creature stared at the floor and her answers had faded to a weak whisper.)
Q: Did your daughter, Ellen, go up with you?
A: No.
Q: She refused?
A: Yes.
Q: She remained in the cab?
A: She did. (The woman seemed intent upon giving the shortest, least revealing answers. Impatience was beginning to strain at the control in Field's voice.)
Q: Why? What reason did she give for refusing to return to his rooms for her clothes?
A: (No answer was forthcoming. The old bawd stared viciously at Field. She was cornered and she knew it.)
Q: Speak, you bloody whore! (Field lashed out at her.) Tell me all, or you will be in Newgate before the hour is out.
A: I don't know the whole truth of it. The girl was queer, quiet queer. All she told I had to wring out of her. (The bawd fell strangely silent. Was she composing her next lie?) The child spoke only in broken fragments. Whatever sense I made of her answers was my sense. She was passing queer.
Q: Get on with it, wretch. Her words. Her words.

A: She said that, when they entered his rooms, he asked her if she desired a leading role in Mister Macready's next play. She answered "yes" as I had schooled her. He said other things to her, things which became increasingly lewd. He put his hands upon her. I had not schooled her for this. She tried to flee. (The hag, lying through her teeth, stopped.)

Q: Continue. (Dickens-the-actor spoke in a resigned voice. He had lost his relish for the part he was playing.)

Q: And then . . .

A: (Summoning all of the tragedian's tricks out of her actress's bag, the bawd drew a deep breath and went on.) And then my daughter said to me "He raped me, mamma. He struck me, slapped me down and . . . he raped me."

A silence fell over the bullpen. The fire crackled in the hearth. We had heard exactly what we had expected to hear, and yet, somehow, none of us had been fully prepared for the brutal reality. I looked at Irish Meg, and I felt like a rapist myself. As I think back upon it now, I realize that Field staged all of this to force Dickens to accept the reality of it all. When Dickens resumed, it was in the woman's role.

A: My daughter was in another world. She could barely speak.

Q: And then what?

A: I went up to his rooms.

Q: Alone?

A: Yes.

Q: Why?

A: My God, she was sobbing into the cushions of the cab.

Q: Why did you go up?

A: I went up to his rooms to accuse him of his
treachery.

Q: Treachery? That is a word used in plays.
You care nothing about "treachery"; it is
your way of life. You knew exactly what
"treachery" Paroissien had planned for
your daughter, before you ever sold her to
him.

A: I didn't sell her!

Q: You did. (Field's voice was even and cold.)
The truth now. Why did you return to the
stage manager's rooms?

A: To curse him.

Q: Just being in the same room with you is a
curse! You went back to collect more
money, did you not? You went up there to
collect your daughter's clothes, and to hide
or carry off all evidence of the crime she
had just committed. Isn't that why you
went back to Paroissien's rooms?

A: No. No. (The woman was waving her
hands wildly before her face.) I didn't know
he was dead. She never said a word.

Q: You entered his rooms. Was the door
open? What did you see?

A: He lay dead on the floor in his own blood.

Q: And you fled with your daughter?

A: What else was I to do?

Q: Call for a Constable perhaps?

A: The police are so new. One doesn't think
to . . .

Q: Especially if one wishes to flee from a
murder scene.

A: I am concealing nothing (the woman was

228

trying to regain her actress's *hauteur,* and not succeeding).

Q: Did you not remove the murder weapon from the stage manager's rooms? A large sewing shears? Did you not remove it along with your daughter's clothes?

A: (The woman's face went grey ad stiff.) No. (It was a whisper.) No. (Louder.) No, I took nothing! (She spat the words at Field.) How dare . . .

Q: Ternan! (Field's voice froze her in the midst of her tirade.) Did your daughter murder Paroissien? Did she stab him with the cutters?

A: (There was a long pause.) She did not say.

Q: Tell the truth, woman!

A: (Defiant, and, I might add, convincing.) She said nothing to me about the murder. I was fully surprised when I entered the man's rooms. I entered, passed through to the bedroom, and saw him. That was all of it. I gathered my daughter's clothes and ran. Ellen said he raped her, that is all!

Q: You lie!

A: (Almost calm.) I do not.

Q: Your daughter murdered him.

A: Perhaps . . . perhaps not.

Q: You say?

A: Someone else could have come in. After my daughter fled, anyone could have entered, and killed the pig. More than half an hour passed between her leaving and my return, perhaps longer. Someone could have waited until Ellen left, then entered to make it look as if she killed the man.

Q: She did it!

A: She is not more than a child. (The actress

resurrects herself, the role of the pleading
mother.) A weak girl. She could not stab a
man to death, drive him to the floor, and
kill him. She has not the strength.

Q: Did you kill him then? (Field mocked her.)
You entered the room after she fled. You
are older, stronger. If she is so weak, how
did she escape her rapist?

A: (The woman ignored Field's baiting. She
sat silent, refusing to answer.)

Q: (Once again, Field walked away.) Where is
your daughter now?

A: I don't know.

Q: That isn't good enough.

A: I *don't* know.

Q: And I say that you do. She is with her, as
you put it, "protector," is she not? With
Lord Ashbee?

A: Yes, she is, but I don't know where he has
taken her.

Q: You just gave your daughter to him, in her
state, after all that has happened?

A: He is the only protector we have. I had no
one else to turn to. We had talked before
about Ellen becoming his ward, he the
patron of her career.

Q: Her career as a kept whore!

A: No. He said nothing of that sort, nothing
indelicate.

Q: You are a artful liar. What he said meant
nothing. You knew his plans for your
daughter. You sold her to him.

A: No. That is not how it was. He said that he
had seen my daughter on the stage. He said
that she had great talent and beauty. He
said that he had heard Stage Manager
Paroissien and others, men of power in the
theatre, discuss my daughter in the most
lewd terms. He said that she needed a

"protector," I swear it is *his* word, more powerful than all of the others. "I can be that protector," he said.

Q: I'll wager that he did, and with relish. (Field was talking to the fire rather than to the subdued Mrs. Ternan.)

Q: What did you do when he offered to be her "protector"?

A: I thought it a jest. Gentlemen make game of actresses.

Q: Did he pursue the subject?

A: Yes, he mentioned it twice more. He suggested that he could get both of us better parts. Finally, he offered me money.

Q: You did sell your daughter for a whore!

A: No, I refused. I rejected his offer. He said that he wished to protect my Ellen from men like Partlow and Paroissien, who would use her badly. He wanted Ellen to live with him, and he would guide her career.

Q: And he offered you money?

A: Yes.

Q: And you refused?

A: Yes.

Q: Yet she is with him now, is she not?

A: I had no other choice. I did not take her to him until we needed a powerful protector, and there was nowhere else to turn. He promised me that she will never be put in prison, and that he will never turn her out into the streets.

Q: Where is your daughter now? At this moment?

A: I don't know.

Q: Would you care to guess?

A: The country. The Continent perhaps. I do not know.

Q: You know. Perhaps you don't think you know but you do. (Field paused to slowly scratch the side of his eye with his meditative forefinger.) Now, quickly, tell me every place where you have met with Milord Ashbee.

A: I and Ellen have dined at his Notting Hill estate. He has entertained us at his Kensington mansion, and, one night after the play, a whole party retired to a large set of rooms in Soho. Those are his places in the city. I have never been to his country house.

Q: (Field's voice is even and menacing.) You are an insolent old slut. You belong in jail. You will end there forever, if I have any say in the matter. You are a monster of your sex. (Field turns and opens the door) Take her away. Take down a full description of each of Ashbee's houses and their location. Hold her in custody.

With those orders, Dickens placed the small sheaf of papers from which he had been reading on the desk and held his hands out palm up in a gesture of *finis*.

"Bravo," Field stood clapping his hands and laughing. "Quite a performance. I wish I 'ad questioned the hag nearly as well as you made it seem I did."

"What is our next step?" I asked.

"We must find the girl, free her from this rake," Dickens insisted, with an urgency that revealed much more, I am sure, than he wished.

"We must find our murderer," Inspector Field corrected.

"'Ow 'sat goin' ta git done?" Irish Meg asked, asserting her right to join the conversation on an equal footing with everyone else.

"I'll bet a bob Fieldsy's got a plan," Tally Ho Thompson said, adding his shilling's worth.

"Indeed I 'ave," Field said, re-establishing his control, "a plan of patience."

Dickens looked at me in disappointment.

"We must wait and watch, until Ashbee and the girl resurface. The old bawd 'as described the neighbour'oods and the 'ouses of Ashbee 'ere in the city. Tonight we must find those 'ouses, and establish surveillance. Then, we must be patient and wait for our principals to return. Mark this, they *will* return . . . and soon, I wager."

The evening had proved so embarrassing, had been filled with so much madness and melodrama that I had completely lost track of time. I reached into the watch pocket of my vest to consult my gold repeater. "My God, it's gone," I could not help but exclaim. "My watch, it's gone."

I vaguely remember Field answering my outburst with a short cough, meant, I feel now, to camouflage an irrepressible impulse to laughter. "Isn't that the second you've lost this year?" His face was struggling as he posed that question.

He did not care in the least that my watch was missing. Nothing had gone properly for me this evening. I had made an utter fool of myself, and now I had lost my gold repeater, which had cost me almost five pounds.

Dickens sat silent but, I sensed, sympathetic to my loss.

Meg tried to be helpful, suggesting I think back to when I last had the aforesaid timepiece in my hand.

Thompson said nothing.

Finally, Inspector Field burst out laughing.

I was indignant. "Just what is so funny?" I demanded.

"It's very funny, Mister Collins." Field spoke through the grin which he could not control. "You are such a green 'un! Thompson," and he turned to that worthy, holding out his hand, "give Mister Collins back 'is watch."

Tally Ho Thompson, with a disgusted shrug, reached into a side pocket of his coat, and produced the gold repeater. "Sorry, Guv," he said. I didn't know whether he was addressing me or Inspector Field. "Just couldn't let such a fine opportunity pass. Snatched it whilst we were wrestlin' with my Bess back at the theatre. Nothin' personal."

Everyone laughed.

Thompson was right. None of this was personal. Dickens and myself were merely slumming, playing a game. Nothing personal. And yet, I could not help but think that for all of us—Field, Dickens, myself—this whole game of *cherchez la femme* had become quite personal indeed.

"CONFESSIO AMATIS"

(May 10, 1851—Midnight)

This memoir continues upon its careening pace. It is my memory of Charles, but I realize now that it has become more than just that. Dickens was responsible for whatever success I now enjoy as a writer. I write of him herein, yet I also write for myself. What I write now is most difficult of all.

The reading of the bawd's testimony done, my watch restored, there was nothing left for we amateurs to do that night. Field, true to his word, had kept us fully posted on the case.

"I 'ave work yet to do this night." Field seemed weary. "The surveillance lists and hours must be drawn. It could be days before they surface. Gentlemen," he nodded to Dickens and myself, "your assistance 'as been invaluable on this case. You shall be in it at the end, I promise."

Dickens answered with a slight nod of the head and a grim smile.

"Thompson," Field continued his dismissal of the troops, "you are earnin' your keep. If you can keep your artful fingers out of gentlemen's pockets, I may make a 'oomin' bein' out of you yet."

Tally Ho answered with that cockeyed grin.

"Meg," Field turned to her, and paused as if searching. "Meg, we are square. I may need you again in this affair. Be alert. You 'ave done well."

Thus dismissed, he ushered us out, and left us standing in the street. It was at this moment, that I realized what a perceptive and sensitive man Dickens truly was.

"Wilkie," he broke the awkward silence, "I need to be alone with my thoughts. I must walk by the river this night. I trust you can find your way home alone." With that, he marched abruptly off, and was swallowed up by the fog.

"I must be goin'," Thompson chimed in as if on cue. "Must 'unt up me Bess an' see if the fire is trimmed in 'er eyes." And he too set off with a wave and that knowing grin.

Irish Meg looked at me and I at her.

"I will escort you home," I said.

"I 'ave no 'ome but Rats' Castle," said she.

"Then you must come home with me."

She raised her head, looked full into my face, and smiled a radiant wicked smile. I had said it. I had said it despite every warning which had been echoing in my rational mind the whole day. I could not help but wonder what on this earth had gotten into me. It was done. Meg's arm was clasped within mine and we were walking together through the gaslit mist. 'Neath the first lamp, its gauzy halo illuminating her face, we stopped. There was moisture on her face, whether tears or simply drops of hanging mist I did not know. She looked into my eyes, and rose slowly to me, her arms encircling my neck, her moist open face drawing up to mine. Our lips met in a kiss that changed everything I was, and had ever envisioned myself to be.

Meg and I did not speak. There was no need for talk. It would have been a distraction from that which was so real between us. Our lips met again, and her mouth opened upon mine with an urgency that I met with both fear and heedless desire. I clasped her in my arms, and met each thrust of her velvet tongue with a clumsy counterthrust. We never spoke.

Twenty years ago, when all of this happened, even ten years ago when I had established myself as a good writer, surely not the match of Dickens, but an entertaining writer of mysteries, I could not have, would not have, written of what I am about to write. Dickens, the greatest, most powerful writer of our age, would never have considered writing of what I am about to write. Yet I must write of it now. It will never be read in my time. If and when it is read, it will show that Dickens and Collins were real human beings. Perhaps it will show that we Victorians were not just a scrabbling race of crabbed hypocrits, dryasdust and as sexually inclined as the pit of a Jersey plum. Our tendency, as novelists in the age of Victoria, is to draw a curtain over all that occurs in the privacy of our sleeping rooms. We attack society at large, we laugh at its institutions, as did Dickens in *Bleak House* and *Little Dorrit*, but we do not confront the most basic emotions of our lives. We portray love in looks, in words, in public ceremonies, but we do not portray love as men and women find it in each other's arms and beds. It is eighteen-seventy now, and there is yet no indication that this subject will ever emerge from behind that curtain. The great painter Turner's rooms were opened some years ago, and what was found there was shocking to some—more than five hundred paintings of the female genitalia. Graphic, obsessive paintings. Lurid in their color and abandon. I was not shocked. We all have our secret lives. That night with Irish Meg, my secret life began, and it has been the salvation of my being ever since. Talk is the stuff of novels, and that night we had little need for talk.

We hurried through the deserted streets to my room. The door closed behind us. We faced each other alone, for the first time unaccountable to anyone but ourselves. When we kissed, the urgency we had felt before, in the street, was replaced by a realization that no one was watching or judging us, that we had only ourselves to please. I felt a new man. Our bodies searched each other out. Our mouths crushed themselves in one long breathless kiss following another.

The light was dim in my room, since I had been allowed no opportunity to ignite the oil lamps. The only real light seeped through the curtained windows. Irish Meg broke our long and passionate embrace, and stepped back. With one uncomplicated motion she unlaced the top of her dress leaving herself, in an instant, naked to the waist.

Wavering shadows played delicately across the ghostly whiteness of her breasts. I fell to my knees before her. We were gentleman and demon lover, neophyte and whore. One cannot fully escape the image of the self engrained by one's continuous hypocrisy in society. Yet we were also people burning in a kiln of desire which turned the shells of our outward lives to ash. Only our buried selves survived to touch each other; hers better, purer; mine lower, freer. My gentleman's world was shut out forever. Within Meg's world of the flesh, I found a heedless refuge. She lowered herself to me, and, as we knelt facing one another like two devout supplicants praying in a darkened church, my lips sought and kissed her risen breasts. The tips of my fingers moved across her skin, her neck, her back, up across the soft roundness of her midriff, so carefully, so slowly, savoring each touch, each contour, each new possession.

She stood, and made herself naked before me. Woman, all openness and acceptance, leading me into her shadowed garden. I rose, still fully clothed, feeling like a fool.

She undressed me. We made love. Our bodies spoke in an age-old language which no modern code could ever match for eloquence or fire. I have never had a sweeter conversation, never entered into a clearer, more honest dialogue. We never spoke. We made love, with no thought of what century, what cold country in which we lived, no thought of what rank in society, what moral status we upheld in the warped mirror of

Vanity Fair. We made love out of desperate need: her need to survive; my need to prove that I was alive. She was too passionate to be a whore, and I, certainly, was no gentleman.

As I look back upon that night from this distant harbor of twenty years, the image of Meg, naked in my arms, does not float my mind back into the past, but rather steams it into the future. Meg, in her determination and passion, is a castaway on this cold island of the Victorian age. She once, later, said to me, "You mark, a time's gonna come when wimmins an't gonna 'ave ta sell themselves as either 'ores or wives ta live. A time's gonna come when wimmins will be able ta work at anythin' jus' like men, do all the things men do. Now, if you tries to do wot a man does, git ahead, you end up like Missus Manning, at the end of a rope, either the law's or your own." Meg is an extraordinary woman, because she was born too soon, but did not let that stop her. Through her, I envision a time when all women will be free to be as passionate as Meg was with me that night.

When I awoke to the grey London sunlight, Irish Meg was gone and my life as a Victorian gentleman was forever changed. My secret life had begun.

THE SIEGE

(May 11, 1851—Dusk)

Darkness was just beginning to descend upon the city, brooding outside of the Wellington Street bay window. The meager sun staggered through the murk of cloud and fog and gas, to disappear into some unmarked sinkhole out in the direction of St. Albans. It was almost five when Rogers rose up out of the fog to summon us once again to an audience with Inspector Field.

As usual, Rogers was chafing at the errand.

Looking much refreshed, after the haggard state in which he dismissed us the night before, Inspector Field greeted us heartily at Bow Street Station. He was leaning in the doorway, smoking a cigar, and watching the lurid sun sink into the lurid smoke of the western suburbs.

"There are stirrings," Field greeted us. "I feel that we may flush them tonight. The beaters are on the 'unt. We must set ourselves in the path of the driven game." He grinned, quite proud of his elaborate metaphor.

"Ah, the hunt is on, is it?" Dickens answered, with more enthusiasm than I had expected, after the melancholy afternoon.

"My surveillance runners 'ave offered two reports. Preparations are bein' made at the Soho flats. Servants, caterers, lights blazin' all through the 'ouse. All is quiet at Kensington Gardens. A few lights. Servants perhaps doing daily maintenance. No sign of Ashbee or the Miss Ternan in residence. The Soho 'ouse is the place, gentlemen. It is surrounded by my Protectives. They 'ave strict orders to allow entry into our little net, but no exit."

"You feel then that the society of rakes plan to meet tonight?" Dickens asked the obvious question.

"All the preparations are in place," Field said, scratching at the corner of his eye with his masterful forefinger, even as that forefinger held his cigar. "I think we should go there. Thompson is bein' fetched. 'Ee may be of use again."

With that, he turned to Rogers, who had been standing attentively at the curbstone next to the horses, and gave what, at the time, I thought to be a rather peculiar order.

"Serjeant Rogers, return to the Kensington 'ouse, use this chaise, and take command of that surveillance."

"But sir . . ." a crazed look of panic came into Rogers's eyes. He knew that he was losing his chance to be in on the *denoument.* I felt a great secret delight at his helpless frustration.

"Your job is to be alert over there," Field said, stifling Rogers's protest, having clearly foreseen it. Field spoke with a cold authority, which intimated that no opposition was to be brooked in the matter. "Your job is to watch every comin' and goin', every light goin' on or snuffed. We aren't sure that the Soho 'ouse is the meetin' place. It would be like 'em to change at the last moment to throw us off the scent. Stay alert at Kensington, Rogers. Our prey may run right into your guns," Field finished with a flourish.

It was clear that Rogers didn't believe Field's words of reassurance for a moment. It was clear that he felt betrayed, sold off in favor of we rank amateurs and a convicted highwayman, who at that moment arrived in a hansom cab with a jaunty wave and a grinning "Evenin', gents."

The hunting party was assembled. Rogers betook his sullen self away.

"Follow me gentlemen. You as well Thompson," Field ordered with a private chuckle.

"Don't mind if I do." Nothing seemed to penetrate Thompson's perpetual good nature. *He's the devil's jokester,* I thought fancifully, *placed on earth for no other purpose than to mock the pretension of we Victorians.*

We four boarded the black coach, which had earlier transported this identical crew of cracksmen on our nocturnal visit to Milord Ashbee's Notting Hill estate. We clattered cross London to a close, fog-shrouded neighbourhood. Inspector Field, eschewing the bull's-eye, which the driver offered, led us slowly through a maze of black and narrow thoroughfares. How the man saw his way through that dark underworld, I cannot explain, yet he led us to a dark doorway, directly across from what Field informed us was Milord Ashbee's Soho house. It was surrounded by a low iron fence, and, unlike any other house in the street, it blazed with light in every window.

"It looks as if something surely is on there tonight," Dickens whispered to Field.

"Let's 'ope," Field growled, then, as if talking only to himself, he muttered, "it's almos' too bright, too invitin'."

We settled into the damp mist to wait for the curtain to ascend, for Ashbee's coach to appear, for Ellen to step out dressed in silks and furs and sparkling diamonds, for other coaches to unload lords of the realm, all evil old men like Thackeray's Lord Steyne. We waited, hugging ourselves, chafing our arms in the effort to stay warm. Every coach that traversed that Soho street clattered by. Seven o'clock passed. The great bells of St. Paul's signaled eight.

"Damn it's cold and damp!" Tally Ho Thompson broke a long dull silence with a quite obvious observation.

Thompson startled Inspector Field into speech. "It's gettin' too late," he said. "It should 'ave 'appened by now." Abruptly, he marched out into the fog to consult, we presumed, with his brother detectives posted in positions surrounding the house.

After it was all over, Rogers, gloating, narrated for us what had transpired at his post as we waited shivering in that Soho doorway. I am sure that he suitably embellished his own role, and exaggerated his ingenuity, but I have no other source for these events, so I am forced to repeat them as he later portrayed them to us.

Serjeant Rogers, on post at Milord Ashbee's Kensington house, is startled by a sound up the way. He sees a coach exit a side street down one set of buildings from the dim house he is commissioned to watch. He notices this coach because it represents absolutely the only movement in the neighbour-hood. Rogers marks it but pays no real attention.

Moments later, however, another coach exits the same narrow thoroughfare and echoes hollowly away. Rogers glances up, but soon subsides back into the torpor of his surveillance. Milord Ashbee's house shows but two dim lights.

More quiet minutes pass and lo, yet a third coach emerges from that selfsame mews and catches Serjeant Rogers's atten-tion. He feels it an appropriate time to stretch his legs. He rises, scratches at his beard, mutters "busy little side street this evenin'" into the oversized lapels of his greatcoat and sets off walking in the shadows of the buildings toward this unusually trafficked street.

The narrow mews in question is empty when Rogers arrives at its mouth. Nothing seems amiss. Nevertheless, he settles himself behind a large dust bin and waits to see if any more coaches arrive.

He does not have to wait long. Within minutes a sleek phaeton drawn by a matched pair of blacks pulls up. A long gentleman in a dark Aylesbury, a silk waistcoat and carrying a cane steps out. The gentleman converses pre-emptorily with the driver. The driver reaches beneath the box, extracts a bull's-eye, ignites it, and steps down to light the gentleman's way.

In the light of the torch, Rogers recognizes the gentleman. He is the infamous Lord Bowes, gambler and rake, a familiar face to most of the detective force in the aftermath of his recent Assizes suit charging two officers from the Park Lane Protectives with excessive force is subduing him one night, when he was brandishing a rapier in the street outside of a Mayfair residence, rumored to specialize in tarts and opium.

The coachman lights the lord's way to a dark and unremarkable door set two steps below the level of the cobbled street, in the wall of a dark and unremarkable brick building. Employing a key, Lord Bowes opens that undistinguished door, and disappears through it.

"Somethin's afoot here," Rogers mutters into his capacious lapels.

He reclines against his dust bin. He considers long and hard. For Rogers, delivering an idea proves equal in effort and pain to the delivering of a pugnacious Irish infant. After agonizing minutes, he remembers the tunnel in Lord Ashbee's Notting Hill residence. "That's it," he hisses into his great coat. "That's it."

At a less-than-discreet run, he seeks out his nearest subordinate and dispatches him with an urgent message to Inspector Field.

That done, Rogers (I am only speculating now) must have

taken a moment to celebrate. *I am not to be left out of it after all. I have done the real detective work this night*, he must have gloated.

While Rogers was making his discoveries in Kensington Gardens, Inspector Field was returning from a quick inspection of his men posted around the Soho house. Field beckoned Dickens, Thompson, and myself to follow him down a foul-smelling alley and around a corner, where we gathered under a single lonesome gaslight. Field lit a cigar. The rest of us followed suit.

"We've been decoyed, lads," he growled. "We've been done." He was furious with himself. "They are not meetin' 'ere at all. He has figured out that we are watchin' 'im and 'ee 'as temporarily put us off the track."

Dickens face dropped. "She is lost," he breathed, barely within my threshold of hearing. But Dickens was not a man to despair so easily. "But where then?" he gasped to Inspector Field. "We must find her, but where?"

"Ashbee's other 'ouse, the Kensington 'ouse, is our only 'ope this night. Rogers is still there. Perhaps . . ." but Field's voice did not succeed, if indeed that was ever its object, in reassuring Charles.

"My God, they could have fled the city, the country, for the Continent by now," Dickens was distraught.

Field, continuing to puff contemplatively upon his cigar, spoke slowly: "I'll wager they're still in London. I'd stake my life on it. Ashbee is a lord. 'Ee don't 'ave to run away. 'Ee can do anything' 'ee wants. Or thinks 'ee can. 'Ee's got the girl, and 'ee's gonna enjoy 'er in 'is own good time and 'ee doesn't feel 'ee 'as to sail to France to do it."

Dickens found little reassurance in this scenario.

"Let us get to the bottom of this, now," Field decisively brought our colloquy to an end.

We followed Inspector Field in single file—Dickens, then me, then Thompson—as if we were faithful pull-toys. He dragged us back through the narrow mews, across the Soho street, through the iron gate to Ashbee's house, up the three front steps to the large brass knocker.

A female servant answered the door.

"Inspector Field. Metropolitan Protectives. Police business. Is your master at 'ome, Miss?" Field fired off his words in the rapid staccato of musketry and the woman recoiled as if hit by a volley. Her retreat two steps backward allowed Field to take the room. He stepped through the doorway leaving his three pull-toys loitering on the windy porch.

The maidservant soon recovered herself, and faced up to him.

"Master an't 'ere," she managed.

"'As 'ee been 'ere this day or these two days past?" Field growled as we stood on the porch eavesdropping.

"Master an't 'ere, 'oi say," the woman was terrified, intimidated, unequal to the task of lying to Inspector William Field, who tapped her three sharp times on the shoulder with his unnerving forefinger.

"Where is 'ee?"

"'As 'ee been 'ere?"

"When?"

"'Ow long?"

"Why are all the lights up tonight?"

"We were hordered to turn all the lights hup by Mister Hutter, who his Milord's hagent," the lying hussy finally answered, through Field's barrage of questions, but he did not relent.

"Where is 'ee?"

"'Ow long since 'ee's been 'ere?"

"Was 'ee alone?"

"Answer me, where 'as 'ee gone?"

The woman was in tears, wet and real, not feigned. They were tears of fear, whether of her master or of Inspector Field, I could not ascertain.

"We don't know. To the country, 'ee said."

"You are lyin', wench. I can smell a lie," Field hissed those

244

words quietly at her. "When was 'ee 'ere? And where 'as 'ee gone? Then we'll know if ye'll sleep tonight in Newgate."

The woman burst into tears, buried her face in her hands. "Left, left, left for the country. We, we, we was told, told, told to stay 'ere. We was, was, was told, told to burn the lights, tonight an' tomorra. He told, told us that, that, that." The woman was quaking with sobs.

Suddenly, Field changed his whole method of interrogation. He became a concerned uncle or a consoling brother. "I know you are not to blame," he said. His hand offered her a handkerchief to wipe her tears. "You are but a servant in the employ of this evil man. I understand your fear of 'im. But you must 'elp me all that you can. You understand that, do you not?"

"Yes, sir," the woman offered, scared half out of her senses, and not knowing what to make of this change of Field's persona from a badgering bully to a kindly counselor. The woman made a serious mistake. She chose to persist in her lying. "Milord went to visit a friend in the country," she lied. "A fortnight, Milord said."

"And 'ee told you to burn the lights, did 'ee?" Field was suspicious.

"Yes, sir."

"And you don't know where 'ee went in the country, is that it?" There was a brittle edge to his voice.

"'At's it exactly, sir," She was so polite, so sure, so false.

"You are a lyin' little 'ore!" Field slapped her hard across the face. "Don't you ever lie to Inspector Field, y'ear?" He was screaming into her face as he pushed her backwards with jabs of his bludgeoning forefinger.

"'Ee didna say where 'ee went nor when 'ee would return."

Field slapped her again. "That is a lie!" he spat.

"'Ee said 'ee went to visit another Lord, 'at's all 'ee said. I promise. Don't 'it me again."

Field slapped her a third time, much harder than the first two. *Does he enjoy it?* I thought. *Intimidating these helpless women, the poor wretches in the rats' castles. Does he like it?*

245

Later, in the coach, I asked him why he hit her so hard.

"I needed the information right away," was his bland answer. "The little 'ore was lyin' to me. She'd been re'earsed. Told to lie. I 'ad to force 'er to tell the truth, and I 'ad no time."

He forced her allright. That third slap snapped her face sideways and made real tears of pain well up in her eyes. He had saved his hardest slap to preface his most telling questions.

"Was there a lady in Milord Ashbee's company?"

The woman's eyes went wide. She began to shake her head in the negative but never completed the gesture.

"Was there a lady?" Field screamed, as he grasped both her shoulders and shook her. "Was there? Answer me," and he raised his right hand to strike her again.

"No. Yes. No," she wailed desperately. "No. It was no lady. She was a trollop dressed up like a lady."

This last greatly distressed Dickens, and he turned away. Inspector Field shook her again, as if trying to jar the words out of her.

"They were 'ere for a few 'ours two nights ago. They left our orders, then they left. They 'ave not returned nor 'as Milord's coach."

Field, having squeezed her dry, discarded the woman like an old sponge. He turned and confronted us on the porch. "This is all only deception. Ashbee is not 'ere. 'Ee and the Ternan girl 'ave, ·for the moment, slipped through our fingers." Dickens groaned.

As if on some stage cue for the very moment when all seemed lost, a uniformed constable came stumbling out of the fog, winded, weary, yet wide-eyed for the recipient of his Marathonian message.

"Inspector Field, sir. Constable Lansbury 'ere," the man gasped.

"Yes, Lansbury, what is it?" We were all suddenly on the alert.

"Serjeant Rogers says for you to come to Kensington Gardens straight away. Says, tell Inspector Field the 'ouse is dark but they're all in there. 'At's it, sir."

Field looked at Dickens, teeth bared in triumph. Dickens met Field's eyes. They rushed from the porch. Thompson and I had no choice but to follow.

Within short minutes, the four of us were rattling at high speed across London.

Rogers was waiting in Kensington Gardens like a smug setter on point. By a back alley he marched us down to peek into the narrow mews where, by his count, no less than six coaches had delivered passengers this night. He pointed out the unremarkable door through which those passengers had disappeared. He walked us the length of the building and noted how that building connected to the adjoining building by a short enclosed walkway roofed over in brick. He next walked us the length of this second building until it ended adjacent to the back garden of Milord Ashbee's Kensington manse.

"We 'ave 'ad experience with Ashbee's tunnels before, 'ave we not, sir?" Rogers prompted Inspector Field.

"Indeed we 'ave. Good work, Rogers," Field complimented his serjeant.

The five of us stood huddled in the darkness staring through the high iron fence and across Milord Ashbee's dark garden to the high, gloomy house. No lights showed on this side of the house, except for a dull glow about midway along the flat roofline to the wing, which rose one storey out of the garden, and ran to the main, four-storey body of the mansion.

"We must get in." Dickens's voice was getting desperate.

"Hold." Field's presence, even when invoked in a whisper, silenced everyone. "We 'ave 'em. We must be sure-'anded in this."

We waited.

"Rogers," he barked, still in a whisper, "you are responsible for securing the outside of the 'ouse, sealing off their escape routes. 'Ow many men do you 'ave?"

"Myself and two constables. Lansbury was sent to fetch you, sir."

"A bit thin," Inspector Field was not pleased, "But others should be arrivin' soon. Station your men as best you can.

When new men arrive, put them on post. We must not allow Ashbee and the girl to get away."

"Yessir," Rogers scurried off to do his master's bidding.

"We must rescue her right away. All those men mean to rape her," Dickens's words exploded.

"She is a suspected murderess, and I am 'ere to take 'er into custody." Field's wooden assertion momentarily silenced Dickens's anguish. "We will prevent any 'arm comin' to the young woman, if at all possible."

"She is not the criminal. Those rakes are," Dickens insisted. "They have corrupted her. They have forced her to violence."

"Whatever is the case," Field clearly did not want to argue either legalities or moralities, "we must find some way to get in without scaring the whole lot off."

"Gents." It was Tally Ho Thompson interrupting their colloquy, "if you'll stand down for a stroke, I'll take a stroll round the neighbour'ood, and we'll see what we can see."

Without waiting for Field to answer, Thompson was out of the shadows and, at a dead run, vaulting himself onto the high iron railings of Milord Ashbee's garden fence. The man scaled those pikes the way the monkeys in the zoological gardens climb about on the bars of their cages. He pulled himself to the top and with a pendulum-like swing tossed himself over. He then ran across the garden to disappear around the corner of the rear wing of the mansion. We waited, five minutes stretched into ten.

"He's not coming back. He's been taken by Ashbee's men." The desperation had reasserted itself in Dickens's voice. "We have to do something. Seven men have her in there."

Field placed a firm hand upon Dickens's shoulder, not a hand of authority, but the hand of a friend which seemed gently to say, "I know how upset you are but we are going about this the proper way. Calm yourself, it will all be over soon." Field's eyes moved from Dickens's face to mine. His head gave a slight nod, as if ordering me to intercede.

I had no idea what to say. I put my hand on Dickens's shoulder as Inspector field withdrew his. My lips were mere inches from Dickens's ear. I, for once, had his full attention.

"Charles, we must be sure. Rogers has, by now, got his men in place. We will move to find her as soon as Thompson returns. We can't just barge in there not knowing what we are going into. That would endanger her as well as us. We shall get her out; I am sure of it."

It was so dark that I could not detect any signs that my words had reassured him, but he said no more.

We waited silently only a few short moments, before Thompson, like a ghost, materialized out of the darkness. That incorrigible jokester had the aggravating habit of doing that, just popping up as if creating himself out of thin air.

"Gents, follow me," he invited us.

THE SKYLIGHT

(May 11, 1851—night)

Mister Tally Ho Thompson proved quite an accommodating tour guide.

"No need for concern, gents," he whispered as we peered out of the deep shadow of the wall, "I met no guards on the grounds. Follow me. It's a simple crack."

We followed this demon jokester. Nothing could make the man stop grinning idiotically. Perhaps it was the idea of his giving orders to Inspector Field which amused him so. Perhaps he simply enjoyed burgling houses under the wing of the police.

He led us along the iron railings to a high gate which stood ajar. Its lock, clearly picked, hung open upon its chain. Like a magician displaying a bird plucked from his hat, Thompson grinned, nodded and led us through the gate. We crossed the lawn of the back garden at a run. The shadows of the rear wing of the house enfolded us. No alarum was raised.

It was as if Thompson had built a set upon a stage and we were his actors. All of his props were in place. He led us to a wooden ladder placed against the wall of the house.

"Pinched it from the coach 'ouse," Thompson declared proudly.

From all evidence, this madman was proposing that the three of us follow him up this ladder. To my perfect amazement, Field and Dickens hesitated not one whit. They were well into their ascent before I even realized that I was expected to follow. It struck me as extremely dangerous and unconsidered, but, when they disappeared up into the darkness leaving me abandoned at the bottom, I reconsidered and followed with little enthusiasm. Housebreaking, climbing ladders, traversing dark rooftops is the stuff of Grub Street hacks and ha'penny novelists, not of real writers like Dickens and myself. Somehow, Thompson had drawn us so far into his romantic, risk-taking career that none of us was capable of turning back.

We crouched at the top of the ladder. Thompson whispered orders.

"Go softly across the roof to the skylight. They are directly below us. We can see it all. Inspector Field," he said, with a professional politeness, "you've got your truncheon in your coat as ever, do you not?"

"Yes, I do."

"Good, I may need it to break the skylight if the scene gets dicey and the script calls for a surprise entrance."

Field gave a silent nod of approval. Even he, I think, was rather impressed with the command Thompson had taken of the situation.

About halfway across the roof, the contour ceased to run flat, and ascended in a gentle slope to meet the side of the main house. From our vantage point near the edge of the roof, we could see the skylight.

On tiptoe, one by one, we traversed the flat expanse of the roof, until all four of us knelt at the base of the skylight.

Because it slanted upward, we could kneel around its base, and, leaning slightly forward, look down into the room below. The skylight was directly over a long, high-ceilinged ballroom. We could see all that was taking place below, but, unfortunately, we could hear nothing. We spied through that skylight like spectators in an aquarium gaping through glass at exotic species performing in another medium.

The gentlemen, seven of them, were at dinner around a long table set elegantly in the middle of the room. They were dining off the finest silver plate. Candelabras blazed at three places upon their board. Bottles of fine wine stood on the table, were passed and poured by the gentlemen themselves. No servants were in immediate attendance.

At the far end of the room, toward the main body of the house, a space, ringed with overstuffed wing chairs, had been cleared, as if for a stage. It is to this small stage that, after our first glances down at the lavish eating scene, all of our eyes were immediately drawn.

Ellen Ternan was chained to the wall at the center of the stage.

My eyes, as if on a leash, snapped immediately to Charles's face. His eyes met mine and were filled with chaotic emotions. I shall never forget that look of anguish. It left no doubt whatsoever, how deeply he was involved with the girl inside his own mind. She was everything to him and seeing her down there . . . like that.

The girl leaned backward against the wall, her eyes wide open, yet strangely detached. She stared at the sumptuous table where the rakes sat, indulging themselves. She was, without question, drugged. The vacancy in her gaze, the docility of her stance, the lolling of her head, all attested to it. She was the complete victim, prisoner, possession of her chains, those men. Her hands, manacled, were stretched apart and slightly above her head. The manacles around her wrists were connected, by short lengths of chain, to heavy iron staples set high in the wall. Her ankles too were in irons, also connected to short chains, terminating in staples sunk in the

251

floor. She was hung on that wall as if on a gallows, waiting for the trap to spring.

"She is safe for the moment," Field whispered.

"We must do something!" Dickens begged.

Field raised his forefinger in a silent gesture of patience.

Dickens visibly sank backwards, defeated.

Lord Ashbee was up, moving around the table, clearing off the plate to a sideboard. He lifted away the carcass of a large bird picked clean. He circled the table, proffering cigars from a wooden box, then uncorking and pouring from a flagon of Madeira. The sumptuous dinner party had clearly reached its conclusion, and the rakes seemed merrily arming themselves for the dessert. They pushed back from the table, lit their cigars, rose from their chairs, carrying their crystal goblets filled with dark, blood-red wine.

I watched Dickens's face. His eyes never left the girl. She was all he cared about in that room. He crouched, tense, like some predator waiting to spring. The others—Field, Thompson—watched the movements of the men in the room below, with the intensity and anticipation of men who knew that they were about to act. For the first time that evening, Thompson was not grinning. His mouth was drawn tight in a look of readiness as if he were waiting to do what he had known all along he was going to do. Dickens's eyes remained locked on the girl chained to the wall. Everyone seemed ready except me. Everyone seemed eager save for me. Only I had not yet formulated our obvious plan of action.

Miss Ternan was dressed in what looked to be nothing less than randomly torn scraps of a red silken fabric. She was barely less than half-naked. The strips of cloth were wrapped around the upper portions of her body and gathered about her waist and hips, giving the effect of a scanty harem outfit, a slave girl's tunic. Her well-formed legs were fully exposed from the tops of her thighs to her manacled ankles. She wore nothing on her feet. *Saint George shall have to carry his maiden to safety*, I, always the practical one, speculated.

Lord Ashbee ushered his guests to their seats in his theatre.

The gentlemen, smoke rising from their cigars, moved beneath the skylight like fish swimming elegantly behind glass. Ashbee seated them in a semi-circle. He left the rakes admiring their captive, and moved to a side table to deposit his wine glass, and dress himself for his role in the performance.

He returned to center stage wearing a soft Australian or American hat with a wide ungovernable brim, and carrying a short riding whip.

Dickens started forward.

Field restrained him with a hand outstretched across Charles's chest.

"He is going to whip her!" Dickens hissed between clenched teeth.

"Wait, she is unharmed as yet. They must commit some crime for which they can be brought before the court." Field was calm, cold actually.

Ashbee turned to his audience seated about his impromptu stage. But it was no longer a stage; it was the auction block, the slave market in New Orleans. Ashbee extended his whip toward the cringing girl chained to the wall, moved it like a pedant's pointer from her head down along the contours of her body to just below her waist.

"What am I bid for this ripe slave girl, gentlemen?" his lips moved but we imagined the words. We constructed the play's dialogue in our minds.

The riding crop, like a serpent, slithered underneath her chin, raised her downcast eyes, her vacant face, up to confront the bidders.

The whip moved along her chin, along the white line of her cheek to the gentle incline of her neck, then down to the white slope of her shoulders. Ashbee handled this whip too lovingly for it to be simply a prop. It was an extension of himself which he had used frequently and well.

"What am I bid for this virgin slave?" Thus, we imagined his exhortation to the rich plantation owners. "Who will bid to take her first?" he cajoled, in our imaginations.

253

With a quick flick of his whip, Ashbee stripped the cloth from her breasts.

Dickens leapt to his feet. He could stand this exercise in humiliation—hers, his—no longer. "We must stop this now!" He clasped Inspector Field by the lapels of his greatcoat, and drew him to his feet over the skylight.

"Control yourself man!" Field barked in a whisper. "She is chained. We must wait until Ashbee unchains 'er. Can't you see? Chained like that, if there is violence, she could be killed. Can't you see what we are goin' to 'ave to do, 'ow this scene is goin' to play? Control yourself. We must wait until she is freed. No 'arm will come to 'er. I promise."

Once again, Dickens had been subdued.

Lovingly, Ashbee ran the tip of his riding whip over and around Miss Ternan's exposed breasts. He stimulated her brown aureola with the whip, while he cajoled the other rakes to bid upon the slave.

We watched as the rakes bid heatedly against one another for the opportunity to be the first to possess the chained girl.

The victim surely had been drugged. She reacted not at all. She hung silently from her bonds, unaware of the liberties being taken with her person, and the six sets of eyes feeding upon her naked breasts.

First one rake, Lord Bowes, raised his hand toward the stage, then another waved his cigar. Ashbee pointed at each in turn with his whip. Then another waved a hand, and shouted. Bowes sipped at his dark red wine, and pointed malevolently at the girl with the forefinger of the hand in which he cradled his glass. Another cast forth a bid. The cigar waved again. Bowes pointed once more. All the rakes, gathered in their circle, laughed at some comment upon the proceedings. We realized that they were bidding for the privilege of having her first, that they all expected a chance with her before the evening was out.

Only two bidders remained, the arrogant Lord Bowes, and the large, mustachioed gentleman who made bids with his cigar. We learned later that he was Denys Walder, the African explorer, and first cousin to Lord Buckingham of the Queen's

Privy Chamber. Milord Ashbee called these two surviving bidders to the stage. They approached the chained girl. He stopped them with the whip.

Milord Ashbee's lascivious whip returned to her body. It moved slowly across her white flesh, to the remaining folds of red fabric hanging from her waist. The whip moved beneath that fabric, slowly descending beneath the gathered rag of cloth down between the captive's legs.

I looked at Dickens. He still stood alone, above and behind us. He stared down over our shoulders at the scene, his face twisted violently with hatred, anger, pain and desire. My eyes jolted back to the captive girl. As the whip explored her body, as the rakes stood as if ready to pounce, life seemed to be returning to her drugged countenance. A start, a widening of her eyes, a stricter control of her head, asserted itself, as she looked desperately from side to side for some path of escape.

Ashbee's whip, suddenly, pulled all of the remaining fabric from Miss Ternan's body. She could not cover herself. She stood naked before the two rakes, who had come forward to claim their prize. Had they purchased her together? Would the two of them possess her at the same time? These perverse thoughts coursed through my mind as the two rakes approached the slave.

Lord Ashbee stepped between his two triumphant bidders and their chained property. "Allow me, gentlemen," he must have been saying, though we could not hear. He drew a key from his jacket. He unlocked first her arms, then her ankles. By one wrist, he led her to the eager buyers.

"Thompson, go!" Inspector Field startled all of us. The only one not startled was Tally Ho Thompson, who was moving upon his pre-determined course before the sound of Field's order had died.

I watched in awe, as Field and Thompson moved in what appeared to be perfect synchronization. Inspector Field swung his truncheon, and, in one sharp downward blow, shattered the glass of the near half of the skylight.

Tally Ho Thompson, without the slightest hesitation, swung

into action. Placing both hands on the side of the skylight, he launched himself over its edge, hung for a short moment in midair, then dropped straight down onto the large dining table. He landed with a crash, amongst the odds and ends of soiled plate and forgotten cutlery, but the table held, and he quickly regained his feet.

To my great surprise, without the slightest hesitation, and before Field could put up his truncheon and follow his man, Dickens launched himself down through the broken portal, in precisely the acrobatic manner by which Thompson had descended. Dickens landed upon the dining table as well, but without displaying the agility and balance of Thompson. Indeed, the alert Thompson clasped Dickens as he landed, steadying him.

Inspector Field, always in control, descended more carefully. Taking two firm handholds on the edge of the skylight, he eased himself into a hanging position in the aperture, waited a long moment until his balance was certain, then dropped, almost softly, to the table.

The members of the Dionysian Circle, in their plush chairs, holding their cigars and crystal goblets of wine, were visibly startled. They turned sharply to the sound with mouths agape, but they did not immediately react, other than to stare in disbelief, as these intruders dropped through the roof, and into their midst. Perhaps they thought it was all part of Ashbee's show.

And there stood I, alone on the rooftop, gaping down at those three madmen who in turn raised their eyes expectantly to me. I confess that I froze. I looked down upon them, and it all seemed too absurd. There they stood, looking up, in the middle of a Lord of the Realm's dining table, about to do battle with a company of rakes, who outnumbered them seven to three. My head was frantically sending all the right messages, but my body seemed incapable of obeying. It was as if I was nailed to that spot, forced forever to be but a spectator at life. It was that last horrible thought which restored my powers of motion.

Even as I slowly began to move, I could see Thompson, Field and Dickens also beginning to move. As if in synchronization, they jumped down off the table, and flung themselves toward the phalanx of noble rakes, who had formed themselves around the naked girl. The Ternan woman had sunk to the floor, as if in a faint, and the last thing I glimpsed, as I hung in the air before closing my eyes for the drop, was Milord Ashbee stooping to that nude figure, pulling at her wrist.

I landed on the stout oak table with a resounding thud, which buckled my knees, and flung me face forward with my arms outstretched, clawing to break the momentum of the fall. In half a moment, I ascertained that no bones nor vital organs had been broken or ruptured in the drop. When I lifted my head, my three comrades were already engaged with the enemy.

The gentlemen rakes had, whether by design or chance, formed a ragged line. Somewhere between the table and the floor, Tally Ho Thompson had acquired a gentleman's walking stick, swinging which, he charged. Field and Dickens, unarmed as far as I could tell, followed directly upon Thompson's lead.

Scrambling down off the table top, a small silver candelabra somehow came to my hand. Swinging it like that fabled biblical jawbone of the ass, I moved in the wake of my detective comrades. In truth, this was not much of an engagement. Only two of the rakes showed any stomach for the fight. The others fled, yet their stumbling around proved an obstacle, preventing access to the girl, whom Ashbee was dragging toward the doors to the main house.

Thompson was engaged with Lord Bowes. The nobleman and the highwayman were duelling with wooden walking sticks, making passes at one another across the floor of Ashbee's temporary stage.

"'Alt!" Field shouted as an order to Ashbee. The temporary distraction of shouting at the fleeing villain allowed Field's closest antagonist, the bulky mustachioed man, to land a blow with his fist to the side of Field's face, which knocked that worthy sideways across the stage.

"'Alt!" Field shouted once more.

Dickens fought his way through the confusion of startled rakes with only one object, that of liberating Ellen Ternan from Ashbee.

"'Alt!" came Field's third command.

"Ashbee, stop!" Dickens shouted.

At that moment, the air was rent by an ear-shattering report. It was a pistol shot. Its source smoked in Milord Ashbee's hand, as he stood on the threshold of the double doors to the main house. The girl was standing, dazed, at Ashbee's side.

To my horror, Dickens lay prone upon the floor.

DOWN INTO THE MAZE

(May 11, 1851—Night)

All was utter confusion. Tally Ho Thompson and Lord Bowes were whacking and flailing their walking sticks, with the abandon of children at Sherwood Forest make-believe. With a sudden move, Thompson sank to his knees. Lord Bowes relaxed for the briefest of moments, gathering strength, perhaps, to move in for the kill. At that very instant, the wily Thompson lunged back into action, cutting the legs out from under Lord Bowes, with a savage swipe to the backs of his adversary's knees. Bowes went unceremoniously sprawling. With that quicksilver agility, which in the years since has never ceased to amaze me, Thompson, in an instant, was on his feet, and standing over the toppled Lord Bowes. Snapping his wrist wickedly, Thompson cut sharply downward with his walking stick, landing a stinging blow to an exceedingly delicate and vulnerable area, just below Lord Bowes's waist. That gentleman, with a cry of extreme anguish, gathered himself into a protective coil, drawing up his knees, and burying his head between them.

To my left, Inspector Field was similarly engaged. He had managed to wrestle the bulky mustachioed man to the floor, and was sitting atop that walrus, pursuant to beating a swift tattoo about the man's head and shoulders. It looked as if, within short moments, that worthy would be as thoroughly subdued as was the downed Lord Bowes.

From all indications, the other four members of the Dionysian Circle had either fled, or were frantically in the process of doing so, as I made my way swinging my field-commissioned candelabra.

All of these skirmishes were sparking around me, yet (though I must have been aware of them, for, after all, I am describing them in some detail now) all I could focus upon was the body of Charles lying still upon the floor, and, in the background, the figure of Ashbee, the pistol smoking in his hand, dragging Miss Ternan by the wrist through the double doors into the house.

The large mustachioed man had somehow disengaged from Inspector Field. Without hesitation, I hit him on the head with my silver candelabra. He crumpled at Field's feet, and I felt as if I had smitten a Philistine.

When I reached Dickens's side, I sank to one knee, and, to my great relief, saw that he was stirring. His breath came in quick little gasps. I searched frantically for a bullet wound, for blood. I found nothing. I ran my hands over his face and forehead, searching for a bruise—nothing. Later, all that Inspector Field could speculate, was that the bullet in Ashbee's gun had somehow misfired, or come apart upon firing. He conjectured that the lead ball in the tip of the projectile had either disintegrated on firing, or had separated immediately upon exiting the barrel, thus deflecting downward from its intended course. Dickens, however, was felled by something—if not the bullet, then what? Field further conjectured, that

Dickens was struck in the neck (a small bruise was later found there) by the wadding of the defective shell, which upon impact expelled the air from his throat and lungs, and temporarily incapacitated him.

I knelt to revive him, but his eyes were already alert and frantic. His mind, I could see in his eyes, was racing, but his body was, quite simply, temporarily unable to obey its commands.

"After them, Wilkie." His lips scraped out the words. "You must not let him take her. I shall follow, as soon as I can right myself."

In the confusion, Ashbee and the naked girl were gone. I left Dickens lying on the floor, jettisoned my candelabra, and ran in pursuit of that villain. I reached the doors, through which they had disappeared, in time to hear scuttling noises at the far end of a dim corridor. I dashed down that passage. One door stood open at the end. I rushed to it, entered a room as dark as pitch. I stood perfectly still, just inside the threshold, listening. All was still as death.

I groped along the walls searching for I know not what, a gas jet, perhaps. As I blundered around in the dark, suddenly the room was flooded with light. It was Serjeant Rogers and his ever-ready bull's-eye. He, upon hearing the gunshot, had abandoned his post outside the house, and rushed into the fray, entering through the front door. (There was no way the idiot could have known, but his precipitate action would prove the key to Ashbee's escape; however, one must be fair, police surveillance was quite a new concept in eighteen fifty-one.)

"It's you!" Rogers confronted me with acute disappointment.

"Yes," I answered, as if we were two long lost brothers meeting by remarkable chance in some far outpost of the Empire.

In a moment, Inspector Field and an unsteady Dickens joined Rogers and myself. Looking round, I immediately realized why the room had been so preternaturally dark. The trail had ended in the library, where the walls, lined with books, digested all natural light. I looked at Dickens, he at me.

It was uncanny how our minds seemed to be taking the same deductive steps. I remembered the secret library in Ashbee's Notting Hill house. A *secret passage*, I thought, *that is how they have escaped*.

"There is a secret passageway here somewhere," Dickens was trying to shout, but what came out was merely a cracking whisper.

Field scanned the room. "We 'aven't time to search it out," he barked, turning to Rogers. "We must seal off this neighbourhood."

Rogers set off at a dead run for the front door.

"We must overtake them in the streets." Dickens, still somewhat dazed, picked up the cue from Inspector Field. "I know these streets."

We emerged onto the front porch of the house, to find the night enveloped in a thick fog. It had also begun to rain, in a cold and steady drizzle. We stood on that cramped porch, staring out at the empty street, seeing little but the shine of the rain on the cobblestones, and the thick encroaching mist.

Suddenly, at the end of the garden well down to our left, a bright white light, a powerful lantern of some sort, blazed up and swung sharply back and forth, once, twice.

"A signal," Inspector Field was the first to interpret this sign penetrating the heavy fog. "That's them, there."

The three of us scrambled down off the porch in the direction of that light, but before we had progressed to the garden gate, I heard, near upon us, the clatter of horses' hooves. From the sound, it was a matched pair pulling a light coach, and moving at a controlled speed under tight rein. I saw the coach as it passed by on the glistening street, and was swallowed by the mist. I could hear, however, the coach scraping to a stop, near where the signal light had been extinguished. We could not get to the fugitives in time. Out of the fog came the snapping of the coachman's whip, the flint-like cadence of the horses' hooves picking up speed on the cobbled street, the terrible finality of the coach's wheels rumbling out of our grasp. They were escaping.

"They are getting away!" Dickens almost shrieked in a desperate voice. "He is taking her!"

Ever analytic, Field tried to calm the distraught Dickens: "'Ee 'as kept this coach in reserve for 'is escape. My men are not in a position to stop 'im." He stated our helplessness as the mere fact that it was. Dickens's shoulders slumped. "Rogers, bring up the coach, quickly!" Field shouted into the fog. "We will pursue, and try to pick up their trail," he said, turning to Dickens, "but the fog, this sharp night, will keep witnesses in. I don't know." He was offering little hope for our success.

"No, he must not take her!" Dickens screamed out his frustration.

We could hear the hollow echoes of the escape vehicle moving off.

I had last seen Tally Ho Thompson as he applied the *coup de gras* to Lord Bowes at the conclusion of their mock duel. For some reason, he had not joined the pursuit of Ashbee into the main house. Where was he? My theory was that he was going through the pockets of the fallen combatants.

The sounds of Ashbee's coach grew fainter.

It was at that moment that Thompson rode up out of the fog. He was sitting bareback upon a speckled grey coachhorse, his fingers entwined in the animal's coarse mane. "I've 'ad better mounts than this," he laughed, "on a carousel. Which way did they go?"

"There," Field pointed. "You can still 'ear 'em faintly. Stay back, but keep 'em in sight or 'earin'. We'll catch up with you."

With no more than that, Thompson galloped off in pursuit.

I stood staring after him, as the sounds of his mount's hooves faded into the fog. How had Thompson known? I tell you the man was uncanny. Somehow he always seemed to know what was going to happen, and what to do when indeed it did. Furthermore, the man had the power of always popping up in exactly the right place, at the right time, properly equipped to do expressly what was required. I remember Field saying, sometime after it was all over, "What a detective Thompson would make, if only 'ee could keep 'is 'ands out of other peoples' pockets."

Within short seconds, Rogers arrived, reins and whip in hand, himself atop the box of the black police post-chaise. I was not surprised, for I knew that Rogers would insert himself into the center of the action, in whatever way possible. Dickens, Field, and myself jumped into the coach, even as Rogers whipped our pair into the fog.

"They are heading toward the river," Dickens said in a quiet voice, as if he were having some sort of vision. Unlike the being who had spent the night thus far in such nervous agitation, he spoke with a reassuring calm. Only later was I able to understand why Dickens's whole posture changed so dramatically, once we took up the pursuit. It was the streets. He was in his own element. "They are heading toward the river. He will attempt to disappear into that maze of narrow streets. We will find them. I know those streets."

"As do I," Field reassured us. "Thompson will keep 'em in sight, and we shall bring 'em to bay."

Rogers whipped the horses along the railings of the park. Dickens stared grimly out into the fog.

"They'll stick to the 'eye-road to the Knightsbridge crossin'," Field said, sounding quite certain, "then they'll make for either Millbank or the Chelsea Embankment. Those are the places to 'ide, those are!"

At a tap on the arm from Inspector Field, Rogers reined in at the Knightsbridge crossroad. A crossing sweep with a broom loitered outside the door of a public house. In an instant, like a vulture, Field was out of the coach and upon the lad.

"A light coach drawn by a pair followed close by a 'orseman," Field was shaking the terrified sweep by both shoulders, "when did they pass? Which way did they take?"

"There," pointed the frightened boy.

"When?" Field demanded with a sharp shake.

"Oney a littul toime. Don't 'urt me. I'se done nothink," the boy begged.

Field removed his fists from the crossing sweep's ragged

shoulders. At a run he returned to the coach. As he jumped aboard, he turned back to the poor creature cowering in the rain. "Wot's your name, boy?" he called.

"Jo it is," the frightened boy answered. "Jo is all."

"I'll remember you, Jo," Field shouted as Rogers laid on with the whip and the coach moved off. At the time, I remember wondering if Field's words were a promise of reward, or a threat to that cowering wretch.

Similar scenes were enacted as we traversed the London streets. Later, Field confided that through that whole tracking of the fugitives in that thick fog, he was all the time afraid that they would make some abrupt turn off, or some doubling back, and both Thompson and we would lose them. But Lord Ashbee never thought to employ such artful devices.

With a hand to the driver's arm, Field would order Rogers to rein in. Field then would climb down and accost the first available passerby, or pound on an inn door with his truncheon, or roust drunken men or painted women out of the shadows of dark doorways. God knows how he threatened these poor souls. We would sit in the coach, and watch him converse violently with them, until, invariably, his informant would raise an arm and point. Field had some uncanny gift for divining which ones had seen or heard the coach and the pursuing horseman. We were close on their trail.

Yet, we were nearing the river. This was the area where, indeed, the pursuit would grow quite tricky. The streets narrowed significantly. The possible turn-offs capable of swallowing a solitary coach multiplied. The fog and the rain had abated not a whit. If Ashbee had led us a fool's chase in order to turn about and run for the safety of Soho or the West End, then we had to be doubly careful not to lose him in this dark maze into which he had lured us. We could smell the river close before us. The houses rose high on each side. The fog closed about us like a shroud.

"Let us alight and walk," Dickens suggested. "We will have a better chance of encountering some sign."

To our surprise, Inspector Field unhesitatingly agreed.

Rogers pulled the coach to the curbstone, tied the horses to a lamp-post, and all four of us stepped down.

"Stay together," Field directed. "Remember, 'ee 'as a gun."

We proceeded slowly down that street through the fog. We could hear the river rushing between pilings and against its banks close before us.

"Did you 'ear a 'orse ride up, just now?" Field held a slinking, ragged, river character hard by the collar.

"'Oi did, guv, a'ead there," the man put himself on point, like some waterlogged retriever. Field unceremoniously cast him off.

We moved in a file along the moldy faces of the buildings. Millbank at night was like the dark side of the moon.

"'Ullo mates. Nice evenin', wot?" Tally Ho Thompson stepped out of the shadows of a recessed doorway.

I honestly feel that Dickens wanted to strangle the fool on the spot.

MILORD RUN TO GROUND

(May 11, 1851—nearing midnight)

"Where are they, Thompson?" Inspector Field demanded. "Were you able to keep up?"

"Is Jack Ketch the Lord's puppeteer?" Thompson laughed.

I felt Dickens tense beside me. Thompson was maddening.

"Where are they, you idiot!" Dickens spat, only to be answered by an artificial cough which I must believe was Thompson's way of camouflaging the laughter that seemed always bubbling up within him.

"'Ee took 'er into a public 'ouse down the way. I know the place. 'Tis a 'ouse of 'ores. I think 'ee's gettin' the girl into some clothes." He gave his report in a conspiratorial whisper. "The coach is waitin' there," he said, pointing, but nothing could be seen through the fog.

"We must get closer," Field looked to Thompson.

"Follow me," Thompson obliged.

We crept no more than ten yards before he pulled us up short.

"We can see the coach from 'ere," Thompson again pointed.

"We don't want to go closer," Inspector Field agreed.

Even as these words were exchanged, two figures, one tall, one slighter, both muffled and hooded, the taller in a great-coat, the woman in a long cloak, materialized out of the fog, and moved toward the waiting coach.

"'Alt!" Field shouted, and he and Dickens took off at a run with Serjeant Rogers in close pursuit.

The two fugitives stopped in the middle of the street as if obeying Inspector Field's sharp order.

"'Alt for the Protectives!" Field shouted.

Time seemed to stop pursuant to Field's order. That water-side street seemed transformed into a still tableau—the two hooded figures in the middle of the way; the detective, the novelist, and the detective's man running as if in slowed motion; the waiting coach tethered near the ghostly buildings; the stones glistening black with rain.

Thompson and I advanced more cautiously. Almost imme-diately, time sped up, o'erstepped itself, careened out of control.

Pistol shot!

Rogers, running before me, tumbled headlong into the street.

Dickens and Field dropped to the ground in front of the fallen serjeant.

When we looked up, the two hooded figures—Ashbee and the girl—were gone, swallowed by the fog.

To our right, a large hulking man was climbing down from the box of Ashbee's coach. Reaching the ground, he charged directly at the backs of Dickens and Inspector Field, who were in the act of regaining their feet.

Beside me there was a sudden blur of movement. It was—who else?—Thompson, darting forward, picking up speed, launching himself into a headlong dive, sailing through the air, and slamming into the midsection of Ashbee's servant, knocking the man, like a nine-pin, to the ground.

I bent to Serjeant Rogers. "My leg," he gasped. "I think I'm bloody shot!" As I remember it now, his incredulity seems nothing less than hilarious, but, at the time, it was no joke.

"Serjeant Rogers, wot is it?" Field's concern wavered in his voice.

"After 'im, sir. After 'im right now." One had to admire the man's dedication to duty. "It's only me leg. Ain't nothin' to mind."

With that, Field and Dickens were up and running in the direction in which the hooded fugitives had fled.

"Stay with him, Wilkie, until help arrives," Dickens yelled back.

Much of the rest of my description of the ensuing events of that evening has been reconstructed from later conversations with the principals, who were in action while I was forced to stay back, and attend to the fallen Serjeant Rogers, who, it was determined later, had been slightly grazed across the forehead by the bullet, but had bumped his knee in the fall.

When I looked up from my charge, Dickens and Field had already disappeared. Only ten yards away, Thompson and Ashbee's oversized lout of a coachman were rolling around in the muddy street. Thompson seemed to be getting the worst of the exchange. Ashbee's servant was sitting atop him with both hands clasped to Thompson's throat. Without even thinking, I ran to Thompson's aid and kicked Ashbee's servant in the middle of the back with all the strength I could muster. I must have caught him flush in the kidney, because he straightened up, and howled in pain. Taking his hands from Thompson's throat, and lunging them to the sudden pain in his back, he gave Thompson an opening. With an upward lunge, Thompson threw off the lout, and regained his feet. The hulking servant knelt on the cobblestones, bent double and holding his back. Thompson hesitated not a moment. Launching himself into a ballet dancer's whirl, he gathered speed, and kicked the kneeling sod full in the face with his right boot. The man toppled like a French king, and lay still on the street.

I returned to Rogers. With a wave of acknowledgement to me, Tally Ho Thompson set off at a run after Dickens and Inspector Field. Within a matter of minutes, my charge, who had been but momentarily stunned, was up, and ready to return to the fray. I left him in the care of a newly-arrived constable, and followed upon the trail of my companions.

Ashbee, meanwhile, was dragging Ellen Ternan by the wrist through the narrow fog-bound streets. He could hear the running footfalls of Inspector Field and Dickens gaining upon him. The girl slowed him down. The pistol's only ball had been expended.

I can only imagine what thoughts raced through Dickens's mind as he ran after that villain and the woman for whom he had imagined this passionate, irrational love. Dickens had that ability, present in all great novelists, to get so caught up in an event, or the fictional creation of an event, that the self is forgotten. As he ran in pursuit of his mistress and her tormentor, Dickens probably was seeing his romantic dream of playing St. George almost within his grasp.

Ashbee jettisoned the girl at the mouth of a narrow alleyway between two stone buildings. She collapsed and lay sobbing in the street. Her hooded cape spread open around her like a dark pool of blood. She wore a lurid scarlet dress, and her bloodless white face, above that bright red slash against that black circular pool, must have looked like one of Turner's violent miniatures.

Inspector Field ignored her. With barely a sidelong glance, he ran past her in pursuit of Ashbee, down that black slit of an alleyway.

Dickens, of course, stopped to inquire of Miss Ternan's condition. No, that is the sort of stuffy Victorian writing that a

Mister Trollope or a Mister Thackeray might be satisfied to offer. I was not there, but I know that Charles flung himself to his knees, took her head tenderly into his hands, kissed her fevered cheeks, gathered her tightly into his arms.

The girl herself had no cognition of what emotions Dickens was feeling. Drugged, cold, wet, brutalized, she was more than disoriented. She was no longer human or sentient. Her eyes looked up into his, with the blank stare of some West Indies zombie, all self blotted out by the strange rites of men into which she had been lured. Dickens cradled her in his arms.

"Ellen, Ellen . . . my love," he murmured, and he bent to kiss her.

It is here that events begin to trample one upon another. Time becomes a palimpsest—the movements of Field, Dickens, Ashbee, the girl all seem to pile up in layers. Violence overlays rescue, danger supercedes love.

After passing by the fallen girl, Field slowed as he entered the darkness of the alley. He proceeded, blind, yet alert in all of his other senses. The running footfalls of Ashbee no longer echoed in the fog before him. Either the man was gone or the man was waiting up ahead in ambuscade. *He is still here*, Field must have thought. I cannot envision Field feeling any fear at the threat of this encounter. It offered the climax of all of his art, the moment when, finally, the detective comes face to face with his other self, his dark side, whom his whole investigation has been intent upon calling up.

In the alley, Field moved, step by silent step, listening. A rat scuttling along the wall to his left. The wind hissing beneath the overhang of the roofs above. The soft scratch of a shutter against the stone. The scrape of a toe across a stone stair. A wooden creak. A sharp breath drawn in. The pound of a man's heart. His own? His prey's?

Dickens's kiss seemed to awaken the girl from her drug-induced stupor. "Ellen, you are safe. I have you now," Dickens breathed into her fear-widened eyes.

The girl's face twisted into a horrible scream, but all that came out was a hoarse plea: "No more, please no more." Pain and fear clawed at her face. Dickens's kiss, the gentle pressure of his arms, offered no solace.

Inspector Field sensed him there, in the darkness, the briefest of moments before Ashbee leaped. Ashbee attacked Field from above, launching himself from a small porch, four stone steps above the level of the alley. Somehow, by some instinctive sense learned in a lifetime of risk, Field knew to put up his arms and drop to his knees to absorb the attack. Nevertheless, Ashbee knocked Field upon his face on the stones of the alleyway.

Ashbee gripped a heavy curbing stone in both of his hands as he sprawled across Field's back. He had hoped to crush his pursuer's head with one blow even as he completed his downward leap. But Field's instinctive ducking to the ground had caused the attacker to miss with his well-planned blow. The stone, however, was still grasped tight in his hands, and his victim still lay, momentarily stunned, beneath him. Ashbee raised the heavy stone to dash it down. Again, Field's uncanny impulse for self-preservation asserted itself. He rolled sharply away. That sudden move saved Field's life, for that heavy stone would surely have crushed his skull. He rolled suddenly enough to save his head, but the blow pounded down upon his shoulder drawing forth a cry of pain.

At that anguished cry, Dickens's concentration upon the stricken girl was broken. He knew it was Field. It was not so much a recognition of Field's sound, as a knowing that Field was hurt and in trouble. Gently, Dickens lay the girl's head down upon her cloak, jumped to his feet and plunged heedlessly into the black alley.

Ashbee was not done. He rose to his feet, both hands still grasping the murderous stone. He loomed over his crippled pursuer. Once again, he raised the stone with both hands over his head to crush out Field's life.

To Dickens, they were but shadows against the deeper dark of the night. A monstrous shadow looming above a small pool of shadow. Running full tilt, gathering all the power his body could muster, Dickens drove low into the backs of that looming shadow's knees. In the silence of that black alley, Dickens imagined that he could hear the crack of bones splitting and the rip of sinews tearing. Ashbee was driven, face forward, to the cobbled ground. His murderous stone careened harmlessly out into the darkness, to crash against the base of the building. Dickens landed atop him and rolled away. But Milord Ashbee did not rise. He thrashed once, then twice, then lay still, his legs splayed out at a grotesque angle.

"Bravo Dickens!" Inspector Field shouted as he struggled to his feet. "Would 'ave crushed me 'ead like a melon if you 'adn't 'it 'im!"

"Is everythin' square, mates?" Thompson straggled up.

"I think me arm is broke," Field's voice was tight with pain.

Thompson moved to Ashbee who lay groaning upon the cobblestones.

"My leg, the fool has broken my leg," Milord spat, in a tone composed half of a whine and half of a curse.

"If you two was 'orses, we'd shoot the both of ye," the incorrigible Thompson laughed.

Dickens saw no need to tarry at Field's aid any longer. At a run he retraced his steps to attend to his beloved Ellen. When he reached the mouth of the alleyway, the girl was gone.

A HOLE IN THE WATER

(May 11, 1851—midnight)

When Dickens returned to find the young girl gone, what thoughts must have whirled within his troubled imagination? As he stood alone, eyes searching for some glimpse of her, yet seeing only fog and dark and the impenetrable faces of stone tenements, his imagination must have taken charge. He must have seen her, muffled in her cloak, running, frightened, alone, fleeing the brutal men who had used her. He must have sensed her reaching out longingly for death, for deliverance. In his imagination he must have seen them all, Nell, Nancy—his own little Dora, Ellen, all of the lost children of his heart—as they fled, in the fog and the rain, from the brutality of men.

I had noticed, since the death of his small daughter, that Dickens had come to rely more upon his inward vision than upon the clear facts that reality places before us. It was as if by the power of his imagination he felt he could transform reality into something less ugly and threatening and . . . final. Perhaps he thought that, through the power of his imagination, he could bring his daughter back; perhaps that is where his love for Ellen began. More and more, he chose to bring his inward eye, his imagination, to bear upon problems which seemed to demand the powers of deductive reason, the powers of Inspector Field's profession. He seemed to be in a trance, yet he was seeing.

"The girl, where is she?" Inspector Field asked, breaking Dickens's reverie.

"The river," Dickens murmured. "My God, the river."

Field's face was twisted with the pain of his injured arm; yet, at Dickens's words, his whole carriage seemed to straighten. "She is drugged, not 'erself." Field was like some thinking machine, processing information, distributing it. "She'll make for the bridge. There are stairs to the water below, or she may go up on the bridge itself."

No sooner had Field spoken than Dickens was gone. Thompson arrived from one direction, I from the other. Dickens, at a flat run, plunged into the fog in the direction of the stinking Thames.

"Go after 'im," Field shouted, through his pain. "All is secure 'ere."

Thompson and myself did as we were bid. It seemed as if the sum of this long evening had consisted of the chasing of phantoms in the fog. Perhaps we knew—I don't remember, because all was happening so fast—that the Ternan girl was out there, ahead of Dickens, fleeing from the one man whose only desire was to help her. As I look back upon it now, the cynicism of the intervening years challenges my last sentence. Who is to know what desires Dickens harbored within his heart? We chased after him blindly. He pursued her. She wandered in a hopeless dream. The fog swallowed them up. The river flowed before us . . . waiting.

Dickens admitted to me, later, that he had no idea where he was going that night. The fog was so thick, and the visibility so poor, that each of his choices, of which turning to take in the maze, was made on pure instinct. He picked his way through that labyrinth of waterside streets. He did not need his eyes because the eyes of his mind knew every turning.

Dickens raced down a filthy alley, then crossed a darkened street between mean buildings. He ducked into another narrow passageway. There, he found her hooded cloak discarded upon the stones. He picked it up, cast it aside, continued on.

Before him, he could hear the river. The tide was coming in, and it broke with a violent slap against the pilings of the bridge and the stone seawalls. The river was close. With a rush, he burst out of that labyrinth of dark, low-lying streets, and came upon wide stairs beneath Chelsea Bridge. Its fog-haloed lights glowed palely in the night, burned dim in a fragile line, up and out to where they finally disappeared into that sea of fog. She was up there in her scarlet dress. He could catch brief glimpses of her as she moved between the gaslamps of the bridge. She was circling, it seemed—not progressing out upon the bridge, but moving aimlessly back and forth. As Dickens screamed her name, and broke into a run for the narrow stairs climbing up the walkway of the bridge, her movements lost their aimlessness.

"Ellen," Dickens screamed. "Stop! Wait for me!" It was a plea.

Thompson and I broke out of the dark maze of tenement-walled streets onto the embankment. Dickens was running frantically toward the bridge.

His cries for her to stop, to wait, were to no avail. She was mounting the railing beneath one of the gas-lit parapets.

"Ellen, no! Please!" it was a scream of helpless anguish.

For one brief second, poised on that bridge railing, his scream vibrating in the night air over the river, she froze, her eyes burning down upon him, as he ran toward her, far below. He stopped running, as if turned to stone by her gaze. Their eyes met for one long second, at the end of which she tentatively stretched her hand out toward him. But her arm dropped limply to her side, and, the next moment, she flung herself from the bridge.

Dickens, it seemed to me, was in motion before she ever made that move to throw herself from the railing. He was sprinting at full speed back in the direction of Thompson and myself, who were standing at the top of the wide, stone boatmen's stairs.

She floated slowly down, it seemed, as if time had slowed, and she was but easing herself into the black current. She floated slowly down, her scarlet dress billowing out around her, catching the swirling river wind, seeming to bouy her up upon the air and break her plummet to the river below. She floated slowly down, as we watched in horror.

"My God, she jumped," I uttered, stupidly.

"Stupid bitch!" Thompson cursed. "We're in for it now."

Dickens dashed past us without a word. I don't believe he even knew that we were there. He leapt down the boatmen's steps, shedding his greatcoat as he went, and launched himself in a long flat dive out into the black water of the Thames.

What was so amazing was the absolute fluidity of his act. He never hesitated. The run along the embankment, the descent of the stair, the dive, were all one decisive act of love and imagination.

Thompson was down the steps at a bound, but was much cooler in his assessment of the realities of the situation. He stopped at the bottom to pull off his boots and discard his greatcoat. He marked the woman in the red dress floating on the surface of the tide, the splashes of Dickens swimming toward her, the speed of the current. That information assimilated, he, too, dove into the river, but not in the direction of the two swimmers. He came up swimming, at an angle well downstream of Dickens and the insensible girl. He was going to let the tide bring them to him.

Throughout our long acquaintance, I have always marvelled at the quick and analytical intelligence of Tally Ho Thompson. He seems the very loosest of beings, and yet, when one observes, one realizes that there is no wasted motion in anything that the man does. He is, indeed, a marvel!

As I watched this drama unfold before me on this watery stage, I was further amazed at the strength and stamina of Charles, as he swam to the aid of his suicidal love. He reached her before the water inundated her billowing gown, and bore her to the bottom of the river. They seemed to briefly struggle, but he later explained that the girl was unconscious, and he was merely wrestling her out of her scarlet dress, which, in its waterlogged state, threatened to pull them both down. He managed to strip the dress away, but the current was too strong, and he could not swim with her in tow.

By this time, however, the river had carried them into the grasp of Tally Ho Thompson. No one must have been more surprised than Dickens when, in mid-river, Thompson tapped him on the shoulder and said, "'Ullo mate, can I be of any assistance?" or something equally as comical. The two men arranged themselves on each side of the stricken girl, and, kicking furiously, made for the shore.

But the current was strong, and the tide almost at the turn. They were being rapidly carried away.

"Come, we must run and catch 'em at that first pier," a voice thundered in my ear. Inspector Field and the revivified Serjeant Rogers had joined me on the stair.

At that order from Field, Rogers set out at a limping run along the embankment. I could not allow that arrogant little bureaucrat to outdo me.

Our headlong dash had the object of reaching a point on the river bank where we might intercept the swimmers, and pluck them from that powerful current. Our only hope was a narrow shipping pier, which extended out into the river. By the time we reached that rickety wooden catwalk, both Rogers and myself were fully blown, and the swimmers were closing fast upon us.

We moved gingerly out upon the rotting pier. It was clear that we must climb down beneath the rickety flooring to the waterline in order to have any chance at hooking Dickens and Thompson, who must certainly have been nearing exhaustion. We managed to swing ourselves down and into position, each standing on a crossbeam nailed between the pilings of the pier. Our shoes were no more than six inches above the rushing current.

"Take me arm an 'old tight," Serjeant Rogers barked.

I hated taking orders from that pompous martinet, but I grabbed a tight handful of his greatcoat, and wrapped my other arm, as far as it would go, around the moldy piling of the pier.

Rogers leaned out as far as he could without toppling off into the rushing water.

We could see the three swimmers bobbing erratically along in the current, heading directly toward our precarious perch, yet bouncing and swerving in their struggles to stay afloat. They were moving too fast. Rogers would have one chance— and one only—to grasp them.

We waited. He leaned further, lower, utterly dependent upon my grip and strength.

Our targets careened toward us on the tide.

Rogers reached. He lunged desperately, almost pulling us both into the river. Somehow I held on, my arm compressing around that piling.

He did it. Rogers came up with a firm grasp on Dickens's foot. He dragged that foot up under the crossbeam upon which we stood and Dickens's free arm clasped the wood. Soon Thompson, as well, was hanging by one arm, and gasping for breath. Their charge, ghostly white, insensible, hung between them, naked, hair plastered to her scalp, feet dangling in the race.

Within moments, Inspector Field and two constables had come to our assistance. Carefully, we passed Miss Ternan up. Field covered her nakedness with his greatcoat. They rushed her to our waiting coach. Dickens scrambled up next, shouting the whole time, even while gasping for breath, that he must ride with the unconscious girl to hospital.

But the coach did not immediately depart. Inspector Field was supervising the revivification of the girl. The two constables were chafing her hands and arms and cheeks. Field himself was pouring short sips of brandy from a bottle, evidently kept in the coach for just such emergencies. He passed the bottle to Dickens, who took a long and uninhibited draught of the strong liquor. The girl sputtered and coughed. Water flowed out of the sides of her mouth as the constables moved her head from side to side. Dickens leaned down, and I perceived that he was speaking with great intensity into her ear as she returned to consciousness.

Days later, I remembered that tableau through the open door of the coach, and asked Dickens what he was so intent upon saying to the girl. It took some prodding, but I finally convinced him to share with me his words, spoken so intently at the very moment when the young woman was being restored to life.

"I simply told her that I would take care of her," Dickens admitted.

"That is all? You spoke many more words than that," I objected.

"No, that is not all," he continued. "I told her that life can be full, that I could help her to live. I told her that in recent weeks one clear thing which I had learned was that one simply cannot run away from reality, whether it be the reality of the world, or the reality of the undisciplined heart. She smiled at me, Wilkie. She smiled at that."

The black police coach, with Dickens and Field ministering to the girl, rattled off to St. Mark's Hospital, leaving poor Thompson, Serjeant Rogers, and myself standing shivering in the street.

"Th-th-thanks all ever, Fieldsy," Tally Ho Thompson shouted after the departing coach. "Bloody guv'ner leaves me 'ere soaked to me skin, and freezin' me bloody stones off. Thanks all to bloody 'ell, Fieldsy."

Another coach, equipped with blankets and, I hoped, a bottle of brandy similar to that with which Field had ministered to the girl, had been summoned, and would, no doubt, soon arrive. Standing there, shivering in that Thames-side street, was but a momentary interlude in what had been a frenetic evening of adventure, the likes of which I had never before experienced, in what (when in the company of Dickens and Inspector Field) I was beginning to consider to be my rather sheltered life.

I turned to Serjeant Rogers, coincidentally, at exactly the moment that Serjeant Rogers was turning to me.

"Serjeant Rogers, well done!"

"Mister Collins, sir, we did it!"

We stopped in mirrored surprise, staring suspiciously at each other.

There was simply nothing else for it. Neither of us could help but burst out laughing at our own awkwardness and jealousy. He clapped me on the shoulder. I stuck out my hand for a triumphant shake.

A RESOLUTION OF SORTS; OR, REALITY RARELY ENDS WELL

(May 12, 1851—Toward Morning)

St. Mark's Hospital is both a lying-in and a convalescent establishment. In its whitewashed rooms, the young enter our violent world and the old, beaten down by the disease of reality, meekly depart. A black police coach, bearing a stricken young woman, accompanied by an Inspector of Detectives and the most famous author in all of London, was, to understate, a singular occurrence in the round of that old stone hospital's grim routine. Because I did not arrive until some time after Dickens and Field delivered Ellen Ternan to the ministrations of the hospital staff, it was necessary for me to piece together what occurred in the wee hours of that morning, yet what occurred there is perhaps the most singular event of this strange history. Negotiations were entered upon, and a friendship between Dickens and Field was stretched to its limits and cemented. I can only report the shards of reality, because much of what happened there that night took place behind closed doors.

When Rogers, Thompson, and myself arrived at St. Mark's, Dickens and Field were sequestered in a small chapel off the central waiting area. Miss Ternan had been taken to a lying-in room. A young Doctor Woodcourt was in residence, and had taken charge of her care. He was a man well-known to Inspector Field, and, as was evidenced later, well trusted.

A blowsy nurse as large as Forster, and with the breath of a dragon, was manning a desk near the hospital entrance. In her own ragged idiom, she described to me what had happened there prior to our arrival: "The two gennulmuns carried the poor shakin' creetur in an' give 'er to Mister Woodcourt, they did. Then they waited, scuffin' back an' forth 'til the doctor come out an' did a lot of 'ead shakin' in a very positive sort of way, an' with that, the tall gennulmun commences 'and-shakin' in an' equally positive way, an' the thick gennulmun takes a share, as well, but not near so positive. An' then, after the doctor escapes the shakin', the two gennulmun 'appen to walk my way. 'I must speak with you . . . in private,' I 'ears the tall gennulman say to the thick gennulman. They looks at me. I points to the chapel door. An' they been shut up in there ever since." She told her story with a kind of desperate hilarity.

We did not have to wait long for Dickens and Field to emerge from their private colloquy. As they came through the door, they paused to shake hands, Dickens placing his left hand over Field's already clasped hand, and clearly offering a fervid "Thank you."

Field, probably due to the pain in his shoulder, looked almost defeated. Dickens looked empty, as if all his words had been expended. It was not until twenty years later, on the day of Dickens's funeral, that I learned exactly what had transpired behind those closed doors. They had struck a pact, out of mutual respect and mutual debt. The "tall gennulmun" had thrown his public position and respectability to the winds, and had spoken from the promptings of his heart. The "thick gennulmun" had chosen to humanely reinterpret the law, to the upholding of which he had relentlessly dedicated his life.

In that pub near the Abbey, on the day that Dickens was laid to rest, I was told the details of the pact. It was an agreement that Marlowe's Doctor Faustus would have nodded at with approval. In exchange for Ellen Ternan's freedom, Dickens pledged that he would be on call for any detective work that Inspector Field required. He promised that he would give Field access to every level of society to which Dickens, in his position as one of the best-loved men in England, could be admitted. Willingly, Charles sealed this pact with this Mephistopheles of the London streets.

I know not what powers of persuasion Dickens employed upon Inspector Field. Dickens had, after all, saved Field's life in that dark alleyway. I do know, however, that Miss Ternan never faced prosecution for any of the crimes of this affair. I learned that, within a week, upon her recovery, she was placed in Miss Angela Burdett Coutts's home for fallen women at Shepherd's Bush. It was not until full five years later, when it became public knowledge that Dickens was her protector— before he, in a public newspaper notice, declared his separation from his wife—that the world learned of the existence of Ellen Ternan.

I could not help thinking, as the "tall gennulman" and the "thick gennulman" emerged from that chapel, shaking hands, of the first time I had seen them shake hands. It had been at the foot of the gallows. Dickens, like the St. George that I always think he thought himself to be, that night in that hospital chapel, saved his beloved Ellen from an encore performance of Mrs. Manning's grisly dance of death.*

Someday the world shall learn the truth about Charles and Ellen, but the world shall not learn of them from me. In the more than twenty years since Dickens took me under his wing, we have become more than friends, more than simply collaborators and fellow writers. And yet, the man that we paid our last respects to in Westminster Abbey lived in close proximity to Ellen, from all evidence a murderess, for the last fourteen years of his life. Whenever I thought of Ellen living under his protection, I wondered if he ever feared that she had the potential to do to him what she did to the first man in her tangled life. When *Great Expectations* was the talk of all London, years after the time of this memoir, the woman Estella was praised as a most interesting character. There was, of course, speculation among Dickens's friends, never voiced in any public way, and certainly never intimated to Dickens himself, that Estella, in all her cold beauty, was indeed Ellen. But, as I read *Great Expectations*, I became fascinated by the

---

*It seems somewhat strange that Inspector Field, a officer of the law, would make such an exception. Yet Field was an extremely intelligent politician as well as a dedicated policeman. He must have realized the public-relations potential of his relationship with a voice in London as influential as that of Charles Dickens. Perhaps the four articles on the Metropolitan Protectives which appeared in *Household Words* in the months immediately following the events of this memoir, all of which reference Inspector Field by name and recount his exploits, were actually contracted for that very night. This does not imply that Field was a shameless publicity hound. Rather, it acknowledges that the Metropolitan Protectives were a new and undeveloped organization and Field was fully aware of the need to get the message of the Protectives' value and proficiency out to the general London populace as well as to the politicians who control the purse strings of law enforcement.

appearance of Lawyer Jaggers's housekeeper. It seems to my dull critical sense that Ellen Ternan could well be both characters: the object of love and adoration as well as the tamed murderess.

There was nothing left to do after Dickens and Field emerged from their private discourse in the hospital chapel. Miss Ternan was to remain there, under the care of young Doctor Woodcourt. That young genius also insisted upon examining the injured shoulder of Inspector Field, and the graze-wound to the forehead of Serjeant Rogers. As it was, indeed, well past two in the morning, we left our two policemen to the doctor's tricks. We clapped Tally Ho Thompson on the back, offering our thanks in that peculiar gruff, male way. When he bid us goodnight, there in the street, he looked as eternally young and brash and bright, if he had just arisen from a night's sleep. He walked off jauntily, as if he had not at all spent the evening scaling buildings, fighting duels, riding at breakneck speed through the fog, wrestling giants, and swimming rivers. "Think I'll go look for me Bess, I will," he offered to no one in particular, as he left us standing there, both bone-tired, in that wet and foggy street.

No hansom cabs were about, as it was so late of the evening (or early of the morning), so we were forced to walk back to our usual parting point at the bottom of Wellington Street. We dragged our weary selves along in quite untypical silence. He was either too tired or too reticent to talk, even to me, his faithful bulldog. To experience Dickens, wordless, was a near-historic event.

(May 16, 1851—evening)

Dickens had no time, whatsoever, to recover from the turmoil of that long and dangerous night. When I looked in upon him at the *Household Words* office the next day at noon, he was miraculously reinvigorated. He did not appear at all a man who had not slept for days. He did not appear at all a man who, only a night before, had knocked an attempted murderer off his pins, and saved a damsel in distress from certain death in the fast tide of the Thames. He was bright and quick and full of enthusiasm, as if the sun had suddenly come out in his life, after a long, dark winter of discontent.

"The play's the thing now, Wilkie," he laughed. "We have but three days, and we are going to rehearse as we have never rehearsed before."

He meant it. For the next three nights, he drove us like a tyrant. He screamed at everyone, but no one seemed to care, because it was so clear that the old Dickens had returned from the abyss into which the deaths of his father and his baby daughter had cast him. It was utterly impossible not to believe his plea, that if one actor falls down in his part, we all fall with him. Thank God that the Duke of Devonshire, who had actually supervised the construction of the stage in his spacious music room, and who had turned all the comforts of his library over to the actors as a luxurious green room, was deaf. During those three nights of rehearsals, it seemed that Dickens was shouting his directions, and repeatedly stopping scenes in mid-line with his impatient "no, no, no, no, that's not it!" in a voice loud enough to be heard out in the traffic of Picadilly. There was, of course, good reason to rehearse so hard. The Queen was coming to our opening performance. Most of the Court would be in attendance as well. The tickets were outrageously priced at five guineas, with all proceeds going to the Actor's Benevolent Fund, and were being unhesitatingly reserved by the most noble figures in London society. Indeed, this Royal Amateur Performance of Bulwar Lytton's new play, *Not So Bad As We Seem*, was taking on all of the appearances of becoming one of *the* social events of the season. Dickens was determined that our performance would be professional, and he drove us like galley slaves.

The Queen's Night, May sixteenth, arrived all too soon. Dickens was thoroughly unsettled, convinced that, due to his personal problems, he had not rehearsed us nearly enough, and that the performance was doomed to a humiliating failure. He could not have been more wrong. More than an hour before the performance, the splendid royal coaches began pulling up and disembarking their elegant occupants at the Picadilly curbstone, outside the Duke of Devonshire's front gate. A ragged crowd had congregated across the street, but soon that small gathering of the curious had swelled to a worshipful mob of gawking, craning faces, waiting for Queen Victoria's coach to make its appearance. As each coach pulled up, and disembarked its passengers, the same scene was played in mannered repetition. A gentleman, in black trousers and coat with a severe black hat upon his head, would step down, turn back, and offer his hand to an elegant, fair-skinned, bejeweled lady, who, upon securing both feet upon the ground, would dart a nervous glance across the street at the huzzaing crowd pushing at the makeshift barriers, which a small detachment of the Protectives in evidence had thrown up. The women's jewels flashed in the gaslight of the palace. The women's hair shown like gold or glistening ebony. The polished coaches rattled off, to be replaced by the next vehicle for speculation.

Dickens and I watched the arrivals from a mezzanine window on the second storey of the Duke's palace. There was the expected and the unexpected. Two days before the performance, Bulwar Lytton's estranged wife, Rosina, had sent a quite mad letter to the Duke of Devonshire, denouncing her estranged husband, as well as Dickens, the actors, and even the Queen. In the letter, she threatened to steal into the performance, and thoroughly disrupt the proceedings. Precautions had been taken to intercept her, but she, evidently, chose to desist, and did not appear that night. However, to my great surprise, another did appear, whom I did not expect.

Dickens, in conspiracy with Mister Tally Ho Thompson, arranged it. As we looked down upon the lords and ladies entering, a hansom cab trotted up. A tall, remarkably handsome gentleman, hatless, in a black evening suit, with a rakish white silk scarf twirled around his neck, stepped down. One at a time, he handed down two of the most dazzlingly beautiful creatures to grace the proceedings of the evening. Dickens howled with laughter when he observed the consternation on my face.

It was, of course, Tally Ho Thompson escorting Scarlet Bess and my Meggy. All were dressed impeccably, both women in elegant dresses, their hair coiffed in the latest London style. The crowd stirred and stretched their necks to view their entrance into the mansion. What speculations must have murmured through the crowd?

"Ladies-in-waiting to the Queen, surely!"

"The son and daughters of the Duke of Devonshire?"

"Irish nobility!"

"I planned it all," Dickens confessed, through his bursts of laughter. "They deserved some reward for all they did. Despite their past lives, they are potentially good people. Thompson is intent upon becoming an actor. Bess loves the rogue blindly. And Meggy . . . well." He raised a comical eyebrow in my direction. "I thought you might enjoy seeing her again."

I could not help but laugh along with him.

"Do you know what Meggy said when I suggested this little frolic?" Dickens asked, awash with mirth. "'Ah, a night among the swells, is it? I 'ope not too many of 'em recognizes me.'"

From the very moment that Meggy had stepped down from that coach, beautiful in her elegant silk dress, her hair a cascade of Irish curls upon her white shoulders, my pulse had quickened, my heart tightened in anticipation. I knew that I would see her after the performance. I knew that I should become her escort for the remainder of this evening, perhaps for many to come.

After Thompson, with his two stunning bookends, passed into the house, my eyes continued to scan the crowd. There was no need to hurry. The actors' first call had not yet sounded. Dickens was summoned away to settle some last-minute production matter. I was left standing in that upper window, watching all the superficial magnificence of London society parade before me. My eyes moved back and forth from the lords and ladies stepping down, to the pointing, jostling, gossiping crowd, and came to rest on a most familiar figure. Inspector Field stood planted in the street, between the fragile barriers and the arriving coaches, like some guardian of the moat between the aristocracy and the lower classes.

One last ugly scene remained to be enacted before the play could begin. A familiar black coach pulled up, driven by a too-familiar hulking giant of a coachman. The door opened, and Lord Ashbee struggled out. He was supporting himself on crutches. He handed down a young girl, who could not have been more than fifteen or sixteen years of age, yet who was dressed and rouged like the most experienced harridan. He was openly flaunting his perverse gentleman's tastes, and not a soul seemed to mind. The Grub Street rumors, concerning the nature and origin of Lord Ashbee's injuries, had been sweeping London for the previous four days. The gossips speculated that his injuries had been sustained in a duel, which had been discovered and aborted by the Protectives, under the command of an Inspector Field of Bow Street. Ashbee's antagonist in the duel was rumored to be a wealthy and decadent lord, who had recently been in trouble with the police, who were observing his movements when they interrupted this affair, and who was also sporting visible injuries.

Afterwards, I learned from second-hand reports, that when Lord Ashbee entered the Duke's music room with his child companion on his arm, he actually had the effrontery to bow to the Queen, before taking his seat. The Queen, I was told, acknowledged his bow with an icy stare, looking right through him as if he did not exist. It does not seem at all right or proper that he should even be admitted into such company, does it? He is the evil nobleman incarnate, unequaled by Dickens's Sir Mulberry Hawk, by Thackeray's Lord Steyne, or by any creation of any of our modern writers, yet he enters perfectly undaunted. Thank heaven that the Queen saw fit to cut him.

Backstage, Dickens called us all to our marks more than ten minutes before the curtain was scheduled to rise. We could hear the audience being seated in the music room. Dickens, the ultimate stage manager, moved from one of his actors to the next, offering each a final word of advice, or encouragement, or a final stage direction. "Wouldn't it be nice," he once, years later, mused aloud on the occasion of another such amateur performance, "if the lives of real people could be blocked and directed in the way that actors can." He stopped a moment to think. "But actors never cooperate when you try to direct them," he laughed, "no more than real people do."

That night, backstage, waiting for the curtain to go up on *Not So Bad As We Seem*, I, for one, was not inclined to cooperate as directed. As soon as Dickens left us onstage to finish his own last preparations, I stole to one of the peepholes in the curtain, in hopes of catching a glimpse of Meggy in the audience. I could not, immediately, find Meggy's glowing face, but, just to the left of stage center, my eyes made what seemed direct contact with those of Lord Henry Ashbee. I knew that I was secreted behind the curtain, yet I felt his demonic eyes boring into my soul, taunting me with the charge, that in my attraction to Irish Meg I was no less a whoremonger than he.

I found Meggy. She and Thompson and Scarlet Bess were enjoying themselves immensely. Sitting in the midst of lords and ladies of the Court, and noble patrons of the arts, they were smiling and pointing and winking knowingly, as was everyone else in the audience. I noticed that Meg and Bess were drawing more than their portion of admiring stares and gallant glances from the gentlemen perusing their section of the audience. More than one elegant nobleman turned to his seat companion to remark enviously upon the extraordinary luck of the young gentleman, just there, who was accompanied by two such striking ladies. More than one time afterward, sitting in a public house with Thompson and Bess, Meg and I would laugh at the utter incongruity of that scene. "If they'd only known we was 'ores," Meg once said, "they'd o' stopped winkin', an' started turnin' up their noses." But that evening, Meg and Bess were two of the most exciting women in London society. Everyone was speculating on who they were, and how big their fortunes might be. In a sense, Meg and Bess were Dickens's private joke on his whole audience.

The Duke of Devonshire's private orchestra struck up the overture, the gaslamps were lowered, the scented oil footlights suddenly blazed up, and the curtain rose. Dickens, playing Sir Henry Wilmot, stood at center stage. I, playing Sir Henry's valet, bustled around administering to him for the whole first act. Bulwar's play went splendidly. The night was, indeed, a triumph for Dickens. He was witty and lively onstage, something he had not been in any of our rehearsals. The Queen enthusiastically led the audience in a standing ovation for, in this order of command appearance, the playwright, the actors, the stage manager, and the host, the beaming Duke himself, who was lured upon stage to take his bow hand in hand with the actors.

Inspector Field came backstage after the performance. Dickens rushed to him with hand outstretched. I joined them, away from the others, who were opening bottles of champagne sent back by the Queen.

"Did you see him out there?" Dickens was asking Field as I came up.

"Aye, I did." Field's smile of congratulation turned instantly to a dour admission of undeserved defeat.

"His evil goes unnoticed," Dickens said, his passion ringing clear, even though his voice was low and controlled, "while the poor and the lost are hounded and hung, for trying to keep themselves alive."

"We shall not get 'im at the Assizes. 'Ee 'as 'ired a quite powerful Solicitor, Jaggers of the Old Temple. We shall 'ave no chance without the Ternan girl's evidence." Field shrugged. "So it goes."

"Ah, but we have gotten him, nonetheless." Dickens leaned in to whisper to Inspector Field. "He is the scandal of both Fleet and Grub Streets. The scribblers cannot get enough of our randy Lord Ashbee. His servants are being bribed for morsels of gossip. Information is leaking to the press in the most mysterious ways." At that Dickens nudged Field in an attempt to cheer him up.

"They write about a mysterious dark lady, who holds the key to the Ashbee affair," I said, adding my tuppence to the conversation.

Field grinned at Dickens, as if enjoying some private joke. "For some strange reason, 'er name 'as never come out," he said, as he tipped me a sly wink. "She must 'ave very powerful friends."

Inspector Field had lost his man, but, in Dickens and myself, he had gained two constant friends, two lieutenants in his detectiving, for life.

"I must get back to supervise my constables. We must not let the crowd get too close to the Queen," Field made an abortive move toward the library door, which opened out upon the Duke's formal gardens.

"The Queen is expected back here. It shall be the better part of an hour before she will depart," Dickens assured him.

"Ah, but I must go nonetheless," Field replied, his forefinger wandering up to scratch at the side of his eye. "I've got me eyes on two swell mobsmen spotted in the crowd tonight. They are a catch I cannot pass up."

Dickens and Inspector Field shook hands. They held their grip for a long moment, their eyes meeting in a declaration of loyalty and friendship.

"That does it then," Field broke their unspoken bond. "The case is closed."

"We have an agreement," Dickens said, speaking directly and sincerely. "The time shall come when we shall work together again."

"Perhaps sooner than you think," Field said, tapping Dickens playfully on the shoulder with his audacious forefinger.

"I shall see you soon," Dickens continued, as if not wishing the conversation to end, not wanting to let this particular adventure go. "It shall not be many nights 'ere I shall need a walk in the neighbourhood of Bow Street."

"Good. I shall expect you." With that, they shook hands again.

Even as the man was moving out of the door, Dickens, almost nervously, continued to babble on: "As they say in America, I shall see you if I don't kick the bucket."

Inspector Field stopped in mid-exit, flashed his sharp ironic grin from beneath his sharp square hat as his sharp forefinger scratched the side of his exceedingly sharp eye, and laughed, "Bucket indeed! 'Tis the bucket that kicks us, my good friend, not us the bucket." With that, he was gone.*

---

*Wilkie Collins's journal comes to an abrupt end at this point at the bottom of the final page of the leather-bound commonplace book in which he was writing. Collins makes no indication that the narrative is complete; nor is there any indication that it isn't. Perhaps other commonplace books existed which carried further the story of the collaboration between Charles Dickens and Inspector William Field of the Metropolitan Protectives. This particular journal, needless to say, exhausted itself at a rather felicitous point. It does, however, leave the fates of Irish Meg Sheehey, Tally Ho Thompson, Scarlet Bess, and Collins himself, not to mention poor Ellen Ternan, somewhat unresolved.